The Chasm of Conspiracy

by D. A. Jennings

*For those of you who never believed the Warren Commission,
think you know who did it, and how it was done . . . this book is
for you.*

Preface

A couple of years ago, I was on the patio going over some changes I needed to make on a new book idea, when the phone rang. By the time I got to it, the caller had hung up. I returned the call, but no one answered and there was no voicemail.

That afternoon when the phone rang again, the caller asked if I was Mr. Jennings. "Yes, this is Doug Jennings."

"Mr. Jennings, I tried to reach you this morning, and apologize if it was too early. I need to speak with you at your earliest convenience. Would you have some time we could meet?"

"Who is this?"

"I'm sorry, my name is Aaron Bubek. I'm staying at the Grand in Point Clear, and if you can't come here, I would be happy to meet you in Mobile."

"Mr. Bubek, before we discuss if, when, and where I might meet you, what is this all about?"

"I assure you, Mr. Jennings, it's important. Otherwise, I wouldn't be bothering you, and I promise it won't be a waste of your time."

He sounded as if it was urgent, and being the curious sort, I agreed to meet him. I suggested we meet for lunch at his hotel around 11:30 the next day.

Aaron said he was a financial advisor in Atlanta, and that his client had asked him to meet with me.

"I won't keep you waiting as to what this is about, but before I begin, I need to ask you to please not discuss this meeting with anyone. Is that acceptable?"

"I suppose so, but why the secrecy?"

"Let's just say that I'm going to show you something that would cause some people to be extremely nervous should they find out what I have brought here today. Going forward depends on whether you decide to take my client's wish to heart. He hopes you will consent to write a book using the material I have with me."

"Aaron, there are hundreds of more experienced and gifted writers than me who would be more than happy to ghostwrite a book for your client."

"Mr. Jennings, this is not about ghostwriting."

Aaron went on to explain that his client wanted me to write the book and asked me to delay saying yes or no until I had a chance to look at least the first few pages of the material. I agreed.

He also emphasized that the journal was given to him to convince me the story had to be told, and no one else could see it.

"Mr. Jennings, the young man who gave me my instructions is the son of a very courageous man who I had the privilege of meeting almost twenty years ago. At the time, he was a successful businessman, whose wife had become concerned about him because of the increasing intensity of his nightmares. When she finally had enough of not being able to get a good night's sleep, and deeply concerned about her husband's health, she asked him to see a psychiatrist, which he did. After her husband's death, the psychiatrist was hesitant to give the family exact details about his patient, but did say he had told his patient to write down what he could remember about certain events in his past. Those memories might have been causing the nightmares; therefore, getting them down on paper could be a way to help ease

4

the level of intensity of the dreams. Whether it worked or not I have no idea.

"When the son became his father's attorney, the old man gave him the journal. Though the son had possession of it, he was not to read it, nor let anyone else see it until his dad's passing. This is what we'll be discussing. It's up to you to write the story as you see it laid out, but it has to be based on the information he recorded. You can have as much dramatic leeway as you need for the characters, as long as you stick to the facts written by my client's father.

"He knew that it was important to honor his father's wishes, but with a wife and family plus a successful law practice, he turned to me for help. I have known the son since he was a small boy, and that's why he called me. You were chosen because my client liked your first book, and he says you met his father when you both lived in Atlanta." Aaron handed me a small card.

Mr. Jennings,

Dad said you most likely wouldn't remember him, but you and he did some work together, and he liked how you handled your ideas and thoughts. Most especially, he was impressed with your desire to keep a tight watch on things that were no one else's business.

I liked your first book very much. I believe you're the person to write my dad's book: so, I ask you to look at the journal, understand how important it is, and create something which will honor my father and the other members of the team who were like a family of brothers. They never gave up on finding out what really happened that black day in November 1963. Thank you for meeting with Aaron and hope my father's last request will be your greatest success.

Sincerely,
DC

I agreed to read the journal, and if I found that it was something I felt comfortable doing, I would accept the young man's request. After the first five pages, what I read had so boggled my mind that I called Aaron to tell him I would start laying out the book within the week. I was completely and totally committed to creating this book.

He made me promise that I would destroy the journal once the book was finished. I promised no one else would ever see the journal again.

I went deep sea fishing a few weeks after the book was finished, and when I got back I couldn't find the journal. Have always wondered if it fell overboard during the high seas. I have never seen nor heard from Aaron Bubek again, if that was really his name.

As a result of writing this book, my admiration for these young men and the man who put it all together goes beyond description. Other than being asked to put the names, places, and actions into a book format, this isn't about me. It's about a son wanting people to know what his father and his group of young warriors did to track down the truth about the assassination of President John F. Kennedy.

Should you choose to read the rest of this book, you will have to decide for yourself as to the authenticity of what he kept in that journal. All of the men in the book are deceased. I did my best to incorporate their stories within the story chronicled once upon a time before truth and honor were cast aside to hide the most infamous conspiracy ever conceived. The lust and greed for wealth and power by a few overcame the decency, the heart, and the soul of this great nation.

D. A. Jennings

PART 1

Chapter 1
Once Upon a Time

Just after President Kennedy was elected, he was informed by the CIA about a planned invasion of Cuba.

The new president trusted the intelligence community, but history tells us that the Bay of Pigs was a complete disaster. President Kennedy was embarrassed by this fiasco and furious that he was used by the CIA.

Robert Kennedy, the President's brother was the Attorney General, and his attitude was that someone did this on purpose. He would find out who it was and see to it that nothing like this ever happened again.

Then came October of 1962 when mankind came so close to complete annihilation. The President, the heads of the armed services, key advisors, and his brother, had just seen photos taken a day or two earlier. The photos showed that the Cubans, with the help of the Soviet Union, had installed offensive ballistic missiles in Cuba which were aimed at the United States. The President kept his cool, avoided military action, other than a naval blockade, and the world was able to breathe again. What no one knew was that this near disastrous episode in our history led the President to seek out a group of young men, whose real names would never be known, to be his eyes and ears as they closely monitored the actions of the intelligence community. In doing so, they uncovered a scheme so dark, so deep undercover that it took them twelve years to put all the pieces together.

This group of men had access to information which allowed them to flourish and grow in strength as they began to find answers to questions no one wanted to ask.

* * *

Three months before the first photos of Cuba were brought to the attention of the White House, the CIA placed two senior agents in Havana. They were there to find out if the information and photos they had discovered about some missile installations were valid. They were to search as much of the island as possible, look for any new activity from the military, count Russians, and get back to their boss quickly. It was all highly secret, and being carried out without the knowledge of the President.

In late July of '62, one of the girls in the phone pool was receiving a transmission from the island. She called her supervisor and asked him to come to her station. She handed him her headphones. "Listen to this."

The static was bad, but it was still possible to hear the voices. The young transcriber had started recording this communication about twenty minutes before, and while she was transcribing it, decided to let her boss listen to it.

It was Russian mixed in with a couple of Cuban voices. One of the Cubans was translating, but what got her attention was the repeated use of *el missal.*

"Sir, do you want me to have this printed?" He agreed and told her to make a copy and give him the original. The transcript was then taken to the Assistant Deputy Director of Covert Operations. What to do next would be his decision.

"When did she record this?" Donald Meriwether wanted to make a note of the time.

Victor Chadwick, the senior analyst, explained, "Sir, she recorded this about two hours ago. It took an hour to translate, have it checked, and typed."

"I appreciate your expediting this Mr. Chadwick. You and your assistant have done a great job. Please tell her thank you for

8

the excellent work and emphasize that she is not to say anything about this transmission. I'll get back to you on this."

"Yes sir, and let me know if there's anything else you need for us to do."

Donald Meriwether, the Assistant Deputy Director, had been around long enough to know that everything is checked and rechecked some more, especially if it could be of vital importance. Many a poor soul had made the mistake of jumping the gun, and were no longer around. He wanted to make a couple of calls concerning two or three things he heard on the recording.

He wasn't going to get into another one of those fiascos created by a group of radical Castro-hating Cubans. This time he would make this available only when the time was right. He knew there had been Russians in Cuba back before Castro. He always thought Batista had been offered extra incentives by the Ruskies to go quietly into seclusion before Castro even got close to Havana.

General Omar H. Turner was Donald's good friend. He had asked the General's military opinion on several occasions, all with the highest degree of confidentiality. Today he approached the General, shared the situation, and asked: "Do you think there's anything to this, sir?"

"Well, obviously this needs more study. Do you have any coordinates on the transmission, any information about where it's coming from?"

"That's my problem, General; I just don't know if it's verifiable or not."

"My advice then would be to sit on this a few days. Give me some time to put an ear to some of my colleague's conversations and see if they know anything. Call me Friday."

As suggested, Donald called the General on Friday to ask him if he had heard back from any of his friends. The General had not and indicated that Donald needed to do some more background work. When he was confident in the source and the situation, he should take it upstairs.

Six days before Russia turned their ships around, and a world crisis was averted, the President was told by his chief of staff that there was a young woman from the CIA who desperately needed to speak to him. He handed the President the note she had given the secretary.

Mr. President,

I have agonized whether to bother you or not. I'm a transcriber at the Agency, and on July 30th, I recorded a conversation between Cubans and a Russian. They used the phrase *el misal* several times. I had to promise secrecy, so I guess I'm in a lot of trouble, but I just had to make sure you knew about that transmission.

Sincerely, Patti Armstrong.

The President handed the note to his brother. "Do you know anything about this?"

The Attorney General read her note and was livid. "Are you telling me the CIA knew about these missiles in July?"

"You read the note, Bob. Find her, meet with her, and get the recording or the transcript. Tell her to say nothing about this to anyone. If any of this is true, I want to know now. I'm not going to ever let them forget this! I'll take down the whole damn bunch if I have to."

When she saw the Attorney General, she could only hope she had done what anyone would have done. He could be coming to arrest her, but he quickly put her mind at ease.

"You did the right thing, Patti." She was trembling when he put his arm around her to help her relax and that the President appreciated her help so much. They talked for a short time, and she gave him all the details about that day and the transcription. Patti also told him about telling her boss, and accidentally overhearing a conversation between two senior analysts.

She said she would have never taken such a chance if she had not overheard those analysts saying that they couldn't believe the President seemed surprised by all of this. What made her extremely curious was when one of them said, "That first set of photos back in the summer should have told the President that something was up."

The Attorney General was back in the Oval Office later that evening, and most emphatically suggested that they start looking into what was going on over at the CIA. He would indict the entire hierarchy for treason.

The President very calmly told him, "No, I don't want them to know. I've been giving this a lot of thought, and I'm tired of trusting the enemy more than I trust my own intelligence community. At least I know what the enemy wants and how he plans to get it.

"Let me ponder this for a few days, and I'll get back to you. In the meantime, give some thought as to how best you think we can go about doing something, anything to get those renegades back in line. If you have a foolproof plan for them to mysteriously be lost at sea, I'll listen." Robert knew or thought he knew that the President was kidding.

"Whatever we decide, only you and I will know. I have an idea, but before I get into that with you, please have Patti promoted and placed on your staff as soon as possible. I want to make sure she's protected.

"Bobby, do you remember my good friend Davis Carmichael? He and I were classmates at Harvard, and we were always arguing about something. I know he can keep a secret, and since what I'm thinking about doing has to be in the private sector, he could be the one to get it done. I have something I'm going to

11

run by him before I discuss it with you any further. Should anything happen down the road, I don't want you to have to be in the middle of it. Talk to you later. Evelyn, could you come in a moment please?"

* * *

"Davis, this is Jack Kennedy. How are you doing?"

"Mr. President, I'm fine. How about yourself, sir?

"I'd rather be on my sailboat. Listen Davis, I've got something important to discuss with you and wondered what you have on your calendar for tomorrow."

"If I had anything, I would cancel it. What time do you have in mind?"

The President thought a moment and suggested they meet upstairs for dinner around six.

"I'll have a car pick you up. You still on the Bay?"

"Yes, and I look forward to seeing you."

The next evening after some small talk during dinner, the President laid out what he had in mind.

"Davis, it's like this: I think something is going on at the CIA, and it's not good. When I say going on, I am most hesitant to use the word conspiracy, but something isn't right. It's as if they have their own set of parameters and to hell with everyone else, including the President of the United States.

"I don't think it's widespread, maybe more like a few people in key positions who seem to have their own agenda. I have an idea, which could quite possibly be illegal, but legal or not, I want it done, and need someone on the outside to make it happen. Here are my parameters: no military, no government, and absolute, total secrecy. Only you, me, and Bobby will know about any of this. Will you help me with this? Before you answer,

12

understand that if our little plan is ever exposed, we never had this conversation."

"Mr. President, the fear or legality of it doesn't necessarily squelch my desire to do this for you, but are you sure I'm the one you need?"

"Davis, I need someone I can trust, and other than my family and you, there are only two others I could ask, but neither one of them has the ability to organize anything like what I want to do. Bobby will be in on the planning, but will have no input as to how or when we do this. In some respects, the less he knows, the better."

The President went on to tell his friend the entire set of facts, how he was tired of having to watch his back for the possibility that some clique at the agency considers the Presidency to be nothing more than one of its playthings. "Somebody's getting a little too big for their britches. We must fix this; not just for this Presidency, but for all who follow. If my idea isn't feasible, then tell me what you think is, tell me soon, and tell me a better way to get it done."

The President went into the explanation about his idea, and if Davis thought it could work, the real development and implementation would be his alone.

"Mr. President, do you need an estimate of the cost? If this is a private undertaking, who or what is going to fund this?"

"I don't care what it costs. If I have to, I'll get the money from my old man. Davis, I need you to give this a lot of thought, but I need your answer as quickly as possible. If you decide you can't or don't wish to do this, you'll have to help me find the person who can. When you've decided, give Evelyn a call. Either affirm an appointment with me or tell her you can't get it scheduled next week. I'll know what you mean."

Davis was on the way to the airport and heard himself talking in a quiet murmur as he looked out the window at all the

13

lights sparkling on the new fallen snow. "Where do I start? Taking on the Agency is like David taking on Goliath with no rock . . . and no sling."

He continued to think about the problem. *Maybe the President is just pissed for the moment and will get over it. I don't blame him for being upset, but this idea would be a colossal undertaking if it can be done at all. And the ramifications of it all, should it ever come to light, God help us all.*

Hours passed, ideas of what to do came and went, but sooner or later he had to find a way. The President trusted him with this most sensitive and secret undertaking; he would do whatever the President needed him to do.

The next day, Davis called the White House and asked Evelyn to tell the President that he wanted to confirm his appointment.

Now all he had to do was design the plan, put it in place, get it ready to rock and roll then live his real life at some other time.

Chapter 2
I Had No Idea

It certainly wasn't what he expected. Rick thought it would be some opulent home in the Garden District, replete with crystal chandeliers, teak and mahogany, and servants all over the place. Instead, it was a neighborhood grocery store.

"Come in sir, and welcome to our little store that has it all," a very enthusiastic man shouted from the counter. "How may I help you today?"

Rick asked the guy, "Would you please direct me to 2145 Canal Street?"

The storekeeper looked at the young man for a moment, then said "Wait here, I'll be right back." A few seconds passed, the guy called him to the back, and showed him a door across the alley. "That's where you need to be, mate."

When the door opened, he was met by a very well-dressed woman with a most pronounced British accent.

"Mr. Charles, it's so nice to see you. Please have a seat. I have a few questions to ask, and then you will see Dr. Carmichael. My name is Helen."

She began to look through several papers until she found what she needed. "Mr. Charles, before I begin, do you have any questions I can answer for you today?"

"Yes, Helen, one in particular: What is this all about?"

"Mr. Charles it's my job to know things, and at times, explain how things work. As to your question, you will have to speak to Dr. Carmichael. You did get a small parcel a couple of days ago didn't you Mr. Charles?"

"Yes, I did. It asked me to answer a few questions and send it back, which I did."

"You're a musician, play a horn of some kind I understand. Are you good enough to play professionally?"

"If you're asking if I'm good enough to make a living at it, I do make a living at it. Why?"

"Again Mr. Charles, I'm not trying to be difficult I promise, but I'm paid by the doctor to ask questions, and that's what I'm doing. If you don't wish to discuss this with me any further, then just sit over there and wait."

"So, Helen, what is your next question, and I apologize for being snippy."

"Thank you, Mr. Charles. Have you ever been arrested?"

"I have not."

"Have you had any affiliation with any political party other than Republicans or Democrats?"

"No."

"Only one more question for you. Are you presently engaged, in a relationship, or married?"

"No, yes, and no. Her name is Nikki."

Helen smiled. "Mr. Charles, it will be just a few more minutes, but Dr. Carmichael will see you as soon as possible."

Chapter 3
What's Up Doc?

Rick knew enough about The Big Easy to get around just fine, but he didn't have a clue as to where they were at the moment. Maybe they were going the back way to another neighborhood store, but by the looks of this car, it must be a prominent neighborhood.

"Dr. Carmichael, I'm very much at a loss here. Why am I here, and why did you want to see me? I thought we had pretty much put all the details to bed the last time we met."

"First of all, you can call me Doc or Davis, and let me answer you like this: if after having lunch, you still have questions, I will be happy to go over it all again."

The car dropped them off at a little place somewhere on Magazine Street. An hour later, they headed to the airport.

Rick was a nice-looking guy of average height around 5'10," and by wearing winter clothes and soaking wet, he could weigh as much as 180 pounds. He was very muscular. When he was in the Marines, he got into this workout thing, and had been doing it every day since. It was a good habit to have considering, his personal schedule.

Lately, he had been spending most of his time playing the music he loved in a small jazz band in the Quarter. It was a lot of fun, paid the bills and greatly enhanced his social life. Rick used the G.I. Bill to get a degree in finance at LSU and that's where and how he got connected to playing with the group in New Orleans.

A girl he met in one of his classes was an aspiring vocalist who had friends in low places, and one of those friends needed a trombone player.

He could carry a tune, but never thought of himself as a singer. One night an elderly lady came up to the bandstand and asked if they knew the song Melancholy Baby. It was she and her husband's favorite song. The band did know that song, and as a bonus, Rick knew the words.

No one could fathom why he knew the words to that song, but he did. She tipped the band twenty dollars and gave Rick a hundred-dollar bill. His vocal style went over so well, he eventually became the lead singer and started to have a lot of success in the Quarter with his voice and his humor.

Rick met some remarkably interesting people on Bourbon Street and became aware of various rules which had been put in place by a very powerful family who managed a lot of New Orleans, especially the Vieux Carré.

For several years Rick lived two lives: During the week he was a young man going to college, but he played a lot of music most weekends, the Mardi Gras season, and New Year's Eve for sure. He was a professional musician with a fairly normal life. It was his contacts, friends, and connections in the Big Easy, plus his very accomplished military background that had brought him to Dr. Carmichael's attention.

They met at 1:30 on a cold Sunday morning. Dr. Carmichael had approached Rick during one of the band's breaks and asked if they could meet after the show was over. When the band was done, Rick told the guys, "Go on and I'll catch up with you in a few." He would meet with the dude, but figured he was just another one of those agent wannabes who swore he could make the band a huge success.

It had been a long night and Rick was hungry; so, they talked over omelets and coffee. "Let me see if I get this right.

You are putting together a team of guys to do some special work for some important dude in Washington, and you have some crazy idea that I'm a good candidate for that? It really is a pleasure to meet you Doc, but I think you've been doin' a little too much smoke." Rick thanked the good doctor and got up to walk away.

Davis paid the bill and hurried after Rick to tell him one more thing: "It pays $20,000 a year."

In 1962, when a gallon of gas was less than thirty cents, and the average yearly income for mid-level management was maybe nine or ten grand, $20,000 would make you very prosperous indeed. Doc now had Rick's immediate and complete attention.

Rick wasn't necessarily mercenary, but he did like nice things, expensive restaurants, rich, beautiful women, and fast cars. Any one of those preferences would find $20,000 most helpful. "Let's talk about this some more on Monday. Right now, I'm beat, and the rest of today is booked solid." They would meet in Baton Rouge on Monday.

* * *

Rick had been auditing a couple of graduate courses to see if he wanted to pursue his Masters. Graduate school wasn't anything like the grind of undergraduate work, which was good because it didn't get in the way of his making music in New Orleans. Also, he had started dating his friend Nikki who had introduced him to Tony Biggers, the guy who needed the trombone player way back when.

Classes would be over by four; so, he agreed to meet Dr. Carmichael for a drink at a place called Rip's around five. The place would be loud and filled with college kids around seven, but before then, they could talk.

"Rick, no one knows anything about any of this except my good friend, a close member of his family, me, and now you. For now, you will only know about a small part of this, and before we can discuss this any further, you will need to sign this document. It isn't too complicated to understand. Anything discussed is considered top secret; therefore, should you divulge any of this to anyone your young ass will probably be locked up somewhere and never be seen again."

Rick smiled and told Doc he had a special way with words. "I understand."

He signed the rather formal looking document. "Now that we have things on paper, what exactly is it you want me to do?"

"We'll meet for lunch on Wednesday, and then we'll take a quick trip to meet my friend. Please make plans to be away for the day, perhaps two."

* * *

It was almost Christmas, and the Capitol was lit up like Fantasy Land, plus it was snowing. Rick hadn't seen this much snow in a long time. He thought to himself, *this has to be someone's idea of a prank, but this is a cool trip.*

Davis didn't tell Rick they were going to the Whitehouse until after the plane landed, and even then, Rick still thought he was kidding. When they pulled up to the guardhouse, he knew for certain it wasn't a joke. He kept asking himself, *what am I doing here?*

It was late, and everyone had gone except the security team. The doctor and Rick were escorted to the President's upstairs study where they were warmly greeted by the President and the Attorney General.

Rick was having a most difficult time trying to determine when he would wake up from this dream and realize he was at home in bed. In the background, he swore he heard President Kennedy welcoming him to the Whitehouse and introducing him to his brother. "It's a pleasure to be here, sir, and to meet both you and the Attorney General." All he could hope for was that he didn't dribble on himself or do any other disgusting thing to embarrass himself.

"Mr. Charles, we've asked you here because the good doctor has decided you would be the right man for the job. Let me get right to the point. What we're doing is creating what I like to call a private oversight operation. To do this will require the best men, with great professional skills, street smarts and a high degree of intelligence. Davis seems to think you fit all of those categories quite nicely."

Rick, in his best attempt at humility, told the President, "Sir, I'm honored to be considered for this assignment and I don't mean to sound disrespectful, but I'm having a very difficult time understanding how I could be of any help. I go to school, play in a band, and otherwise, just have a good time. How is it I am so privileged to be part of something you consider to be so important?"

The President turned to his friend and smiled. "Davis you failed to tell me he was a politician."

The Attorney General took over the conversation at this point, telling Rick he would be working with Dr. Carmichael exclusively. The training, operational information, assignments, and logistics would be forthcoming over the next two or three weeks. Most of the operation would be about gathering information, and there could be times when some assignments could be dangerous. "We considered that possibility before choosing you as the leader of this group. Our vetting indicated that you don't take much crap off anyone, but if they insist, you seem to handle those types of situations just fine. Most impressive to us was that the men in your outfit admired and respected your

20

character, strength, and leadership. All that made the decision much easier."

They had a drink, had a few minutes of idle small talk, and the meeting was over. Operation Oversight was underway. Rick said he would strive to be the best he could be. Under his breath, he muttered, "Man, that was lame!"

Dr. Carmichael told Rick that they would begin putting things together on Monday. Rick would work with Davis during the week and then go back to his usual routine on the weekend. One casualty of all this would be graduate school, which to Rick was a good trade for twenty-thousand dollars a year.

"Doc, I probably know the answer to this, but will ask anyway. Can I tell Nikki anything about this?" Doc gave him a snide look and said nothing. Rick understood.

Chapter 4
A Lovely Couple, Don't You Think?

Nikki and Rick hadn't seen each other in almost two weeks. She had concerts in Connecticut, Rhode Island, and New York, and was just now getting back. They had talked a couple of times while she was away to tell each other they were missed. This time she was calling to tell her sweety that she was on her way over.

She loved to go to Rick's little hideaway. It was only one room, but it was so cozy and quiet. Sometimes they would sit and talk for hours, discussing subjects like ETs or politics or even relationships. And then sometimes they didn't talk much at all.

Elizabeth Nicole Meredith was a beautiful woman with an incredible voice. Her beauty wasn't just her looks, but more her willingness to help other young women not as privileged as herself. She loved to run around the house barefooted, wearing one of her dad's old white shirts and a pair of shorts, but when she went outside the house, she always looked like a fashion model. Five foot six, long blond hair, and eyes that looked right through you, Nikki Meredith was the woman several young men in New Orleans wanted to wed. Wealthy, charming, beautiful, and talented were only some of her attributes. She was having none of that marriage discussion for now. Her career was first in her mind, followed closely by her interest in Mr. Charles. You wouldn't find her in any of the clubs other than when she was on a date because her talent was dedicated to the world of opera.

She had starred in several operas in New Orleans and major cities all over the US and Canada. Four years before, she was Miss New Orleans and runner-up to Miss Louisiana. To all who knew her, they fully understood why she was so attracted to Rick.

Other than her father, Rick was the only man she respected. He had the audacity to tell her that he wasn't necessarily available just because she thought he should be. Besides that, he wasn't overwhelmed by her looks as most other men were. To Rick, she was a great friend who he loved and adored and didn't mind at all that she had a highly successful career. He was quite secure in his unique and private world of the French Quarter.

Nikki was doing all she could do not to fall in love with this enigmatic man, but the closer they became, the more she wanted him all to herself. At this moment, his little one-room Lair in the woods was her favorite place in the world.

She had two brothers, but neither one would ever be as strong as Nikki. Her father spent more time talking to Rick about his business than to his sons. There were times when he would go to great length to explain why Rick should marry his daughter, take over a part of the business, and give up all this music stuff. Big John Meredith was a successful maritime lawyer, who also owned a shipbuilding company, a large commercial real estate agency, and several prime pieces of real estate in the downtown area. He had a piece of Lloyds of London, and just in case he was bored, owned part of an Indy racing team. His friends thought he bought into the team just to make sure he had tickets at the finish line for the Indy 500.

Rick was dreamingly special to Nikki, even when she couldn't find him. Since they met at LSU, there were times he would just go somewhere without telling anyone, stay a few days, and then reappear. It would drive her crazy, but he would always laugh it off, and tell her, "At least I know you missed me."

Nikki had just turned twenty-eight, and as they sat by the fireplace, they were trying to calculate how many times she had been proposed to since her first one at the age of eighteen. He had written a number down on a piece of paper and put it in his pocket, and now as they drank their favorite wine, she began to go down the list.

What was cool to her was how much fun it was to tell Rick why she would have never married any of them. As best she could remember, she had turned down twenty-two proposals, not to mention the number of invitations she had received for live-in arrangements. She would have none of either possibility. Rick had written seventeen on the piece of paper.

He smiled as he reached for her. "Don't you get tired of being a sex symbol? I can't tell you how much it means to me to be able to sip a glass of wine in your presence, my fair princess. I shall treasure these moments forever."

"Rick Charles you are a pain in the ass, but you have such a cute little ass that it's okay, I guess. She put the glass down and started to have her way with her playmate. Don't you think you should take off that good shirt? You wouldn't want to get it torn, would you?"

"Well, what about that really beautiful dress. Heaven forbid if we spilled any wine on it. Let me help you with it."

The phone rang about 7:30 the next morning, and it was Dr. Carmichael. He needed to see Rick later in the morning.

He leaned over and kissed his roommate and went to take a shower. Around ten they went to breakfast, and they were off on their different paths for the day. "I love you Miss Cute Butt, and I will see you later."

She loved him too, but didn't do the casual love you too thing. When she told him she loved him, it was a most private and serious matter. He was the only man she had ever wanted for more than fifteen minutes. She smiled, thought about it a moment, and realized he was the best thing that had ever happened to her. She damn well knew he could never do any better than her.

* * *

Rick had been playing in the Quarter, at private parties in the Garden District, and some other clubs in and around New Orleans for about two years. In the audience this night was Sheila Morgan. Miss Morgan had ownership in a successful burlesque club, and was also a most gifted exotic dancer with a unique and somewhat provocative style. Not only was she a great success on stage, but when it came to something she might want, someone made sure she had it. Her boyfriend had a strong Italian heritage and a big family. It was true: whatever Sheila wanted . . . Sheila got. Sometimes she received little gifts she didn't even know she wanted.

Sheila loved Rick's voice, and sent word to him that she would like for him to meet her after her last show the next night. There was a large man standing next to the door, who told Rick to turn around, which he did, and the guy frisked him for a weapon. Rick had no clue why they thought he would be carrying a gun. She had asked him to come by, and he did. "Rick, I love to hear you sing. You have sort of a Mel Torméish sound, and it's sexy as hell. I was told that you go to LSU and are only down here on special occasions and weekends. Is that true?

"Pretty much, but sometimes I've been here for a week or so at a time. He wondered how she knew he didn't live here all the time, and why she needed to know.

"Where are you living when you're here?"

"Right now, I have a room about four miles from here, which I rent by the week. It's not much, but keeps me dry, and it has a window air conditioner."

"She laughed and asked him if he would join her in a nightcap, and call me Sheila, please."

There must have been a button on her dresser, because a moment later, the big guy outside was inside being told to get them a brandy. He took the order and left.

"Now, while we're waiting, I have a good friend who was with me last night taking in your show. We both loved the comedy, the music, and of course the way you sing, and thought you might be a good act for the club. I told him I would talk to you about it soon. Do you act on behalf of the band's interests or do I need to speak to someone else?"

Rick had been acting as the band's manager ever since Tony Biggers was reluctantly taken on vacation to someplace in south Louisiana. "Sheila, I can make decisions for the band, but I still discuss things with them before making a final decision. What did you have in mind?"

"Talk this over with your guys: Tell them who it is you're dealing with and that my friend wants this to happen. We will pay $1000 a night, you keep the tips, and you, as the band leader, get a bonus. And would you like to live closer to your work?"

"Damn, if that doesn't entice the band, I will get a new one." She laughed, the door opened, and they had their brandy.

"I would love to be nearer to the club, but even with your generous offer; I don't have the funds to get a place too much closer."

"Did I say anything about money? We have a small place on Royal Street, and it will be available to you when you are here. It is completely furnished, with maid service, and fully stocked kitchen and bar. We have three or four apartments just like it which we let our friends use when they are in town. Consider yourself a close friend, Rick.

"Sheila, I can't begin to say thank you enough for such a generous gift, but . . ." She interrupted him with, "But what? It's yours, and even though it's not large, I'm sure it's nicer than where you are now. Now I've got to get my beauty rest. Can you and the band start next weekend?"

"We'll be there if the guys agree, and I know they will. Who do I contact about what we'll need for sound and lights?" "I will have Émile give you a shout sometime in the next couple of days. What's your number?"

"Tell him to just give me a call at this number. It's the office where we're playing now, and they'll give me a message if I'm not there. And thank you again, Sheila. Thank you so much." The guys in the band told Rick that he must be one cool dude to get them booked into Sheila's club. The tips alone would be more than they made now. Nobody makes that kind of money unless they're from New York or Hollywood. That wasn't exactly true, but the guys in the band now thought they were pretty damn cool.

Chapter 5
A Bit More Interesting

Dr. C was most emphatic. "Rick, you're leaving for a couple of weeks, and you won't be back here until the work is done."

"Where am I going, and why? We just signed a deal with Sheila Morgan's club, and they aren't going to be in a good mood if I'm leaving for a couple of weeks. Any chance you could postpone whatever this is?"

"I wish I could, but because it's so secretive, we only have one shot. I'm afraid you're going to have to go to a rehab clinic to rest your voice for a couple of weeks."

"Doc, can you get me something on paper about this problem I'm having? These people aren't very understanding, and they trust no one. Her club is too good of a gig and too good of a source to let it just go away."

"Rick, I know this is a problem for you, but you'll just have to figure something out."

"Who is this Dr. Landingham? Why him? Why Dallas? We have some great doctors here, and I have guys depending on me?"

Rick was going whether it caused problems or not. It wouldn't be the last time he would have to make excuses for why he had to be gone, but the timing of this one was going to be tough to explain.

"Sheila, I am so sorry, but this was a complete surprise to me. I had no idea my voice needed therapy and rest. It was just a sore throat at first, and then it began to hurt in the back of the throat. Dr. Widmark took a look and referred me to this guy in Dallas.

"Had I known about this I wouldn't have signed the contract. I'll be ready to go in a couple of weeks. There's nothing I can do about it. The doctor said if I put any more strain on the chords, it could become very serious." He hated the lie, but it's all he had for the moment.

Johnny Faretta was pissed off in a big way. "You're telling me the kid has voice problems and he didn't know anything about it? You make a deal with me; you keep your part of the bargain. And you're saying he can't sing for two weeks? Where's he gonna' be recoverin'? This rehab thing better be on the level. I catch him hangin' with some broad, he'll wish he had never seen the Quarter."

Johnny Faretta ran things in the Quarter for the Dianatti family. Johnny, once upon a time, was a young, brash, and brutal two-bit thug. He most likely would have stayed that way had it not been for a very off chance meeting he had one night with Joey Dianatti. No one knows exactly what happened, but if someone did, there had not been, nor would there ever be any discussion of it.

All that's necessary to know is that some dude from Chicago got into it with Joey because of Sheila and pulled a gun on Joey. Faretta hit the guy over the head with a bottle of red wine, and that pretty much took care of the problem. Chicago's tough guy population had one less idiot.

From that point forward, Johnny had the gratitude of a powerful ally. He rose quickly in the family and took care of more and more business. One night in May of '63 he was called to the home of Joey's father. There was a problem with a guy stirring things up with the dock workers, and he needed to be persuaded to stop the conversation about a strike. Andy Swenson didn't take well to being told what to do. He told Johnny that he had been the leader of this union for twelve years and no one was going to tell him how to run it. If they needed to strike, they would strike. Two days later, Andy's body was somewhere on the bottom of Lake Pontchartrain wearing very heavy chains. Sometime shortly after that, Faretta became a made man.

Rick wasn't going to be in a clinic in Dallas. His therapy would be in a very lovely home in Vermont. For two weeks he was to study, memorize, configure, and live the part of an undercover agent. He was to know the face of every major player in the Dianatti and Vinzzetti families. He would be able to move

28

across the southern part of Louisiana without a map, and know the name, number, and call code of everyone in his group. All the above would have to be accomplished in two weeks.

One of the last things, but maybe one of the most important parts of his time in Vermont was learning phone numbers, call codes, and all the drop point locations. Rick was beginning to understand why he was getting five figures for this, but not sure he would ever get to spend any of it.

Two weeks were done, and now it was back to a real world that might not be as much fun as it was when he left. The guys in the band were more than glad to see him. Things had not gone well with the guy Sheila chose to step in for Rick. And Johnny Faretta was always asking about their leader's condition. He was not a happy man.

Maybe now things would settle down for a while . . . have a little break in the tension . . . or maybe not. They had checked out this Dr. Landingham out and found that Rick hadn't been in therapy there. Faretta wanted to know why the kid had lied. He invited Rick to come over for a drink.

"Hey, my man, how are things with the voice box?"

"Not too bad now. Doc said I could go back to work but have to ease back on some of the high notes."

"I forgot, who was your doctor?"

"I was supposed to go to a Dr. Landingham in Dallas, but he wanted me to spend four to six weeks in his recovery unit. There was no way I could be gone that long. I got a second opinion from Dr. Perry in Montpelier, Vermont. This guy has worked with a lot of opera stars and was recommended by my girlfriend. She was there with me for two days, but since I couldn't talk, she decided to go home. I spent most of my time reading and watching old movies on TV."

Johnny was relieved by that little bit of information. Maybe the kid was okay after all. He called to tell Sheila that everything was okay for the time being, and in a roundabout way, apologized for questioning her tolerance level. Rick had no idea how close he came to being a memory in the Big Easy.

* * *

Dr. C was sipping a glass of scotch. "Rick we know that the CIA or a small group within the agency is selling drugs to finance something extremely secret. We need to know what that plan is and to find out where the drug link begins. We do know it's coming through New Orleans, but from where is just a guess. They are selling tons of it in Harlem and Queens. They have even expanded into New Jersey. They're destroying a lot of lives and must be stopped for two reasons: First and most obvious is saving lives, and secondly, put a stop to their revenue stream. You need to get to know Johnny Faretta a lot better. I know what happened was a little too close for comfort, but it may have given you a way to befriend him. He's a made man, so whatever you do, don't get in his face. Take your time and work into a nice friendly conversation with him, if there is such a thing. He is extremely dangerous; so, be careful."

He patted Rick on the back, and they went in separate directions. Rick kept asking himself if I'm going to be making friends with a guy like Faretta, shouldn't I get a raise?

Rick didn't know how Doc did it, but he did think he was damn smart. A bill came in the mail from the office of Dr. Ernest Mallory in Vermont for the tidy little sum of $2860. There was a list of all the procedures, treatments, and therapy sessions and a request that the bill be paid immediately. Rick's bank account didn't come close to having that kind of money in it.

* * *

"Rick, we've never advanced anyone four weeks of their salary, and pretty sure we're not going to do that now." Sheila was doing her best to be a little provocative while she told him not to get his hopes up.

Sheila was a good businesswoman, and though she liked Rick, giving him an advance didn't fit in her cash flow projections. On the other hand, if she did this, he would owe her big time. She thought about it and decided she would loan him the money, but no interest and no repayment schedule. For the moment, it was more of a gift. She decided Ricky boy might be a fun way to spend an afternoon now and then.

"Johnny, this is Rick Charles over at the club. Do you have some time I could meet with you? It's important."

"Sure guy, come on over. I'll be here."

Today would be the first time Rick had ever been to the place known as the tiger den. It was just another bar until you made the mistake of going toward the back without an okay from the bartender. You would quickly find out there was a very well protected no entrance zone on the other side of the little red curtain.

The guys up front didn't know who he was; so, before he was allowed back, he was frisked. He was given the nod, and he went on back.

There was a poker game in session, and he didn't want to interrupt. He just stood there for a few seconds. He heard this big macho voice ring out. "Hey Big Rick, whatcha got goin' on for me today?"

"Johnny, I can come back later. I need to talk to you in private."

"What's it about?"

"We can talk later."

Johnny folded, went to the bar, poured himself a drink, and told Rick to follow him. They went up a flight of stairs into this rather opulent looking office with photos of local and national celebrities and politicians on the walls. "Okay kid, what can I do for you?"

"I do understand what could happen to me for bringing this situation to you, but I'd rather have it on the table now than later." He pulled out the invoice from the clinic in Vermont and told him that he had asked for an advance on his salary to pay for it. At first, Sheila didn't think it was something she wanted to do, but then she decided to loan him the money with no interest and no repayment schedule. He had thought that was strange, but at the same time, it helped him out a lot.

"Yesterday, I found out what the repayment was all about. Sheila called me to come to the club to talk about one of the celebrity guests who would be in the audience on Friday night. When she opened the door, she was wearing nothing under her very see-through gown. She told me to take my clothes off and get in the bed. "Johnny, I told her it wasn't a good idea, but she told me she was just collecting a little interest on the loan."

Johnny had yet to move or say anything. He just took another sip of his drink.

"I'm here to tell you this, understanding I'm in a lot of trouble, but couldn't let this go on without you knowing. I didn't want you to find out from someone else."

"Rick, my boy, she's always had a thing for singers, so don't let it worry you. You're cool with me and loyalty is everything. If she calls you again, maybe you should have something else that you have to do."

Elizabeth Taylor was going to be in the audience that night, and Sheila was to do her first show at ten. When she didn't show, the MC said she was not feeling well. There was a substitute act for her, the band was on again, and Sheila's second show was canceled.

No one seemed to know where she was. Elizabeth Taylor would not have another opportunity to see Sheila's act. Sheila had been retired.

Chapter 6
Yo Hablo Espanol

The messages were coming from Baía de Guanabara, a small waterfront area near Rio de Janeiro.

Rick had discovered the name of the place on a piece of paper in Sheila's dressing room when she had asked him to drop by to discuss his show. He immediately sent it to his associate Chip Hagen, who was pursuing leads in South and Central America for drug connections with the New Orleans area.

Doc had brought Chip into the group because of his background in communications, his degree in romance languages, and overall great guy that he was. That was his assessment even though he had been chosen because he was more like an Americanized James Bond.

The guy was smooth as silk, no doubt about it. If you didn't know he was from Kansas City, you would immediately have thought him to be Spanish or maybe Italian. The ladies were quite taken with him, and he was quite fond of them as well. He had been in Brazil for two weeks, and already found a sexy friend named Camila. He had an uncanny knack for working himself into whatever situation in which you needed him to be involved.

She didn't pick him; he chose her. The daughter of a very wealthy importer/exporter Camila was very much daddy's little girl, and whatever she wanted, she got. Her figure was almost sculpted, and many wanted to see it up close. Her eyes were dark, full of mischief, and the facial expressions might indicate interest, but could also put a man in his place. Chip paid her driver a lot of money to have them introduced, and they immediately hit it off.

His Portuguese wasn't as good as his Spanish, but she offered to help him with that.

He knew she could be his direct connection to her daddy's business. If Señor Estoval wasn't directly involved with the drug train, he knew who was.

Camila had invited him to a party as her date at her home on Saturday, but daddy would have to meet him first. "Señor Hagen, what kind of work are you doing here in our quaint little town?" And please, call me Alejandro."

"Thank you, sir, for allowing me to use your first name; I am honored. As for my reasons to be here, I am acting as an advisor and translator for a maritime attorney in New Orleans who is the intermediary for a company interested in setting up a revolutionary oil and gas storage concept in this area. I cannot reveal any of the details at this time, but when all of the papers have been signed, I'm sure I can tell you more about it then."

"Mr. Hagen, you seem to have an important part in this rather large undertaking. Do you have a background in oil and gas?"

"No sir, I'm not involved in the oil and gas business per se. My value to the attorney is making sure everyone on both sides is comfortable with what is being said. A lot of translators take it upon themselves to generalize what is being said rather than being precise. In that respect, I am most valuable to my client."

"It has been a pleasure to meet you, and you have my blessings and permission to be with my daughter at our very humble festa this weekend." Mr. Hagen had now been successful in getting a foot in the door and possibly his tail in a crack as well.

Anytime there was the possibility of drug activity the cartels had radio searches going 24/7; consequently, any communication between Chip and Rick would have to be done very creatively. For now, they were using a runner and a very well-paid runner at that.

From Rio to Miami to New Orleans and back again was an every-six-day routine for a young associate attorney in the Meredith law firm. He was being paid a lot of money, but he was yet to handle his first case. What the hell was all of this about? He had a lot of time to think about it and was also becoming quite well read during his various round trips.

Aaron Rothenberg graduated with honors from the Virginia Law School, and clerked in the 5th Circuit before being hired by John Meredith. The guy was insanely smart; so, to keep him happy during his running days, he could take his girlfriend and stay at the nicest hotels while they were away. She loved it; he didn't.

On this particular trip, the message from Chip was urgent. "Do not stay over, do not delay; this needs to get back to New Orleans ASAP."

Rick wanted to get Chip a little more noticed and would do so by having him place large bets on sports events back in the states. To do that, he would need cash and lots of it. Two hundred thousand dollars had been placed into a Swiss account which was accessible from a transfer account in Montreal. Any bank in Rio would immediately honor a transfer of funds from there. It gave Chip continuous and instantaneous liquidity, the knowledge of which would be passed on to Alejandro by his banker.

With all of Chip's moves easily traced, he wouldn't be suspected of trying to hide anything, and whoever was watching would know he had access to large sums of money.

The festa was very lavish, and Camila was breathtaking in her new gown personally designed by Hubert de Givenchy. Chip smiled, thinking how much the dress must have set the old man back considering how much fabric was involved. Camila knew she had an exquisite body and didn't mind showing it off to tease the men and anger the other senoritas. She gave Chip a small kiss on the cheek and took his arm. Let the gala begin.

She was the only child, and there was nothing she couldn't have, except a man who might love her for herself. The thing she liked about this mysterious man from New Orleans was that he didn't put her on a pedestal. If anything, he didn't pay as much attention to her as he did some of the other senoritas there that night. She would soon take care of that.

While they sat at their table talking to the other guests as well as her mom and dad, she kept running her hand up Chip's pants, playing with his zipper, and squeezing him just enough to notice he was becoming increasingly uncomfortable. She was doing this while engaged in serious discussions with various guests at the table. He wondered how in the hell was she able to concentrate on both situations? Chip couldn't concentrate on anything with her hand moving in all the right places.

After most of the guests were gone, she walked him to his car, and let him know how much she enjoyed the evening . . . especially the time at their table. If he would like to discuss it further, she would leave the door open at the pool cottage. She also wanted him to know that she would not be wearing the gown she wore to the party. She might not be wearing anything. He wasn't going to fall into that trap. He went home and stayed there. *Admittedly, it was a hard choice for him to make.*

* * *

When Nikki threw a party, she hired the very best to make sure that hers was by far the most attended by the who's who of the old money in New Orleans. There were families attending whose great-great-grandparents moved from New York when New Orleans was nothing but a small river port. Some of Jean Lafitte's

36

descendants lived near the Meredith's and were frequent dinner-party guests.

This evening's party was to celebrate Nikki's recent signing to play the role of Baby in the opera, The Ballad of Baby Doe. She would be leaving for New York in a couple of weeks; so, she wanted to have a send-off fit for a queen. Nikki enjoyed the thought of nobility. She told Rick he needed to buy a tux because he would be using it a lot from this point forward. It seemed as if Miss Nikki had it in her mind that she was going to be a star.

A string quartet played during the first phase of the party, and then during the second half of the evening, a piano quintet played very romantic music for those who wished to dance. Dinner was served buffet style with guests seated inside and out. The night air was less humid than usual and much cooler as well. Nikki had to do her three hours of mingling, but eventually, she and Rick had some time for a glass of bubbly and a few minutes of being alone.

No one could miss the huge cake being rolled out onto the pool area. It was at least four feet tall with sparklers lighting up the night. Everyone was being served Dom Perignon, and there were toasts from her father, friends, but the private, personal toast from Rick, would be shared later in private.

It was a hugely festive night for this most radiant and beautiful woman. Rick stood to the side and watched the elegant Elizabeth Nicole Meredith graciously accept all her many well-deserved accolades. She would be leaving for New York on May first and be terribly missed by everyone but especially by Rick. He had grown quite used to her being there with him, but being in New York . . . who knows who she'll be seeing. All he could do was hope that she would miss him as much as he would miss her and remember how close they had become. Rick wasn't a worrier, but he did understand that she was not only special to him, but a

37

woman who could have any man she wanted. She had many from which to choose, but for the moment, Rick's heart was all that mattered.

When Rick got back to his apartment, there was a note from Dr. C. He and the President were in constant touch, and the last time they spoke, Prez wanted to know if anything had been found which could link the agency to the drugs coming into New Orleans.

Rick replied to the message the next morning, and left it at drop number four. It read, "Doc, we're going as fast as we can. The answers aren't going to just fall into our laps. Chip has made inroads, but nothing yet connects the Estovals to any drug smuggling operation. I will let you know the minute I think we have something."

Chapter 7
Some Guy from Russia

"Boss, there's a guy here to see you. Says he just got in from Russia and is supposed to see you."

"Tell him to come back later; I'm busy right now."
It wasn't going to be quite that simple. Johnny's phone rang about twenty minutes later; it was Mr. Dianatti. "Damn it Johnny, get the kid back, and call Joey. Don't screw this up again."

Johnny went to the door and began yelling at Jeremy to get the guy back in here. He kept thinking why didn't the kid say who sent him here? If the Don told the kid to come here, you didn't tell him to come back later. It always made Johnny edgy when he messed up. No one was indispensable, and that could make anyone a little edgy even when it was something as innocuous as sending the kid away.

Jeremy found him across the street having a cup of coffee. Jeremy had become Johnny's right-hand man ever since Sheila mysteriously disappeared. The big guy showed the kid back to Johnny's office.

"Hey, kid, I'm sorry I didn't know who you were when you first came in. I get people dropping by all the time; so, again, I'm sorry for the mix-up. What can I do for you?"

"My name is Harvey, and I was told to get back to the states as soon as I could. I've been in Russia, but when my contact sent me my last set of directions, he said it was important that I see you as soon as possible. After this meeting, I'm supposed to meet up with a couple of dudes who live on St. Charles."

Johnny was puzzled. "They told you to see me first? Why don't you go to the bar, get whatever you want, and I'll be back with you in a few minutes. Joey, there's a guy outside, name's Harvey, and says your dad wanted him to see me first. You know anything about this?"

Joey said that he'd be over in a minute. When he did get there, he asked Johnny to step out for a few minutes, and when Johnny was asked to leave, it was business at the highest levels. Twenty minutes later the door opened, Harvey and Joey shook hands, and now things might get back to normal.

* * *

Myer O'Steen and Craig Benson were almost like an old married couple. They could finish one another's sentence; they had known each other for years. Both were very wealthy, shared a beautiful 7000 square foot home in the Garden District, owned several valuable pieces of property in the downtown area, and almost half of the ninth ward had their company's name on the deeds.

They both had day jobs as owners of a financial corporation which in of itself operated a large real estate firm, several beauty salons, nightclubs, and a very secretive, well sheltered, prestigious escort service run by a woman named Jacqueline Du Monde. Her real name was Susan Lockhart, but that didn't sound very sexy.

Craig was a good friend of Wendell Jeffreys, the recently promoted Director of the Special Activities Division of the CIA. Not many knew about that connection.

Rick passed along to Doc his thought about how small the world seems to be. New Orleans underworld figures, highly successful businessmen, a young ex-Marine just in from Russia, and the CIA all having an opportunity to get together and talk over old times. It was all a little too cozy.

* * *

Paul Hudson was Rick's communication expert and very adept at setting up surveillance anywhere and under any circumstances. Doc had used his influence with the President to have Paul sent to New Orleans to help with, what he thought, was an FBI sting operation. Paul spent six years in the Navy, and installed everything pertaining to electronics when the so-called advisors were first sent to Viet Nam. Rick needed to meet with him right away.

After a couple of calls, they set up a time to meet in Baton Rouge. Rick didn't want to take any chances of them being seen together in New Orleans.

He told Paul. "Here's what I'm thinking about doing, and you can tell me if it can be done and how. Also, if what I want can't be done, then I need you to find some way we can hear what's going on in a very private office.

One of the key figures in our investigation has an upstairs office at 630 Ann St. I'm sure it's virtually impossible to get a bug in there, but is there anything you can set up close by that we can use to eavesdrop on him?"

"Rick, you're right about one thing: a bug won't be going in there. Maybe I could come up with something via the next-door office space. I will spend some time looking at old blueprints and see what, if anything, I might be able to rig up for you. I'll be in touch when I have something."

* * *

Camila and Chip were on a private yacht somewhere off the coast of Cancun headed for a weeklong cruise to get to know one another better. If this didn't get them closer together, nothing would. Camila had controlled most every man she had ever dated. She loved the chase, and then just as soon as she caught them, she forgot their names. She kept their gifts, but nothing else.

Now she had on board the one man she hadn't been able to figure out. They would be together on the boat for a week. She would have him when and where she wanted him, and if he didn't treat her right, give her what she wanted, he would pay the price. What she so wanted was that he wouldn't give in to her wanton, lustful needs. He didn't, she was pissed, and very happy. He dared to tell her that maybe when she was a little older, they could take another shot, but for now, she was still too attached to daddy. Maybe she should grow up some more.

The crew had never heard noises and screams like that. Camila ran up one side of the ship and down the other telling Chip that he was the most despicable individual she had ever met. He had a good idea as to her thoughts about him, but she was going too fast for him to understand it all.

"Are you one of those sweeties who like other boys? Why else would you not want my magnificent body next to you every moment we're together?" She screamed at the Captain to let this asshole off at the next port. She was through with him.

He was in their cabin reading. She was so mad that for once she couldn't find the words. She laid down next to him and went to sleep. Eleven hours later they were making deeply passionate love. She was most happy, and *right on top of the situation.*

Chapter 8
Some Things to do in Washington

The President, Robert, and Dr. Carmichael had scheduled some coffee time to get caught up on a few loose ends. "Davis, has Rick found out any more about that kid who dropped in from out of nowhere? And what about that O'Steen guy. Bobby said he was fairly sure that the guy was mixed up with the mob down there. Any idea if that's true or not?"

"Mr. President, I can't give you anything on that front because we don't know anything conclusively, but will tell you this, Chip Hagen has gotten close to Camila Estoval, the daughter of Alejandro Estoval. They are out on her father's yacht as we speak and should find out soon if there's anything unusual about the boat and who some of the passengers have been over the last few months."

Bobby indicated that the connection between the Dianatti family and O'Steen and Benson was about money . . . a lot of money. "Doc, it's vital that Rick finds out how all this fits pdq. Something big is up, and we've got to find out what and where before all hell breaks loose."

The President indicated that he had a source which told him that over three tons of heroin was on its way from South America to the Gulf, but they didn't know where exactly. Bobby told Doc, "They're pretty sure it came from somewhere in Brazil, and I'm assuming it was from somewhere close to where Chip is living. We desperately need that drop point or there's enough of that poison to take out the entire east coast."

Donald Meriwether was now the acting Assistant Deputy Director of Covert Operations because of the passing of Harold Stewart. Harold seemed to have been in excellent health, but one morning during his three-mile run, he had a heart attack and died before they could get him to the hospital. He was only fifty-six.

Donald and the newly appointed Director of the Special Activities Division, Wendell Jeffreys were classmates at Duke Law School. They had similar backgrounds and similar interests. They both lusted for power and money, and could be unscrupulous to get what they wanted.

It was a hot, humid day in Dallas, which made some afternoon storms possible here and there, but for the moment it was clear blue skies at Love Field. The small Lear jet came to a stop at one of the private hangars and a couple of interesting looking heavyweights got out and stood by the stairway as a very well-dressed man and young friend departed the plane. He stopped to give the stewardess a note, and then came down the steps to get into a car which was waiting to take them downtown.

Johnny and Harvey arrived at a little bar called the Carousel Club, which had some exotic dancers, some of whom were more exotic than others. Jack Ruby was able to keep the club afloat because he was a small-time hood who did favors for the big boys. He always saw to it that when they met at his place, everything they wanted or needed was there for them. There was a door in the back, which led to a stairway to what looked like a combination office and bedroom. It was rather gauche but served its purpose for the time being.

"Harvey, I want you to meet a couple of friends of mine from Chicago. They've heard you're a crack shot and they may be able to use you on an upcoming job. Why don't you guys talk

43

about this while I go to the bar and have a drink or two? I'll take you to a favorite restaurant of mine later if you have the time." Johnny stuffed a c-note in Harvey's pocket and told him, "When you're done here, I need you to take a cab to the hangar. The plane will be waiting to take you back to N.O."

When the meeting was over, Jack asked if there was anything else they needed. He did know of two exciting new girls who had just arrived in Dallas if they were interested. Johnny thanked him for his generous offer, but his friends were leaving after dinner.

Johnny would be staying over for a day or two. There was some merchandise he had to see about, and he was having a meeting in Fort Worth the next night. He called Jack later in the evening to ask about one of the girls he had mentioned earlier. Her name was Estelle, and she liked dark Italian types.

* * *

"Mi amigo, do I call you Chip?"

"My first name is Charles, which is a great name, but the family started calling me Chip when I was a kid, and then my friends at school called me Chip. I almost forgot I had a real name. You may call me Chip if you wish, Señor Estoval."

"Chip, I wanted to spend some time with you for two reasons: first, of course, is Camila, and secondly, I would like to find out more about you and your business here, if you don't mind. But before we talk about business, I hope you enjoyed your cruise with Camila."

"I would be happy to answer any questions you have that I have permission to discuss, and yes, I enjoyed our time together on your yacht. Senor Estoval, I will say one thing for certain: She only knows one speed."

44

"That's so true, and for a long time I thought she would never be able to settle down, but since meeting you, not only is she more settled, she is halfway civil to the house staff. They all asked me to extend to you their sincerest appreciation.

"There's no doubt I have spoiled her rotten over the years, but it's because I could. My lovely wife Marianne says it has made life more difficult for Camila, but one thing I do know: it's one hell of a man who could take her away from me. I compliment you, Señor Hagen."

"Sir, it was never my intention to take anyone away from anyone. Maybe she likes me because I'm so difficult to control. Were we to become a serious couple, she would most likely be bored soon thereafter. I'm afraid she's still yours."

They both had a good laugh with that comment, as they made a toast to Camila's Latin temperament. "So, tell me Chip, what exactly is it that you translate?"

"Sir, I'm sure it's difficult to think that there would be a need for a French translator in Brazil."

"I assume then that you represent a French company?"

"I actually represent the attorneys who represent an American company which is taking care of the French company's business. It's complicated, but I'm sure as well-known as you are, someone might be able to find that information for you. With no disrespect intended, sir, the names can't come from me."

"How long do you plan to be here? Once your present task is concluded, you could be of great help to me as I grow my companies internationally. Perhaps we can talk about that at some point in the future."

"It would be my pleasure sir, and I appreciate your confidence in me."

Camila had flown to New York to do some shopping and would be back home tomorrow night. "Chip, why don't you plan to join us tomorrow night for dinner? We'll have something out on the veranda and make it just the four of us. Would you accept my invitation?"

"Certainly, Alejandro, I would be most happy to join you and your lovely family. You might need to double check that with Camila, just in case. She may have found her a very wealthy, powerful boyfriend in New York."

Alejandro smiled and told Chip, "Now you know better than that, don't you son?"

Chip smiled, and excused himself. He had to be in his office within the hour. "Buenos Tardes, Señor Estoval y hasta mañana por la noche.

Chip called Rick to see if he had anything to hear as to messages or recorded conversations. "Not yet, but I will call Paul later to see what he's found out. How are you and the energetic Miss Estoval getting along?"

I must admit, she is one wild and wonderful woman. I've lost five pounds and haven't missed a meal. I'm having dinner with the Estovals tomorrow night, and almost dreading what will come after.

"I am so sorry that you have to suffer like this, but I've got work to do. I need to call Paul about a couple of things, and I'm sure he'll have the same sympathy for your situation as I do. Take care old stud."

* * *

"Hey Paul, this is Rick. Any decision as to whether we can get a listening device close enough to make out what's being said?"

"Rick, I've been looking at some old drawings, and I think I can come in from another building, but not sure yet. I'm meeting with a guy who used to be an inspector for the city; so, after we have looked at the drawings and talked about it, I will let you know what the chances are of getting something close by.

"Thanks, Paul. I appreciate your help on this. Call as soon as you know something.

* * *

It was as if you were going back in time to maybe the twenties or thirties. There were big black limos arriving every minute or two, and forty or fifty ominous looking dudes moving in and out of a small café in South Cicero, Illinois. There were five important family members having lunch and didn't want to be bothered. For every three moving around, one FBI agent was assigned to take pictures.

It wasn't so much about the individuals enjoying their meals as much as it was the discussion they were having after lunch. "I want the son of a bitch dead, and I don't give a rat's ass how it's done." That pretty much set the tone for the rest of the afternoon.

"This guy that our New Orleans friends have, is he as good as they say he is? How much do we really know about him?"

"All I know is that he's the perfect hit guy. Hate's the government, volatile, stupid, and thinks he's a part of a broad conspiracy to kill off five people on the same day. He wants to be famous, and we're going to help him."

"Do we have any timetable on this going down?"

"We're waiting to hear back from a guy we have in Washington who will give us information about possible times and locations. We'll only need a week or two to get this ready; so, I'm thinkin' it could happen at any time. You guys have anything else to talk about?"

"We just gonna use this one guy? Shouldn't we have some back up just in case?"

"Yeah, Joey says he's got that covered. We'll have two of our guys there to make sure it all goes down like it's supposed to, but it'll be the kid who gets all the credit." They had a big laugh and with that, started closing down the meeting.

One of the Dons said, "This will be our only sit-down about this. If you got somethin' you wanna say, get it out now. Otherwise, we're turning this over to Joey and his dad, and we're gonna' stay out of their way."

"Okay, if we are all agreed, I will call them to say it's on." As quickly as it started, it was done. The FBI got a lot of pictures, but that was about all they had.

* * *

"Joey, this is Donald Meriwether and just wanted to let you know that Mrs. Stewart and her family wanted to thank you for your most generous gift. Her husband had worked a long time to rebuild the reputation of the Agency and his passing shocked everyone. His widow wanted you to know how very happy she was that you recognized his commitment to his country, and appreciated the token of your sympathy so much. She also said that you are more than welcome to visit anytime, and that her cousin Eileen also wants to thank you personally whenever you're in the area."

Joey was smiling and thinking Johnny was pretty cool to get the body cremated so fast.

"Donald, I'm happy we could be of help. Mr. Stewart was a good man and too bad he was such a young man when he passed. Again, thanks for letting me know, and I know you will be great with your new promotion. Oh yeah, what does this chick, Eileen, look like?"

Chapter 9
It's Good to Have Friends

Johnny Faretta placed a long-distance call. "Jack, you have anything going on that would keep you from coming down this weekend?"

"No, Johnny, I can be there . . . when and where?"

"We'll pick you up at the hangar around 3 pm; so, make sure you're at the Love Field hangar by 11:30 Friday morning. You okay with that?"

"Sure Johnny, I'll be there, and thanks for flying me down."

Jack would be taken to his hotel, have a chance to clean up, go to the bar for a drink or two with his date, and Jeremy would pick them up around seven to take them to dinner with Johnny. Vanessa, Jack's date, talked a lot, but didn't say anything. Though she was very sexy, her voice could be compared to fingernails on a chalkboard.

Jack was doing all he could to blot out the sound of her whiny voice by thinking about this meeting. Why would one of the most powerful families in the country want to have a private dinner with me? He wondered too if there was something they needed him to do, why didn't they just send a runner to Dallas? Maybe he was finally getting somewhere for all his loyalty and assistance with the drugs. Oh well, he thought, I'm having a great dinner, and have an all-night plaything; so, might as well just enjoy myself.

After dinner, Johnny told Vanessa to go powder her nose and have a drink. He would let her know when she could come back to the table. Jack was smiling. Man, she's going to think I'm a big shot. A private conversation with Johnny Faretta was impressive.

"Jack, we have a major hit going down, and you're going to be a big part of it. You have a lot of contacts with the boys in blue in Dallas, am I right?"

"Let's put it this way, I take care of them, and they take care of me; so, yeah, you might say I'm pretty connected down there."

"Depending on how this continues to develop, we may have another chance to talk, or maybe not. I'm going to give you a little bit of information, and you're going to need to start thinking about how you will handle your end.

"In a couple of weeks, you'll get a call from your little sexpot Vanessa. She's going to want a job at the Carousel. You'll tell her to come on up. After she gets settled in, you will introduce her to your good friend Harvey, and tell her she's getting a large bonus for doing her part for the family. You got that?

"If she balks at that, you know what to do. Now you and Vanessa have a lovely dinner, and we'll talk again. You're a good man, Jack."

Johnny hated the little greasy asshole, but needed to keep him thinking he was moving in the big time. He tossed four crisp Franklins on the table and went to the car. Vanessa wasn't feeling well and said she was going home. Jack couldn't understand why she would want to go home, sick, or not. After all, he was now a big-time player.

* * *

Craig Benson handled a lot of money for various clients all over the South and Midwest. He had clients from New York to Hawaii, but most of the larger accounts were in Louisiana, Texas, and Chicago. He specialized in helping the very wealthy avoid paying higher taxes. There was nothing illegal about his business. He merely helped wealthy people keep more of their money by paying less taxes. Because of what he did, his business was constantly under the microscope. Not so much by the government as it was by certain CPAs for certain accounts. Mishandling of funds would not be tolerated, and it had other not so pleasant ramifications as well.

He graduated from Tulane with honors and then got his Master's in accounting. That was a great start, but to fill what he thought was a wide-open niche in the financial advisor business, he needed one more degree. Craig Riley Benson received his law degree from Tulane, and that concluded the educational requirements. The first offshore account he opened was in Bermuda for a very wealthy contractor in New Orleans. He very skillfully tucked away about $4 million, and from that referral, Craig's reputation began to spread far and wide. One of his clients in 1960 was Frank Sinatra, and he specifically wanted Craig's help to manage a slush fund, which was created to provide money for large campaign events and very private parties.

Hollywood would become somewhat enamored with Craig's work, and soon he was on the inside of money, power, sex, the mob, and politics. One thing was certain, Dick Nixon had no clue as to the power, money, and organization he was about to meet head-on.

American politics was being royalized by the media. Integrity and honesty might be taking a hit as well. No doubt about it, the fifties and its Ozzie and Harriet image would soon be history in so many ways. Ethics would take a hit.

The club once known as Sheila's Place had been renamed and not all that creatively according to some. It was now known as the Quarter Past Club, the newest and coolest place where everyone wanted to be seen. Anyone that was anyone could be found there on Friday and Saturday nights. This Friday evening found Mr. and Mrs. John Meredith and Mr. and Mrs. Craig Benson at one of the tables close to the stage area.

John had started small, and once he had an idea what Craig could do, began to give him more money to manage. There was now something like $2.8 million in the Meredith Financial account in Montreal, which was linked to a small financial holding company in Bermuda that would occasionally receive and transfer funds from a numbered Swiss account.

Rick received a dinner invitation to the Meredith home for the evening of May 31st, 1963. He was going to have to wear that damn tuxedo again. John wanted Rick to meet his friend Craig Benson.

John was telling Rick that this Benson guy is really smart, and knows a lot of people. I want you to help me take care of some things if you can find a few extra hours in your schedule. I will pay you well, and you'll need it all, if you keep dating my daughter. After everyone leaves on Sunday night, you and I will have a brandy in my study. That okay with you?"

"Yes sir, it's fine with me. Should I keep this just between us, or will Nikki know we're meeting?"

"She'll know, and might even be there, if that's okay with you."

"Your daughter is quite welcome to be around me all the time, but she always has things to do."

This next gala was to give Nikki a big send-off as she went to New York to pursue her career. She was leaving first thing Monday morning, and it was John's way of making her feel special. Nikki suffered terribly from not getting enough of daddy's attention.

She had just found out about the management offer from William Morris. With her talent and an agency contract, her future would simply be up to her talent and stamina. Daddy's money wouldn't have anything to do with it, or so she hoped. No doubt she was driven to succeed, but she was also her father's choice to succeed him when the occasion arose. The woman was beautiful, smart, and let nothing get in her way. She was just like her father, and probably more ambitious than he had ever dreamed.

Rick had come a long way since this quest to find the bad guys had begun. He had reported to Doc that he was getting a little bit of gossip that something very unusual was in the mix, but what it was, he had yet to find out. He would love to talk privately with some of the waiters and waitresses. They could write a book about what was happening in the Quarter, but they preferred staying alive.

One of those waitresses, who loved to talk was Misty Raine. She had a thing for Rick, and when he was trying to get information, he turned to her when he needed a favor. He would return the favor with her staying overnight at his place.

Misty had told him that Johnny Faretta had a guy from Dallas come down for a dinner meeting. Her roommate Vanessa was the guy's date. He was kind of sleazy, but money's money. Anyway, Vanessa told Misty that she would be going to Dallas in a few days to do something for Johnny. It must be big because they were giving Vanessa a thou to work at this guy's club for a week, and she was to give the guy a package when she arrived. Misty said Vanessa thinks there's going to be a hit, but also said that she was just guessing. She had heard Jack say something which sounded like a hit to her.

When Sheila disappeared, he thought he would be moving. He was, but Johnny told him there was a great place with a courtyard, study, and one bedroom that was owned by Joey and his dad. Rick could lease it for just a couple hundred a month. Rick jumped at it, but was joking with Johnny about why a place like that only cost $200 a month. Johnny told him, "Hey kid, we like you, and besides, we haven't gotten all the blood off the carpet yet."

Johnny thought he was funny, and Rick wondered if it was true.

It was a bachelor's paradise. More like something out of a movie, and what a cool place it was to have a close friend over for the night. His friends now thought he was rich. Hell, he thought he was rich. The boy had come a long way in a very short time. Rick's analysis had things going pretty well, but Dr. C. reminded him he was going to have to pick up the pace.

"We've got to make some inroads into the organization down there." For that reason, Doc told Rick to meet him in Baton Rouge the following Tuesday. They had a lot to discuss.

Chapter 10
Bro Ain't Happy

"I don't give a damn what we have to do, just do it! Robert Kennedy was not in a good mood. "It's like we've been spinning our wheels, not getting anywhere down there. Something is going on, and I want those sons of bitches taken down. I will prosecute them for treason, first degree murder, drug smuggling, and kidnapping just to name a few felonies, but I need something, anything to get the warrants issued."

"Mr. Attorney General, I can understand your frustration, but if we go too fast, it could screw things up big time. These guys know all about how the government works; so, we're doing our best not to come off anywhere close to acting like agents. Chip is making real progress on the drug side, and Rick is getting in tight with Faretta. If either of them was found out in any way, they're dead. We can't let that happen."

Dr. Carmichael had put this team together, and he wasn't going to let an irate Attorney General push him around.

* * *

Myer O'Steen and Craig Benson now had the most profitable and prestigious financial firm in New Orleans. Myer handled all the details and Craig was the sales guy. Every party given was certain to have them on the guest list. Some of the financial advisors downtown said they were mere charlatans and one of these days a lot of people were going to pay a heavy price.

Craig told his clients the brokers were just jealous and thought no more about it. At that time, it was estimated that the financial company was managing close to $170 million, which, in 1963, was an incredible amount of money. So, what could O'Steen and Benson possibly have to do with some poor guy from Dallas staying in a ninth-ward shack in New Orleans?

There wasn't a lot of information Darren Leitner could find on O'Steen and Benson other than what they had filed with the state and the SEC. From that data, it appeared they were extraordinarily gifted financial gurus who had picked a lot of winners over the past few months. They were handling funds for some of New Orleans wealthiest and no one seemed to be unhappy with their results.

Rick and Doc met with Darren to discuss a plan which would hinge on getting John's permission to let Darren work with John's shipyard account. Darren would be employed by the shipyard to manage the pension fund, discuss the investment side with O'Steen and Benson to see where their investment suggestions might lead him. Rick would approach John about a meeting with Darren next time they met.

Darren Leitner from Columbus, Ohio was another Naval Academy guy who decided a career in the Navy wasn't for him. He loved flying, but he loved making money more and had done quite well in that pursuit over the past three years. He was an excellent stock trader and was most hesitant to get involved in something that might hurt his business.

At first, he agreed to do some assignments, but with some stipulations. When he realized that something was in the works, and he was needed on several different occasions, his role continued to expand. He enjoyed the feeling that he was a part of something much bigger than a commission check.

His first job had been to do a full workup on the activities of Myer O'Steen and Craig Benson. Darren had been able to do that work on a part-time basis, and it didn't seem to be a problem for him.

* * *

"Are you kidding me? How did you find out?" Rick couldn't believe what he was hearing. Dr. C met Rick at a small place just off Magazine Street to tell him what he had found out about Vanessa.

"I couldn't believe it either, based on what you had told me. She has an undergraduate degree in Chemistry from Northwestern and a law degree with honors from Yale. Her real name is Susan Arthur from Oklahoma City. Her father was a successful criminal lawyer there for years. He died in '59 and left his family in excellent financial health. From what I could tell, Susan had a million or so in the bank." Doc had a friend to look at Vanessa's background. He told the guy it was about a sting they were working on.

"She may be working undercover for the Feds. Otherwise, what's the point of this dumb blond stripper charade? My other thought is that if I found this, wouldn't it seem that Johnny would know about it too? Maybe they do know, and that's why she's here. There's more to this than I'm comfortable with at this point, and if she's not working for the cops, and if she's not working for Johnny, who in the hell is she working for and why?"

* * *

There's a little place not far from Metarie where people meet who don't want to be seen. Good place for lovers, and on this rainy, overcast day, a good place for two quite different people to chit chat and not be noticed. The rather remote bar and grill was just the right venue for Craig and Harvey to meet. They could talk and when it was time to leave, they could exchange a couple of packages, and no one would care.

Harvey had a wife and child, and though he was convinced he would someday be highly successful, it hadn't happened yet. There aren't many full-time jobs for extremely accurate snipers, but jobs do come up now and then.

This one was going to make Harvey famous, and then he could charge enormous sums of money to do it again. Just you watch, this boy was going places. After all, his down payment was $10,000 with $10,000 more when he finished this job. He and his family could live on that for a couple of years while he was getting other jobs.

Harvey had picked up his package at a downtown bar from a guy who owned the place. This Jack guy was okay, and to show his appreciation for taking the package to New Orleans, Harvey was given a night with one of the girls at the Carousel. He was somebody important now, and would soon be making a lot of money.

The one thing he didn't understand was the part about standing on corners acting like he was some weirdo communist dude. What did commies have to do with him? Yeah, he was over there, but other than a pretty bride, he didn't think much of it. When the guy approached him about doing undercover work, he wanted to help his country, so he signed up. It didn't take long before he called his contact, "Man, I don't want to hand out these damn pamphlets anymore. It's not me. I quit."

"Listen, Harvey; we have to give you some cover, and as bad as you feel about it, it gives us a way to keep you on TV and in the news, making waves about the cold war. Just let this go as best you can, and I promise when this is all over, you'll have money, a business reputation, and everyone will know your name. That's not so bad is it?"

Johnny could be quite persuasive, and if words weren't enough, he also had other ways to get his point across. In this case, he didn't want to put any fear into the guy's head. Just making him feel important should do it. Johnny liked to play chess, and knew the value of a well-placed pawn.

* * *

Wendell Jeffreys was on the red line. "Donald, I'm sorry to bother you with this, but I thought it was important that you know. I have the name of a young guy who is a runner for a law firm in New Orleans who has been making a lot of trips between Dallas, New Orleans, Rio, and D.C. That got my attention; so, I had the kid followed. He started at the Meredith Law Firm and took a flight to Mexico City, then left there for Rio. All he had with him was a small overnight bag and his briefcase. Do you want me to keep after this, or do you want to take it from here?"

"Wendell, you do good work. Where did you get the name, and how did you find all this out?"

"One of the girls in a club in N.O. dates a guy named Swanson, and he does investigations for that firm. Bottom line, the young runner talks too much, and the girl works at one of Johnny's clubs. She wanted her boss to notice her more. Swanson called me last night about meeting me at the Holiday Inn at the airport. I told him I would run it past one of my sources, and then get back to him. It's your call."

58

"Yeah, go ahead, meet with him, and then let me know what he says. After that, I will decide if we need to put a tail on the kid."

"Why does some law firm have a kid running back and forth between the places where we have a lot of our business? Could it just be a coincidence?"

"Donald, there's one way to know for sure. I will leave how you want to handle that to your judgment, but I'm quite sure this Rothenberg kid would be scared out of his mind if he was interrogated about his travels. He's not going to know anything about his trips, but it could stir things up at the law firm.

"We'll tail him, and when he gets to N.O. we'll take him for a little ride to see a part of the country he hasn't seen before. No rough stuff, just a little intimidation to scare his ass. Johnny will take care of it, and we'll see what happens. Talk to you later."

Chapter 11
South of the Border

Alejandro had a most lucrative business about which most of his friends knew nothing. It was called, innocently enough, Oil Rig Supply, Ltd. It certainly didn't cause anyone to notice, and its number one product was supply boats for the offshore rigs.

The company recently sold thirty supply boats to a small oil and gas company in Venice, Louisiana. Each one of the boats was required to have an extra storage area for various tools and extra barrels of cleaning supplies.

Chip and Camila were having dinner at one of her favorite places, and she just knew he was going to tell her how much he loved her, that he couldn't wait to spend the rest of his life with her, and it was time she settled down with him. It didn't exactly happen that way. He did tell her how beautiful she looked, but then she was already being told that about twenty times a day . . . Yawn.

He loved to dance with her; so, this place was his first choice for great music and great food. It was most romantic, quiet, and more than expensive. "Chip darling, don't you care about me more than just being your date?"

"Of course, I do darling, why would you ask that?"

"Aren't we ever going to talk about anything in our future? Something about always being together 'til' death do us part?'"

"Sweetheart, I told you that in my line of work, it's not conducive to long-term relationships, and I know you don't want to leave the lifestyle you have now."

"And how do you know that? You think you know everything, but I love you, and want to be with you . . . not my lifestyle here."

"You say that now my love, but what about when you have to go to some grungy part of the world, while I'm doing my job."

"Okay, I could visit mom and dad then, or just stay in our little house while you were gone. How long would you have to go to this grungy place?"

"Honey, you'd have to go with me, because I could be gone for months, maybe a year or more."

"What? No man has to be away at work for that long.

"Why don't you just work with my father?"

"Camila, my love, let's enjoy tonight, enjoy being together, and we'll think about the future later."

They danced away the night and went to his place for the night. He had started running every day, and it had helped him with his stamina because she was a marathon unto herself.

* * *

60

"Chip this is Alejandro. How are you doing today my son? Is my daughter there?"

"Just a second, sir. It's your father."

They talked for several minutes before she told Chip her dad wanted to talk to him.

"Yes sir, what can I do for you? . . . Sure, and I will see you around two this afternoon, if that's a good time for you?"

They went to breakfast, and Camila took her car to head back home. She smiled as she thought of how she was going to have this man forever, and that was that. There was no doubt as to how much she loved him. Camila had never loved anyone but her mom and dad and herself.

Alejandro knew good material when he saw it, and this young man had more going on than some translation job. He was either overly modest or up to something, and though he liked Chip a lot, he wasn't going to miss anything.

"Chip, my boy, we need to talk. When will your contract be completed?"

"Sir, as I said before, I am employed by a law firm in New Orleans, and this assignment is just one of the many jobs they want me to do."

"Where will you be going next, or do you know?"

"I believe they've got me headed to Dallas, but for what I do not know yet."

Getting Alejandro very curious was what Chip had been working toward ever since he arrived. He would find out how curious in the next few days.

Chip called Rick to tell him he would be on a plane for Dallas on Thursday. "Meet me at the airport. I will be there around 3 pm. See you then." He didn't tell him why on purpose.

Chip wasn't in the habit of being followed, but he had been taught enough to be able to spot key things when someone was tailing him. That was exactly what he planned for on this trip, and he got what he wanted. The dark suit and the bright red tie stuck out like a sore thumb, but Chip let the guy think he was a super tracker. Chip slowly left the plane and headed for the main terminal.

Rick saw Chip first and waved for him to come over to the table at a small bar. Chip acted as if he was angry, and at first, Rick didn't get it, but Chip winked, and Rick went along with the drama.

Rather loudly Chip snarled, "So where's the money Rick?" Chip threw something on the table and then very quietly told Rick, "Hey, thanks for doing this on such short notice. I've been tailed, and this is just what I needed. Now we'll look like we're deep in conversation.

I will ask to see your wallet, you'll raise hell about it, but give it to me anyway. I will look at something, put it back, and give the wallet back to you. A few minutes later you're going to get really mad, call me something awful, and storm out. I'm going to look around to see if I'm being watched, and quietly leave the bar.

"Okay, but tell me again, why are we doing this?"

"Rick, it's just for the appearance that I have an accomplice and it's you. We're having a big disagreement about something so important that it brought me here.

"I know this for sure: The old man is trying to find out what my job is. We set the trap, and now he has fallen into it. I want to help him get out of it without having him injured in any way. I thank you for going along with this. At this point, everything is super important; so, let's start having our heated discussion and the wallet exchange."

They both did an excellent job, and then went their separate ways. The acne-pocked ugly dude who had been following Chip didn't know whether to stay with Chip or go with the other guy. Alejandro didn't say anything about two guys. He would stay with Chip as his boss had told him to do.

Alejandro was most anxious to know what happened. Miguel told him all that he saw and had no way of knowing what they were saying. He told his boss that Chip looked at the other guy's wallet, gave it back to him, they raised their voices, and Chip left. That's all that happened, but the hook was set.

"Camila darling, would you do your father a big favor? Call Chip and ask him if we could have the honor of his company this evening."

She called him, and in her sultriest and sexiest voice she wanted him to come to the house to meet with her father this evening, and of course, he would be treated to their warm and loving hospitality.

Dinner wasn't anything elaborate. It's not often you have an Italian style pizza in this part of the world. It was delicious.

Camila and her mother had some excuse to leave the dining table; so, Chip and Alejandro had a Cuban cigar and a very soothing snifter of French cognac. Nothing was cheap in the Estoval home.

"Chip, if that's your real name, I'm not going to waste your time or mine any longer. I want to know what the hell you're doing down here, and I want to know now. You either shoot straight with me, or I could get angry big time. Do I make myself abundantly clear?"

"What exactly makes you think I'm not doing what I said I was doing? And one other thing Señor Estoval, don't threaten me. You have no idea the mistake you would be making."

Chip tossed the napkin on the table and headed for the door. When he opened it, his old travel buddy Miguel was standing there with a gun pointed at him. He turned to Alejandro, and said, "Really . . . is this how you treat your guests?"

He was summoned to sit back down at the table. Alejandro whispered, "Maybe I was a little too harsh. Perhaps I should have asked the question differently. Very politely and very quietly what were you doing in Dallas on Tuesday?"

"Before I answer that question, let me ask a very quick question of you: what makes you think I was in Dallas on Tuesday?"

"Because, damn it, my man Miguel was following you."

"Oh, was that your guy in the dark suit and red tie. I thought he might be one of yours, but didn't have the heart to tell him that he was lousy at his job. Did he like the performance we gave him before my friend left?"

Alejandro was smiling, but maybe more of a sneer than a smile. "Why are you playing me like a fool Chip? Have I done something to cause you not to trust me?"

"It seems it should be the other way around Alejandro. What did I do to lose your trust?"

"Son, let's start over. Who knows, we both might be of service to one another."

Chip smiled, thinking how best to reel in the big one, but be careful not to let it get away.

Chapter 12
Esta Muy Grande

Rick flew to Rio on Friday night to meet with Chip. He hoped that Chip would be followed, but not sure that would happen after getting the call from Chip about the meeting he had with Alejandro.

Everything was riding on the next few days, so they would play it by the script. There was a strong connection between rig supplies, Alejandro's company, and drugs. This alliance could be the way to see how the connection fits in New Orleans. This meeting would give Chip all he needed to start getting on the inside.

Time didn't seem to be on their side because Dr. C had told Rick that it looked like whatever was being planned had an early October date on it. He wasn't sure, but that's the time period they were targeting now.

"Chip, you need to make your move tomorrow. Give him a price, an opportunity, whatever you need to do, but find a way to get into his operation. Be careful, but don't piss him off anymore. I have gotten to where I like you." They laughed as Rick asked for the bill. "Hasta luego mi amigo."

"Alejandro, this is Chip. I need to see you soon. It's important."

"Are you ready to tell me what it is you're really doing here? If not, don't waste my time, but if you have something to say, we'll meet at my office."

This meeting could be tricky, and dangerous, but it had to work. "Alejandro, I hope you and I can have a more pleasant discussion or at least a more peaceful discussion than the other night. I sincerely apologize for offending you with my rather childish behavior."

Alejandro smiled, "No, no, sometimes it's best to shake things up a bit, so that good things rise to the top. How can I help you, or maybe how can you help me?"

Chip began with an explanation of sorts. "I had to clear this before going any further on my own, and now maybe we can do some business together. I already know a good deal about your operation and can have access to certain information which gives me better insight into your money and where it's going.

"It's not the money, nor what you do which interests me; it's how you do it. You already know who I work for and I am, on the surface, a damn good translator. Nothing gets by me when I'm in the conversation. It is not a place to make mistakes or guess at what was just said.

"My partner and I would like to lease your services. You will have all our personal and company business and what we do scrutinized from top to bottom. I'm hoping you like what you see, because I'm going to be coming to you soon to ask for your daughter's hand in marriage, and I want you to be proud to say yes. Before going any further, any questions you would like to ask?"

"Not at the moment, but you have my attention."

"I'm not going to insult your intelligence by beating around the bush Alejandro. My partner and I would like to lease a couple of compartments on one of your supply boats twice a month. You may set the price for your service, and for the moment, we only need one unit. Depending on how things go, we might need more, or maybe even ask you to build us one of your special units. I know about the storage area, and what they're supposedly for; consequently, no questions asked, can we do business?"

"My son, you seem to know a lot about me from our short time together. Have you been spying on me, perhaps?"

"Alejandro, I confess. Yes, we have spied on you, and your clients, and we know a great deal about all of you. You see, my partner and I have a lot of friends in powerful places, and they are interested to see how we handle our business. If you like, I can provide you with written transcripts of the phone conversations you have had with various individuals over the past several weeks. That should give you an idea as to how well we take care of our business."

They say the first one who blinks loses, and Chip wasn't going to lose this one. After what seemed like ten minutes, Alejandro rather abruptly said, "Chip, I don't need any transcripts.

As a matter of fact, I don't need you, and furthermore, neither does my daughter. You are no longer welcome in my home."

With that the meeting was over . . . for now.

"How did it go?" Rick was anxious to know how the meeting with Alejandro went.

"Just like we thought it would. He was buying no part of it for the moment, but maybe he'll change his mind after you do your part. Are you ready to get this done?" Rick wasn't about to let his buddy down. The game was on.

* * *

"Hey Johnny, you have some time we could talk?" Rick told him that he needed his help and advice about something important.

"Yeah, come by anytime, and we'll see what you got."

"Two o'clock okay?"

"I'll be here."

It was something like a test to see how the microphone worked. Paul Hudson had found a way to get things set up in an adjacent building. He had gone in as a city inspector and determined that he could drill a couple of holes, cut out a small crawl space, and assemble a small microphone. It would be connected to a receiver nearby and record on a large reel to reel tape deck in the basement. They would frequently change the tape, but it could be tricky when there wasn't much traffic on the street. For now, it's all he could do.

Rick had gone over all the points he had put on the page, making sure he had the details clear in his mind. Johnny Faretta wasn't someone you took a proposal to without having your act together. He didn't have much patience with amateurs. He also knew when he was being used and didn't take well to that.

It was two o'clock on the dot. "Come in kid, whatcha got?"

Rick very humbly began, "From the very start, you've been nothing but great to me, and I thank you for that more than you can know. My idea may be one of the stranger ways to say thank you, but a buddy of mine and I have come up with a way for us to make a little extra cash and make you a little extra as well.

"Being a musician, you meet some strange dudes, but one night about a month ago, a guy, I think they call him Tin Man, asked to see me for just a minute or two after the show. I don't usually do that, but this time I did. Anyway, he had someone he wanted me to meet; so, my buddy and I met the guy.

"About twenty miles south of Pensacola, on some oil rig, they have a friend who can supply a ton of weed a month, but they need someone to handle it from the rig to the drop off point. This group is no big-time drug ring, just some guys in the oil and gas business wanting to make some extra spending money.

"There's this Brazilian dude who makes supply boats with extra storage units. It's cool how they do it, but in any event, we asked to lease one for a couple of times a month, and he said no. I was hoping that I could give you the guy's name and number and you could see if he would change his mind. We lease it from him, make the deliveries, and you tell me what you would think was fair for our split. That's my proposal."

"Kid, I knew you were smart, but had no idea you had a business head on you. Let me give it some time, and I will get back with you. You know you don't owe me anything, but it's good to know you want to take care of your friends."

"Thanks, Johnny. Do you think I could hear somethin' back in a week, maybe ten days?"

"I'll let you know sooner than that."

Alejandro was sitting at his desk having his morning coffee when his secretary said that Mr. Hagen was on the phone. "Chip, my boy, why didn't you tell me you had such good friends. We could already have been doing business. Tell me, what is it you need, and when do you need it?"

When Chip hung up the phone with Alejandro, he stood there for a moment, wondering how Rick had gotten things handled so fast. He then called Rick to tell him about the call to Alejandro. "Hey man, Big A just told me that whatever we need we got. You do good work brother."

Rick hadn't heard from Johnny yet; so, he figured he would probably find out later today. Sure enough, about three he got a call from Jeremy telling him to drop by the office at five.

"We got you set up, and now you owe me one. I will let you know when you can return the favor, and there's no split required. Be careful kid, and if you get into something you can't handle, tell them to call me." Johnny laughed, "Now get outta here kid; I'm busy."

Alejandro asked Chip to come by the house any time after five. There were a couple of things they needed to discuss. As always Chip was about ten minutes early, and Camila was so happy to see him. She didn't think her daddy would ever let her see him again, but this morning he told her he had changed his mind.

She knew her father well, and when he exorcized someone from his presence, he didn't suddenly change his mind. She wondered, who is this man she wanted so much?"

"Come in, come in Chip. I must apologize again for my temper the other day. I have good days and bad, and obviously, you caught me on one of my bad days. So now, let's talk a little business. How many boats will you need, and for how long?"

"Señor Estoval, for the moment we need one boat, twice a month. We need the boat docked in Pensacola under the name of The ADCH Company, Ltd. While I do thank you for this gesture, what changed?"

"Let's just say that I overreacted and thought better of it later in the day. Besides my daughter adores you, and I'm not sure she would have ever spoken to me again. That's another reason I wanted to see you. I want to give my permission for you and my daughter to wed, and as a small wedding gift, there will be no charge for the use of my boat now or boats you may need later as you grow your business."

"Mucho gracias, Alejandro; your kindness and your gracious apology are most happily accepted and appreciated."

* * *

Rick needed to talk to Dr. Carmichael fast and wasn't going to leave any messages. It took four calls, but at last doc answered the phone.

"We're in, and we need you to make sure those bales are in place. The plan has to work like clockwork. You know we're going to be watched like a hawk because Johnny Faretta is helping a friend and doesn't take well to surprises of any kind."

"Rick, you and Chip are amazing. I think you both are having way too much fun with this. Just don't get so carried away that you forget who these people are. They can stomp the life out of you in a heartbeat. You'll have everything you need, but for God's sake, you guys be careful down there."

"Doc, I appreciate your fatherly advice, but if we look calm, that has nothing to do with our minds. We know the situation. You wanted us to get more involved, and we are. Tell the President, we'll know more soon. You take care and let me

70

know when and where the pickup is to be by tomorrow. I've got to get things set up here."

A half ton of pot was neatly baled and hidden in used pipe on Thunder #2, a small rig about fifty miles south of Pensacola. Chip would leave Rio and stay close to the shore until he got about twenty miles or so from Brownsville. From there he would head directly for New Orleans, pick up Rick, and head for the rig.

Once they had all the recyclables, which were contracted to be removed on board their boat, they would arrive at a small inlet a few miles east of Pensacola. They would deliver the product, collect the money, drop Rick off in NO and Chip would head back to Brazil. It was a long trip, but worth it. These two guys were now players in a dangerous game of hide and seek for adults.

Camila ran to the pier and couldn't believe how much of a beard he had grown in such a short time. She didn't care about that; she was just so happy he was back. Now they could start planning the wedding.

No doubt Chip had a real love for this woman. She was the sexiest woman he had ever known, very smart, calculating, and relentless in the bedroom. Now that he and her father had an understanding, maybe it would be good for them to be married. If for no other reason than making sure she was well protected.

Rick wasn't so sure about Chip's decision to marry her, and neither was Doc. Things could get extremely messy, and no way to walk away if things didn't go well.

"Chip you have to be very sure you can do your job while being married to Estoval's daughter."

"I believe that this could help us tremendously in the long run. I won't get you involved in anything down here, and no matter how I feel about this woman, I won't let her get in the way of what I have to do."

"Chip, I truly hope you're right. Good luck my friend, and we'll see you in a couple of weeks."

Chapter 13
Nikki's Choices

It had been a month since Nikki arrived in New York, and the first week was incredibly exciting. She started rehearsals, had a chance to shop, went to a couple of parties, and met several interesting people. The second week the rehearsals were grueling, she had developed a cold, but the show would go on.

Shopping and men weren't on the top of her list, but she did enjoy her phone calls to Rick when she could get him to answer. She had left him several messages with his answering service, but he must be terribly busy not to answer. She had a little pad next to her phone which read that there had been twenty-two attempts, she had left eighteen messages, and he had only called her back three times.

Was Rick going to be here on opening night with the rest of her family? She loved the man; she was rich, beautiful, and smart; so, what was his problem?

Nikki knew one thing: if she didn't get a ring this coming Christmas, she would start getting the word out that she was a lot more available than ever before. She was going to give him a chance, but if he didn't come across, that would be the end of their relationship. Her problem was Rick Charles had never been intimidated in his life.

John Meredith had invited Rick over for a couple of drinks, dinner, and maybe a little snooker afterward. By now they had become great friends, and John was always dropping little tidbits about Nikki, hoping that Rick would find them intriguing enough to want to know more.

On this night, Rick gave John a jolting surprise. "Mr. Meredith, we've known each other for a couple of years or so, and during that time, you've been to where I work, seen what I do, and must have an opinion about it. I need to know what you think about my present employment when it comes to me asking your daughter to marry me."

John Meredith looked like he was going to pass out. "Are you serious son? You're considering marrying my Nikki?

"Hey, John, are you going to be all right?"

"I'm fine, but do you know she thinks you don't love her or care about her and isn't happy that you don't return calls or write her? She is even considering giving you your freedom and deciding to just concentrate on her career."

"Yes, I know all of that, and if she wants to do that, then that's what she needs to do. On the other hand, I have never been one to jump because someone thought I should. I love her, love her family, love her career choice, and I'm going to ask her to marry me, with your approval of course. So now, how do you feel about my musician status as it relates to my marrying your beautiful Miss Nikki?"

"Rick there will be a point when you give up entertaining and start becoming more involved in the business side of music. You certainly have all the tools for it, but I'm afraid Nikki will be performing while they're moving her body to the cemetary."

"I don't mind that, but want to make sure you and Mrs. Meredith are comfortable with me. I have more than an interesting past; so, if you choose to have me investigated, I can save you the expense by simply telling you anything you want to know. That's up to you."

"Son, when do you plan to let Nikki in on all of this?"

"Let's see how long she gives me." John made a toast, and they started into the dining room for dinner. Both men were incredibly happy.

In New York, Nikki's director, Wallace Johnson had a friend, Larry Tyson, in town from Atlanta. He had asked his old friend out to dinner and thought maybe Nikki might enjoy meeting Larry besides just having the night off.

Wallace didn't care much for southern belles and was determined this one wasn't going to get her way about anything. But over the past week or two, he had been watching her closely, and had to admit that she was steady, worked hard, wasn't temperamental, and might be just what this role needed.

"Nikki, you have a second? Would you join me and my friend from Atlanta for dinner? You've been doing a lot of heavy lifting; so, thought you might enjoy having some fun."

Nikki didn't hesitate. "I would love to have dinner with you, but are you sure you know it's me your asking?"

He gave her a big smile, and said, "Yes, I know it's you. Go home, get ready for a few hours of R & R, and a car will pick you up at seven."

When she stepped out of the limo, she immediately got Larry Tyson's complete attention. He looked at her body up and down and back up again, and by the time he saw her beautiful face, he was in a sort of a lust 'n love mindset. Larry offered her his arm, thinking she was stunning and saying to himself, this woman is single? Wallace smiled at Larry's reaction.

After a most wonderful dinner at the Four Seasons, they decided to have a nightcap at the Oak Room. A couple of hours there, and it was time to go back to her apartment for a good night's sleep. Larry insisted that he walk her to her door. She was saying she had a lovely time, when he interrupted her with, "Wouldn't it be good to have one little drink for a nightcap?" She most emphatically told him good night, opened the door, and went inside; smiling of course, and very relaxed. It had been a fun night, and she needed it.

Larry was smiling too, but for a different reason. He was going to see this woman every night. His firm in Atlanta was in negotiations to create an extraordinary dual tower office complex, and he might have to be in New York for at least two weeks.

When Nikki arrived at the theatre, she was amazed to find three dozen long-stemmed red roses in her dressing room. The card simply said, "I enjoyed the evening so much, would you care to help me with another one tonight? Larry"

He was very charming, nice looking, must be doing well in his business, and wanted to be with her tonight. She would think about it. No sense rushing into anything. Nikki Meredith wasn't about to get involved with someone because he sent three dozen roses. A lot of men thought that the number of roses was equivalent to showing her how interested they were in seeing her again. One morning she had received twelve dozen, but she didn't remember the guy's name. She was smiling as she looked at the card again. *Larry my man, you have no clue about the woman you're pursuing.*

When he called her, she thanked him for the roses and declined the invitation. She wanted to go home and get some rest. They were fast approaching dress rehearsal, and she wanted to be ready for anything.

Larry Tyson was used to getting whatever he wanted, and he wanted this woman. He would be relentless because he knew there must be someone else for her to turn him down.

Nikki handled him like this: She would go out with him again, but not until after her opening night performance. She would only see him backstage for a moment or two. Her mother and father were going to be there, and the man whom she had been dating would also be there. If after that evening, he was still interested, he was invited to give it his best shot.

Opening night came and Nikki didn't understand why Rick wasn't there. Her mom and dad knew how hurt she was. With

Rick not being there, and her telling them about Larry, John had more than an uneasy twinge. Her dad thought to himself that Rick needed to get his ass up here and soon.

She now had a friend in New York, her reviews were outstanding, and she was on her way. A couple of weeks later she and Larry flew to Atlanta in his company plane, met his parents for dinner, and flew back to New York. During that most wonderful night, she didn't care whether Rick had called or not.

Nikki thought about Rick now and then, but if he didn't have time for her, she most certainly would be too busy to bother him. John and Rick did talk about what happened on her opening night. Rick was at sea, but couldn't tell anyone; thus, he explained that he had to stay at the club because of all the celebrities who were on the reservation list. He would fly up on Wednesday to see her performance that night. She didn't know he would be there.

Rick was excited as he made his way backstage after the performance to see her, but the excitement ebbed greatly when he saw Nikki kissing some guy quite passionately.

He went back to his hotel, called the airport for an early flight back, and left at 2 am. It hurt like hell, but his double life made it difficult to let her know that. It was probably for the best to let her go. She was a part of his life he could never forget, but he always looked at things head on. To Rick, everything worked out like it should.

Chapter 14
And the Rocket's Red Glare

July fourth was a busy time in New Orleans. It might have been hot and humid, but it was still the Big Easy, and people came from everywhere. A fun time was had by all, and back then, business in the Quarter was under the control of a very powerful family. Consequently, you didn't have a bunch of crime aimed at the tourists. If someone had to leave this earth, it was usually connected with those who made the family unhappy in some way.

After a very fun-filled night, the club had closed, and Rick and the band went to a small out-of-the-way club where there were no tourists and a lot of the local musicians hung out to jam until all hours of the morning. Jimmy Snyder, better known as the *saxiest* man in town, was stopped by a couple of guys just as they were about to go inside the club. Rick told the rest of them to go on in, and he and Jimmy would be there in a few minutes.

The best way to describe these guys was Ugly and Uglier. Ugly had an awfully bad attitude and wasn't thrilled to have Rick interfering. "Listen, kid this is between us and Jimmy boy here. You go on in, and you won't have any problem with us."

"Hey guys, I don't know what Jimmy has done, but is there any way I can take care of this? He's the best sax man down here, and I need him healthy. Ugly drew his piece, and asked Rick one more time if he wouldn't rather just go on in the club?"

Most of the time, 99% of the time, Rick wouldn't have tried this, but he needed Jimmy to be able to play. "I have to ask you boys this question before I leave Jimmy with you. Does my friend Johnny know about this little get-together?"

Ugly asked, "Johnny who?"

"Boys, there's only one Johnny down here that I know of who needs to know about crap like this; so, one more time, does he know? Johnny, and I are more than acquaintances. We work together."

They put the guns back inside their coats, began telling Rick that Jimmy boy owed them $1500 for weed he bought a couple of weeks back. They just wanted their money.

"Okay, now that makes sense. You sold Jimmy some weed, and he hasn't paid for it yet. Is that about it Jimmy?"

Jimmy stood there and nodded that in fact, it was correct. Rick told the Ugly brothers that they could come to the bandstand every Friday and Saturday for seven nights and he would give them $300 on each visit. Jimmy would be most happy to pay $600 in interest. Jimmy kept his face, Rick had his sax player, and the ugly brothers had their money back with interest. Crisis averted.

Funny how news gets around, but it wasn't too long until Johnny had Rick over to tell him he was in the wrong business. "Rick my man, I'll say this . . . you've got a pair. I'm beginning to get used to hearing about you, and believe it or not, it's all good. Those two thugs you ran into the other night would rather kill someone than have sex. I think I'm gonna put you on my payroll full time."

Johnny let out one of his belly laughs and told Rick how glad the kid was on his team.

Johnny had an infectious laugh, and everyone sitting around the table was laughing too. Rick had to laugh, or he might have thrown up.

"You mean those guys were dangerous?" This time the guys laughed 'till they had tears in their eyes.

When the laughter died down, Johnny told them all to leave except Rick. "How did everything go down the other night? Did you get your packages delivered okay?"

"Yeah, and I want to thank you so much for helping us do this. We think maybe we can do at least a ton a month, and maybe more if we do everything right."

Chapter 15
Connection Problems

Aaron Rothenberg will always have nightmares about his little side trip in New Orleans. All he knew was that one moment he was on the curb checking his baggage, and the next thing he remembered he was riding between two large men headed down some dark road and no one was saying anything.

Finally, they arrived at an old house which looked like it was about to fall to the ground. Inside was a light hanging over a table where it seemed to move slowly back and forth, and when they drove up, he could see a couple of other guys sitting at the table.

"Kid, I'm going to ask you one time, and if I don't hear what I want to hear, you won't have to worry about us asking any more questions. We'll just dump your skinny little ass in the swamp. Now, why have you been going to all these different places, with just a briefcase and no baggage? And don't tell us your clothes are in your girlfriend's suitcase because you'd be lyin' and, we hate liars."

They knew not to hurt the kid, but they could scare him to death. One of the guys picked up something shiny and began to put his fingers through the holes. Aaron knew he was now going to be beaten to death and left on some lonely road or worse in the swamp. His mother and dad would take this very badly.

"Okay, kid, you've got to the count of three."

"I swear I have no idea what I'm carrying, and never see anyone when I leave the briefcase. I'm told by a different secretary every trip where I will be headed and my flight numbers. That's all I know. If you don't believe me, ask any of the secretaries."

Aaron didn't see it coming, but one of the men put a needle into the kid's neck, and after a wince of pain, his head fell forward. His nap would last about fifteen hours. He opened his eyes gradually and tried to make out the blurred images in front of him. He was lying on something hard, but where, he had no clue.

He could hear them talking, but about what he couldn't make out. Someone came over and asked him if he was okay. He didn't know if he was or not, but at least they didn't seem to be there to hurt him. He seemed to think he was in some police station, and guessed it was in New Orleans. He didn't know that for sure. There were a lot of blue people walking around, and radios going on and off continually.

There was a roaring avalanche in his head, and about all his body could do was lie there. Finally, a woman said she was a doctor and was going to give him a shot. Hell no, he thought, not another one of those, but before he could attempt to resist, he felt the needle. Over the next ten minutes or so, he slowly began to come to his senses.

The doctor gave him some water, and then a cup of black coffee. His girlfriend would never believe this. He didn't believe it either, which reminded him, where was he, and how long had he been here?

Back in the offices of John Meredith, the boss wanted to know what happened to Aaron. The receptionist had just gotten a call from the fourth precinct that they had found a guy on a park bench who was claiming he worked for the Meredith law firm. John pondered how all of this happened and knew that it couldn't happen again. How did they find out about this?

It must have been around ten the next morning when Johnny got word that the Rosenberg kid had been picked up by the cops and taken to the fourth precinct. Johnny wasn't quite sure why he was asked to do this, but if it helped keep things on track, he saw to it that it happened. They all knew the kid didn't have a clue about much of anything, but now someone who needed to know was aware that the little game had been exposed.

John Meredith's firm was no longer a viable conduit; consequently, it seemed that a different kind of communication would have to be put in place. Otherwise, the whole damn operation would have to be shut down, and that couldn't happen. Rick called Doc to let him know that the plan was changing.

* * *

Two recent shipments had been blown out of the water. The first one literally, and the second one was discovered by the Florida Highway patrol which almost by accident was patrolling a small inlet near the Alabama/Florida border. Almost in this sense, meant they had to have been tipped off. Losing $6 million doesn't sit well among business associates, and with all that was at stake, Johnny was told that it better not happen again.

Donald wanted to know what the hell was going on and to get it fixed. He told Wendell, "We don't have much time, and we can't afford to lose our partners in this. When you find something out, call and ask my secretary for an appointment. She'll give you a time and place. Be there and whatever you do, don't tell anyone where you're going."

Something big seemed about to take place in New Orleans, and once again, Misty was a most valuable asset when it came to hearing things. She told Rick that while Vanessa was in Dallas, she heard that there was going to be a major hit, and the target was called lay back or way back or something that sounded like that.

"That's not much information," she said, "but do I get something for it?" She hadn't exactly been thinking about money, but she would take a hundred or two any time.

Was Vanessa right about a possible hit? Was it going to be in Dallas? Rick turned the information over to Dr. C immediately and asked him if he could get someone on the streets to see if they knew if there was word of any kind of big-time hit being planned. If it was very big, no small-time snitch would know, but they had to be asked.

"On the other hand, Doc, do you think this Vanessa is being given bits of information and being told to pass it along, and secondly, to tell her friend to pass it along as well?"

Doc reminded Rick, "Anything's possible, but why would they take the chance with her? Either she's not as smart as we think she is or it's just part of the act. I may have to get David involved in this. Maybe he can find out if anything is happening that we need to know about, and if he thinks it's connected to Big D."

David Atwater was a graduate of West Point, served as an aide to a four-star general, and had just finished his Masters in Economics at Wharton when approached by Dr. Carmichael. Having arranged every event, photo session, PR opportunity, and dinner party for the general, he had a vast amount of experience in giving and taking orders as well as knowing how to move in the upper circles of society. He was going to love his first assignment for the group because he was about to become a very wealthy heir to a very notable New York family.

John Meredith sent his most accomplished property and estate planning partner to Albany to start working on a specific lineage dating back to 1693. It took her almost a month, but when she was finished, David Atwater became David Calvin Flynn III, a direct descendant of Robert L. Calvin, one of the most successful importers/exporters in the King's colonies.

David Flynn, III would be involved in businesses in Argentina, Brazil, France, the US, China, Japan, and if that wasn't enough you could add Italy and Germany. His travels and especially his schedules would not be noticed.

Rick just sat there trying to come up with some reason why Vanessa would go to so much trouble to cover up her real identity, and then it occurred to him: *Maybe Misty knows about her? Misty is very cooperative when it comes to sex and money; so, I could find out what she knows or doesn't know.*

Chapter 16
Play Misty for Me

"Misty, this is Rick. Do you have plans for tonight?"

"I hope so if they're with you."

"Could you drop by my place about nine? Maybe we could have a drink or two and just spend some time talking."

"Sweety, I would love to talk to you about anything you want to discuss. I'll see you at nine.

Misty would sometimes hang out at the club during the day when the band was rehearsing a new number just to hear Rick sing. She had a real thing for him, but she knew it would probably never be anything serious on his part. She had seen the women he dated, especially that hussy opera singer who thought she was Miss Big Time. Misty referred to her as Miss Alaneous.

She didn't care if being with him was only a physical thing. They were great in bed, and she would greatly enjoy whatever he had in mind tonight.

"Misty my dear, come in. I love your dress. You look gorgeous."

"I thought I might get your attention with this little outfit." She had decided to give him a night to remember, and if he wanted to talk, she could do that too. For right now, all she wanted was a small glass of wine and his attention. She got both.

Misty said she was twenty-eight, but then again, she might have misread her birth certificate at some point. She was a very striking woman with very green eyes, auburn hair, and a figure which men always noticed, especially the way she dressed. She loved to dress rather tacky most of the time, but that was simply to enhance her image as a hot-to-trot sex symbol. What was surprising about her was that she was only hot for this man, but he would have never thought that about her. She didn't want anything permanent, but then she wouldn't have refused it had he offered. He wouldn't, and so she was perfectly content to have whatever of him she could get.

They had a glass of wine, kissed several times, she was very ready to get comfortable, but he just wanted to talk. She wondered, *why in the hell does he want to talk at a time like this, and what could be so important that they couldn't talk about it later . . . like in the morning?*

"Misty, we do have something rather incredible when we're together, and I know you think this is just about sex. You do things to me that are most incredible, and I hope I make you happy as well. I'm not promising anything, but if by chance we both decided that we wanted to become more involved, don't you think it's a good idea to know more about one another?"

"What else would you like to know about me, and why?"

"I don't know where you're from, or anything about your mom and dad or if you have brothers or sisters. Hell, Misty, I don't even know your real name. So, let's start there, and I'll tell you why in the morning."

"Rick, darling, I'll answer your questions. I'm not sure why I'm going to do this, but if you tell anyone about me, you'll never get anything from me again, and I mean nothing. Do we understand one another?"

He nodded yes and whispered, "Misty, I'm not going to hurt you, I promise. We just need to have more than one-night stands in this relationship. This discussion is more for me than you, and none of this will ever leave this room."

"Okay, first thing on the list is I'm not Misty. . . I'm Candice Dawson, from Los Angeles. My dad left before I could ever know him, and my mom raised me by herself until she died with brain cancer at thirty-six. I was seventeen and all by myself.

We were living in Madison, Wisconsin at the time, but I wanted out of there. I hitchhiked to Canada, near Montreal, got a job as a waitress, and moved in with an older guy for a few months just to make sure I had a roof over my head. He was a nice guy, but was always high on something. I'm not a druggy, so I left one night, and never looked back.

One day I was at the movies, and part of it was about New Orleans, and here I am. When you first met me, I was working in the kitchen at a small café over in Algeria and working here part time.

I had met this guy who wanted me purely for sex; so, he offered to put me up over here. We were already having sex; so, I stayed in his apartment for almost a year. He evidently was a little more notorious than I knew and must not have been very smart either. One night a friend of mine let me know that Tony was no longer with us."

"You're not talking about Tony Biggers, are you?"

"That's him. How would you know someone like Tony Biggers?"

"This is funny. I know how much you dislike Miss Alaneous, but Tony was an acquaintance of hers, and he gave me my first job here. He didn't play in the band, but he managed it. He needed a trombone player, and I was hired. I was told he moved to south Louisiana."

"Well, your hotty was good for something. Tony did go south, but he didn't know it."

"May I still call you Misty? I do love that name."
"I wouldn't know you called me if I weren't your Misty. Aren't you getting tired, maybe a little sleepy?"

"We'll get there soon enough, but you have a roommate, I have a very wealthy friend, and wanted to talk to you about setting them up."

"Which friend are you talking about?"

"My friend's name is David, and he was in the Carousel Club in Dallas one night and saw Vanessa's act. He asked the bartender to see if Vanessa would meet him for a drink, but

Vanessa refused the invitation. The guy told David she was headed back to N.O. after her week was up."

"Rick, my love, don't you know who she works for?"

"I thought she was an exotic dancer over at Star's place." "Yeah, she's over there, but she told me she sorta works for Johnny Faretta. I don't know for sure, but I don't think it's all work between them. Not sure Johnny would like her out with someone he didn't know."

"Misty, don't you know that Johnny and I are friends?" I'll ask him if Vanessa can go out with my friend David. It's just a date."

"Let me first see if she would be interested, and then we'll see what we do or don't do. Now I want to get these clothes off and move our little chat to your bedroom."

She didn't leave until ten the next morning, and Rick was going to take a long nap. He had no idea how much she cared about him. Misty may have lived a very checkered past, but since she met Rick, in her mind they were a couple, and there could be no one else in her life. She didn't just have sex with Rick; she gave every bit of her heart and soul to him. She loved the guy.

Chapter 17
What's the Rush?

Craig Benson arrived a little after 2 pm and went straight to Jack Ruby's office. Before they went to dinner, there were a couple of things they needed to talk over as it pertained to what was known as payback. It didn't seem to be all about the money, but that was some of it. They now had a pretty good idea of when this was going to happen, but it still wasn't for certain. For Jack's information, it didn't matter. Whether it was today or three months from today, his work would be the same. Craig simply needed to make sure all the details were in place.

None of the girls had come in yet so they wouldn't be disturbed. "Jack, I was asked to come visit you to make sure of your responsibilities and to make sure that you understand the financial arrangements. The time is getting closer, and as we draw closer to the time, there won't be many opportunities for us to meet like this.

Your account in Montreal is in the name of J.D. Travers. Your passport, driver's license, and account number will be delivered to you in about a week. Your actual name will be Johnson Davis Travers. Your age is 52, date of birth is July 6, 1911, and you will be living in Taos, New Mexico.

The account will have $1 million in it, but under the agreement, you will not be able to use any of that money until three years after the hit. No one is to know about this account, but you. You don't need to ask what happens if you break any part of this agreement. Anything else we need to cover?"

"When do I get my final instructions as to the who, where, and the when of all this?"

"Jack, I can't answer that because I haven't been told when I can discuss that with you. They have someone who will contact you a week or two before, but since the exact date isn't known for sure, just be ready when you get the call. Now let's get something to eat; I'm starved."

* * *

In another part of Dallas, "Harvey, it's good to see you. How are things goin' man?"

"Hey Johnny; things seem to be okay, but I could sure use the ten thousand. With a wife and kid, things are runnin' a little tight right now. Is it time to get things going? Do you know what the date of this payback thing is?"

"We don't have a firm date yet, but it's getting close for sure. You'll get the money the week before you handle your part of the plan. In the meantime, we've got you a job at a place downtown.

We do know where payback will take place; so, we wanted to make sure you would have great visual clearance and an easy way for you to get away from downtown. I know you're a great shot; that's why we picked you. You take care of your part, and we'll do the rest. A couple of days later you'll have the rest of your money."

"Johnny, thanks for being here. I need to get this done soon. Man, I need the money."

"We'll do what we can but we're not speeding up the job to solve your problems. It'll happen when it's time."

At a steakhouse near the stockyards in Fort Worth, Craig, Jack, and Johnny had dinner, talked about the club, women, money, football, and drank almost a fifth of vodka. When Craig and Johnny got to the hangar, they were already flying. Jack had gone back to the club thinking how cool it was to be a millionaire. By the time he was sixty he'd be living in Italy. It was a good day.

Harvey's wife had prepared some Spam concoction with a baked potato. It was awful.

* * *

The Kennedy brothers were close, sometimes maybe too close. When they happened to disagree, it might start at a normal decibel level, but would quickly escalate into a very vocal argument which could then go to the rather boisterous level. In this case, it had to do with the trip to start with, why he had to go, and some of the key worries that the Secret Service had.

"Jack, you can't go to Dallas now. Let Lyndon do this. Hell, he's been chomping at the bit to be important again, and this could be the way to help him with that. Just think, he could be the guy saving the reelection of the President. I can see the Dallas headlines: Johnson Helps President Win Texas . . . President Kennedy says he couldn't have done it without Lyndon. You don't need to go down there, Jack. Some of those people are crazy."

"Bobby, do you think I'm going to let a bunch of red neck nutcases keep me from doing what I do best? You can stop all of this now because I'm going and that's that, and besides, Jackie is going with me. They want to see her more than me anyway. I will make four stops and be on my way back in forty-eight hours. As for the Secret Service, worrying is what they do best. They love a challenge."

Matthew Fitzgerald was the Director of the Secret Service and was aging much more rapidly than he should be. President Eisenhower had not been a problem at all, but the mood of the country and the President were vastly different now. Jack Kennedy loved the idea of reaching out to the people, shaking hands, chit chatting, and making himself an easy target. Now he was going against everyone's advice and going to Texas, and to make matters worse, one of his stops was going to be Dallas. There had been numerous death threats coming in from Dallas in just the last few weeks.

The President said, "I'm going to Dallas damn it!"

Chapter 18
Blind Date

Johnny and Rick met for a late breakfast and had been discussing Rick's little side business, when he asked Johnny, "Are you and Vanessa a couple? Let me explain why I'm asking. My good friend David Flynn is coming down for a few days to visit, and I had asked Misty if her friend Vanessa might be interested in going out with the guy. She told me that I should ask you first because she thought maybe you and Vanessa were close."

"Rick, there are a lot of girls to pick from down here so why Vanessa?"

"You're right about the selection, but David wanted to ask her out when he saw her in Dallas. The bartender said she was headed back to New Orleans when her week there was over. I didn't want him to find himself in a jam by asking her out if you and she were a couple."

"Tell you what RC, tell your friend that Vanessa and I are good friends, but she can decide who she sees without my help. My only advice is that if he wants to have a long and happy life, don't hurt her in any way. You understand what I'm saying don't you?"

"Absolutely, and that's not a problem. David is just your average rich guy who likes to go out with beautiful women. Thanks for your time, and I know my friend is going to be happy. Now all he has to do is see if she's interested in him." He smiled and, on the way out the door, turned back to say, "Thanks my friend."

Susan Arthur, aka, Vanessa went to work for the FBI immediately upon graduating from law school. Though her father was a defender of those who broke the law, Susan was more like her mother, who was a compassionate woman, but she didn't like those with money getting away with things that regular folks couldn't. The justice system was anything but fair.

At the time she went to work for the Bureau, drugs were coming in from everywhere, and something had to be done. The President, Congress, everyone in the communities effected wanted something done about it. What exactly that would be was yet to be determined.

Vanessa volunteered for an undercover assignment, but on her first attempt, she was excluded from the mix. The women in the Bureau, at that time, weren't supposed to be in the direct line of fire. She kept after them until they relented, and thus she became Vanessa Adkins, but seldom ever used the last name.

She was 5'6" dark brunette hair, and well built; thus, her decision to work in some of the clubs as an exotic dancer. Jack had seen her in New Orleans a few times and kept asking when she might come back to Dallas to be a headline act at his club.

Vanessa met Misty the first week she was in town. She had gotten a job at a place called Stars, and did two shows a night, five days a week. Misty, at that time, was working at Sheila's club as a part-time waitress. Both were having a late breakfast, and because they were sitting almost side by side, they started talking about the heat, the men, and where they worked.

Over the next couple of months, they met a few more times, talked, and finally decided that to save money, they would share an apartment and see how that worked out. Vanessa could talk in a strange way that would drive you insane, but thankfully she reserved that part of her acting career for those men who thought she didn't have a mind. At the apartment, she was so different, according to Misty.

"Misty, it's me, and wanted to let you know I talked to Johnny, and he had no problem with Vanessa dating whomever she wishes. Can you ask her tonight?"

"Sure, and one more time, who is this guy?"

"He's an old friend of mine, and he comes from an old family from somewhere in Ohio, I think. Somewhere up in that area anyway. He's a cool guy and thinks Vanessa is the hottest thing around. He is a nice guy, and if you want to tell her, he has more money than the mob. Okay, maybe not that much, but almost. And one more thing, would you like to go with me to the

Symphony on Thursday night? I've got great tickets, and they're playing two of my favorite symphonies."

Misty almost dropped the phone. *He wants me to go to the Symphony.* "Rick, I would love to go with you. How formal is it?"

"I'm wearing a suit so whatever you think goes with that is fine with me. You'll look great whatever you're wearing."

"I will tell Vanessa, and see what she wants to do, and I'll tell her I need to know by tomorrow night. Is that okay with you?"

"Sounds good.   See you tomorrow about 5:30 for dinner, and we'll go from there."

She sat there and kept thinking. *Did I just get asked out for dinner and the symphony? I don't think I'm dreaming, and I know I'm not drinking. I have to get something perfect to wear. I can't believe this." . . . She kept smiling . . . "I can't believe this.*

After Misty told Vanessa about the Symphony, the next subject was about Rick's friend. "He tried to introduce himself to you in Dallas, but you declined the invitation. He's here and would like to see you, but only if you want to. No pressure from anyone, I promise."

"What's the guy's name again?"

"David Flynn; He seems to be a good guy according to Rick. They've known each other a long time, and if you talk to anyone down here about Rick, then you know that his friend must be okay. Yes or no, just let me know by the time I meet my sweetie tomorrow night."

"I'll let you know. Just need to check it out with Johnny."

"Rick has already done that, and if you want to go, it's okay."

"What's with this crap about everyone running my life? I'll go, but just this one time."

"Hey, I'm sorry to bother you with this. I thought you might enjoy it, but don't do this unless you want to. It's supposed to be about having a good time."

"I'm sorry, just a little tense about a couple of things. Tell Rick his friend has a date with Miss Fabulous." Misty poured them a glass of wine and they talked some more.

Chapter 19
The Closet

Dr. C called Rick near three in the morning to tell him that something was up, and somehow, he had to get in close to find out what. "We think something important is either in Johnny's office or on the way. We need to know. There's been a lot of discussion about a black box with some kind of code in it. I had Jack's phone tapped, and let's just say that Jack Ruby has interesting friends. One of them was calling about the box and we think it was Johnny. Couldn't tell for sure because of the static on the line. If it's not there, we need to find out where it is and get it."

Also, from what they could glean from the conversations, the day of the hit was getting close, and still there was no clue who the victim was or where it would take place. Doc said, his best guess is that it's to be in Dallas but can't figure out the New Orleans connection. Rick had to find the link and quick.

"Paul, this is Rick. How close can I get to the office in that crawl space?"

"Right next to it; why?"

"I've got to get in there somehow."

"Should I call someone about burial arrangements, just in case they find your body?"

"I'm serious. Is it ever vacated, and the lights turned off?"

"Rick, I don't know about the lighting, but yes, on occasions, there's no one in there. Not very often, but sometimes it's empty. But we also don't know what kind of security they've got in there. Cutting in might not trigger an alarm, but you can't put it back without leaving a hole or signs of where a hole was made. Either way, they'll know someone broke into a place that no one would ever, in their right mind, break into."

"You're right about that, but I have to get in there. There has to be some way to get into that place."

"This is a long shot, but while I was working on getting the microphone close, I was able to see the layout of the downstairs area. There's a space between the kitchen in the back and the bar up front. It's nothing more than a storage area about the size of a closet, but if you could hide in there, maybe you could wait until everyone was gone, go upstairs, get what you're after, and leave. There wouldn't be any alarms unless it's a safe you're after, and you couldn't crack a safe anyway . . . could you?"

"If I managed to slip in there and hide, how long do you think I could be in there?"

"Hey guy, I have no clue. Get in there in the late afternoon, and you could be out in six or seven hours unless it's when they have something going on that keeps 'em in the place for several days. One thing you could do in that situation is to sneak out of the closet while the guys are not watching, which is easier said than done. If anyone saw you coming out, you'd be a dead man. Besides, there wouldn't be much air in there. Thinking more about it, hell it might be better just to burn the place down." "Thanks, Paul, I'll let you know what I'm going to do. By the way, have you heard anything interesting on those tapes?"

"It's like they know I've got the damn thing running. If something is said that's in any way important, I feel sure it must be in a code of some kind."

Rick had total access to come and go as he pleased, but it was mostly about him there to see Johnny. If there was going to be a time to do this, it had to be now. They knew something was going down in late '63, and it was fast getting close to that time. They had to know if that little black box had gotten into Johnny's hands.

Rick prepared to be in that closet in the next day or so. He wanted to make his entrance at the busiest time of the day, whether Johnny was there or not. Fortunately, Johnny was there, and after a short meeting, Rick slowly came back down the staircase, stood next to the closet door for a minute or two, and when he hoped no one was looking, he opened the door and got into the corner. It was hot, smelly, and his only air vent was a small crack under the door.

There were some old dirty shirts, what felt like a coat, and a couple of boxes which he placed over him just in case someone opened the door. That was about 4:30 pm on Wednesday.

It had only been a few hours, but the way he was wedged in there, his legs had to be almost tucked under him, and his knees were hurting. Just as he was going to try to move, a couple of guys just outside the closet were asking about the broom. One said it was in the back, and the other one insisted it was in the closet where Rick was.

Rick stayed just as still as he could and waited. The door opened, the guy took a quick look, and shut the door. At least there was some fresh air in there, but he still hadn't moved.

Time seemed to have stopped, but finally, a guy yelled upstairs, "Hey Johnny, I'm leavin'. You wanna come down and lock up?"

Yeah, hold on, I'm leavin' too.

Rick could hear the footsteps on the stairs, a muffled conversation, and then the light under the door went out. Now he could move a little.

He had a method to relax by simply counting backward. It also served as a timekeeper. In small numbers, he could keep up with the minutes, which became ten minutes, twenty minutes, and all that time he listened to see if there was any movement from anywhere.

His legs were killing him. He had to take a chance to see if a light was on anywhere. As he opened the door very slowly, he stretched his legs little by little. It took him thirty minutes to be able to move his legs without excruciating pain; he began to crawl outside into the hall.

There was no sound and no light; so, he decided to take the risk of making a little noise. One of the old boxes was near the door. He hit it lightly with his fist, but hard enough to make a sound which could be heard upstairs. He was almost back in the closet just in case someone was still hanging around, but nothing happened. It was time to take the biggest risk of his life: He very slowly started up the stairs.

At any moment, someone could have heard him on the staircase and blown his head off, but so far, he was okay. At least he was still alive. He was now upstairs, but the office door was shut. What if it's locked, he thought? That hadn't entered his mind until just now. He slowly turned the doorknob, and it opened. He would get on his knees just in case there was a gun waiting for him on the other side. Rick could take care of himself in a fight, but he wasn't armed, and might not get a chance to defend himself unless he stayed as low as possible.

Either there was a light outside the window, or the moon was very bright. He could see a shadow across the floor, but no movement. Going out the window would be his way out. He crawled inside the room, pulled himself up, and waited. Nothing happened, at least for the moment. Something moved, and he froze. It was a small cat. When his heart started beating again, he and the cat were alone.

Rick had a small light at the end of something that looked like a ballpoint pen. Not much light, but enough to make his way around the office, looking high and low for a place where a small box might be hidden. It did occur to him that something this important could be at Johnny's home, but if it were here, he had to find it.

Rick looked under, over, in and around, everywhere, but no safe, and no box. He noticed the clock on the desk said 2:35 and no telling what time one of the guys would show up. Look another twenty-five minutes, and then he had to get out of here. The room didn't have much in it: a desk, a couple of chairs, lamps, and a small bar. The floor hadn't been carved up, or at least it didn't look like it has any trap doors in it.

As he looked around one more time, he heard the front door open. Did he go to the closet, try to hide up here, what was he to do? "Hey Johnny, you up there?" Whoever it was, maybe he would stay down there. The window was an antique. It had one of those handles that let you roll the window in and out. There wasn't a lot of space, but he had to get out that way and fast. He heard the footsteps on the stairs, and the only place he could find to hide was under the desk.

The guy came in, checked something over by the bar, and left. Rick's heart had now stopped beating twice tonight; it was time to leave. He rolled the window out, squeezed through the small opening taking out the screen with him. He was able to turn himself around, get a grip on the edge of the window and drop about fifteen feet. It hurt a little, but he was out of there.

Whoever got there first would immediately notice that someone had been in there. Johnny would wonder who had been in his office, and how they were able to get in. God forbid if he ever found out.

Johnny also knew enough about the law to figure it wasn't the Feds. They went by the book for the most part, and besides, if one of them decided to do something on their own one of his buddies would let Johnny know. There was a lot of money donated to all the branches of law enforcement.

Rick wasn't in much of a mood for the Symphony, but he wasn't going to break the date. Besides, he loved the music, and it might help him get some mental relief from the past thirty-six hours. Most importantly, Misty was so looking forward to this night, and he wasn't going to disappoint her.

The band had a small room where they met each night before they started the first show. It wasn't much, but a place to go over a few things, have time to go over the show, and relax. Misty said she would meet him there around five.

They had reservations for dinner, and then the concert started at eight. She had spared no expense with her hair, nails, her dress, and accessories. She was a knockout tonight and felt like a princess. She had not been this happy since she was a little girl. Mr. Charles would not forget what a great decision he had made when he asked her to be with him this night.

The dinner was incredible, and since Misty had never attended a symphonic performance before, her entire idea of beautiful music would be forever changed. This would be the most magnificent night of her life. Not even her incredible lust for this man's heart could equal the excitement and thrill of being treated like a real woman. She could now understand why his high-pissy opera singer and hopefully ex-girlfriend loved the atmosphere of the world Misty had first enjoyed tonight.

He hailed a cab, and on the way to her place, he held her hand, kissed her on the cheek, and told her how much he thanked her for all she has had to go through to reach this night. For the first time, it was as if the two of them were beginning to see one another in a completely different light. She already knew he was a wonderful man, but he was even more gentle, loving, giving, and aware of her need to be adored and respected.

His thoughts wandered back to the first time they had sex. Misty knew everything to do to make a man happy, and he accepted those pleasures without considering how much she ached to be loved. At first, he thought she was like that with any man, but he came to understand that wasn't true.

When she finally did tell him how she felt, he too was having an awakening of sorts. He wanted to keep her safe, let her know that no one was going to hurt her again. Maybe part of him was beginning to understand that love, compassion, emotion, and desire could make a wonderful relationship even closer. Whether or not Rick could take time to love someone was a question he couldn't answer. For now, holding her close to him was a good start.

* * *

If they kept this up, people would soon start to assume that Rick and Misty had become a full-time couple. They did have a lot of fun, and even as he struggled with his other life, she helped him keep things in perspective. Tonight's date was just about helping David and Vanessa get off to a good start. Just before he and Misty left his apartment, Chip called Rick to tell him that they needed to meet as quickly as possible. It was urgent.

Rick knew about a woman in Houma who wanted to start a restaurant, but for the moment was using her home to cook incredible steaks for a few people at a time. He had called her to see if she had a table available. She did; so, that's where the four of them would be headed. The food was incredible, the wine superb, and everyone had a really good time. Misty was terribly disappointed that Rick was leaving, but she'd make up for it when he returned. When Rick called Chip back, they would meet in Miami.

Chapter 20
Roger Dodger to T-bone Charlie, Come In

"We're only about 500 yards to the tie-up. Can you see what it says?"

"With that stack of pipe up there, I can't see anything."

"What about the supply boat. Can you see it?"

"We're going to have to get closer than this to make sure it's up there."

Rick and Chip had begun a look out almost five hours ago when they were dropped into the Gulf a few miles south of the drilling rig known as Offshore Thunder #3. They knew this rig very well.

The pair planned to quietly paddle the dinghy as close as they could and find some way to get on the supply boat. The Angel's Breath which was tied up at the rig had expensive cargo bound for New Orleans, but this time they weren't concerned about the heroine. They were there to find a small black box which had made its way on board somewhere in Brazil. They thought Johnny had it, but found out it had been in Alejandro's safe all the time. Now it was headed to New Orleans.

There was no moon, which made them almost invisible. The Gulf was calm, making it easy to move toward the rig. Getting there was easy, but leaving, maybe not so much. They moved through the water as quickly and quietly as possible, but they had to stay on schedule.

Sources told them that the supply boat would arrive between one and two. One hundred thirty men were on the rig plus the two or three on the supply ship, but all Rick cared about was getting onto the supply boat without being seen. The box he was after was supposed to be in the Captain's quarters; so, while Chip attached the timed explosives to the hull, Rick would find the box and get back in the water. They had figured they would have at

100

most twenty minutes. The reason Rick couldn't find the box in Johnny's office was simply because it hadn't been sent yet. When Chip found out it would be on this supply boat, both men knew they might have only this one chance to get it.

For the past seven months, there had been increasing communication between Alejandro Estoval and Craig Benson about a very secretive black box. Chip had been able to intercept a communique from Brazil that said the box would be leaving on Angel's Breath, a new cargo boat headed for Venice, Louisiana. It would tie up at Thunder #3 to supposedly take a load of garbage to the mainland, or so the oil company was told. The real cargo was 500 kilos of pure heroin headed to New Orleans.

Having set up a local fisherman to let them know when the boat was headed out, Rick and Chip would be at the rig when it arrived.

Now they were here and could see the boat. A lot of the heroin and marijuana being smuggled into New Orleans arrived on various offshore supply vessels, but this load wouldn't be one of them. The plan was that when Rick had the box and they both were out of harm's way . . . things would go boom in the night.

He was close to being out of time, but Rick found the box under the Captain's bunk. As he came out of the room, all hell broke loose. There were gunshots, and Rick ran like hell to the end of the hall. He was on the stairs and onto the deck in a heartbeat, but now there were lights everywhere. Bullets were coming in from his right, but all he could do was keep moving and hoping nothing hit him as he jumped into the water.

Chip had already set the timer and was several yards away. On the other side of the cargo boat, someone started an engine on a small motorboat. It had a huge light on it which was searching everywhere for any sign of the intruders. Rick quickly submerged, but knew his exhaling could get him killed. He took a deep breath and then discarded the breathing apparatus.

If they kept firing at the bubbles, he could get away by moving as fast as he could to the north. He had to come up for air and could only hope that they weren't able to see him. Chip was waiting for his buddy, watching, and listening for him to surface. He was beginning to fear that they had killed Rick. The wait was excruciating, but finally Rick came up for air just a few feet away. They had a rendezvous with their ride five miles to the north and needed to get moving. In all the commotion, they were able to ease the dinghy away from the rig and get to their pickup point. Once there, they put a yellow stain in the water, so the chopper would be able to easily find them.

As they climbed aboard, there was a huge fireball and a moment later the sound of a tremendous blast. They did what they had come to do; get the box and destroy the heroin.

Chapter 21
Follow the Money

"Hey Johnny, there's a call for you on your other line," someone yelled out from the bar.

"Okay, I got it, thanks. Yes sir, I'll be there in twenty minutes." When the boss called and wanted to see you right now, twenty minutes was too long.

Johnny was met at the door and asked to have a seat in the study. A few moments later a large, rather over-powering man entered the room and asked Johnny to follow him to the pool area. Johnny thought he knew everyone in the immediate family, but didn't remember ever seeing this guy. He thought to himself, something big must be happening, or I wouldn't have been invited here.

"Johnny, my boy, how the hell are you doing?" The Godfather, Francesco Dianatti, was seated with a couple of other men dressed in their swimming attire and a very striking woman in a gray suit. "Have a seat, and can we get you a drink? I've been telling my friends about your loyalty, your abilities, and that I trust you explicitly to carry out any orders I give you. With that in mind, I have something I need you to do for me today. I know it's short notice, but I need you to take this case and its contents to my good friend in Chicago. They will give you something to bring back to me, and I want you to deliver it directly to me the minute you return. The details are in this envelope." Francesco handed him the sealed envelope, and told Johnny the plane was ready to move when he got there.

A few minutes after he was airborne, he opened the envelope and read who would meet him at the hangar, where he was going, and the person to whom he was to give the briefcase. The flight took almost three hours, which was time enough for a quick nap, and after landing, it was an hour to deliver the case. Johnny was quickly back on board the plane with a larger case than the one he delivered.

By around 7 pm, the round trip was over, and he was on his way to the big man's home to deliver the case. When he arrived, he was immediately shown to the study. The large dude he met earlier took the case and told Johnny to wait. When Johnny said he was told to deliver it personally, he was again told to wait and this time in a more convincing tone of voice. Ten minutes or so passed, the door opened, and there was Francesco again.

"My son, I know it's been a long day, but the importance of what's going on depends on you and me. We will do whatever we have to do. You will now take this case to Dallas. You are to leave it in the hangar, pick up a brown envelope which will be handed to you, fly back here, and give the envelope to Joey. One of these days I will tell you about all of this, but not now. Here's a little bonus for your time and being the one man, I can trust to do all this right."

Johnny wasn't going to count it until everything was finished. He got back to his apartment around three in the morning, took a shower, had a drink, and counted 250 excellent photos of Ben Franklin. Nice day's work, he thought, but he kept wondering what was in that case.

* * *

Myer O'Steen arrived at Love Field and was waiting for the car to pick him up and take him to the home of Dr. M.L Townsend, a very prominent cardiac surgeon in Dallas. They were meeting to go over all of the doctor's holdings, do some estate work, and then transfer funds to Dr. Townsend's Canadian account via his private Swiss account.

It seems the good doctor had received a large amount of money, which he needed to keep secret. No one was better at that particular activity than Myer. By the time anyone ever found out about the money, none of it would be able to be traced. For the moment, there would be a purchase of some maritime equipment in Brazil, which would be handled by a company in Mexico which had a bank account in Bermuda.

For the moment, everyone who was supposed to receive goods and services had received notice of deposited funds for that purpose. With that all settled, the parameter of possible times was set. All that was now needed was the exact route and the day which payback would be traveling. When Joey had that information, he would set things in motion.

* * *

Vanessa had enjoyed meeting Rick's friend, David Flynn the third. He was rather cute, had a great sense of humor, and thought she was beautiful. She thought so too, but more than eager to hear him say it. After all, she hadn't had much time for a social life, and being around Johnny all the time wasn't helping that situation to get any better. According to Johnny, she was a good lay, but not much of a brain, as if he could tell the difference. It was all disgusting to her, but if that's what it took to keep her on the inside, then that's what she had to do.

Her contact lived in Denham Springs just east of Baton Rouge. Debra Ingram was there just to make sure Vanessa had a place to go, should things get rough. Johnny thought it was Vanessa's sister, but had her vetted anyway. The cover for both women was good enough to get past the guys checking them out, but all it would take was one stupid mistake, and they would quickly disappear.

Vanessa had passed on to Debra what she overheard in Dallas. It sounded like a hit to her, and it had to be something big, or there wouldn't have been such a covert approach to it. Usually when someone was removed, it took a phone call with one of their codes, and the deed was done. The best she could guess it was some politician or other prominent individual who had reneged on a deal. For that matter, it could be someone in the media who was about to make his or her final appearance. According to her superiors, they were probably about to take out someone at the top. Before a family could make a hit on the hierarchy, they had to run it by all the other families and get their approval. It must have been something like a Board of Directors meeting before deciding to fire the CEO? The FBI assumed that's why the meeting had taken place earlier in Cicero.

Devin Akers had been with the FBI since he got his MBA in 1956. His primary role in the organization was to help trace drug money back to any one of the families. With the money the mob earned, they could afford to hire the best lawyers and buy off just about anyone they needed for their illegal activities. There were so many layers between the bosses and the street that it could take years of around-the-clock surveillance to have enough evidence for an indictment. Whoever they arrested was usually back out on the streets in a few hours.

J. Edgar Hoover's patience was running thin. He let it be known that he wanted agents seen taking down some mobsters, and he wanted it done now. He told Devin to create a plan to infiltrate the Dianatti family, and get someone inside and close to the heart of the family. Devin chose Vanessa to be the one who would take the risk. She was smart, devious, and beautiful. He told her it would be the most dangerous work she could get, gave her ample opportunity to back out, but she insisted that she could do it. If she were successful, she would rise quickly in the ranks. If unsuccessful, most likely she wouldn't have to be concerned with her career. Some soldier who wanted to make a move up in the family would be chosen to take her for a moonlight boat ride, dressed in her finest chains.

Vanessa moved to New Orleans and started hanging out at some of the smaller clubs. She used the dumb-blonde approach, and was soon getting to know some of the small-time hoods who directly or indirectly worked for the Dianatti family. She could play these guys pretty good, and sometimes she had them thinking she might come across to get what she wanted.

When she told her dad that she was going to work for the FBI, he wasn't surprised. She had spent countless hours at the jail and the courthouse watching her father defend some of the sleaziest looking people who were guilty as sin but needed someone to help them. One of her first heroes was a guy who would come in on occasions to talk to her father about some case. When he entered the room, he would flash this big shiny badge, and announce his purpose. On one of his visits, Susan asked him if she could be an FBI agent. In a somewhat flippant tone, he told her, "Sweetheart, a pretty girl like you wouldn't want to get involved in something as complicated and dangerous as what we do." That was all it took. Susan decided right then that she would show him.

Now here she was in a place which was kind of different in a lot of ways because they had a jukebox with nothing on it except Sinatra records. Maybe that's why they called it Sinatraville. Her appointment was at 10 pm, and in some ways, it was going to be like a blind business meeting aka a date. She had been asking around about how to get into the exotic dancing business, and some guy called her and told her to meet him here tonight. They would talk, and then he would show her some of the places that might be able to use her. Maybe afterward they could go back to his place to discuss it further. He didn't know who he was talking to and had no idea how resistant to his charms she could be.

Vanessa had about decided she had been wrong to agree to this meeting and was getting ready to leave, when a very handsome, very hard looking, well-dressed guy walked in and she knew immediately that he was there to see her. He walked directly toward her.

"You Vanessa? He asked as he waved to the bartender. He showed the bartender two fingers, and within about three minutes he and Vanessa were served a couple of very dry martinis.

He looked her over as if he was buying a car and said that she had all the goods to be a hit. Vanessa used her unpleasant whiny, I'm-stupid voice, and though he hated that sound, that body definitely deserved his full attention.

After going to four or five bars where this man seemed to know everyone, he took her to a small restaurant that had closed thirty minutes earlier. If Johnny Faretta wanted a late-night meal, no one complained.

Johnny had decided during their little tour that he was going to take this one home tonight for a test run. On the other hand, Vanessa may have sounded less than smart, but she had been here before, and wasn't going to just fall backward for this guy because of what he wanted. Not yet anyway.

Vanessa knew she had hit the jackpot. Johnny was the guy who had a direct link to anything and everything in New Orleans. He had the ear of the Don himself, and though she was going to play the hard-to-get card, she would let him have his way with her when she thought the time was right. For now, she would have a nightcap at his place, but that was it, or so she thought.

He had a temper and almost threatened her if she didn't take her clothes off and get in bed. She drew a gun on him, and said something to the effect, "If you're interested in ever using that thing again, I suggest you back up and let me out of here."

Johnny started to laugh. "Ooh lady you're scaring me something awful; so, get your ass out of here, and don't let me see you around here again. Got that baby?"

Vanessa shot the lamp, and it was dark, threw the gun down, and went over to him, kissed him hard, and walked out. He just stood there smiling and thinking that he liked this woman. She had balls.

As Vanessa told her contact, "I just danced on the edge of a four-story building and thank God, I'm still here. Debra asked her what got into her head that she could pull off something that brazen, and with Johnny Faretta? "Girl you're crazy; very courageous, but crazy none the less.

It took about a week before she got a late-night call from Mr. Faretta. In his own way, he apologized, but she knew he just wanted another shot at her.

"Johnny, you're a great guy, and I do appreciate that you took time out of your busy schedule to help me, but I don't make it a habit of bedding down with someone I don't know, much less just met. I know who you are, and I suppose I'm lucky to still be here, but I have principles and don't think those rules deserve being abused for your pleasure."

"Let's do this Vanessa: why don't we start over and see where it goes. I won't violate your rules until you want me to, okay? By the way, you start at the Star Club on Friday night, so you better get an act together. You'll be doing two twenty-minute shows on Friday and Saturday. You start at $200 a night."

"Johnny, sweetheart, thank you so much. Do you think you could be there for my debut? I would feel so much better if you could be there."

"Baby, I'll be right up front. See you after the show."

She was on the inside, but it was going to be difficult to get out and about without having someone always knowing where she was. Johnny was very protective of his assets, and to him, Vanessa was to be watched and protected. She damn sure wasn't trailer trash by any means. This woman could handle herself. He would see to it that she became very well known in the quarter. After all, she was his woman now.

Chapter 22
What the . . . ?

The chopper was on the ground around seven, and Rick and Chip got back to Destin, cleaned up, and headed for a little place on the beach that served an excellent ham and eggs with home fries. After last night's adventure at the rig, they were tired, but too hungry to hit the rack without eating something.

On the way back from the pickup point, they talked about the little box but hadn't looked inside yet. Chip had been told that it was imperative that they get the box and its contents to Dr. Carmichael as soon as possible.

There were two items in the box: Some kind of financial code and a key, which appeared to be from a safe-deposit box at some bank. There was a note which read: "Payback on the move with three in place. Santa ready for early Christmas. You know what to do with this."

Rick called Doc, told him about the contents, and asked how it was to be forwarded. Doc would send a courier for the pickup in about an hour. "Eat slowly, and he'll be there soon." After giving the package to the courier, they went home to get some sleep.

They could have died under that rig, but now they were calmly having their second round of caffeine and talking about what they were planning to do on Christmas.

Thanksgiving was only two weeks away, and both were talking about where they were going to spend turkey day. Chip was going to be with Camila, and Rick would just stay in New Orleans to feast on some of the best cooking in the country. Rick's mom had never served oyster dressing, and who said you had to have just turkey? Rick had made a lot of friends, and they all wanted to feed him. He was just a nice guy they would like to have over to their home anytime.

Misty wanted him to baste her turkey several times, and she would see to it that he was well fed. She loved to be bad, but just for him.

Chip was flying out in a couple of days, but before either one of them could think about some wonderful time off, they had work to do with their now very profitable second source of revenue.

Thank God no one suspected that either one of them had anything to do with the problems that were being experienced trying to get the heroin to New York. Johnny Faretta was under a lot of pressure to get the problem fixed, or he might not have a Christmas or any other holiday for that matter. He knew what pressure was, and he knew how to fix things.

Johnny's grandparents first arrived at Ellis Island, New York in the early summer of 1912 on an old steamer called Le

Marque. It had the stench of rotting animal carcasses lingering in the bowels of the ship which had once proudly served the French maritime in its building of international trade.

When they got to America the little family existed by selling homemade baked goods and delivering milk from a local dairy. One afternoon the grandfather was approached by a couple of tough looking guys who not so politely discussed how they were now going to be his new partners in the baking business.

Known by his friends as Ernie, Johnny's grandfather didn't need any partners and told them to kiss his ass. When one of the thugs pulled a knife on him, Ernie promptly took it away and damn near removed the left side of the guy's face. There was blood going everywhere. He kicked the other one in his balls, and that was the end of the discussion about a partnership.

The news got around very quickly that Ernie Fratella had attacked two of Carlos Barbaro's men and lived. Not only did he live, but damn near killed one of them. A few hours later, Ernie was in a large home surrounded by a couple more guys with unpleasant attitudes.

"Mr. Fratella, please come into my humble home. You are my guest. Would you please share a glass of Campari and soda with me? Don Carlos Barbaro was feared by all, and everyone knew that being told to be at his home meant one of two things: you were about to be very dead, or you might wish you were dead. Odds were that Ernie wasn't asked over for dinner.

"The reason I suggested you come see me Ernie . . . may I call you Ernie?"

"Yes, absolutely, yes, don Carlos, please call me Ernie." He was a tad bit nervous and could barely get the words out of his mouth.

"As I was saying, the reason I wanted you to come to my home was that I understood that you didn't feel comfortable having two strangers approach you and suggest, without properly introducing themselves, that they wanted to become a part of your little business. I do apologize for the abrupt manner in which you were contacted. "Our visit today doesn't have anything to do with them, but has a great deal to do with you. When I heard what happened, I was most impressed with your ability to get matters, shall we say, put into a different perspective. You handled yourself very nicely under such conditions. "Ernie, I apologize for the misunderstanding and would like to make it up to you by offering you a small job, which you could do for me instead of delivering milk."

Ernie stayed with the Barbaro family until his life ended somewhat prematurely when he was gunned down by some thugs from another family as he and three of his buddies were delivering some beverages for a small party during prohibition. There was a small funeral, a grieving widow with three children, and a couple of Ernie's friends who had known him since he arrived.

His son Stephen would eventually follow in his father's footsteps and rise to the top of an infamous New York family. You might say, it was in the Faretta genes to take care of family business, and most likely little Johnny Faretta's future was pre-determined as well. Johnny's grandfather would have been proud of what his grandson had been able to do for the Dianatti family. As his grandfather said proudly, "It's such a great country, this America."

Chapter 23
Something Isn't Exactly Right Here

Harvey was being pressed from all sides and needed money now. He called Jack and told him to find some way to get him some of his fee or he was backing out of the deal. A call was made to a guy in Chicago, who then called Johnny. Johnny was more than pissed. No pipsqueak like that was going to dictate how things would be going down. Harvey was just about to buy the farm, but after Myer called.

"Johnny, this is Myer. How's it goin'? Or should I ask?"

"I take it you heard what that little bastard was trying to pull?"

"I did, and it's not a problem. I sent the kid $5000 by courier, and that'll take care of everything for now."

"So, everything is still in place, I take it?"

"Yes, we're moving nicely. You can tell Joey that we'll have all the specifics by tomorrow night. With that information, the deed is done. If I don't talk to you for a while, it's not that I'm not sociable, but I'm headed to Italy for a little vacation."

"That's cool man. We'll see you when you get back. Take care."

Johnny thought to himself, *if it had been me, I would have knocked the kid around a few times and saved the money.*

* * *

A big black Cadillac pulled up in front of the Western Hills hotel in Fort Worth, and the driver opened the door for a very attractive woman in a black business suit. When she approached the desk, she was warmly greeted. "Mrs. Townsend, it's so nice to see you again. How long will you be staying with us this time?"

Nancy Townsend, the wife of Dr. M.L. Townsend, would only be staying for a couple of days and had reserved the Executive Suite. She made it quite clear that she would be having guests and would need a second bottle of scotch.

Dr. Townsend was sixty-eight when he married Nancy. She was thirty and had already amassed a great deal of money from various investments she had made with her late first husband's insurance proceeds. He had died in an auto accident in South Texas a few years ago. His $1.5 million policy yielded her

$3 million because it was an accident. She was twenty-five at the time of his death. What no one knew was that the night when her husband was killed, she was with an old boyfriend in the backseat of his '56 Chevy. Ronnie had asked her to marry him when they both were nineteen, but then he changed his mind when he caught her playing house with his best friend. Loyalty and trust weren't everything to Nancy.

Nancy looked twenty when she was twelve, which attracted every male in Lufkin, Texas from age ten to thirty. Her mom, who was a looker herself, had married a cowboy named, Robbie Woods. He rode bulls and made a living of sorts, but his real gift was helping a lot of young women ride him. He damn near got himself killed by a jealous husband a couple of times, but just couldn't resist the urge to have one more for the road.

When Nancy was fourteen, she heard something outside her door, and before she knew what was happening, old Robbie was trying to rip off her clothes. She started screaming, but didn't know Robbie had sent her mother to the store for some beer. He pulled her panties off and unbuckled his pants, but that would be all he would do. There were two gunshots, and both went through Robbie's head.

Nancy's mom got ninety days for a weapons charge, and Nancy was severely reprimanded for shooting the guy. With that punishment she headed to Dallas. What she would do there she didn't know, but at least no one knew who she was.

Someone was always there to help her, and usually, it was an older man. She never knew her dad, and most likely spent most of her life living and loving anyone who might take care of her like a father. She wanted the security from him, but not the sex, which as one might imagine caused a lot of problems. Finally, she met an attorney who was a partner in a small firm in Dallas. It was a strange relationship because when he went to work, she went to school.

At work, he introduced her as his younger half-sister. She had come to live with him after her mom and stepdad were killed in an auto accident. Nancy did care about this guy, and he taught her etiquette, tact, grammar, and making love. Besides that, his home was gorgeous. They married when she finished high school, but soon after they were married, things began to go sour.

Marcus Ryan was eighteen years older than Nancy and had become very possessive. He didn't trust her and started to have her followed. She met with the private eye who was hired by her husband to keep tabs on her and made him an offer he just couldn't refuse. She would meet him two days a week for sex, and he would tell Marcus that she was pure as the driven snow.

Through her romps in the sack with the private eye, she learned a lot about the Dallas underworld. There was a guy she met briefly from time to time who had a small club in Dallas. He had some friends who could take care of things like getting rid of people who had overstayed their welcome.

She paid the owner of the club in such a way as to keep him happy, hired a local hitman, and told him it had to look like an accident. He did a great job, and at a tender young age, Nancy Ryan was a very strong, beautiful, and wealthy woman. No man would ever use her again.

The possibility that the hitman would attempt to blackmail her or try to reduce a sentence by ratting her out was eliminated. She called her friend Jack, sobbing, almost wailing, and told him what Tony Rodriguez had done to her. Tony, the affable hit man, never saw the guy who pulled the trigger.

After a few months of playing the grieving widow, she moved to New Orleans. Nancy Ryan had a lot of money, was beautiful, and immediately had the attention of several prominent men; one of those being Eric Summers. He wanted to introduce her and her money to the old money that could give her prominence in the New Orleans social circles. They were seen at several high-society parties, and as a result of their continued social relationship, he finally determined it was time to make his move. That didn't go so well. He had assumed that since he had introduced her to all the right people, she would naturally want to reward him. His idea of a reward and hers were two different concepts.

One night after attending the ballet, he had invited her to a small gathering at his home. The guests began to leave, and before Nancy had called her chauffeur, Eric, having consumed a few too many martinis, started to paw her and then rip her gown. She told him quite unceremoniously to get his hands off her. When he didn't, she pulled her Derringer out her bag and once again told him to stop. He didn't, and she shot him.

Nancy was not one to panic. She had been in New Orleans long enough to know that if there was a serious problem to call Johnny Faretta. She did and within a few minutes he was there. He told her not to worry and called the police. She explained the situation, her driver was given the night off, Johnny took her home, and not much else was ever known about the unfortunate accident.

Just as most men felt, Johnny wanted to get to know this woman better. She was beautiful, rich, and bad which met all his requirements for the ideal woman. She thought he might be interesting as well; so, over the next few months they began to get closer. They would meet for coffee, have dinner, go to his club, and of course spend time exploring their sexual fantasies with one another. Though she always had some well-known man with her at those tuxedo-only outings, it was Johnny who would be waiting for her when she got home. She loved how it felt to be conquered by a man who would kill for money. The harder he drove the point home, the more she loved it.

After a fun night of raw sex and three bottles of champagne she thought it best that he understood her parameters.

Nancy wasn't about to let him think he owned her. She told him quite bluntly that if he thought he was going to get into her pants whenever he wanted just because he was some macho tough guy, he was sadly mistaken.

He laughed and told her, "Baby, once you're with me, you're with me. We understand one another, and nobody walks away from me unless it's my idea." She laughed and told him "I might have to run that thought by Joey. I wonder what he would have to say about that Johnny?"

Johnny had no idea the power this young girl would have once she understood the way the game was played. He wanted her for his very own, but she had let him know that she was out for bigger things, and Johnny couldn't provide it. He was great for a lust-filled afternoon now and then, but not for much else except his friendship. While no one was paying attention, she had been having a lot of phone conversations on Joey Dianatti's private line. One thing turned into another, and soon she and Joey were having regular secret liaisons at his private suite in the Roosevelt Hotel.

It was after one of those nightly trysts that Johnny saw her give Joey a kiss goodbye. He knew he couldn't say much about it if he wanted to stay healthy; so, with that, Johnny said he was just too busy for just one woman. He reluctantly let go of the idea that Nancy would ever be more than just an acquaintance.

After she had unpacked and made herself a drink, Nancy called downstairs to let them know she needed ice and four glasses. Also, would they mind terribly showing her guests to her room? She wanted to make a good impression.

Joey Dianatti, Myer O'Steen, and Jake Whitsel arrived about thirty minutes later. She was cordial but rather abrupt when she finished her drink.

* * *

117

Way out in west Texas, about a hundred miles east of where the movie Giant was filmed is an old run-down shack that once was a pretty nice place to live. It has two wells, two outhouses, a rock foundation, four bedrooms and big room next to the kitchen where Mrs. Wanda Winslet used to cook and feed her family of seven children and her not-worth-a-damn husband Mel.

One day back in May of 1922, the kids were all outside playing when they heard a loud bang and went running toward the house. Their mother was standing there with blood coming out of her nose and her mouth, holding a shotgun, and on the floor was one very dead Mel Winslet. He had hit her for the last time.

When the sheriff came to take her to the jail, he left the kids out there by themselves. Jake was the oldest; so, he did the best he could at being mom and dad, but at fourteen there was a lot he didn't know how to do.

Mrs. Winslet was convicted, sentenced, and hung all within two weeks. Two aunts came for the kids, but Jake had left the day before. He would never see his brothers and sisters again.

He was almost nineteen when he landed in a place called New Braunfels which is between San Antonio and Austin in the hill country of Texas. He got a job on a road crew and stayed pretty much to himself until he met a guy named Lyndon who became a good friend.

Lyndon had a regular home life, and knew a lot of people. He was hard working and down to earth and Jake liked to be around him as much as he could. In 1928 no one ever thought about two guys like Jake and Lyndon as anything other than two damn good ole boys who got things done.

Jake was laid back and Lyndon seemed to be charging uphill all the time. If he needed something done all he had to do was get in touch with Jake. Their friendship wasn't like most of Lyndon's other buddies. Jake preferred to stay in the background while Lyndon was the guy out front. His other cronies wanted to stand next to the big man, so people would think they were as important as Lyndon.

Lyndon had to teach school for a year while he was in college and there were several girls in his class who wanted to make an A without doing much. It may have been a different time in Texas, but girls still understood what motivated men and did their best to help them with their enthusiasm.

One of those girls was Susie Collins. Some of the girls at school wouldn't even talk to her because they said that she had done it with an army boy from Abilene out behind old man Johnson's General Store. It made a good story, but who knew for sure? Susie let 'em talk because she liked the boys to think she was bad.

There was one guy who his buddies called Blue who liked to think he was meaner and tougher than any other boy around. His real name was Webb. The reason they called him blue was because that's what color his balls were after his dates with his girlfriend Jennifer. He almost had her bra off, but then she told him to stop. When he kept trying, she hit him with her hand and the ring scratched his left eye.

After he took Jennifer home, he was still so mad that he was going to find how bad Susie could be. He threw a few small pebbles at her window and got her to come down. She played with him for a minute or two, and he didn't have any more problems with blue balls. Susie thought it was funny and didn't think anything more about it. She spent her time fantasizing about Lyndon doing her in his office after school.

One day Webb saw Susie talking to Mr. Johnson and she had her hand on his arm. Webb figured that since they had shared mutual masturbation, she was his property.

Next day Webb approached Mr. Johnson in the hall, told him that Susie was his, and threatened Lyndon with bodily harm if he as so much looked at Susie again.

119

That was on a Wednesday, and late Friday they found Webb damn near beat to death and lying in a filthy pig sty on the outskirts of town. Six months later, he finally recovered, but who beat him senseless was never known. Webb never really got over the beating, and never bothered Lyndon or Susie again.

* * *

Nancy was dressed in her business look, but casually began the meeting. "Gentlemen, I thank you for accepting my invitation. I assure you that I won't waste your valuable time. On November first I sent $2.5 million by courier to a small bank in Bermuda. For your purposes, it doesn't matter which bank, but the funds were deposited in the name of a close friend of mine who is overseeing a great deal of this operation. His share of the $2.5 million is for making sure that all the details of our project are locked into place. We now have everything we need to take care of payback."

She went on to tell them that they would receive instructions as to where and how to deposit her $3 million as per their agreement. She had planned for the young man to be in place at around nine-thirty the morning of the hit. When the motorcade first came into sight, Harvey would simply pick up the gun, and take care of payback.

Everything was timed to the second. Nancy would be at the trade center where she would be so overtaken by it all that she would have to be taken home by her driver.

She poured another round for everyone and asked them if they had any questions. Joey asked Jake, "Are you absolutely sure that this guy can get the job done?"

"Joey, let's think about it. The kid can hit a moving bird at a hundred yards; so, do I think he can get the job done . . . next question. If the cops don't kill him, I've got that covered as well."

120

Myer asked a simple question: "How do we know that this Harvey kid won't go to the Feds?

"That's a reasonable question, but let me ask you: If you were hired for a job and had a wife and family, would you take the chance of them being killed because you changed your mind? I've had several discussions with the young man and explained to him the repercussions of a change of heart."

As the guys started to leave, she asked Joey to stay for a few minutes. "One more thing gentleman, before you go: The funds have to be in my account by November sixteenth. Let me just emphasize that I have good friends in very high places who would be most interested to know that there might be a conspiracy in the works. She smiled and showed them to the door.

She asked Joey, do you trust those two?"

"About as much as they trust you."

She smiled and told him that while Myer was in Italy, she wanted him gone.

"Baby, are you serious? What the hell for?"

"Let's just say that loose ends need to be cut off, and while we're cutting, make up something about Marco that would piss off the guys in New Jersey."

"Damn, woman, you on the rag?"

She reached down and started rubbing his crotch, pulled him closer and kissed him, and provocatively whispered that she just wanted to make sure things worked out just right. For the next couple of hours, she was all his. She loved wild sex and might even love Joey. Not really, because she loved nothing but herself, money, and power and in that order.

Chapter 24
The Rick and Nikki Show

Rick and Misty had become a couple, but there were times he would be having a drink or maybe listening to an opera and think about Nikki. She was everything he had envisioned a woman to be and besides missing her love and her body, he missed their most interesting diatribes on how life started if you took God out of the equation.

But now Nikki was gone, and her father told Rick that she was living with that rich guy from Atlanta. Rick wondered if she ever thought of him, but for now, he had things to do. He'd think about Nikki some other time, which lately seemed to be about 10:30 every night when he was alone.

Larry Tyson was a key man in the upcoming construction of the World Trade Center in Manhattan. There would be two one-hundred-plus story structures side by side. It would be an architectural masterpiece. If Nikki thought he was doing well now, no telling what he would be worth when the towers were finished. For all his fame and fortune, there were times when she believed that he didn't even know she was around.

Once in a while Larry would mention marriage, but that could only happen after the project was finished. They could be in the same room, and both be alone. There were many nights she went to bed longing to be loved the way Rick loved her, but she knew that was impossible. No one had ever made her feel secure, sexy, and adored like Rick. She had made a terrible mistake and wasn't sure Rick would ever forgive her for it.

She and Rick had shared an intimacy that went beyond ecstasy. They both gave all of themselves and their hearts. Every particle of their being was involved in each moment of their passion. Every nerve in her body could feel Rick deep inside her, holding her so close she couldn't breathe, kissing her, vowing to never leave her side. How could she have ever left such a man? What was wealth when it cost so much more than it was worth. She had to see him, or at least try. He might not want to see her again, but she had to try.

Nikki had access to Larry's private plane, and though she had asked him if she could use it to visit her mom and dad, she most likely wouldn't see either one of them. They were in Bermuda and she was going to New Orleans.

Rick had been with Chip for almost two weeks and finally was headed back to New Orleans. A lot had been taking place, but no one seemed to be able to find out why things seemed to be closing down. No one was talking, and everyone seemed to be on edge. There had been a lot of discussion about who was sabotaging the heroin shipments, but that didn't seem to be what was causing the pissed off attitudes. Must be the full moon, he thought.

A nice hot shower, a couple of drinks, and hit the rack would help him recover from the trip. Rick unlocked the door, flipped the light switch, and put his jacket on the coat rack. When he turned around, there she sat. "Nikki, how did you get in here?"

That wasn't exactly how she hoped to be met, but it was a good question. "Rick, my love, you know better than to ask a lady how she got in your apartment. She might think you weren't happy to see her."

"It's great to see you, but what are you doing here? Am I a break in the action while your boyfriend closes another deal?"

"Oooh, aren't we in a snit. And to think I came all the way down here just to see you. Hope I'm not interrupting too much."
"Nikki, I am deeply appreciative that you wanted to see me, but I'm tired. Maybe we can have lunch tomorrow."

"We can do that if you like, but I really hoped we might talk about some things tonight."

"Okay I'm here, and you're here; so, why is it you wanted to see me?"

"Because I love you damn it, and I have missed you so much I can't stand it anymore." With that, she walked to him and asked him to please kiss her. As much as he wanted to push her away, he couldn't. They held each other, they kissed, and stood there in each other's arms. He was feeling all those feelings he knew he wasn't supposed to have. He and Misty had become very involved, and this wasn't right. Nikki could be very convincing when she wanted to get her way.

Rick wasn't the kind of man who had a woman in every city. He thought Nikki had gone away forever, and he was now in a committed relationship with a woman who he loved and adored. Nikki just wanted him for the moment, and she had to leave. She did leave, but it wasn't until after ten the next morning.

* * *

Venice is a small town in south Louisiana. In '63 there was a lot of traffic coming and going from this little port town because of the increasing number of drilling rigs. Men and supplies were constantly going back and forth; consequently, a new face wouldn't necessarily be such a big deal. Johnny had only been to Venice a couple of times, and November 17th would be his third visit.

Joey had sent Johnny to meet a guy who had arrived as an employee of the company which transported supplies to fourteen new rigs. Freddie Lantano didn't know an oil rig from a gas station, but he knew he was supposed to be dressed like a rig worker when he met some guy from New Orleans. They talked for twenty minutes or so, Johnny gave the guy a small case, and then headed back home.

124

* * *

Rick had done some isometric exercises and taken a shower. He was on his third cup of coffee when the phone rang.

"Hey doc, it's been a while. Where are you?" . . . What? . . . When? . . . I'll be there in fifteen minutes."

Dr. Carmichael met Rick in the lobby and went immediately to room 322. Lying there in a pool of blood was Donald Meriwether. What the hell was he doing here? This had all the markings of a hit, according to the detectives in the room. Rick whispered to doc that this could be the hit Vanessa thought she had overheard the guys talking about in Dallas. Why Meriwether and why now? Rick wondered. Doc had no choice but to call the Attorney General to let him know about this before it hit the press.

The calendar said 11/20/63. Rick and Chip were talking about Meriwether, and it occurred to Chip that if Meriwether was going to be anywhere other than D.C., it should have been Dallas. It had been announced that the President was going to Texas to mend some fences, and get things rolling for the second term campaign. The security there was going to be intense considering all the death threats and hate mail the FBI had uncovered. The Secret Service had pleaded with the President not to go, but the plea had fallen on deaf ears.

Rick considered that the Assistant Deputy Director might have been doing some company business in New Orleans and then would be leaving for Dallas.

Johnny sat in his office reading the Times-Picayune, which had a banner headline that read, "CIA Exec Murdered." He put the paper down and thought, this must have been the guy in Venice?

* * *

Nancy Townsend was on a plane on her way back from Paris. She had gone there to look at several pieces of art and was now on her way to Dallas. She had a date with a well-known attorney for lunch at the Trade Center in Dallas on the 22nd.

Before leaving for Paris, she had asked her friend Donald Meriwether to meet her in New Orleans. She told him it was especially important and let him salivate thinking she was going to make it worth his while. "I just bought the most beautiful little black cocktail dress, but I forgot my panties. Do you think that I should get a pair or not? See you tomorrow."

Donald was notorious for intimidating young girls at the agency and had an addictive appetite for oral sex. He would move his schedule around to make sure he didn't miss this chance with the insatiable Nancy Townsend. He had been trying to get in her pants since the first day he saw her. Nothing at the Agency could be as important as having one night with her.

She had asked him not to tell a soul where he was going. She laughed that seductive little laugh of hers, and told him, "Baby, I don't want us to accidently create some promiscuous, covert little scandal. He chartered a private plane using an assumed name and headed to his rendezvous with destiny which would soon to make him very dead.

* * *

Rick, Chip, and Dr. Carmichael were somewhat relaxed as they sat on the balcony of Doc's beautiful home on the Chesapeake Bay enjoying a scotch and soda. Most of the conversation was about the Director's murder and the increased tonnage of heroin headed for the northeast via the Gulf of Mexico. They were making plans to find out more about the possible routes

126

which were being used when Dr. Carmichael's wife rushed out to tell them that the President had been shot.

They watched in utter disbelief as the situation unfolded. It would be another forty minutes or so before Walter Cronkite made the unbelievable announcement that the President of the United States had died at 1 pm Eastern Standard Time. All they could do was sit there in silence and despair.

The man who had brought them together, who had given them enormous support, and who believed that something or someone was undermining his relationship with the CIA was dead. Through the tears, all Rick could say was, "I failed him so badly."

PART II

Chapter 25
And the Winners Are . . .

It had been seven months since that most horrific day of November in 1963. President Johnson had reluctantly tried to be civil to Bobby Kennedy, but it hadn't worked.

Bobby knew it had to be the CIA, but had no proof. No one in Washington doubted that Lyndon Baines Johnson had more power than most any of his political brethren because of what he knew about most of them, and that included the FBI Director. Some Senators wrongly deduced that during his tenure as Vice President, Lyndon relinquished some of his authority as it pertained to the ugly lives of the rich and powerful. They were majorly incorrect in that assumption.

The companies that thrived on the production, sales, and distribution of weapons had the man they wanted in office. Their profits would soon explode as the United States became mired in the sewer called Vietnam.

The youth of America became increasingly more involved in the war between North and South Vietnam. Had Kennedy lived and his plans for the Vietnamese prevailed, most of those young men and women who died in that so-called war against communism would have lived to be doting grandparents as opposed to a name on a huge monumental wall in Washington D.C.

The group of men originally brought together by Kennedy was now secretly wedged among the powerful elite in Washington and the international drug cartels, arms dealers, and the Mafia.

Underneath the outward appearances of increased drug usage, indiscriminate sex, and student unrest, was a constantly evolving labyrinth of connections between the vile elements of the covert wing of a corrupted bureaucracy, several crime families, huge banking interests, maritime shipping syndicates, and weapons production.

The closest thing to this kind of vertical power had not been known since the days of the robber barons, and those guys paled in comparison to what was going on now. It was equivalent to creating a plan for world dominance as a logical result of the rise of corporate greed. America the beautiful was for sale.

The age of experimentation with psychedelic drugs and free love was extending its reach far beyond the private parties of the extreme left in northern California, but that was old news. Television was beginning to smell something cooking in Southeast Asia and foreign unrest was much more interesting than what was happening back home.

Doc's group started probing the interactions between crime, government, and business one little piece at a time. It was their strategy to bring down those at fault by taking out the foundation one block at a time.

Rick, Chip, Darren Leitner and David Atwater were the first four chosen, but now Vince Williams, Becker Caldwell, and

Justin Maxwell were becoming more heavily involved with the objectives and the strategies which had been put in place.

* * *

Doc told Rick and Chip that the group wouldn't be complete without Mr. Caldwell. Whether he was kidding or not, it made Becker feel extra special. The young man was one of a kind for sure. The silver-tongued fox, aka Mr. Cool, and always best dressed on campus, had more girlfriends in college than most men have in a lifetime. He also had a very analytical mind and a vivid imagination. Becker Caldwell was too good to be true. He mesmerized everyone with the way he made joke into a saga which combined with his personality made it even funnier.

He could write, play the piano, compose, act, race cars, emcee various gatherings, and sing. He loved History, English, math, science, and once upon a time won an award for writing the missing scene in Hamlet. He was the prototypical Renaissance man.

After he and Doc had time to talk, after all the questions had been asked and answered. Beck wanted to know one more thing: how would this effect his social life?

Doc laughed and assured him that he could do anything he wanted to do, but only after he had taken care of the business he had been given him to do. Mr. Caldwell was all in for the long run. He was known for taking risks, loved mysteries, thought he could be the next super spy, and loved the fast lane. He was perfect for what Doc wanted him to do. Dr. Becker Caldwell was going to be the smartest, coolest, baddest, and most debonair assistant college professor ever, and possibly the youngest.

Beck asked, "Dr. C., why is it you need a college professor for the project?"

"With all your abilities, I need for you to get a lot of visibility, show up at all the functions on campus, maintain a high profile in the Quarter, date the socially elite debutantes, and all and all be the most eligible bachelor in New Orleans. Your credentials and reputation precede you from your prior positions as assistant to Dr. Morey Simpson at the University of Michigan. He has agreed to help us with this but has no idea as to the real reason we need him.

"Your specialty is the History and Formulation of Analytical Psychiatry. Can you handle that?"

"Dr. C, I will dazzle them with my footwork, and make up some BS they'll never understand." Doc wanted to laugh, but hadn't decided if it was funny or not.

"You will be working closely with Rick. He and Chip Hagen will be taking care of the uglier side of New Orleans and you will be our front for the life here that few know exists. At some point in time, things could start to get a little edgy, but you did tell me that you were a natural James Bond. Is that correct?"

"Dr. Carmichael, I admit I do shoot a good line of bullshit from time to time, but I can handle myself just fine, thank you. You tell me what needs to be done, and I will see to it that it gets done. Is that good enough for you? Just one other question: wouldn't I have been better as one of those financial guys who make all that money?"

"Mr. Caldwell, all I want you to do is simply put together a semester's worth of classes for your new subject, be in the paper constantly, and find out who killed Donald Meriwether."

"You got it Doc."

* * *

Vince Williams was one of those macho grandé types. He had a black belt in Karate and could hit a moving target at two

130

hundred yards with most any rifle. At 6'3" and 240 pounds, he was a most intimidating man.

He graduated from Virginia Law School in December of 1962 and had landed a job with a very prestigious firm in Chicago. His destiny didn't include practicing law. He was added to the team for one purpose: to infiltrate the Chicago mob and to work closely with Rick and Chip in their pursuit of how the Vinzzetti and Dianatti families worked together. It would be extremely dangerous, but Vince knew he could take care of himself. There was no Mrs. Williams, no girlfriend, and only one necessity for an excellent day: A daily two-ounce love fest with a glass of Scotch.

Then there was the Kid. Justin Maxwell got that name growing up in New Jersey looking like he was nine until he was nineteen. At first it had been a bit of a problem because almost daily some bigger kid wanted to beat up on someone smaller. It took about six months of that until Justin realized that if he let the other guy hit him first, he was going to always wind up on the pavement. He started working out with weights, and eight months later won the Golden Glove title for lightweights at the age of fifteen. No one bothered him again.

At the Naval Academy he had gained more weight, taken down several challengers, and won the middleweight championship by knocking out three seniors and a junior. He would be heading back to Jersey and getting a job on the dock. From that vantage point he would keep a close watch on all the shipments to and from Brazil. He didn't meet any of the other guys until after the assassination.

* * *

It was a formidable group of young men who had been brought together to help the President, but now would dedicate themselves to finding out what really happened on the twenty-

131

third. All of them were fully aware of what was at stake, and what each of them would be doing in the months ahead. It was going to be difficult for those with wives or girlfriends, and though they hated to have to lie to those whom they loved, no one, for the moment, could ever know what they knew or what they were trying to do.

All of them were extremely smart, resourceful leaders, loyal, and intent on finding out who took their President away. They had access to millions of dollars, which had been deposited in a numbered Swiss account. No expense would be spared to help them in their quest.

Chapter 26
Rick Took It Very Hard

Three weeks after the President's funeral, Rick decided that he needed some time away. He called Nikki and asked her to come to his place when she had a day or two she could spare. Though her career was growing one successful appearance at a time, she knew that if Rick were asking her to be with him, she would find the time.

Nikki couldn't believe the place when Rick opened the door. The smell of stale beer, maybe some pot, and three-day old pizza combined to make one want to throw up. Nothing was clean, and he looked like he had been on a week-long binge. What the hell was going on with him, she wondered.

"Sweetheart are you sick," She asked, though she didn't think he acted sick.

"Nik, I've been a little under the weather but nothing major. I'm sorry about how the place looks, but I didn't want to be bothered by the maid. I've just been upset by what happened to the President. He was really a great man, and it made me so angry, so vulnerable that some son-of-a-bitch could shoot down the leader of the free world. It's not right, and I feel partly responsible."

"My darling Rick, what could you have done about it? You're no different from me and every other American. We all feel terribly violated, wish we could do something about it, but understand that's impossible. You have nothing to feel responsible for; so, let's not go down that road anymore."

"You don't understand all of it, won't ever understand it, but that's okay. It's my problem, and I swear to God, I will do anything and everything to find out what really happened."

"Sweetheart, what's gotten into you? What are you going to do, join the FBI? I love you and I appreciate your allegiance to your country, but this has nothing to do with you."

Rick smiled and told her she was probably right, but he was really angry about some idiot thinking he could change the world. Rick had promised himself that those responsible would pay with their lives.

Nikki insisted that he come with her, and he reluctantly agreed. They grabbed a po-boy and she took him to her home. There she would see to it that he got some rest and lots of TLC.

The first thing her father asked was, "What's wrong with Rick? Is he sick?

"Daddy, I don't know exactly what it is, but he's really upset about the assassination. He said he felt responsible. I don't understand where that came from, but that's what he said. I got him out of that apartment of his and thought he could use some sleep and good food for a few days. You don't mind, do you?"
"Of course, not darling, but why would he feel responsible? Maybe when he's had a few hours rest we can all talk about it. I love you and glad you brought him here. He's a good guy, but as stubborn as my favorite daughter." He smiled and went back to the den to watch a football game.

Nikki didn't know it, but Rick had showered, put on clean underwear, and passed out the minute his body hit the bed. It would be noon tomorrow before he opened his eyes again.

* * *

The past few days had been a nightmare for Rick. He couldn't get it off his mind. Why didn't they see it coming? They knew it was going to be a hit, but they never considered it would be the President. Who in the hell was Lee Harvey Oswald to take it upon himself to shoot the President? He was that little red-leaning asshole who kept flying in and out of New Orleans. Rick told Doc that Oswald had handed him one of those flyers one day down on Carondelet Street.

When Rick wasn't trying to figure out what they didn't see coming, he was going back over every clue he knew about to find a pattern of behavior with those with whom he intermingled there in the Quarter. He told himself, it might take a while, but he was going to find out who did this.

Now it was New Year's Eve and Rick tried to celebrate, but just didn't have it in him. They went to her home early and watched the New Year come in on TV. Rick still wasn't himself. He looked as if he were off in some other dimension. Nikki was worried that he had some type of illness.

New Year's Day he could hear his lovely Nikki doing her practice upstairs and loved to hear her sing. For the moment, he was enjoying talking to her father, especially since it was about something besides November twenty-second. Rick was originally from Texas, but went to LSU and his favorite uncle was a graduate of Texas A&M; consequently, he didn't much care for Texas University. He thought for sure that Navy with Roger Staubach at quarterback could beat Texas. He and John bet on the game for fun and a bottle of their favorite beverage. John won a bottle of brandy.

The following day Nikki finished her two hours of technical work by 11 am and wanted Rick to go with her to pick up the dress she was having made to wear to the Grammy's. She would be going with the Conductor of the New Orleans Symphony and hoped Rick would go as well. He politely and very tactfully declined, telling her he couldn't leave at that time of year. She pouted, but not for long. Rick didn't really react much to that type of behavior.

While they were out to pick up the dress, they went by his apartment to pick up his car. Since he had been gone, the maid had been there a couple of times and finally managed to get the place clean. When Rick walked in he didn't recognize the aroma, but it was wonderful to see that everything was sparkling clean. One other thing he thankfully noticed before Nikki did was a note lying on the table. On the envelope it read: I miss you darling! Your Misty Forever

He had quickly put the note in his pocket and would have to read it later. There was little doubt about the language she probably used. Rick usually referred to her little notes and letters as sex on steroids. He laughingly once told her that he figured she must ovulate at least two-thirds of the month.

At this moment in time, Rick had a lot on his mind, and although he loved the attention of two incredibly beautiful women, business was business. It was time to get back to the real world.

He kissed Nikki goodbye at the airport and headed back to his place. Just as soon as he got in the apartment, he looked at the envelope and slowly opened it.

To the dearest and most wonderful man I have ever known, I am so horny right now I don't want to move. Every time I place my head on my pillow I can smell you so close to me. I touch myself all over and imagine what it would be like to have you inside me right now. I want you so much. I'm hoping that you feel the same, but not sure you could ever feel as I do. I've never loved, desired, or craved a man as much as I do you, my darling.

Everything I am, every emotion I could ever consider, and every moment of my life I commit to you. However, you want me, whenever, and wherever you want me, I am yours forever. With all my body and my soul, I love only you.

Misty

Rick smiled and felt the passion growing with every image his mind created reading the note. He felt terrible that he loved two women, and he knew sooner or later that he would have to make a choice. For now, he was going to call Misty and spend the rest of the weekend with her in his arms. He knew he should be hung upside down and shot, but the woman was incredible.

He was also thinking how bad things could have been if Nikki had found this note. Maybe bad wouldn't be the appropriate word to use in that case. How God-awful would his body have hurt having been thrown out his apartment window? Miss Nikki had a temper and was very possessive. Put those together and what he was doing while she was away was getting terribly close to signing his death warrant. Nikki would never kill him. She would simply make him wish he were dead.

He heard the knock at the door and knew it was her. When he opened the door, he almost fell backwards. There was Misty dressed in a short black skirt, a blouse which left little to the imagination, high heels and holding her little black bag. "May I come in?"

Rick pulled her tightly to him, she dropped the bag, and he picked her up and took to the bedroom. He almost ripped her dress off, but let her help him. She quickly unbuttoned his shirt and pants. She reached into his pants to feel how hard she had made him so quickly. All she could think about was him loving her so hard she would cry for more. He licked and sucked everything he could find. This wasn't making love; this was primal passion and they couldn't get enough of it.

A couple of hours later they lay there exhausted and very satisfied. All his passion, his aggression, and his anger he combined with a lust he never thought possible. They drank a glass of wine, dropped the glasses, and started again. He wanted more and so did she. It would be a night to remember. It was Saturday afternoon before they awoke and started all over again. The realities of life would have to wait a few more hours. Right now, he was quite happy to be with this wonderful woman, have a few days to rest, and get ready to get back to the realities of what he had to do.

Chapter 27
August 1964

"What's going on with you Rick? I've called you at least six or seven times and no answer. Are you okay?" Doc had become quite worried about Rick, and had they not connected today, he would have been on a plane for New Orleans that afternoon.

"Hey doc, I'm sorry, but I haven't been close to that phone for hours. I've either been with Misty, at the club, or over at the Meredith's. And yes, I know, that's not the smartest combination of things to do, but sometimes I just don't give a rat's ass anymore about any of this crap."

"Son, you can have all the self-pity time you want, but I'm calling a meeting of everyone in the group very soon and you had better be there."

"As they say, 'What's up Doc?'"

"If we can be serious for just a moment, you will have a set of instructions at drop point two on the twenty-third of this month. Read it, memorize it, and burn it, and do what it tells you. Got that?"

"Yes, almighty leader, I will obey."

"You know what kid? You can be an absolutely perfect and total ass. I think it comes naturally to you."

"Aye aye sir, mi comprende!"

"One more thing Rick: Shove the attitude."

* * *

Though they didn't know it at the time, there would only be two meetings during the life of this group when they would all be together. It was time to make sure what was going to be necessary to keep going forward; consequently, Doc called for everyone to be at the meeting in Sainte Therese Canada

There's a small building not far from the Ste. Therese United Church. There were always meetings scheduled there for church business, and this time of year, which was beautiful, there were hundreds of residents and tourists everywhere. No one would think twice about a few guys meeting at the church.

They had been sent instructions as to where they would be staying, and when they would meet. Some would land in Montreal, some in smaller airports located within a few hours' drive of Sainte Therese. No one would be staying close to anyone else; consequently, they would have cars which were registered to various shell corporations which had been formed for just this situation. Their rooms were near where their planes landed. The meeting would begin the next morning at nine, but their arrivals had been structured so that there would be at least ten minutes between entrances into the building.

Doc thanked them all for their sacrifices, for staying the course through some of the most difficult days this country may ever know. Also, he wanted them to know that he and the former Attorney General had been sharing tidbits of information as it related to anything that might help define how the assassination was carried out.

With all the information that the group had in their files, Bobby Kennedy was convinced that this had been a massive conspiracy, and he would find out by whom and why and make sure some form of justice was rendered. He had a front row seat to how the Warren Commission appeared to disregard certain information and focus on something that would help give them an adequate, though somewhat dubious resolution of what happened to the President. In the meantime, he needed to talk to Doc.

One of Bobby's questions, was how much would it cost to keep the group going? In 1964 dollars, his estimate was around six hundred thousand dollars. New funds would be deposited in their highly secret Swiss account and only three people would have access to those funds: Bobby, Doc, and Rick. Any cash withdrawal would need two signatures in person. Doc had been assured that if they needed more money, it would be available to them. No one would ever know about the account.

It was decided that the group would meet to analyze what leads they had, what they needed, and how each man would be redirected. Chicago, New Orleans, and a yet unidentified location in New Jersey would be the three key areas from which to start. Though most of the drug money came out of New York, the supply was being controlled elsewhere.

Another important piece of business was solving the killing of Donald Meriwether just before Kennedy's assassination. There was more to Donald's death, especially the timing, than they first realized. Did he know what was going on? Maybe he was going to go to the cops? Was his death tied to the killing of the President? Was it simply meant to be a tragic diversion? Why him and why New Orleans? So many questions and too few answers.

Robert Kennedy was now the rock of the family and asked Davis if he would stay on and keep the guys together. What started out as a six-month project was now coming up on two years. Doc thought about it, and decided he couldn't walk away now because he wanted the sons-of-bitches who did this to die a horribly slow death. He would see to it that the group would find out for certain who had killed his good and loyal friend.

There had been so many clues, so many situations; yet, they never figured out that the hit would be on the President. How did they miss that? Rick told the group that he had failed to put the pieces together and felt that maybe he was too concerned about structure. Going forward, wherever the lead took him that's where he was going. For the time being, he was going to get deeper into the Dianatti family's business in New Orleans, find out if they had participants in the assassination, and he didn't care whether the evidence was admissible in a court of law or not. Those responsible had no idea what payback really meant.

For now, they would go back over every call, conversation, meeting, or anything else that pertained to those individuals in New Orleans. This group would find a way to avenge the death of their President. The bad guys started all of this, but these eight men would finish it.

Chapter 28
Chicago

Vince Williams aka Vinni Pertinelli arrived in Chicago after doing a nickel at Talledega in Alabama. He was a big man with a temper, and when his one-night stand told him to go fuck his mother, he beat the life out of her. He got off easy because she shot at him. He pleaded guilty to manslaughter with extenuating circumstances. The day he walked out of that hell hole, he got on a bus for the Windy City. One of the inmates had mentioned the name of a guy who might be able to get him some quick money.

Cardello Mandilossi only let his three closest friends call him Bondy because he only had three friends. He got the nickname because he sent clients to one of the sleazier bail bond guys near the county jail. No one messed with Bondy for fear of losing their life. The man was a walking time bomb. With his new referral job, he had become a little nicer, but that only meant he wouldn't cut your balls off before he killed you.

Doc had warned Vince about Bondy, but also told him that if he wanted to get close to Big Jim Vinzzetti's family this was the man who could help with that.

They had worked on Vince's identity, family history, and criminal background for several months and now it was time to see how it would play out.

It had been raining all day, it was cold, and the wind was blowing off the lake around thirty miles per hour. It was a rotten day to be out, but if Vinni was going to meet Bondy about fast money, today was the day.

"Why Chicago, Vinni? Seems like an old southern boy like you would have stayed where it was a lot warmer."

"Well, Mr. Mandilossi, I might not have decided to come this way had it not been for Kevin Sorrenstein who said you might help me make a few bucks to get me back on my feet."

"How well did you know Kevin?"

"We washed dishes after breakfast and lunch for over a year, and with that job, it's nice to have someone to bullshit with now and then. He got out about a year ago."

"Tell you what Vinni; I will think about this for a couple of days and then give me a call, say on Friday, and I'll let you know."

"Hey, appreciate anything you can come up with Mr. Mandilossi."

"Call me Cardello. I ain't promisin' you nothin' but call me Friday around two." The contact had been made, now Vinni would know on Friday if all his background had checked out okay. If not, he would be out of Chicago in a heartbeat, if he still had one.

Vinni's phone rang. "Vin, meet me at eight at the Solar Club and don't be late. I don't do late. And for God's sake wear somethin' to keep you warm."

"Hey Cardello, you don't sleep?"

"And what's it to you?"

"Nothin' man, just kiddin'."

About the best he could do for protection from the cold was an old windbreaker and a Cubs sweatshirt he bought earlier for fifty cents. Bondy's car was a new Dodge Charger, and it was fast. Vinni was ready for anything because for all he knew Bondy could be taking him for one last ride. His mind eased a bit when they pulled up to this old building at the back of some trucking company.

"Take this and come with me." Bondy gave Vinni a small caliber gun and a crowbar. When they got to the door, Bondy told Vinni to yank the lock off, and follow him. The flashlight didn't work very well, but they could see a couple of boxes under some dirty rags in the back of the room. Bondy told Vinni to take them to the car and wait. Whatever this was about,

142

Vinni didn't like it. Once he set the boxes down, he moved away from the car.

About five minutes passed and no Bondy. Out of nowhere there were two squad cars with lights flashing. A bullhorn told him to lie down and put his hands behind his back. "The son-of-a-bitch set me up," He said as he lay there on the cold asphalt. Vinni was more than pissed.

He was fingerprinted, arraigned, and put in a holding cell along with twenty other guys, and all of that before midnight. The place literally smelled like shit and marijuana at the same time. Throw in a little standing piss, and Vince wanted to throw up.

He huddled over by the wall to keep warm and stay out of the way. All he wanted to do was sleep. This was the first time he had been almost warm in the past twenty-four hours. Sleep wasn't easy considering the noise, the stench, and the comings and goings of drunks and druggies all night. Around eleven the next morning, the cell door opened, and he was told he could leave.

What the hell was this all about he wondered, and how was he getting out of this place?

Bondy met him at the door and was laughing out loud when he asked Vinni how he was doing.

"What the hell are you doing here, you asshole?" Bondy pretended he didn't hear that and kept laughing.

"You didn't think I was just going pal up to you without makin' sure who the hell you were, did you? Somethin' to say about those fingerprints Vin. You're a bad dude beatin' up a broad, but you'll find that some of the boys here are a lot rougher than she might have been." Bondy started laughing again.

"Dude, tell you what I'll do. Here's five c-notes. Get you some clothes, a good meal, a decent room, and for God's sake get a coat. If you have anything left over, get yourself laid. You can pay me back later. Let's have dinner at the Solar Club tonight, I'll give you some choices, and we'll go from there, okay? You're a good sport Vin, and I like you. See ya tonight around eight."

Vince told Doc that he wasn't paying him enough to play this game, but did say he had passed the initiation and his sheets came up as the bad guy he's supposed to be. With that he would meet Bondy and see where things might be headed. Right now, as Bondy suggested, he was going to get a coat, a better place to stay, and a few z's before tonight.

* * *

They had a couple of drinks before they ordered. It was mostly small talk as they ate, and then it was time to talk business.

"Vinni, my friend, I hated to put you through all that shit last night, but when my boss wants something done, I don't ask why, I just do it."

Bondy handed Vinni an envelope, told him he had taken six hundred out, and said this was from the boss. Then he explained that the boss wasn't giving him a gift. He wanted Vinni to run a little errand for him.

"Vin, tomorrow afternoon at 4:30 I want you to be at Gate 25 at O'Hare. A guy dressed in a security uniform will hand you a package. Put the package in this briefcase and head to where they repair some of the American Airlines planes. When you get there, tell one of the repair guys you need to see Benny. He'll tell you what to do next. I'll see you tomorrow night at the club around ten, and you can give me what you are supposed to pick up. You got all that? Whatever you do, don't fuck this up or this will be the last pick up you'll be asked to make. Capiche?"

Vinni nodded that he understood and told Bondy he'd see him tomorrow night. When he got back to his room the envelope held four one-thousand-dollar bills, and four one hundred-dollar bills. Bondy charged a hundred dollars interest, but Vince didn't care. He had some cash to live on for a while.

When he got to the hangar Benny did tell him what to do next. A small twin-engine Cessna was parked just outside. Vinni was to take a short ride to a small airport just outside of Duluth, Minnesota. He was to give the briefcase and its contents to the limo driver, and in turn the driver would give him another briefcase. It was locked.

Vinni gave Bondy the case, they had a couple of drinks, and Vinni was told that they would be back with him in a few days. For now, he could enjoy some of his new-found earnings.

Chapter 29
Meanwhile, Back on the East Coast

Justin Maxwell, now known as Max Justin, had been getting a lot of attention because of an incident he provoked between one of the foremen and himself. He needed to get the attention of the family's liaison with local 1285 of the longshoremen's union. Max got attention alright, but damn near got himself killed. To start with, he was no match for the jerk who hit him with a chair. After a couple of days in the hospital, he was back on the job, but none of the men wanted to be seen with him.

Rick and Max had spent a couple of weeks together in Bermuda before Max started working at Port Newark. They had a lot of time to go over what he would be looking for, who he needed to get close to, and most importantly, noting anything that remotely looked like merchandise coming out of Brazil. The second part of that discussion was about staying alive.

It was almost four in the morning when Max's phone rang. When he said a very sleepy hello, whoever it was hung up. Ten minutes later it rang again, and just as Max was about to say hello, some guy with a mouth full of something told him, "Be at the dock in an hour." Before Max could say anything, the call was over. He had no way to contact Rick, but he knew he better be on the dock and be on time

There was a heavy, cold fog. Only one or two lights could be seen through the mist; so, knowing who it was standing by the phone booth was impossible. As Max started to walk over, the voice told him to stop, put his hands up, and turn around. This didn't seem to be going well, and yet, Max knew he couldn't run. The last thing he remembered before waking up was excruciating pain from a hit on the back of his head. As he slowly regained his senses, there was still a throbbing pain over the left ear.

"Wake up asshole, somebody wants to talk to you."

Max tried to sit up, but it took a minute or two to get his bearings. "Where am I, and who are you?" The blurred looking image slapped Max's face and told him to shut up.

The guy that slapped him, then handed Max a cup of coffee, laughed, "You're one lucky asshole. Drink this and come with me."

"Well, if it isn't Mr. Justin. How's the head?"

"I think it's still attached, why do you care?"

The dude who had just about taken his head off was sitting across from him smiling. "I have to say I was impressed that a newbie like you would take on one of our best men. The fact you're still breathing is an indication of how impressed I am. I don't like my guys to be upset."

"The asshole wouldn't have been upset if he wasn't taking money off the top and leaving us in the dark about where our dues are going. Speaking of which, what's with the three percent increase?"

"Now, now Max, you know that's not true. We take good care of all of you. And the three percent? The bosses have always had a little extra to make sure things go smoothly on a day to day basis and they needed a raise. I'm going to let you get away with being stupid this time, but if there's a next time, you won't have to talk to me again. Do you understand?"

"And who the hell are you?"

"Let's just say I'm one of those guys who keep things running on time. My name's not important; it's what I can do for you, that matters. Take the day off to get your head straight, and I'll be in touch.

Once again Max had the day off, but went back to work the next day making damn sure he watched what was going on behind him. A few days later it was almost time to clock out when one of the guys came up to him with a small envelope. Max, I found this in my locker, and it said to give it to you today. The message read: Smart guy, meet me at the union office after you clock out, Felix.

Who was Felix, and was Max in trouble again? He couldn't figure out what he could have done this time. He had made sure to lay low when he went back to work.

"Max, my name is Felix, and I run this dock, and wanted to apologize for some of the ugly stuff you had to go through with some of my over-eager managers.

"I needed to see you because it's not often we get someone like you. Not only are you a lot smarter than the others, but I read that you have a black belt in Karate. Is that true?"

"Yeah, but don't usually get too many opponents who use a chair."

"I like your sense of humor, kid, and like your style. Any chance you would be interested in something a little more complicated than moving shit around here?"

"I suppose that depends on what you have in mind."

"I'm the VP of Operations for a small company in Newark that helps oversee the operations of the Port. What I could use is someone with a good sense of knowing a little about all the working parts of the organization. I could start you at thirty thou and see how you do. Do a good job, and there's more where that came from."

"Nothing this good comes without a hitch; so, what's the punch line?"

"Max, take the job, and we'll get more into the specifics later."

"When do I start?"

"I will meet you here on Monday morning at 6:30."

That night, Rick heard Max's message: "I think I'm in."

* * *

Camila had only been pregnant for two months, but already she was holy hell to be near. She was gaining weight, felt ugly, didn't like sex as much, throwing up non-stop, and hated Chip for getting her in this condition. Not that she had anything to do with it, but this was no way for the sexiest woman in the world to have to live. She was mad when she woke up and stayed that way the rest of the day.

What made matters worse was Chip having to be gone all the time. She continued to live with her dad while Chip was away, but where did he go all the time? He called her almost every day from somewhere, but never told her exactly where he was. Sometimes he would tell her that he was a few miles from Miami, or just outside of Chicago, and one time he even told her he had taken pictures as he was flying over the Alps. What the hell was he up to she wondered.

Her father would try to appease her, but there wasn't anything he said for which she didn't have a tart reply. What made everyone even more uneasy was that her condition was only going to get worse. Not that having a baby is a bad thing, but Camila would just as soon she didn't have nine months of this hell.

Alejandro and Chip thought about sending her to a convent, but then they would laugh and say how excited they were that she was pregnant. Those discussions happened when Camila was not around. Blessed was the silence.

Chapter 30
Queen Elizabeth

It took Rick several months to be able to entertain an audience again. It wasn't that he had forgotten how to do it, but since that day last November, he hadn't felt like it. Now he had determined what he would be doing for the long run; so, playing at the club fit perfectly into his plans.

He had created a monster for himself by loving two beautiful, but incredibly different women. They loved him too, but would have first killed him, then killed each other had they known about each other's intimacies with their Rick. At some point in time the man knew that shit was going to hit the fan. All he could think was maybe it would be much later than sooner. Sometimes it's what you don't know that will get you killed.

The phone rang. "Hey there cutes, what's for dinner?" Rick loved to eat at Nikki's home because Annie, the Meredith's cook, loved to watch how much Rick enjoyed what she cooked for him. It wasn't going to be about dinner. Nikki wanted to see him alone and would come to his apartment about nine that night.

"Is there something going on that I need to know about," He asked her somewhat hesitantly.

"You'll know soon enough," as she slammed the receiver down.

Oh crap, he thought. *Something's up and I can only hope it has nothing to do with Misty.* "Please God, keep me safe," he uttered out loud. If Nikki knew about Misty, it was going to be a

149

short night and a very long forever before she would speak to him again.

One thing he could say about her: she was punctual. Just as the clock began to chime nine bells, the doorbell rang. Why she didn't use her key, he didn't want to know. She was dressed for dinner and dancing, but the way she had sounded on the phone, it must be with someone else.

"Sweetheart, you look exquisite. What's the occasion?" She stormed in, threw down her coat and almost screamed, "Rick Charles, are you going to marry me or not? I want an answer now, or you can kiss this private little pussy of yours goodbye."

He just stood there staring at this beautiful woman and trying to think of the words that might be appropriate for that question. "Nikki, you know I love you, but I didn't really think you wanted to get married." He thought that might give him a few moments more to come up with the next thing to say.

"If that's all you have to say, you can take that horn of yours and shove it up your ass." She was headed toward the door.

"Baby, baby, slow down a second, and let's sit down for just a minute and start talking to one another. Please sit down, please."

"Rick, I don't want to talk. I love you, but I'll be damned if I'm going to be tossed aside for another woman or your job or anything else. Either you give me an answer, or we're done."

"Nik, I will give you an answer right now, but you have to answer just one question first: what are your plans for your career?"

"That's fair. I am giving up the idea of becoming a member of the Met. I will do some private appearances, an occasional opera here in New Orleans, and raise our children if we get that far."

Rick pulled her close to him, kissed her passionately, and told her how much he loved her. He told her he would be back in a minute. When he came back in he got on his knee, and asked her, "Does this answer your question?" She looked down to see that he had the most beautiful diamond ring she had ever seen. It had a big-ass diamond in the middle, surrounded by several blazing red rubies. When she looked back at his face, he said, "Literally, baby, you did ask for it." She was going to be Mrs. Elizabeth Nicole Meredith-Charles, and they celebrated in various positions all night.

Nikki couldn't wait to get home and tell her mother. They would start planning the most fabulous wedding ever, plus they would have to begin planning the party to celebrate their engagement. She was so excited, and her father was smiling from ear to ear. He really liked that kid and now he was going to be his newest son. He rang out with, "Hot damn, I'll have the best damn grandkids ever."

While everyone else was celebrating and planning, Rick sat alone in this apartment thinking about Misty. This was going to kill her. He knew he couldn't have them both, but if Misty had come to him first like Nikki did, maybe she would be doing the celebrating today. He called her and told her that he needed to see her soon. It was serious.

Chapter 31
All Hell Is Breaking Loose

First, there was a call and whoever it was hung up. Five minutes later there was another call and again, this time no one was there. Ten minutes later the banging on his door made him aware that someone urgently needed his attention. In his disorderly confusion caused by drinking too much last night, he slowly made his way to the door. When he opened it there was a very sexy woman standing there, but he didn't understand why Vanessa would be banging on his door.

"Rick, you little bastard, I should just shoot you and put you out of your misery, but on the other hand, I prefer to watch you die a slow and horrific death. Why have you done this to my best friend, the woman who loves you more than life, and how could you have done this and not even had the decency to tell her? She had to find out about it in the la de dah section of the Times Picayune. The woman is devastated. I'm damn sure not devastated, but I am here to tell you that this time you've really fucked up more than you can ever know. You've just lost the best thing your puny little ass ever had. I am disgusted that I even know you."

Vanessa picked up what looked like a stale drink and threw it in his face, and as she left, slammed the door so hard that one of the paintings fell off the wall and shattered the glass.

As he was drinking his second cup of coffee, the phone rang again. He hesitated to answer it, but he did. It was Nikki, and she wanted to know if he had seen the announcement yet. "I'm sorry darling, but I haven't even seen the paper yet. What announcement are you talking about?"

"Are you serious? What announcement? It's our engagement announcement silly. I'm not happy with the photo mom chose, but now it's official. I've had at least twenty phone calls already, one from the Mayor, to wish us all the happiness in the world. I am so happy. Want to come over for brunch?"

Rick told her the absolute truth, which was that he had a terrible hangover, and just wanted to be still for a while. Nikki laughed, but understood. "Then I will see you for cocktails at five and we'll have dinner around seven. Do we have a date?"

"Yes, my love, I'll be there promptly at whatever time my body says it's safe to travel. I love you."

* * *

Rick finally began to feel his body coming back to life around noon, and by this time he had decided there was only one way to go about this. He wasn't going to call her. The only thing he could do out of respect for the woman was to go see her. If she wouldn't let him in, at least she would know he was trying. Of course, there was the possibility she might just shoot him through the door, but at least he wouldn't suffer too badly or too long.

He didn't even have to knock or ring the bell. She opened the door and threw her framed photo of them at a Mardi Gras party right at his face and slammed the door. It hit him, but the cut wasn't too deep. Rick stood there a moment and asked her if he could please have a few minutes to talk to her. There was no answer. He waited a few more minutes and asked again, but no answer. Before he could ask again, a patrol car pulled up in front of her place and two officers started walking toward him.

"Hey Rick, what the hell are you doing trying to break into this woman's home?" One of the guys who knew Rick from the club thought this was a joke. Rick sort of laughed and told the officers that he wished he could break in, but she would probably shoot him the minute he got inside.

One of them yelled out that he was the police and asked her to open the door. Misty opened it a little bit, asked them to make him go away, and shut the door. Rick agreed to leave voluntarily, and they all left. Maybe he could find a way to talk to Vanessa again.

Rick was moving into the upper set of New Orleans society, but there was a healthy price to be paid for admission. Not only was he going to have to find a way to talk to Misty, but at some point, he would have to tell Nikki about Misty. It was quite possible that he was going to wind up very alone. He decided he would have dinner with the Meredith's and then leave for a few days. He needed some time away from everything in his life.

Before leaving the next morning, he sat down to write a letter to Misty. There was no way to say he was sorry, no way to ask her forgiveness, and certainly nothing he could do to make the situation any better, but at least he could try.

My Sweet Misty,

You didn't deserve this, and if saying I am sorry would help I would do that in a heartbeat, but only being able to say I'm sorry just won't do it. I am guilty of falling in love with two women, and not having the balls to own up to the obvious outcome of my selfishness. I used you both for my own lust and need for love and deserve everything that is about to happen to me.

There is a reason for all of this, but to tell you what that reason is will require us to meet. I'm going to spend a few days in Mobile at the Grand, and when I get back, I hope you will meet me in a private place of your choosing to listen to what I have to say. I promise you it's not about trying to acquire your forgiveness, seeing you again, or any other personally self-satisfying reason you think I might have. It's just about the truth.

Please think about it, and I hope to see you soon,

Me

The Grand is an awesome hotel on the east side of Mobile Bay, very private, and very exclusive. Rick was thinking, *considering how angry Misty was, she's probably already paid Nikki a visit, and either shot her or better yet, made her miserable by telling all the bawdy details of our wild and crazy sex.* To Rick it didn't make any difference. His demise was imminent, and

154

what impact that could have on the work he was there to do only time would tell. As he sat there on the patio drinking one scotch and soda after another, he began to think of a plan. It would be dangerous, but a plan, nevertheless.

Later that afternoon, Rick answered the phone; it was the front desk. A small package had arrived for him. Did he want to pick it up or would he like them to bring it to his room? He told them he would pick it up when he went to dinner. He started to ask them if it was ticking, but decided that might not be such a good idea.

The bartender had cooked up a very dry martini and sat it down next to the little pink package on the bar. He asked Rick if it was his birthday, but Rick was so deep in thought he almost didn't hear the guy. "Oh, uh, no, I think it's someone's way of saying ole buddy, you had your shot and now this is your parting gift." Zach, the bartender, asked him if he was going to open it, and Rick said, "Sure, what the hell, but you may want to step back."

He just sat there staring at it. It was a beautiful antique English Silver Hunter pocket handmade in 1873. It had a description and a small photo about the watch. Also, tucked neatly into the small watch box was another piece of paper. It read: *Rick, sorry about the picture frame toss. I wanted you to have this watch to always remember our time together. I got your note, and if you still want to talk I'm in room 236.*

Rick just sat there for a moment, and finally realized that she was here. Zach had been talking to another customer and noticed the box and Rick were gone. He smiled when he picked up the hundred-dollar bill that was left behind.

When Misty answered the door, she wasn't dressed in anything sexy, but no matter what she wore she always looked fantastic.

"So, Ricky boy, you wanted to talk, let's hear what you have to say."

"First of all, this watch is beautiful. Not sure I understand why you gave me this instead of a Timex, but I thank you with all my heart. What I wanted to talk to you about is extremely dangerous for me and could be for you as well. Consequently, before I say anything, having given you that caveat, do you wish me to go forward?

"Rick, the way I feel about you right now, I don't really care one way or the other. You can tell me or not tell me, but let's try not to make everything so melodramatic, okay?"

"Actually Misty, I'm really not going to say much of anything today. I so appreciate these few moments to at least start a conversation about how two lives came together for a reason, and then became so much more than a random circumstance. For all it's worth, I fell in love with you. I wasn't supposed to do that, but I did.

What I'm asking you to do is consider a hypothetical situation which involves me and some, shall we say, interesting people. At some point in time, and hopefully it will be soon, I can tell you several things which can partially explain some of the things I've done. For now, I can only say that in some respects I live two lives. Those two lives cannot be combined. I love you so much that I must decide between what I have to do with my life and the life I hope you will have. All I'm asking from you is to believe me when I tell you that it's breaking my heart to lose you. Someday you'll understand all of this, but for now, my darling, goodbye.

Tears were streaming down her face as he closed the door. How could this have happened. How could something like they shared be torn apart and thrown to the floor in a matter of hours. She laid down on the bed and wished she were dead.

Chapter 32
He Waited

Rick and Nikki were having lunch when the waiter approached to ask Mr. Charles if he could come with him to the kitchen. Rick had no idea why he was asked to the kitchen area. He had barely gotten through the door when he saw Chip. "Hey buddy, what the hell are you doing here, and why the kitchen?"

They had a brief hug and Chip explained that he only had a few minutes and had to give Rick a message in private.

"Rick, you have a problem and Doc wants it fixed muy fasto. It seems as if Misty called Johnny to ask him if he knew anything about why you just dropped her. During their little chat, Misty mentioned that you said you were doing something dangerous that she couldn't know about until later. She knows you love her more than Nikki and wants to know what's really going on with you.

At first, Johnny apparently didn't pay much attention to what she was saying, but yesterday he made a call, which we have on tape, wanting to get more information about you. Doc wants to know what the hell is going on here and that whatever it is, he wants it stopped. I'm headed back to Alejandro's plane; so, do what you need to do to get this fixed. Take good care my brother."

Nikki asked him what that was all about, and he told her it was a secret. It was, but not anything like she imagined. They spent a couple more hours together, and then he took her home. There were things at work he had to fix.

"Johnny, this is Rick. Would you have some time to meet with me this afternoon? Just need thirty minutes or so."

"Sure Rick, whatcha need? And by the way, congratulations on your engagement. My boy is movin' up the chain around here."

"Thanks Johnny, and that's part of the reason I need to see you."

"Three this afternoon okay for you?"

"Thanks guy. See you then."

Rick wrote a short message and left it at drop four. Doc wouldn't see it for a few hours, but at least he would know that Rick was at work on solving the problem.

Johnny always locked the door when he was working on something important; so, when he heard the knock he started putting things away and told Rick to hold on a second.

"Ricky boy, how's my favorite celebrity dude?"

"Very funny, and I'm fine. Maybe not fine, but when we're through here, I may feel better. I've gotten myself into a very unpleasant situation, and it's simply because I am a selfish little bastard who loves two incredible women."

"Johnny, you saw the result from announcing that I apparently love one a little more than the other. I'm not proud of myself, but I really didn't want to lose Misty forever; consequently, I indicated that with the work I'm doing might be dangerous and didn't want her to be in the middle of it. I hoped that would quell her anger, but obviously I was wrong."

"Ricky my boy, you are one of the best con artists I've ever met. You have to admit that making yourself out to be some strange mystery guy is a bit much just to keep yourself from getting kicked out of her bed."

"If you've ever been in her bed, then you know why I would do just about anything to get back in it. Like I said, I love two women. Anything you can do to help would be great. Also, if you think I'm overdoing it, remember when we first met I was the most naïve guy in the world. You have to admit I've come a long way."

"Rick, you were a complete nerd and now here you are a man of the world, with two very sexy women who adore you, and you have my friendship. They shook hands, and Johnny said he would see what he could do with Misty. Rick thanked him, and Johnny nodded. "Now get the hell out of here, I'm busy."

* * *

Misty knocked on Johnny's door, and he had to ask her to wait a second. Lately it seemed like Johnny had more picky crap to do than ever before. If he had wanted to be an accountant, he would have gone to college. Probably not anything that drastic, but he was not a detail kind of guy.

She was dressed very sexy, and for just a moment Johnny considered not letting Rick see her again. Maybe he could take better care of her and just appreciate her more than Rick.

"Misty, thanks for coming. I need to talk to you about some things I have in mind for the club and want to get your input. You've been a good employee for quite a while, and I think it's about time we moved you up to management. What do you think about that idea?"

"I'm really surprised you even noticed, but I'm certainly capable of managing your club. I do get a raise, right?"

"How's fifteen g's sound to you?"

Misty almost passed out. Considering that her job now with tips barely made four thousand a year. With this new job, she could finally have some nice things of her own. "When do I start?"

"I'll have you meet with Henry on Monday to work out a transition arrangement. He'll be taking over the restaurant and bar at the Roosevelt.

"While you're here I need to talk to you about Rick. As you know, I like the boy, and he's never done anything to make me become suspicious. He's been straight with me about everything; so, this conversation about him being something other than who he says he is disturbs me to no end. You mind talking about it?"

Even if she had minded, she couldn't tell Johnny Faretta to kiss off. "Johnny, I don't mind discussing him, what he is or isn't, but there's nothing you can say to make me ever want to see him again."

"That's too bad Misty because I asked him to come over to meet with us." Misty looked amazed and angry but knew better than to leave.

"Why would you do that to me? The man has lied to me and besides that he's marrying someone else. I hate the bastard."

"Baby, if you had just said you didn't care, maybe I could buy into this I don't give a damn thing. You still love him, or you wouldn't have gotten so worked up. Sit back and relax a few minutes."

She jumped when Rick knocked on the door. When he entered the room, he saw her and almost forgot to shake Johnny's hand.

"Okay, here's how this is going to work: I've got some things to do downstairs, but when I finish, I'll be back. During that time, you guys are going to talk, and by the time I open that door, one of you will have shot the other, or you've worked this out."

"Misty, I figure we've got fifteen to twenty minutes before he gets back. All I have to say is that I love you, I'm sorry I fell in love with you, and yes, I'm sorry about Nikki."

She sat there for at least five minutes before saying anything, and then, "Why did you do this to me? I thought you and I were together forever. Why didn't you tell me that you and Miss Bitch were serious? I'm a big girl. I could have dealt with the truth. Sure, I would have still killed you, but at least I would have been nicer when I did it."

He reached for her hand, and whispered, "Misty, at some point in time you will find out all there is to know about me. We could have a good life together, but selfishly for now, it has to be on my terms. I'm sorry I hurt you, but I swear I love you with all my heart. Sometimes business can cause a lot of problems. Take care of yourself, remember our times together, and should there ever be a time that you need me, I'll be here for you. Goodbye sweetheart."

As Rick was going down the stairs, Johnny was on his way back up to his office. When he opened the door, Misty was crying. "I take it things didn't go too well?"

She wiped away the tears and started to get out of her chair. Johnny held her a second and told her to give the boy a chance. "Who knows, the kid might be the guy you can't ever forget."

Chapter 33
Back to the Salt Mine

There seemed to be a lack of enthusiasm, energy, and especially productivity. Everywhere they turned someone had a theory as to why the President was shot.

Max had been the only one really getting anything done. He was now a foreman on the dock, had some authority, and was getting to know a lot more about the hierarchy in Newark. He was a regular at a small club a mile or so from the docks. Mindy Watson had a great little bar to go to before heading home. After her husband was killed by a crane line, a bunch of the guys got some money together for her to help take care of her and her little boy's living expenses. She worked for a while at one of the nearby cafes, but asked the union for a loan to buy the club where most of the guys spent their money. It had suddenly become available, and after she took over she called it Mindy's Place.

Max had begun to spend a lot of his after-work time hanging out there. The reason was a cute little waitress who made sure that Max's beer was always the way he liked it. She gave him the nickname Frosty because he loved the beer cold with ice on the glass.

Laura had tried melting his ice several times, but Max didn't seem to be interested in getting any closer. They did go to a union dance one night, and on a couple of occasions went to the movies. Laura was divorced when she was twenty-two. Her husband thought the word faithful had something to do with religion, and he had none. She had a son, Donnie, who was now six, and Max really liked the kid. The problem as Max saw it was that he was too deeply involved in things which could get him killed, or worse yet, get those he cared about killed. He told Laura upfront that his business was dangerous, but she assumed he was talking about the dock.

Rick, Chip, and Doc were to meet up with Max at a club in Manhattan. From there they would head to a place near the Tonawanda Wildlife Management Area which wasn't too far from Buffalo. Max had no problem getting away because he had been working seven days a week for the last month. He told his boss that he was going on a fishing trip, but he mostly just needed some time to rest. In case anyone asked, he took some pictures to make sure they knew he had been in the woods fishing.

The cabin was big enough for two families. The fire was already dying down by the time they arrived, but a couple of logs later and it was nice and warm.

The four of them needed to meet because of what Doc had learned from one of his confidants in the FBI. In the next two or three weeks, there's going to be a large shipment of high-grade heroin, which will be working its way to New York. Chip would be working on his end to find out where it was coming from and by what route. Max would be on the lookout, and Rick would coordinate what to do once it was located.

Doc went on to explain, "I have an undercover cop in New York who will be watching there, and Max, you'll need to be on the lookout for anything suspicious or which has more than adequate security. If you see or hear of anything like that, get word to Rick as quickly as possible.

"Most likely those crates will be well hidden, and the heroin even better disguised, but you have to find a way to let us know what it is, how it's packaged, if you can find a way, check the lading docs. We think the heroin will be in the midst of several containers of artwork, curios, and cheap pottery. My guy doesn't know that for sure, but two shops in South America seemed to be thriving without much business."

Chip and Rick's little business was flourishing, but they had not moved anything except marijuana. They had started with a little less than a ton and one boat. They were now moving three and four tons every month and were using four of Alejandro's boats. Chip told Doc to hell with dangerous undercover work. He was going to start spending his time becoming a drug king. Doc didn't smile.

After two days, Max and Chip took the car and headed back to the city. Chip always had access to his father-in-law's plane, and Max would get a taxi back to his place.

Rick knew it was going to come up sooner or later, and it appeared today was the day.

"Pardon me Rick for being old fashioned, but it appears to me that you've done a great job of getting a lot of attention with the saga of your love life. Anything you want to say about that?"

"Nikki is a woman not every man can handle, Doc, but I can. She's strong-willed, ornery, emotional, and outspoken, but everything about her is what I love about her. When she came storming into the apartment, she caught me off guard, and I succumbed to her fierce determination before thinking about the consequences it might have. I have agonized over everything, and if you want me to step away, I will."

"Rick, no one is asking you to step away. At the same time, it's imperative that you have Misty on board. You do whatever has to be done, but be warned: if she makes the mistake of talking about this to anyone, I'm not responsible for what happens to her. If you really care for her, take care of this problem."

"Doc, she has been invaluable to me when it comes to information. She knew way before any of us that the President was going to be killed, but had no idea that Vanessa was talking about the President, but then, neither did Vanessa, nor anyone else. Misty's taken over the management of the club. I'm going to ask her to help me?"

"Are you suggesting you bring her in on what you're doing? She could get you killed in an instant."

"Doc, I wouldn't ask that of her or you. I just need to think about how I'm going to handle the relationship. I'll think about some things for a few days and make some decisions. I know what to do if she fails me, but she won't. At least we'd be working together."

"I will allow you to test the water. If you feel that you can do this, that it will be successful, and she has your absolute trust, I give you my word that I won't get in your way. Just be careful, for God's sake. Oh, this may not be the best time to say this, but give Nikki my sincerest hope for her happiness."

"You're right Doc, not good timing." He patted Dr. C. on the back, and they headed out to the chopper that had been waiting on them for a good twenty minutes. When he got back to the Big Easy things might get better . . . or not.

* * *

164

When Rick walked into the club the first person who spoke to him was Misty. "The receipts have been down now for several days, and it seems that it may be attributable to your absence. The boys in the band are good, but not good enough to hold the house while you're away. How long will you be with us this time? Johnny wants to know."

"Calm down, I'm here now and will be for quite some time. I just needed to get away for a few days. Do you want me to do two shows a night or not?

"You know Rick, I really don't care as long as the audiences are happy. It does seem to me like you would want to do both shows, but then marrying a wealthy woman means you won't have to worry about money anymore." With that said, she quickly turned and walked away. He just stood there and thought to himself that Misty may never be civil to him again. At the same time, he knew she had to be for both of their sakes.

After leaving the club, he called Nikki to see if she wanted to meet him for a drink and dinner before he had to be back at the club. She wanted to, but she had a fitting and she and her mother were meeting the lady who would be baking the cakes.

"Honey, after your last show, why don't you come over for a nightcap? If you're hungry, we can raid the refrigerator.

"I'll see how tired I am, but thanks for the offer. I miss you, and if not tonight, maybe tomorrow?"

The last show was over at one. The club didn't close, but the band did. Rick told them to go on without him because he had some business to take care of before he went home. He had parked the car across and down the street from the club. As he waited, he went over the conversation he wanted to have with Misty two or three times. It never seemed to make much sense, but this was going to be his only shot at making his case. Right now, he was beginning to think she might not be leaving. She could be in there doing Johnny for all he knew. *God, I hope not,* he thought, *but she wouldn't be in that situation had it not been for me.*

When she did come out, she headed down the street and was about to cross the street when Rick pulled up in front of her. He got out, ran around the car, and basically forced her into the car. She was about to scream when he pleaded with her not to, and they sped away.

He only had ten blocks to drive, but he had figured it was going to be the only way he could get her alone. Then too, there was the possibility that she would file kidnapping charges against him, but he'd worry about that later.

"Rick Charles, what the hell do you think you're doing? Take me home and do it now! I'm serious Rick. Either take me home or I'll call the police."

"Well baby you're gonna have to call the police because you're going to listen to me or else. Give me five minutes, then I will take you home.

"Okay, you have five minutes."

"I need you to work with me. No sex, no romance, and no dating. Misty, when I first arrived here it was you who befriended me. Not only did we have a non-stop passionate relationship, but you were always passing along little tidbits of information that was useful to me. It amazed me how you found out so much. I could use that ability you have to help me now.

My good friend Chip became involved with a girl in Brazil, married her, and now they're having a baby. His father-in-law is in the business of supplying drugs to several hundred thousand people. One day I looked around and Chip and I were working with him. Now it's even bigger, and I need extra eyes and ears to let me know if there's anything I need to know going on when I'm not around. Johnny and I are in business together;

so, if for no other reason, I just want things to be nice and relaxing. Would you help me with that?"

"You want me to spy on my boss? Not one single second, buster. If you're in over your head and you're asking me to help you with that, not a chance. That would guarantee me winding up very dead."

"That's clear enough, but just one more thing before I take you home: Before I arrived in New Orleans, I went to school in Baton Rouge and that's where I met Nikki. I didn't know anything about her wealth, but I did know she had a lot of friends. I knew too that her father was an attorney, but nothing about the business empire he owned. I was told she could help me, and I used her as much as I could. It's cold and calculating, but that's what I did.

"I could never have imagined that she would want to have anything to do with a musician in the Quarter, but it worked out that she did. In the meantime, I fell harder for you than I thought possible. You are the most giving, loving, and caring woman I've ever known. I still love you, and therein lies the problem. I can't be married to two women. Don't misunderstand me, I love the Nik, but she's nothing like you. Maybe I feel like her dad and I are closer than she and I are, and I'm supposed to watch out for her when he can't.

"I have a very unorthodox situation right now, and I need your help. You have two choices: you can turn away or you can help me. If you work with me, you'll know very soon that I'm for real. I'm asking for your trust for at least three months. Can you, will you give me that time?"

She started to tear up. He handed her his handkerchief. "Rick, I love you so much. I can't stand the thought of you not being with me. Every night I lie there wondering where you are, what you're doing, and when I will see you again. I'm going to help you do whatever it is you are needing from me, but we must do all we can to make sure that . . . oh Rick, just take me home."

He made the mistake of walking her to her apartment. She unlocked the door, and pulled him close. They kissed, pressing hard against one another, and she pulled at his shirt. She wanted him right now, she needed him to love her, to want her, touch all of her body. The moment they were inside, she unzipped his pants, tore the button, and took him into her mouth. She just wanted to love him. He pushed her back on the floor, ripped her blouse, and seemed to be consuming every part of her body. She screamed for him to love her, take her, give her everything he could. When he came, he didn't want to move. "Misty, I love you so much. Whatever we have to do, I will never be without you again. Before they went to sleep in each other's arms, he whispered, "Goodnight my sweet darling, I will love you forever.

> *"Tomorrow, and tomorrow, and tomorrow,*
> *creeps in this petty pace from day to day,*
> *to the last Syllable of recorded time; and all*
> *our yesterdays have lighted fools the way*
> *to dusty death.*
>
> *Out, out, brief candle!*
> *Life's but a walking shadow, a poor player,*
> *that struts and frets his hour upon the stage,*
> *and then is heard no more. It is a tale told*
> *by an idiot, full of sound and fury,*
> *Signifying nothing."*
>
> William Shakespeare

Chapter 34
Now He Has Three Lives

Rick moved from the sofa, got on his knees, drink in hand, and decided that he needed to get it out of his system. *Lord in heaven, we've got to talk. I have no idea what my life is about anymore. I thought I knew at one time, but now I'm just wandering around with no meaning, loving two women, getting nowhere with my life, and feeling as if I've let everyone down. I know you can't be happy with me, but at first, I thought this is what you wanted me to do and where you wanted me to be. Now all I'm doing is reacting to one crisis after another; all of which I have created. Please don't let me hurt anyone else. It really isn't my style, but it seems that lately I've been doing a really good job of inserting pain everywhere I turn. I am sorry Lord, but me being me is a load for both of us. Anything you can do would certainly be appreciated. In Your holy and precious name, amen.*

Rick knew that Nikki would never forgive him if she found out what he had done last night. More importantly, he now hated himself as much as she would when she realized he had another woman in his life. Why would any man put himself in this kind of position? He kept going back over that question time and again. It really wasn't about the sex with Misty, though that part was beyond ecstasy. It was how much she needed him to be there with her, for her, and to have a real love for the first time in her life. She was such a precious woman. He couldn't let her hurt ever again.

Deep down, he wanted to believe that if he went to Nikki today and told her the truth, she would be terribly hurt, betrayed, and go into a crazy tirade. However, in a week or two she would justify that Rick wasn't the man for her, and would move on with her life. Hell, she could have any man she wanted, but then so could Misty. It was flattering to be loved by two such exquisite women, but one of those women had never known the agony and pain of rejection plus the suffering of mental and physical abuse. Rick needed to protect Misty from the world around her and protect Nikki from himself.

He had so much work to do, but at least for now, he could sleep knowing that, for the moment, he had averted the worst possible scenario . . . his demise. Not by either of the women, but by those who might think he really was a dangerous little liar. He had to ascertain where he now stood with Johnny. It wouldn't take long for him to find out.

"Hey kid, be at my office in an hour if you aren't too tied up picking out colors. I've got something we need to discuss, and it can't wait."

"Give me fifteen minutes."

Rick could only imagine what this was all about, and nothing said so far made him feel more comfortable. He was nervous as hell, and that wasn't a good way to walk into a meeting with Johnny. Jeremy told him to go on up, but he didn't exactly leap up the stairs. He took a couple of deep breaths, knocked, and opened the door.

Johnny was seated behind his desk and Misty was standing by him with a notebook and pen. Their eyes met, but they only said good morning to one another before Johnny asked Rick, "You want some coffee?

"Misty, we'll talk later," which meant she would be leaving. He got him another cup of Cajun coffee, which really didn't pour; it just oozed into the cup like syrup.

"Ricky boy, how big do you want your little operation down in Brazil to get?"

"Johnny, I haven't given it much thought. We started with all of us making a little money, but not enough to get noticed. I talked to Chip the other day and he said we did a little over a million dollars last month. Does that mean you need us to cut back a little?"

"Hell no, I don't want you cutting back. I want you to join with me and my partners, so we can help you get even bigger. Of course, if you get bigger, we make more money."

Johnny grinned and told Rick that he should give it some thought. "You talk it over with your partner and get back with me in the next forty-eight hours. We're willing to give you whatever money you need, but we want sixty percent for our generosity."

"Why in the hell would I want to give up sixty percent?"

"How about having working capital of ten million dollars and grossing five, maybe six million a month. Don't you think you and Miss Honeydew could live on twenty percent of that? If you didn't need all that maybe you could give Misty a nice little gift here and there. Speakin' of which, what are you gonna do about Misty when you marry the other one?

"Misty's a hell of a good businesswoman and loves your ass too much in my opinion. Here you are going to break her heart and she still loves you. You must have a giant twanger to have both of those women thinking you're such hot shit."
Johnny at his raucous best, told Rick to go do something productive, and went back to work. Rick went down the stairs much more relaxed.

Chapter 35
Decisions, Decisions

Based on the conversation he had with Johnny last week, Rick had an idea. It was a big ass idea and would mean that he and Chip would have to meet with Doc to discuss all that it entailed. They decided on a small island just off the Carolina coast. The weather was changing to spring like temperatures, but it wasn't time to walk on the beach without a windbreaker.

"Here's what I want to do, and if we do this right, I think this could make us a major player, get us deep into the culture, and find out firsthand what's going on with the New Orleans connections. With what I'm proposing, I would want to bring in one of the guys as President of the company, and that would give Chip and me a chance to become more visible. Both of us are a lot more powerful together than when we are acting alone. We could set things up as an import/export business specializing in various pieces of art for interior decorators in and around the major cities of the world. Wherever there's a need for big time big deal art we could be involved while at the same time moving through the maze of drug dealers and their suppliers. What do you think so far?"

Doc wanted to know what he had in mind for the money. Drug money wasn't going to be made available to the group under any circumstances.

Rick began to explain how he got the idea in the first place. It could be very tricky and dangerous as well, but Johnny wanted to give Rick the money for sixty percent of the ownership.

Chip was the first to respond to that. "Rick, that's crazy. We do all the work, make things fit, and all we get is forty percent? I won't vote for that."

Doc didn't say much for a few minutes. In the meantime, Rick tried to show the big picture to Chip.

"We didn't start all of this to be in the drug business, but that's where the money came from that paid for murdering the President. The way I see it, we get inside the operation at whatever percent, follow the money, and we'll know what happened and why. Isn't that what we need to know? Whatever amount we have will go to the offshore account to help pay for what we've been doing here to start with."

"I guess you've got a point there. My only problem with being the minority owner is that we won't have any say over

172

times, amounts, pickups, and deliveries." Chip would eventually get on board, but he still didn't like the numbers. Doc asked them when they could get this underway.

Rick was considering hiring one of the larger law firms in New Orleans. "I happen to know from what I've heard on the street that a couple of the partners, Jason Jennings and Michael Underwood are good friends with the Dianatti's mouthpiece. When they find out what we're really doing, we might have a better chance of being protected. There are no guarantees, but attorney-client protection gets us some space."

Rick was going to strongly suggest that Darren help them to get things set up. He was a master of making sure all the details were securely in place, and Rick was anything but a minutia kind of guy. By the time they all met for the July meeting, the Company would be in place.

Both young men knew the peril they were adding to their lives, but it didn't matter for now. They were going to nail the bastards who killed Jack Kennedy.

* * *

Now that Darren would soon be on board to handle the day to day operations, Rick and Chip had more opportunities to get involved in some of the financial aspects of those who they suspected of being a part of the conspiracy. If that wasn't enough to get them going, Rick's marriage to one of the wealthier women in New Orleans was practically a permanent invitation to every formal party in the city.

A name that kept coming up at various parties and charity events was Nancy Townsend. Chip noticed a column in the paper about her conversation with the police after the death of Donald Meriwether. It seems she was the last person to see him alive.

"Rick, did you see this?" Chip showed him the excerpts from her statement, "And not only was she the last person to see him," as Chip laughingly noted, "But apparently she had been with him for several hours."

"You don't really think she killed him, do you? I mean the guy was way up the chain at the CIA. Why would some New Orleans socialite kill him?"

Chip replied that it was a reasonable question, but he did add, "The guy arrived on a plane using an alias, and checked into the hotel under an assumed name. He may have been CIA, but it looks and sounds suspiciously interesting to me."

"You know his reputation in Washington. Maybe he was just taking in some of New Orleans' southern hospitality."

"Nevertheless, I'm going to start a file on her, and see what I can find to put in it. I'm headed back on Thursday. Anything you need me to do for you?"

Rick thought for a minute, and told him, "Yeah, there is something I need. I'm not sure how hard this would be for you to get but see if you can find some old drawings of the supply boats before and after they made the changes to the size of the storage area downstairs." "I'll do what I can, but it may take some time. Why do you want the old drawings?" "I want to calculate how much storage space was added. We know what it looks like down there, but I want to know for sure. Get me the drawings and I'll show you what I'm talking about Mr. Camila."

Rick and Johnny were now working together a lot more since business had gone to another level. They were now partnering in a different sense; yet, both men made sure they kept a close eye out for the other guy. Doc decided that after the agreement was given the okay by the Don that there would be no more interference with the shipments. The goal now would be to trace everything to the source, follow the shipment, and connect the dots. The manufacture and transportation were Rick's main concerns. Unfortunately, there was no way they could have any impact on the ultimate distribution. They would certainly pass along as much information as they could to the Feds, but it was sent anonymously and from different places in the Midwest.

The group's sole objective was to use the drug connections to help lead them to those who had a hand in the killing of the President. In time, there would be a piece that didn't fit the puzzle, and that's how they were going to track down the bad guys.

* * *

The law firm of Jennings, Underwood, and Holt had been hired by Rick's company to oversee the legal aspects of international and maritime law and how best to navigate within those parameters. On a very chilly day in late March there was a meeting of the senior partners of the firm, with Rick, Darren, and Chip attending. The law firm had no idea as to the background of these men, but as clients they knew there was a great deal of money backing them up.

They also didn't realize that they were chosen because with whom they often played golf and attended various society events in the city.

Halfway through the meeting, Rick stepped outside for a few minutes, made a private call, and returned to some discussion as to off-loading of certain goods, customs, and making sure of the proper papers required at that time. An hour later, a secretary opened the door to tell Rick that Mr. Meredith had arrived. "Would you show him in please?"

Everyone in the room knew John Meredith, but not because he would soon be Rick's father-in-law. John was an expert when it came to Maritime Law, and Rick had hired John's firm as his personal legal counsel. John not only knew the law, but knew everything about each of the men across the table. After the introductory chit-chat, they got down to business.

Chapter 36
Looking Back

Darren Leitner used the direct approach this time and seemed to have made a much better impression. The first time he tried to work with Benson and O'Steen it didn't turn out so well; consequently, his research, background information, and specific questions about operations had to come from outside sources. He and Rick both agreed that Craig and Myer were more sophisticated and credible in their world than Darren or Rick had expected.

On a very rainy Tuesday afternoon, Darren walked in the door and asked to see either one of the partners. They of course were busy, but he sat down and waited and waited and waited some more. He sat there for almost four hours when Craig Benson came out to ask him to step into his office.

"Mr. Benson, I apologize for intruding upon your time, and thank you for seeing me. You most likely don't remember me, but I tried to get your firm involved in a pension fund I was overseeing, but the timing was probably not the best, all things considered. Subsequently, I thought this time I would submit a different type of proposal. I have studied your firm, like what you represent and what you do for your clients and want to be a part of it."

"Darren, believe me, I am flattered that you would want to work with us, but exactly what did you have in mind? We don't hire brokers, and we have several analysts who give us our recommendations hours before the market opens."

"First thing is that I do not want to be a broker with your firm. I started my career several years ago with a small firm in

Ohio and I was a terrible broker. The company wanted to sell stock and I wanted to make sure my clients had the best possible service for placing their trust in me. What I'm proposing is letting me associate with your firm as I manage my clients' portfolios, share my revenues with your firm, and learn from the best in the business. Of course, I would have a long term non-compete agreement with you, and work within the framework of your company's guidelines."

"What kind of share of the revenues were you looking to offer us in return?"

"I think seventy-thirty would be more than adequate, don't you agree, Mr. Benson?"

"So, we give you an office, our insights, and you handle your clients while paying us seventy percent of your revenue? Is that correct?"

"I pay you thirty percent."

"I always worry when something seems too good to be true. How many clients do you have and how much are you managing?"

"It's not relevant as to how many clients I have, but I'm managing in excess of twelve million dollars at the moment."

"Darren, I'm going to talk to my partner about your offer, and I will give you a call about our decision sometime in the next day or two. Thank you for coming by, and let me say, I do like your style."

"Thank you, Mr. Benson, I appreciate your time, and look forward to your call."

"Hey Rick, this is Darren, and let me say your idea made old Craig sit up and notice. He was almost drooling. We should know something in twenty-four to forty-eight hours. Call you when I have something."

Rick told Darren that he had done a good job, the bait was excellent, and he would expect that they would call within twenty-four hours. It didn't take that long.

"Mr. Leitner, this is Marjorie Simmons, Mr. Benson's and Mr. O'Steen's secretary, and I'm calling to ask if you could come to the office this afternoon around four? Mr. Benson and Mr. O'Steen would like to have a follow-up meeting with you."

"Mrs. Simmons, thank you for the call and tell them I'll be there."

The rest of the day Darren spent with Rick going over all the ideas they had to set up shop inside of the financial firm owned by Benson and O'Steen. It would be difficult to get close in the beginning, but it was the long-term relationship that was of the most interest. There were too many red flags when it came to all the connections between those two men and several of the suspected parties involved in the events before the assassination. They were going to find out how the money was spent and see where it led them.

"Darren, please come in. Myer, this is Darren Leitner, and it seems Darren already knows you." Craig suggested they have a glass of wine and talk some more about Darren's offer.

Myer had a question about Darren's background. "Craig told me last night that you managed something over twelve million but didn't want to share the number of clients you have. Why is that? If you asked us, we would gladly tell you how many clients we have. We're damn proud of it."

"That's a reasonable question which I will answer this way: Without seeming to be a smart ass by it all, what difference does it make? Whether I have one client or a hundred, when commissions are earned, you get thirty percent, so again, why is it so important to know how many clients I have?"

"Basically Darren, should we decide to do this, it would be something akin to a partnership between our firm and yours.

We'll drop the question for now. Depending on whether we do business or not, we reserve the right to come back to this question at some point in the future.

"We spent some time on the phone with your previous firm, and even though you were correct in your assessment as a broker, you were well liked, respected for your work ethic, and adored by the secretaries. The women in the office felt as though you respected their thoughts and ideas as well as making sure they knew they were a vital part of the organization. We liked that about you the most. Marjorie probably wishes we were that sensitive to her needs."

"Eighteen is the number."

"Eighteen, Mr. Leitner?"

"That's the number of clients I have at the moment and working on bringing in another twenty or thirty by the end of the year."

"One last key question, and you will understand why we're asking: What was your commission from the eighteen clients last year?"

"I assumed you would ask that question; so, I brought this to show you." Darren handed them his most recent tax return and waited.

"That's a nice return on your work, but how much did you make for your clients?"

"Their gross was a little over eight percent, less my one-point- eight percent; consequently, they made a reasonable return of just over six percent. If I do that for them every year, there will be no complaints. I do assure you and them that I can do better. Let's say this in closing, your share will more than cover my office space."

Myer looked at Craig then reached out his hand to Darren and smiled, "Welcome to the firm Mr. Leitner."

Darren didn't really expect this, but he was happy to accept. "Thank you both so much and let me say you won't regret your decision. I'm really happy to be able to tell my clients where we'll be from this point forward."

"Darren, this will take our attorneys a couple of days to get the papers ready; so, let's set up a time to meet to sign the papers. What about dinner on Thursday at eight? Will that work for you Myer?"

Everything was set up for Thursday provided the agreement was accepted. It was, and the dinner was fabulous.

"Rick, it's Darren again, and wanted to let you know it's all done. I will be moving in on the first with kitchen privileges and a key."

"Darren, you've done very well with this, and you've made me proud. Let's get together in a few to talk about how we're going to manage this. I'll call you later."

"Great, but don't forget, I need the list of my clients to add to the company's mailing list. Are you sure we've got all that covered tightly?"

"I will have it for you later this week, and yes, it's all covered. Great job guy."

After moving into the very plush surroundings of Benson & O'Steen Investments, Inc., the next thing on Darren's list was a secretary. He called a headhunter downtown, told her what he needed, how much he would pay, and Jennie Ledbetter got right to work on it. Not for any of her clients, but for herself. Jennie wasn't going to let this go by without at least an interview, which she set up for the next morning.

"Mrs. Ledbetter, I didn't expect you were my interview, but happy you found the job interesting."

"Mr. Leitner, it's more than interesting. It's the job anyone would die to have. Here's my resume, and feel free to call my references if you wish."

Let me ask you a couple of questions and we'll go from there. First, may I call you Jennie?"

"Yes, please do."

"Jennie, what is it about this job that got you so excited?"

"It's just the way you described it to me as not being just a job but being a part of and learning about the ins and outs of a career in the investment business. Another point which was almost breathtaking was the salary you're offering. I might be the only woman in New Orleans in 1967 being paid $15,000 as a secretary/office manager.

Just to make sure you understand the importance of this opportunity to me; my husband was killed in an auto accident almost two years ago. I'm a single mom with a three-year-old son and, want to take good care of him during the day when I'm at work. I'm quite good at what I do. I'm organized, punctual, have a great work ethic, and my motto is doing whatever it takes to get the job done right the first time."

Darren liked her from the moment she sat down and hated the thought of having a lot of interviews. "Mrs. Ledbetter, you're hired."

She almost teared up, but quickly got things on track. "Thank you so much Mr. Leitner. I promise you will never have reason to regret it. When do you want me to start? I can give notice this morning and see what they want me to do about staying on for the two weeks."

"Let me know what you find out and we'll go from there. Thank you again for coming and look forward to seeing you again soon."

When she drove away she was smiling and singing and so thankful that she now had a real job. Mom and dad would be so happy for her.

Jeanine Harding was from Shreveport, LA and attended Tulane to study business. While pursuing her degree, she met and fell in love with Donald Lindstrum. They married after she graduated and while he was working on his law degree, they had a little boy named Byron. These two young people could have never been happier, and then Donald went to a bachelor party for his best friend Carter. On his way home, he was killed when he went off the road and down a steep embankment. It was assumed that he went to sleep at the wheel. He was only twenty-seven.

The employment agency where she worked told her that she could leave when she had brought her replacement up to date on all her files. It took four days, and then it was off to work at her dream job.

"Craig, Myer, I would like you to meet my new secretary, Jennie Lindstrum. Jennie, this is Craig Benson and Myer O'Steen. They are the founding partners of the firm. Most importantly of all, this is Marjorie Simmons. She's the best and has the unenviable task of keeping these two organized. Watch how she handles everything and you'll both be famous."

Darren told her to make whatever aesthetic changes she wished for both her office and his, and then let her know her main job would consist of making sure he knew where he was supposed to be next. At first, she thought that was just him making a joke. Jennie soon learned that he was telling her the truth. He was not the most organized person in the world, but his smarts and her office skills would be instrumental in bringing him even more success.

She had never seen so many celebrities coming into one place ever. It was almost like being in a room with Wall Street, Hollywood, and Washington who's who. They weren't there to see her boss, but that was okay. She told Marjorie to let her know if Tony Curtis happened to drop by.

After two months of phone calls, letters, and personal visits, Darren had added eight more clients and about fourteen million to the money-management side. It was time to look at some new investment opportunities; so, he asked for some good advice from Craig and Myer. They gave him a two-hour tour of offshore accounts and a few more ideas about what to put there. This was what Darren needed to start looking around for other similar accounts.

With all of this going on, Jennie managed to redecorate their offices, find a new apartment just off St. Charles, and get a live-in sitter for Byron. If that wasn't enough, she bought her a 1965 Mustang and sometimes took Byron on long drives. She loved to drive that car and Byron loved to sleep. It was a wonderful time for mom and son.

Chapter 37
Speaking of College

Back during the difficult days prior to the President's murder, Becker Caldwell had managed to get himself involved in one of those triangles which can get you killed. The wife of a powerful banker preferred spending her time in Beck's bed, and decided she would let her husband find out about their little fling. She figured he would try to settle with her to keep it out of the papers, but instead, the husband killed the wife, got life in prison, and Beck escaped with his life.

Now that he was safely ensconced in New Orleans society he would be keeping an eye on anyone who might be close to Benson and O'Steen, while trying not to get caught or killed. Beck provided a lot of information about who was spending the most time with the financial gurus, and what kind of connection they had with the various families. His smile, subtle wit, and charm caused many of the women to tell him all the juicy facts about the other women in the group. In doing so, they gave him valuable inside information which no one could get without blackmailing someone.

Beck did find out from Clarisse Simpson that her good friend Nancy Townsend was a close friend of a very well-placed executive-type with the CIA. She knew that because Nancy told her how much she loved to taunt the guy by making him think he was going to get lucky. "As a matter of fact," the woman went on to say," she had a plan to lure him down here for a little playtime. I'm sure she was just heartbroken when he was killed."

Professor Becker's schedule at the University wasn't necessarily flexible, but he did find a lot of free time for a round of golf or a few sets of tennis when needed. Besides his responsibilities as an assistant professor, it was imperative that he maintained his contacts with the city's social set and helped the charitable organizations so dear to all those wealthy families. He had become a very sought-after fund raiser. Raising money and staying in the limelight created excellent links to all the business dealings downtown. Not only did the charities love him, but so did several of the women who gladly donated their time and money to various fund raisers that Becker chaired. There were those who wanted to help him even more in so many more creative ways.

One woman who quietly took quite an interest in Dr. Caldwell's work was the mysterious Mrs. Nancy Townsend. She was a generous giver in so many ways. A shrewd businesswoman and avid supporter of the arts, Mrs. Townsend was often seen on the arm of some Hollywood heartthrob or rising political star. Her present favorite date was an older man from the Chicago area who owned a considerable amount of downtown Chicago acreage among other assets.

They were often seen together at social functions in New Orleans, but there was one club where she loved to spend a few hours on Friday or Saturday nights. The music and the drinks were excellent, and she was always treated like a celebrity when she was there.

184

One night she arrived with someone new and one couldn't help but notice that Mrs. Townsend seemed to be having a most enjoyable time. Her table of six included a congressman and his wife, a successful real estate broker, his wife, and Nancy with her date, Dr. Becker Caldwell. Dr. Carmichael was ecstatic. Beck was happy too, but for an entirely different reason. He had told Doc about the date he had a few days ago and in describing how it came to pass there was little doubt as to whose idea it was.

The previous Tuesday Nancy had called Beck to see if he would be interested in helping her with the upcoming annual French Quarter fundraiser for the arts. She asked if he would meet her at her home, which he did, and there they discussed the details of the upcoming event. She invited him to lunch and while they were dining she told him that she would be most appreciative if he would be her escort on Saturday night. His first question was how Dr. Townsend would feel about his wife being escorted by another man. She laughed and explained that their arrangement allowed her to attend various functions with whomever she chose. "You will accept my invitation won't you Dr. Caldwell?"

Beck liked good champagne and there was plenty of it at their table. Rick and the band did a lot of their best songs and skits and entertained the crowd royally. They were now the star attraction, and the place was packed on weekends. Everything was coming together nicely. As an Asst. Professor of Psychology, Beck had no problem with throwing out a lot of BS when he was in front of a group of wealthy and attractive women. His social schedule damn near required a private secretary.

Because of the situations which put Beck and Rick in the same crowd, when it was necessary for them to meet, they did so in Baton Rouge. On Wednesday, they spent the first hour with Rick giving Beck a rough time about his various photographs in the Times-Picayune where he was escorting one beautiful woman after another. "Don't they get jealous old stud?"

"Well, when you've got it you better damn well not lose it; so, the more jealousy there is the more they talk about me. I do ask myself, when will I wake up from this dream? Enough about my love life and to what do I owe this special private meeting?"

"I need you to do whatever is necessary to get Mrs. Townsend to want to spend a lot of time with you. While you're doing whatever the job calls for, and I know you will suffer, I want you to find out all you can about her tryst with Donald Meriwether, how close they were, and obviously, anything which would put a hole in her alibi the day Meriwether was killed.

"Let me remind you that this woman is bad and can be worse. If she thinks you're any kind of threat or even if she loves your ass, she'll kill you if it seems like the thing to do to protect herself. Just watch her closely and be careful my friend. She is the epitome of the female black widow."

"Damn, and I was so getting used to becoming a man among many women. Do you want me to get really close to her or just close enough to find out what you need to know?"

"Beck I don't care if you have to marry her, we need to know the connection she has among some of our more infamous people here and her relationship with Meriwether. The faster we get that information the better."

"Rick, I have a fairly good war chest, but not the size that would tempt Nancy Townsend. She has a lot of expensive trinkets, and anything less would probably not endear her to me."

"Becker, my boy, it's the other way around. She has tons and loves to give it to her favorite man of the month. You need to become her number one for however many months this might take. Consider you're fundraising for yourself. As a matter of fact, make her want to give to you as much as possible. Both of you will feel so much better for it."

"You know Mr. Smartass, when Doc and I first discussed

all of this, he at no time, ever mentioned how much fun you could be. I will do this for you, and yes, I will suffer, but if I get my ass shot, you better be somewhere close by to call the ambulance." Becker left a twenty for the waitress, smiled, and told Rick, "I will see you later and I do mean later."

After his Thursday morning class, Beck called Nancy to make his first move on the offensive. She wasn't in according to the maid, but if he wished to leave a message, she would tell Mrs. Townsend he had called. He had a better idea. He called a very fashionable florist and had a dozen yellow roses sent with a card that read: Would you celebrate National Professor's Day with me tomorrow night . . . The Beck

He thought that was kind of cute and hoped she did as well. When the clock hit three and he had not received a call back about the flowers or the card he figured maybe he had made a mistake. There was a faculty meeting at four and after that he would take care of a couple things before leaving his office.

After the meeting, he made a quick stop at the bookstore, and headed for his office. When he unlocked the door, there at his desk sat a most seductive woman who wiggled her finger for him to come to her. He did, and she, in her own inimitable style, thanked him for the roses. As she walked toward the door, she turned to tell him that she would pick him up at seven tomorrow night. When she was gone Beck had to sit down again. He was very relaxed, and smiled for the next two hours.

Nancy was the center of attention at the restaurant, and she made sure her date was having a good time too. She would, from time to time, rub the inside of his thigh while she licked her lips. After dinner they went to a couple of clubs, had a glass of bubbly, a dessert, and then she took him home. Nancy didn't wait for an invitation for a nightcap. She told her driver to go on home and in the door they went. Nine hours later she went home.

He was not himself during his ten o'clock class as he discussed some of the studies which had their beginning with the results of research using two different methods. He couldn't concentrate because there was a part of his body which had never been used like that and for such an extended duration. Never had there ever been a woman like this. When she wanted you, she wanted you badly, and she combined passion, lust, love, sex, and pain with being playful, creative, and an endurance reserved for exceptional athletes. The woman could make love all night and not stop at daylight. He had to get to class or else. He couldn't stay erect forever.

She liked what he did to her and how he did it; consequently, the papers picked up on it and began speculating about their relationship. Beck couldn't figure out how a married woman could be on the front page of a newspaper, answering questions about her possible marital plans with him.

This was a crazy deal and he wasn't so sure he wanted it to go any further. Then again, he didn't have a choice. Rick told him what he had to find out, but hell, he couldn't find out anything because they had sex for hours and the discussion was mostly about what she wanted next.

Beck had lost nine pounds, was sleeping at most three hours a night, drinking more than usual, and watching time disappear. He was being screwed to death.

"Rick, we've got to meet. I'm not a well man."
"Yes, I can tell by the way you look in all of your photographs. Are you sleeping any at all?"

"Yes, I believe it was last Tuesday. I think it's evident from my side that I know why Donald was probably doing whatever he could to see her. She's a human fucking machine . . . literally."

"Doc has made arrangements for you to have a few days in Bermuda at an Economics Conference. Your meetings will be on the beach or anywhere else you would like to rest and relax."

"That would be great, but she'll want to go with me."

"Lucky for you she is going to be named Chairperson for next year's Mardi Gras parade and will have to attend several meetings while you're away."

"God love him, but how in the hell can Doc arrange things like this? He must know everyone."

"Just enjoy, sleep, and get ready for the next round of Mrs. Townsend. So far, I think she's much more durable than you are. Get her talking soon. Have fun Studulous."

It had never occurred to Becker that five days alone could be so magnificent. The first two days he was there, he barely got out of bed. There were some beautiful women at the resort, but he absolutely did not want to meet any of them. There were times he hoped she wouldn't be there when he returned, but when he did return, she met him at the airport. On the way back home, she told him she thought they should talk. She loved his lovemaking, but it was time to talk. He instantly agreed.

Nancy didn't elaborate too much on some of her less feminine moments but did give him a chronological breakdown as to where she started and where she was now. He could see in her eyes that she did have a vulnerable side, but also that in her actions and her words covered up any possibility that anyone could ever outmaneuver her. She got to the top on her own merits and she'd be damned if anyone were going to get the best of her. That's when she stopped talking, took Becks hand, and told him she loved him.

For the next ten seconds, which seemed like ten minutes, he sat there looking at her. Finally, he squeezed her hand, and flippantly said, "I bet you tell that to all your guys." He didn't get a favorable response to that remark.

She stood up, glared at him as if she were saying I hate you, and walked toward the door. He couldn't let this happen. He moved in front of her and told her he was sorry and didn't mean to be so childish. Her shoulders lowered somewhat, and he asked her to please sit down. Being told she loved him had left him speechless and made for a poor choice of words.

"Sweetheart, what makes you think you're in love with me? I'm just a college professor and you could have any man in the world. How did I get this lucky?"

At first, she didn't want to say anything, but finally she lowered her head and told him that, "You're the only man that wants me just for who I am and not for what I own or possess. You're the first man who has ever made love to me this passionately, wanted to not only love me but control me as well. I'm tired of being the pants in every relationship." She began to cry.

In the back of his mind, he could hear Rick warning him, always be on guard. "Darling, I had no idea you felt that way about me. You mean so much to me, but as I said, I'm just a college professor. I admit I'm an incredible college professor, but that's not important."

He hoped he might bring a small smile to her face. They had a small glass of wine and continued to talk. "Nancy, pardon my bluntness, but what about your husband? Are you going to tell him about me?"

"Darling, I may love you to pieces, but I don't want to marry you. I'm not giving up thirty million dollars because I crave your body and love everything about you. You do understand that, don't you?"

"Absolutely and thank you for saying that. A thousand pounds of stress just left my shoulders. I was positive we couldn't live on $60,000 a year." This time she did laugh.

When the conversation was at an end, she told him one more thing that he would remember for some time. "Honey, you do realize that if something happened to my husband not only would I love you, but we'd never have to worry about anything again."

He looked away for a second and thought, did she just ask me to put a hit on the old man? Before he had too much time to consider the question, she was unzipping his fly and getting him how she liked him best . . . long and hard.

He could resist, but there was no way he could stop her. She laid back on the sofa and told him she wanted him now. Take me, make me scream, hurt me baby, and love me with everything you've got. I want it deep. C'mon, give it to me, and then she screamed for him to suck her tits until they were raw. She reached an orgasm and then another and another and then she was quiet. This man was magical. She would keep him for always until she tired of him. For now, he would be there all night.

* * *

In August of 1962, a message arrived for the President, which after reading, needed a response. He scribbled a few lines, put it in an envelope, sealed it, and gave it to the young man who had brought it to him.

Around 11 pm that evening a small blue Ford arrived at the security gate and was immediately let onto the grounds. A member of the staff opened the door for the woman and took her directly to an upstairs bedroom. She and the President talked for several minutes while they enjoyed a glass of wine. He made a call to someone about not being disturbed, and a little over an hour later the young woman was shown to her car.

This had been her second visit and assumed it wouldn't be her last. After all, she made him extremely happy and why wouldn't he want her again soon?

Her third visit was to a large but rather bland looking home in Georgetown. When she arrived, she was met at the door by a business-like, well-dressed woman who took her to a small cottage by the pool. She simply thought the President had decided to have their little tryst in a more romantic setting.

A few minutes passed and when she heard someone coming she looked up to see a man she didn't know. He was attractive, but he wasn't the President.

"Who in the hell are you?"

"Honey," he grinned, "I'm your entertainment for the night."

The young woman stood up and started to leave when he put his hand on her shoulder and forced her onto the sofa.

This was not what she had in mind and told him not to touch her again. "Baby, I don't know who the hell you think you are and you damn sure don't know who I am, but when the President says that you're the best fuck he's ever had, you can bet I'm gonna find out for myself.

Now get your damn clothes off and get ready for something big in your life tonight."

Again, she tried to leave, but this time he ripped her dressed, forced her down on the sofa and was going to have her one way or the other. She decided that resisting was exactly what he wanted and so she began work on her acting career. She took a large chunk of his hair and pulled him down on her. She whispered loudly, "Come on baby, let's see what you got, and it better be your best."

He almost came in his pants, but she made him get up and take her to bed. In the back of her mind, she couldn't believe that the most wonderful man she had ever known had passed her off to someone like this dickhead.

All of this was over in a matter of minutes, Nancy pushed his arm off the top of her chest, and five minutes later she was gone. Someone was going to pay big time for this night.

* * *

The Fort Worth police officer at the scene had radioed headquarters that two bodies had washed ashore on Eagle Mountain Lake. Both men were dressed in suits, nothing in their clothes, hands cut off, and all the teeth knocked out. This had to be a double hit.

For the moment, about all they could do at the morgue was hold the bodies until someone upstairs told them what to do. The police tried to come up with some way to identify the bodies, but without fingerprints or dental work, there wasn't much they could do.

After the appropriate amount of time had passed, the two men were buried in some unknown grave without a name.

Chapter 38
Chicago 1965

Vinnie had made real progress in his goal of getting deeper and closer to the heart of the Vinzzetti Family. At first, all he did was make some low-level drops, but then they let him do more hands-on work. He sure as hell didn't want to do any rough stuff, but not doing it would get him killed or worse. There was a guy who had decided he didn't need to make any further payments to have his place protected; so, a guy named Jamie (the Dude) Castle called Vinnie to tell him he was needed to fix a problem. With

Jamie standing by the door, Vinnie made sure that the store owner understood that his escape clause was at the bottom of the lake.

After that, there were a few other misunderstandings that Vinnie had to deal with, but three weeks later, he was told to be at a small restaurant on the south side around 9 pm on Tuesday. "Vinnie, I gotta tell you man, for a guy who acts like nothing bothers him, Jamie says you can get kinda intense. Tonight, though, I need to talk to you about a job I have in mind for you. It ain't nothin' dangerous or even interesting, but I need someone I can trust for this. You in?"

Vinnie sat there for another minute or so, and finally asked, "Do I know you?"

His new friend across the table laughed and said, "No, you don't know me, but you will. Now are you in or not?"

"For all I know you could be the chief of police, and no, until you tell me who you are and what this is all about, I'm not in for anything."

The guy across from him got up and went to the back of the place to a pay phone. Vinnie wasn't sure if he should stay or leave. Either way he could be asking for a lot of trouble. When the guy got back to the table he had a little more to say.

"Vin', my name is Carl Montano and from now on, you work directly for me. I like the way you handle yourself. "You and I are going to be doing some things together, and I needed to find out if you are as good as they say. Bondy recommended you highly, and he's knows talent when he sees it. So, one more time, are you in or not?"

"Carl, you don't mind if I call Bondy, do you?"

"By all means make your call."

When Vinnie got back to the table, he looked at his new friend and laughed. "Carl old buddy, I'm in for whatever you have in mind."

It seems that Carl Montano was way up in the organization. A made man several times over, and in charge of the operations on the south side of Chicago. He was a very bad man, and one hell of an overseer. Vinnie was now in the fast lane. Any mistake now, and Vin wouldn't be seen nor heard from ever again.

The first job Carl had for Vinnie was to meet with Joe Feronti in New Jersey to set some guidelines for the use of pension funds. Up until now there hadn't been a lot of noise coming from Jersey, but in the last few months, the Feds had been spending a lot of time watching how things were moving along on the docks. Some of the boys over there were getting a little too generous with their payoffs and it was starting to show.

"Vin, tell him that I want one of his men in my office every Monday morning to tell me what was brought in, paid out, and nothing better be missing. If he balks at that, tell him I will give him twenty-four hours to change his mind or he's dead. Be sure to tell him how he will die."

"You have something in mind, Carl?"

"Fuck, Vinnie, make it up, or just tell him how you're gonna do it. I don't care, but if he doesn't cooperate, kill him any way you think would be the most fun." Carl grinned and told Vinnie to show up at hangar ten around seven in the morning.

"You should be back by late afternoon, maybe sooner, unless the guy is stupid enough to say no. If you stay over, make sure everyone knows who sent you."

As soon as Vince knew all was clear, he called Rick to tell him what had just happened.

"Hey Rick, this is Chicago and I've got to see you in Jersey tomorrow or give me a protected number where we can talk."

Rick called on another number and asked what was up. He quickly found out. "Hey Vince, we can't have this happen to you. Do you think the guy would say no to that kind of threat?"

"I don't know, but my ass is on the line either way I go if the guy tells me to shove off." "Let me call Doc and I will be calling you back shortly. Can you wait?"

"Yeah, sure, but make it quick."

Ten minutes felt like an hour, but at last the phone rang. "Rick, what did Doc say?"

"You're not going to like this, and I don't either, but if you don't do what you've been told to do, they'll either kill you or make you irrelevant. About the only advice he could give is for you to be as intimidating as you can be and make him agree to your terms. The other thing Doc offered is that if you want, we'll pull you out of there tonight and get you to a place where they will never find you. It's your call."

It seems there was much ado about nothing because Feronti guardedly acceded to Vinnie's request and now Vince could take a nap on the way back. That night he was considering drinking until the next morning. Instead, he decided to have dinner at a place called The Black Rose. The place was owned by the family, and run by the world-renowned chef, Carlo Beinvinutto. His cuisine was the talk of the town, and a lot of very prominent people went there to celebrate special occasions and to be seen.

Darlena Velasquez was a beautiful young woman who aspired to be a great chef. Her family could be traced all the way back to a sixteenth century artist, Diego Velasquez.

Senor Velasquez, Darlena's father, owned over three million acres spread out over Spain, Mexico, and Louisiana. His millions of tons of rice and sugar cane had made them one of the wealthiest families in Europe, but no one in the states, except Darlena, knew that. She wanted to earn her place at the table as opposed to being given anything because of her father's wealth and prestige. She had left Spain to live in the United States to have her choice of the best culinary schools available. Her plan was to get her basic training done in the states, and then move to Paris to study with the greats and to hone her many talents.

When Vinnie introduced himself, she was somewhat taken aback because she didn't even know he was standing there. He had been watching her going back and forth from the kitchen to the dining area several times, and this time he decided to find out who she was.

She had something on her face and that made her look like a young girl sneaking a bite of her mother's cooking. "Miss, I'm sorry to bother you, but I was wondering if you could spare me a minute or two when you get off?"

"Right now, sir, you're going to have to get out of the way. I have work to do and unless you cook, I have nothing to say to you. Goodbye."

"I cook a mean tuna-casserole so could I see you after work to share my recipe with you?"

At least she smiled. "I'm Vince and just want to have a cup of coffee and have a chance to meet you before you leave."

She was exasperated with him, but agreed to give him five minutes after she had finished for the night. He didn't know that would be after one o'clock in the morning. *Oh well,* he thought, *I'll take what I can get.*

True to her word, she gave him five minutes and she headed for the door. As she was hailing a cab, he offered to take her home, but she refused. She handed him a card and told him that was her schedule. She closed the door and was gone.

He poured himself a glass of scotch before he hit the rack and looked at her card. The woman was working at least twelve hours a day, six days a week. He doubted seriously if she would have any time for him on her one day off, but you never know until you ask.

It was a few days later when he went back, and now that he knew her name, he asked the waiter to take her a note. It said: This is Vince – Do you remember me? Yes _____ No_____ Would you have any time at all to see me on your next day off? Yes___ Possibly_____ Absolutely Not _____ If yes, when _____ If No, Rats. If Possibly, how can I make it a yes? _____

When he looked up from the menu there she was with the note. Vince, here is your note, and may I recommend the Veal Piccata. She went back to the kitchen. She checked yes, yes, and Sunday at 1 pm. Her address and her number. He was very happy indeed.

* * *

He rang her doorbell promptly at 1 pm on Sunday. She answered the door and was wearing her jeans, a man's white shirt, and barefooted. "Come in Mr. V, and could I interest you in a glass of my favorite Chianti? I should have told you that I didn't want to go anywhere, and because of my thoughtlessness you can take off your shoes and relax."

"You know I should have guessed that because you have a schedule from hell. I sincerely thank you for giving me some of your valuable time."

"Well, you better appreciate it because I don't do this for just anyone. You made me laugh when I needed it, and so I thought you deserved time to explain how you prepare your tuna casserole. And by the way we're having a delivered pizza for dinner. You can stay for pizza, I hope?"

"Miss Velasquez, you honor me, and I would love to have dinner with you. May I ask which recipe you have chosen for the pizza?"

"This week we'll be tasting a very exotic and precocious concoction called Dantoni's Deep Dish. It's more like an Italian casserole. I believe you're quite familiar with casseroles?"

Vince couldn't believe that she was taking her day off with him, and it was so nice to be normal for once. He really wasn't cut out for the mob, but that's what he did. How was he going to hide that from Darlena, or was he going to hide it? That wasn't on today's agenda, but maybe later if she enjoyed being with him as much as he felt that way about her, he would tell her.

She didn't have a whole lot to say about her background or her youth. It seemed to him that her whole life was in the kitchen, and that was where she was the happiest. He gave her a brief excursion through his other life, but stopped at the point of how and why he was in Chicago.

Her little apartment was well furnished and had some wonderful pieces of art. He kept looking at one small canvass. It was bright, colorful, and had the strangest looking face he had ever seen. Darlena noticed him admiring it and told him it was a gift from her father. She didn't tell him that it had been a gift to her father from Picasso. Her father gave it to her for her twenty-fifth birthday. No telling how much that little canvass was worth.

They had a great time, and both learned that they enjoyed some of the same things. They liked art and music, both had thought about graduate school, but decided it was too boring. Besides that, she only wanted to be a chef. She loved the Cubs and so did he; so, they must be masochists.

The pizza was delicious and then she did something he didn't expect. She poured another glass of wine, put on a beautiful piano concerto, and turned off the overhead lights. It was now very dark and very romantic. She made a short toast to their meeting, took a sip, and asked him to kiss her. He was quite happy to oblige. It didn't get past some very enjoyable kissing, but it was wonderful for them both. She told him she hadn't been kissed in almost a year and that was only because it was her friend's birthday party. They all had too much of the grape and someone kissed her. To this day she still didn't know who it was.

"Vince, I can't tell you how special it was to have you notice me. I don't feel all that feminine anymore. The kitchen in restaurants is a man's world, and I'm just one of the guys. When you came back, I was so flabbergasted I didn't really know what to do. I'm so glad you were tenacious."

She kissed him again and this time she pressed her body much closer, much harder than before. "That was just to let you know how much passion I have for whenever the time comes I need to bring it to your attention."

It was getting close to nine, and he thought perhaps he should go. He wished she hadn't agreed but it was time for this most wonderful day to conclude. "May I see you again the next time you would like to relax by my side?"

"Let's do this, that is if you want to. Tuesday night, one of the guys owes me a cleanup because I helped him when he had a date one night. I will be off around ten; so, could you be here around ten thirty?

"Young lady, if you wish, I will arrive at nine and wait on your doorstep."

"Just be here at ten thirty, and maybe I will bring you some dessert."

He gently kissed her goodbye and was off to the house. Vince had never known a feeling like this in his life. All he could think about on the way back to his place was what she was going to think of him when he told her about his life. All he could do was say that whatever happened was God's will and he would abide by the outcome. Vince could still smell her body and feel her lips. There was a big grin when he said, "I love Tuesdays."

Chapter 39
A Choice to be Made

Chip had called his father-in-law to ask him for an hour or so of his time. Alejandro was always willing to meet with his son-in-law. After all, the several hundred thousand dollars that was going in the family's pocket was because of the business that Chip and his associates were running from New Orleans.

Alejandro was a very smart man and he fully understood how strong Chip and his friend Rick's organization was. Alejandro saw to it that whatever Mr. Hagen needed he got. This visit seemed to be more about family than business.

"Alejandro, I'm here because I wanted you to know first about the new plans we are putting into place. Camila doesn't know yet and she may not be happy about it, but after the baby is born, we will be moving to another location. It may be New Orleans or Puerto Rico, but wherever it is, I'm certain Camila will be visiting you quite often. I'm meeting her for lunch at eleven; so, if you hear a loud scream, you will know for certain from whence it came. I'm sure you'll hear from her soon. I wish I could change the plan, but I can't."

Alejandro laughed, told Chip good luck, and continued to drink his coffee.

It wouldn't matter if it were New York or Spain or Dallas, she wasn't going to be at all happy with the idea of moving. Camila was daddy's girl and her home in Brazil not far from daddy is where she assumed she would always be.

At first, Camila just sat there and then she took a sip of her drink. No screaming, no cussing, nada, and then she just stood up. She blew Chip a kiss and walked away. He just sat there thinking that his beloved and beautiful wife must be in a rare catatonic state. He left a couple of twenties on the table and caught up with her as she was about to cross the street.

"Sweetheart aren't you going to say anything?"

"Chip, my darling, I will let the lawyers do the talking for me. I'm not going anywhere. If you want to be married to me and take care of me and your child, you will be here with my family. Otherwise, I will see you in court."

This wasn't how it was supposed to go. She loved him, and he loved her; so, obviously wherever he went she would go as well. Never did he think she would divorce him rather than move a few hundred miles away.

Chip's plane was leaving at 3 am and it was imperative that he make the flight. He could probably postpone it for an hour, but he had to be in New Orleans by noon. Leaving her now was not going to make things any easier.

"Alejandro, I assume you've talked to your daughter?" "Yes, and she was very calm. Almost too calm for me. She told me what she told you, and I am sorry that my spoiled little girl is now a spoiled mother-to-be. I promise you that I will talk to her and do my best to encourage her to be with her husband, but my son I know she can be one very stubborn woman."

"Do you suppose she would be willing to live with me if she could be with you two or three days a week?"

"All I can do is ask her, but at this moment, I will let her just think about the situation for a while. You go take care of business, and I'll handle Camila for you." "Gracias senor y hasta luego."

Chapter 40
The Group is Gathering

"Hey man, it's good to see you." Rick picked up Darren and they headed over to the hangar to pick up Chip. They stopped for lunch and then went back to the Roosevelt. Doc arrived the day before and had been catching up on his reading for a good part of the morning.

"It's about time you guys got here. Chip I'm glad your flight went well, and you're ready to get to work. I'll try not to bore you too much, but if I do, you'll have to live with it." Coffee was ordered, and they got down to work.

Most of the afternoon was spent going over the connections which were being put in place and took some time to match the timeline with the number of people involved in the bigger picture. Certain individuals had a star by their name, while others just had a check. Becker was late, but that wasn't unusual. David Atwater alias David Calvin Flynn, III was in Dallas and of course Vince and Justin were doing their job elsewhere.

After the break, Doc explained, "Guys, we're not going to use our time here going back over all of the minutia. Now that we're running the operation from here, there will be plenty of time to catch up. My purpose for this meeting was to give you the plans which I am proposing we follow going forward.

"So far, we have managed to set up a drug operation, make inroads into two crime families, get Beck's photo all over the social section of the paper, and you can see how much he's suffering." They all got into the fun of giving Beck and his poor little pecker a lot more hell before getting back to business.

Doc continued, "We have to find all the connections between the money, and there's a bunch of it, and the people who either handed it out or received it. To date, we know that almost nine million dollars has gone through New Orleans from a London bank. Those funds were then funneled from the London bank to the Swiss via banks in Montreal, Seattle, and Bermuda. I don't want those conduits to be jeopardized, but we must find out who's sending and who's receiving those dollars. Other than that, gentlemen, what we are doing here is just a walk in the park."

* * *

Not far from this meeting, Johnny Faretta was taking a call from a guy in Dallas who said he worked as a PI for a small law firm. "Mr. Faretta, my name is Terry Sanders, and I wouldn't bother you if I didn't think that what I overheard last night at the old Carousel Club wasn't something you might want to know." "Okay, Terry, you have my attention. What did you hear?"

"Like I said, Mr. Faretta, it's my job to be aware of things that just don't seem right, and this guy was acting like he wanted to be heard. He was talkin' real loud about how he knew what really happened at the book depository. He kept sayin' it was those Chicago guys that really did it. The dude was going to tell the FBI and that would get some things movin' about who shot the President. You couldn't blame this on Texas because those boys were from Chicago."

"So, Terry, why do you think I should know about a guy who was evidently just trying to get attention?"

"Mr. Faretta, he said you, his old pal Johnny Faretta, made it happen."

After a second or two to digest what Terry said, Johnny responded, "That's the craziest damn thing I've ever heard. I appreciate your concern Terry. He can talk about me all he wants, but I damn sure never had anything to do with any shooting of a President. Thanks for calling, and when you're down this way come by to see me. I'll buy you dinner."

"Sure thing, and thanks, Mr. Faretta."

David Atwater aka David Calvin Flynn, III aka PI on the phone was evidently very convincing because Johnny immediately called Joey to tell him what the guy said. Joey didn't seem too interested.

"Johnny, relax; there's no way anyone would believe some idiot like that. If they did, the guy would still have to prove it. Let it go, and do what you do best. See ya later guy."

* * *

Chip had a lot on his mind, but he managed to acquire a very nice apartment in the Quarter and hoped it would be enough to lure Camila to forget all the nonsense about divorce. She was a load, but he loved her very much. Every time he was away from her he spent a lot of time thinking about her and remembering how they met. To think he would have to live without her, and their son was heartbreaking for him. She had to know how much he loved her. He had called her several times, but she wouldn't talk to him.

Rick told him that he had to get his mind on the work at hand. There was much to be done and the work was going to get much tougher and more dangerous.

Doc also put in his two cents worth, but went one step further. "Chip, if you want out, do it now. We can rearrange things at this point which will become impossible to do the deeper we get into this. Make your decision now and live with it."

Chip Hagen was not a quitter. If he continued to be a part of this privately funded covert activity, there was every reason to believe he would lose his family. On the other hand, if he left the group, he would second guess himself for the rest of his life. He told Doc to make sure that if anything happened to him, that Camila and his son would be protected from those who might do them harm. That done, Chip turned the page on his life as it was at this moment, and committed himself to finding those responsible for the President's death.

Chapter 41
The Conflict of Caring

Tuesday night finally arrived. Vince figured it took his mind three hours to live every real hour in the time since he last saw Darlena. He arrived promptly at 10:30 and thought the house looked a little too dark on the inside. The third time the doorbell rang, a very sleepy woman in pajamas answered the door. He almost didn't recognize her, but it was Darlena.

"I'm sorry Vince, I fell asleep on the sofa. Would you like a glass of the sedative I just had?" She was trying to laugh about her glass of wine, but he could tell she was almost sleepwalking.

"Hey cutes, why don't we reschedule our night for another time and let you get some sleep?"

"Absolutely not young man. If you can handle my silk jams, we'll have ourselves a late date."

"Are you sure? I hate that you are so tired."

"Mr. Vince, I assure you that I do my best work when I'm pooped. And I am officially pooped." She smiled, asked him to sit down beside her, and when he did, she kissed him quite passionately.

"I bet you didn't know that you have captivated my mind. Not only that, but I've found myself daydreaming about you. Apprentice chefs aren't supposed to daydream. One other thing: "I'm sorry, but I didn't bring you dessert from the restaurant. I decided I would be your dessert." She yawned, and told him he could kiss her again.

Darlena had been working since seven this morning and after fifteen hours and two glasses of Prosecco could have probably gone through outpatient surgery and not known it. She put her head on Vince's shoulder, and about a minute later was breathing very heavily. It wasn't a snore which would have embarrassed her beyond words. She was out like a light.

Vince laid her down on the sofa, covered her with a beautiful throw she had placed on a chair, turned off the lights, and went home. He was so happy that he got to see her.

Wednesday morning around 10:30 the most beautiful arrangement of yellow roses was delivered to an exceptionally beautiful woman who at that moment had flour all over her face. Everyone wanted to know who they were from and why. The card read: Cutes, I thank you so much for trying to stay awake for me. Let these roses remind you of me whenever you're not too busy. Your Vince.

She didn't know how to call him to thank him. Maybe he would be in tonight. She took a break to use the phone in the lobby. It took ten minutes for the call to be set up, but she wanted her dad and mom to know how happy she was. She had to tell them that she was on the edge of caring for someone special.

Vince had almost forgotten he was Vinni, and that he was getting a lot of attention from the other members of the family. They weren't as enamored with him as was Carl, but one benefit of being Carl's friend was that no one else was going to bother Vinni about much of anything. The downside of the Capo's friendship was that Vin was on twenty-four-hour call. Something needed to be done, it was Vinni who Carl called first, and he called a lot.

"Hey Vin, I need you to do something for me. It's important; so, be here around seven in the morning, and pack for three or four days."

"Where am I going? Weather hot or cold?"

"You'll be going to Fort Worth for a few days. I'll have a car pick you up at seven and I will give you all the details when you get here."

Vince decided he would have dinner at The Black Rose and when and if she had a moment he could tell her that he would be gone for a few days. He didn't want her to think that he in any way wasn't thinking about her.

He had two glasses of a vintage cabernet, sat for another twenty minutes or so, and then ordered. He asked the waiter to give Darlena a note, and then waited some more. She came with the waiter to serve her most interesting customer. She had cooked this especially for him, and with almost a tear in her eye, asked him when he would be back.

"Sweetheart, I don't know for sure. I've packed for four nights, but hopefully it will be less than that. Could I see you a week from Sunday?"

"You'll see me before that, or I won't speak to you." Darlena's smile was infectious and she just wanted him to know she couldn't go that long without seeing him. "I'm considering being sick one day soon, if you could handle me for a whole day."

"That would be wonderful. That's like having three dates with you all on the same day. Just tell me when."

Right there in front of all the customers, waiters, and busboys, she kissed him goodbye and turned to walk away before he could see the tears in her eyes. She was so happy but sad at the same time. She didn't want him to leave.

Vinnie left Carl's office around nine and flew to Meacham Field in Fort Worth where a car was waiting to take him to the hotel. This would be his center of operation for the next few days. Depending on what he found would determine when he would be headed back to Chicago. He had called Rick to tell him what it was about, and it meant that the message to Johnny from David had worked. Rick wanted to add one more thing for Carl to think about.

"Vince, interspersed among all of the conversations you're going to have, this is the one thing you make sure Carl hears first: Tell him that while you were in a precinct on the west side of Fort Worth, one of the officers told you in passing that they think they had identified one of the men by the small flag they found tattooed on his left leg. That's all the department knew at that time. There's no truth to it, but Carl doesn't know that. Let's see where it goes. Good luck and for God's sake be careful."

He did talk to a lot of people while he was there, and even had time for a drink with David Atwater. No one knew anything other than what they had already told the Feds, but Carl would most definitely become concerned. Vince was at the airport on Monday afternoon and would go directly to Carl's office when he got back.

"Carl, I must have talked to a hundred people, but there was only one chat that you may find interesting. The officer at the precinct didn't think it particularly important, but did say that they might be able to identify one of the guys by a flag tattooed on his leg."

"What? That can't be right. A damn flag tattoo on his leg? Did he say anything else about the guy?"

"No, and I don't think he really thought much about it one way or the other. To him it was just another dead guy they were trying to identify."

"If we needed to talk to the guy further, think he would be up for a fun night and a sleep-in date?"

"Carl, not many guys on the force are going to miss something like that. After all, he's just being helpful."

After he left Carl, he went directly to the restaurant to see his lady. There she was in all her radiant splendor to give him a big hug and kiss. She faked a cough and told him to be at her place tonight. She would leave a key under the rail by the door. Help himself to a beverage and she would see him as soon as she could get there. When he left her, he went across the street to call Rick.

"Rick, this is Vince . . . You have a minute? . . . Great . . . I just wanted to make you aware that Carl may want to meet this cop who told me about the tattoo. I don't know that he's going to go down there, but he might. I had a drink with David while I was there and maybe he could be that cop. . . . What do you think? Rick thought about it a second. "Only if it's absolutely necessary."

"Okay Rick, I will let you know what happens, but if for some reason he tells me at the last minute he wants a meeting, you better have David or someone else ready. He's going to need a badge . . . Yeah, okay, and you too guy." He hung up and headed for Darlena's place.

He couldn't believe it when she opened the door. She did her fake cough again and told him she had never played sick in her life. Her ailment meant that they were going to have a wonderfully lovely night.

The very first thing he noticed after being surprised was how she was dressed. She was beautiful to start with, but tonight her clothes and accessories made her look like a model. He smiled; *Vince, my man, you are one lucky dude. And she likes me.*

She made them a very tasty and refreshing gin and tonic, sat down on the sofa, and told him how happy she was that they had this time together. "Vince, I have to tell you something I've done, and I hope you won't be upset with me. If you are, I will understand because I don't really know all that much about you. But first, please tell me that you're not married."

"No, darlin', I'm not married, but not against the idea either. Now what have you done?"

"I called my mom and dad to tell them that I had met a man I really liked. My mother was ecstatic, but my father will take some time. He'll resist, but I'll get him there."

"I don't see anything wrong with that. I called my parents too, and they were so happy. So, if you did something wrong, so did I. Okay, now that we've got our little sins out of the way, would you like to go out tonight or just stay at home?"

"Vince, you can take this any way you want to, but you're not leaving my side until I leave for work in the morning, and we're staying right here."

He was smiling and told her that the sofa was too narrow for two, but he would let her have the throw. She had contained herself quite well until now, but she wanted him close to her and she wanted to kiss him so much. Vince, my darling, promise me you won't disappear tomorrow. I don't think I could bear being this close to happiness and not getting to enjoy it for at least a few days or a month. I treasure the time I have with you."

Words got put away for a while as their bodies ached with each touch of their lips. He felt her breasts, caressed her thighs, and gently brushed her face with his lips. He nibbled at her ear and her neck, rubbed his face in her hair, touched her any place he could find to pleasure his lovely lady.

She wanted his body close to hers. She had never known such feelings before this night. Darlena had never been with a man before, because young women from wealthy families in Spain don't have casual sex. She was in the here and now with Vincent and this was the night she planned to give herself to him. The question kept running through her mind, how could she make love to a man she barely knew, but loved desperately? They both would soon find out.

He carried her to her bed, laid her down very gently, and slowly began to take her dress off. He would stop and kiss her, softly bite her nipples, and her breathing became more excitable. When she looked at him, his eyes were looking at her beauty and then into her eyes. She was precious to him, and he was going to make this night something they would never forget.

The dress was placed in a chair over his shirt and pants. She was waiting for him. For him and for this moment, there was no underwear.

Vince wanted to consume her, and he began to try.

Her body was trembling, her hands were clutching at his face, there had never been a moment like this in her entire life. How could she be this possessed? He had his hands under her and had his mouth doing wonderful, excruciatingly delicious things to her delicate and trembling vagina. She wanted to scream, but it was too intense to take her mind off his mouth and his touch. When she reached one orgasm after another, she almost passed out. Nothing had ever felt like that in all of her life.

"Vince, darling, I love you, I love with all my heart. Take me any way you wish, but I must tell you, no one has ever been where you have been my love. Take me over and over, and never stop loving me. She was about to have another orgasm, and he had yet to give himself to her.

"Oh my God," She gasped for air, she almost pulled his hair out, she screamed, and her body arched and tensed hard. It took several minutes before she could relax, but even then, she didn't want to move. He was holding her close, letting her know he was there to love her and take care of her as long as she wanted. Now it was time and she pulled down his shorts. He was so muscular and so tan. He was beautiful to her. He was so hard, and she wanted him inside her now.

Vince went very slowly, very carefully until she was no longer a virgin. He made sure he didn't hurt her because he knew this was her first moment of fulfillment. They made love for hours. She was more than complete. He was aware that he had given all his love to the woman of his life for the first time, and for a million nights beyond forever she would know how much he loved her. They fell asleep in each other's arms.

When he awoke, he began kissing her back and letting his hands gently rub her breasts. She made him smile with constant desire, and as she stirred, he told her, "I love you so much." She turned over and kissed him and whispered, "Darling, I will be in love with you forever." They made love again, and then they showered. She wouldn't be going to work until she was feeling much better, or that's what she told her boss when she called him. They would have breakfast, but Vince needed to call Carl just to make sure everything was clear for a few hours. With those two things done, they could relax and revel in the passion of the rest of their time together.

Considering that she was a chef, her breakfast was a great deal more enjoyable than what he was used to having at Bernie's Place. Her idea of ham and eggs was incredible plus she had Prosecco, which made for delicious mimosas. They were probably the happiest two people in Chicago.

As Vince sipped his drink, he was thinking that he wanted to be with this woman forever, if she would have him. He wondered *if she would still care about him after he told her what he did when they were apart.* He wasn't going to wait to find out.

"Sweetheart, I have several things I need to talk to you about; so, what do you say we just get snuggled in and let me tell you some things you need to know?" She was wearing her terry cloth robe, and he had on yesterday's shirt and shorts, but that was just fine for sipping mimosas and talking.

Darlena was glowing and her eyes would tell anyone how happy she was. "Vince, I know you wouldn't lie to me, but you do promise me that you're not married, right?"

"No darling, I'm not married, nor have I ever been married. I've been engaged, and I am so happy it didn't work out. Since I've been in Chicago, I've had a few dates, but nothing I care to remember."

"So, my love, what is it that you want to talk about?" He took a deep breath, smiled, and said, "I want to tell you about me and why I'm in Chicago. It's not easy to tell you this, but I want you to know who I am and what I do. If, after hearing my saga, you ask me to leave, understand there's a reason for everything."

Darlena tensed up a little bit because he sounded like what he was about to say wasn't going to be a good thing. "Vince are you in trouble?"

"Not yet. I might be after spending the next hour telling you about the man you love, or at least love right now. It's complicated, but as I said, you need to know.

"Darlena, do you happen to know who owns The Black Rose?"

"Not really because I don't have time to think about it. My boss gives the orders and that's about it."

"The owner of your restaurant is the Vinzzetti Family. Do you know who they are?"

"Not really. Are they from Chicago?"

"Yes, they are an old and powerful family here in Chicago. They are also known as being a part of the Mafia, and I assume you know what that is?"

"My father has spoken many times about the Mafia and fought with them on several occasions as well. I know they can make things bad for you if they want to."

"Darlena, darling, I work for that family."

She just sat there looking at him. "What do you mean you work for them, the Mafia?"

"The guy I just called is a very high-ranking member of the Vinzzetti family, and I am what you might call his assistant. When he calls me to do something I have to do it or else I can kiss my bony little ass goodbye. I don't like it, but that's the way things are for the moment."

"But Vince, you're so gentle and loving. How could you be in a group of people like that? Don't you have a choice or tell them you're going to get another job?"

"No darling, it's not like that. Once you're inside, there's only one way out and I choose not to have that happen. But before I go any further, let me also tell you that sometimes there are extenuating circumstances which will only be known and understood when the time is right. For right now, I am who I say I am, and I love you with all my heart. If you will allow me to be with you, to take care of you, and adore you, what I do at my so-called job doesn't matter. I don't kill people, I don't rob banks, I just work for someone who does."

She just sat there looking at him. He could tell she was confused, but he wanted to give her time to think about what he had said. He thought he saw a tear in her eye, and he was sure that she was going to tell him he had to leave. Vince was a very compassionate, sensitive man, and certainly wasn't going to overstay his welcome.

Darlena went to the kitchen, fixed another drink, and when she came back told him, "I don't know that I've ever had to think about anything too involved or complicated. I've been cared for, pampered, indulged, and spoiled rotten all my life. Maybe I just can't imagine anyone having to live like you do. Let me explain myself a little better.

"My family tree reads like a royal family without the crown. My father is one of the wealthiest men in Europe. There are lands in my father's estate that were given to his great-great grandfather by the King of Spain. There is acreage in Louisiana that was a gift to my family from the King of France for their heroic participation in some war. What I'm saying is that I had to leave Spain and come to America to be me, to earn my way; otherwise, I would have been caught up forever in the wealth and power of my father's estate. So, Vince, do you think I could ever judge you for being a man who does what he was hired to do? "I'm going to love you, want you, and depend on your trust in me, for as long as you will have me. There is nothing that could change that because you have told me the truth, and because when I am with you, there is nothing I fear except that you would stop loving me. If you want us to be together, I am yours forever. My only request is that if you decide to leave me, just leave one red rose at my door: no goodbyes, no note, just a single red rose"

If she thought she had been loved last night, the next few hours brought her to the most exquisite passion life could offer. Every part of her body had felt his mouth and his hands. She had never considered how absolute and total pleasure could be endured for hours.

When at last they rested, he told her that he wanted to consume her, suck her, and love her until she couldn't move. She laughed and told him he had just about done all that already, but when he was ready again, she would be happy to let him do whatever he wished.

"You do understand Vince that I do have to work tomorrow, and I need to be able to move without thinking about what you are doing to my body. God forbid I could have an orgasm cooking the pasta because I was thinking about you."

They had emptied their bag of reality and could be together now for as long as they wished. He would be who he said he was, but with one more secret he couldn't tell, and she would continue to learn about cooking and about being with the man she loved. For them, life was now complete.

Chapter 42
It's Been Over for Awhile

As far as the country was concerned, the death of this young president was one of the most horrible times in American history. A very affable, intelligent, and charismatic man, the leader of the free world, was gunned down in a heartbeat of unforgettable reality. The recovery would take some time, but sooner or later the day when the country lost its innocence would fade into the abyss of history.

For these very dedicated men, they would continue to wade through an immense number of names, phone numbers, connections, and lives to get to the bottom of the mystery of who killed the President. Slowly but surely the team was more confident that soon they would have the men behind the shooter and the money and the motive behind this tragic event.

What they couldn't know was how deep the facts were buried, the enormous size of the haystack hiding the proverbial needle, and the endless hours and days and even years before they could rest. Faith and trust were being pushed to the very limits, but those responsible for Kennedy's death had to be brought to a kind of justice, yet to be determined.

Robert Kennedy had met several times with Dr. Carmichael, and his lack of patience was always a problem. He wanted answers and thought yesterday was too late. Funding for this continued investigation was becoming a source of contention. Hundreds of thousands of dollars were being spent each month, and it couldn't go on forever. The money coming via the Kennedy family would have to be replaced at some point, but from where, Doc had no idea at this point.

His main purpose was to help keep things on track, give advice when asked and sometimes when not, and constantly change the dynamics of the search. Other than Vince, David, and Justin, the others were in New Orleans to operate the investigative mechanism now in place. This seemed to give everyone a better sense of organization.

The one very crucial part of this quest, which had not been an issue before, was now an almost daily twist and turn of the reality of life: men, women, and their relationships. What was really going on was young men becoming husbands, fiancés, and thus taking on a great deal more responsibility. Chip was having issues with Camila, Rick had his problems trying to love two women, Vince was deeply in love with Darlena, Darren recently began to think about someone special to him. Becker was up to his eyeballs in his covert attempt to keep Nancy satisfied, keep his teaching at a peak level, and stay involved in the overall picture of what was going on downtown. David would be soon moving to Chicago where he could help Vince and be closer to Justin just in case there was a problem in New Jersey.

The drug traffic had been isolated by merging Rick and Chip's business with Johnny's group. Darren, with Jennie's help was now handling all the financial transactions. Records of the names, amounts, and transportation costs were now being kept in a large safety deposit box at the Hibernia Bank. Darren made entries in his office and transferred them to the lock box twice a month but at different times. Soon they would be adding another bank, but for now Hibernia was the home base.

Darren had already made a big difference in the way things were done. His secretary's ability to handle details was a hundred-eighty-degree difference from Rick. Old stud muffin was good at taking care of any number of undercover activities, but Rick was never cut out to take care of the stacks of minutia. Having Darren and Jennie to handle things made everything work together in a much smoother and more secure environment.

Chapter 43
I'm Sorry, She's Busy

Darren had started with a solid slate of clients who had committed funds to his management, and Craig and Myer were most happy to be receiving thousands of extra dollars and not having to do much to earn it. Giving up a few square feet in their very pricey building was perfect for them. They also enjoyed the opportunity to get to know Jennie. She could have been his daughter, but Craig spent a little too much time in Jennie's office. Neither Jennie nor Darren were happy about it.

"Craig is there something we can help you with today?" Darren asked in a rather sarcastic sounding tone.

"Oh, hi Darren, no I was just telling Jennie about my new boat I bought last week. It's a beauty, and just letting her know she and her little boy were welcome to come aboard any time."

Craig left, and Darren went back into his office. A few minutes later Jennie stuck her head into his office and thanked him for encouraging Mr. Busybody to leave. "He makes me kind of nervous Darren, and he's either asking a lot of questions or trying to find a way to get me to his place. I don't want to make him angry for your sake, but it's hard to work sometime when he's hovering."

"I'll see what I can do to make it a little more private for you to get your work done."

He didn't think of it at first, but what if he and Jennie were dating? That would let Craig know that Jennie was off the market so to speak.

"Jennie, could you stay for a few minutes after work? I have an idea I would like to pass by you."

"I hope it's a good one."

"Jen' I forgot I have a meeting uptown at five; so, do me favor, if you can. Meet me at Two Sisters when you're finished here. I'll have a table reserved and if I'm a few minutes late, just wait for me. That okay with you?"

"I'll be there.

Rick, Chip, and Darren were meeting to discuss adding a couple of accounts to Darren's list and how best to manage each of the new clients. The first client would be Rick and Chip's company, and they wanted to make sure that Myer and Craig knew about the account. The second was going to be a little tricky because Chip had spent a lot of time procuring a small amount of money from Alejandro. The big man wasn't too excited about turning his money over to someone he didn't know, but Chip assured him there was nothing to worry about. Alejandro had Darren and the firm checked out from one side to the other, but all he found was a small but stable and conservative manager of millions of dollars. Alejandro's new best friend was going to be Darren Leitner.

"Jennie, I'm sorry I'm this late, but we went on longer than I first thought. What are you having?"

"I like gin and tonic with a squeeze of lime. It's refreshing after a hard day at the salt mine." Darren loved her smile. Even when she had too much to do and not enough time to do it, she was always smiling. How could anyone always be this happy?

"Waiter, I'll have what she's having, and could you hand me a menu please? Want to join me in an appetizer?"

"Anything but calamari. I just can't get over the fact that they're tentacles. What's up with this private talk we're having?"

"As I briefly told you in the office, it occurred to me last night that if you were dating someone or interested in someone then Craig might back away."

"That's a great idea, but who am I supposed to be interested in or dating? I think I've had three dates in the past year. It's not something I really want to do."

"You mean to tell me that you would turn down your boss, if he asked you to attend a fund raiser this weekend?"

"Darren, I'm flattered, but do you think that's a good thing to do?"

"Well, you don't have to fall in love or anything, but going out a few times might keep you from having to fend off your friend. It's completely up to you."

"Okay, but don't get it in your head that I'm looking for any kind of relationship out of this."

"I promise all you have to do is have dinner now and then, maybe a movie, or a concert, and let Craig know how much you enjoy our time together. After a week or two, I'm quite certain he won't bother you, unless of course he wants to know what kind of guy I am. You can tell him that I'm wonderful."

"Darren, I would love to be your girlfriend du jour. Today is a great time to do this because my son is staying with his grandparents for a couple of weeks. They love to take care of him, and I really will enjoy some time alone."

* * *

"Marjorie, this is Darren. May I see Craig for just a few minutes?"

"Darren, Mr. Benson said he's free until eleven."

After Darren got to his place last night, he and Rick had a few things to go over before taking the new accounts to Myer and Craig. Rick told Darren that because of the oversight Doc required, Darren would tell Myer or Craig that he wanted to be in on the details of setting up any offshore accounts. "If my clients want to know how it works, I need to know how to answer that question."

Myer wasn't very enthused about the prospect of Darren's inclusion, but he did tell him that he would check with Craig and let him know. "Darren, you may have to take your clients elsewhere. It just depends on what Craig thinks about the idea."

"I understand, but tell Craig that we could be looking at moving fifty to sixty million if that helps him with his decision."

"Okay, I'll let you know."

Darren was confident that that neither partner was going to let that kind of money go somewhere else. He went back to his office.

"Jen', will you go with me to the fundraiser on Saturday?"

"What's it for, and what would I have to wear?"

"They're raising money for the symphony, and wear whatever you'd wear to hear the symphony. I'm wearing a suit and tie."

"Darren, I'm just a hard-working regular girl, and not sure I would fit into your group. I'll think about it and let you know tomorrow."

Jennie had several conversations with herself that night about going with the boss to a party for high income music lovers. She started talking to herself, rationalizing about going. *On the positive side, it would help to eliminate Craig from her coffee time and her work. On the other hand, I would have to find a dress, get my hair done, and it cost money to do all of that for one date. But then, Darren is being super nice to invite me, and I hate to make him think I don't trust him or want to be around him. I mean I like him, but I'm just not ready for dating. He did say that it wasn't really a date."*

She continued her attempt to find a reason not to go, but she thought *I will do this, but any other outing would have to be less of a hassle. I can handle Craig without having to burden Darren, even if the guy is getting a little pushier all the time. No, I will go and let Darren become my guy . . . just to make sure Craig leaves me alone.*

While she was eating her breakfast, she was still thinking about it. This is only to keep Craig out of my office.

Darren was in a good mood, and when she told him she was going, he seemed to be even livelier.

"That's great Jen. I'll pick you up around seven and have you safely and comfortably back home by eleven, eleven-thirty at the latest."

The crowd was quite large, everyone was enjoying the champagne and the socializing. Darren introduced Jennie to several couples, and she was excellent at mixing and meeting. He also noticed she looked ravishing in her gown, and her hair was beautiful as well. He rather enjoyed the idea of helping her with her problem. As promised, he had her at her front door at ten minutes after eleven, she told him how much fun she had, and they said goodnight. He had told her on Monday, when Craig made his way over, he would come out to tell her how much he enjoyed the fundraiser, and that he had dinner reservations for them at 8 pm on Thursday night. If that didn't help get the message across nothing would.

She really enjoyed herself even more on their dinner date because she could be more of herself, and not be worried about what she was wearing or who was who. It was just the two of them talking about the office, their interests, and a little about themselves. Having dinner with Darren was fun. Once again when he took her home it was just, "Darren, I had a great time and see you tomorrow." No muss, no fuss, and off he went.

* * *

The gentleman at the London bank had a code which he used to confirm receipt of funds. He had another group of numbers which meant those same funds were in a Swiss bank account. Two days passed, and Craig and Myer received a call indicating that a deposit of $55 million had just been made at a small bank in Bermuda. The transfer of those funds to Darren Leitner's firm's account in Bern, Switzerland took two days to complete, but tracing the transaction was near impossible. It was a much simpler time.

Chapter 44
On the Dock

Max had settled in very well to his routine, but he was a bit frustrated by the lack of any sound leads about shipments coming from South America. There had been several large containers which were handled suspiciously off to the side of the dock, but nothing was found when they were investigated by the Coast Guard. Maybe it was all a ruse to clear a different way into the area. The only way Max could find out was to get a look at the books. He was now in charge of about forty guys, and with that responsibility, he could pretty much come and go as he wished into the office area. One afternoon he decided to stay a little later than normal.

While his friend Dix was wrapping up the afternoon reports, Max very quietly moved toward the back office and hid in a supply closet. He was hoping that Dix would think he had gone home and lock up and leave too. About an hour after getting into the closet, he heard the door shut, and then it was very quiet. The cleanup crew wouldn't be there until after eight; so, that gave him plenty of time to look around. What he was looking for he really didn't know, but figured he'd know it when he saw it.

File after file he looked to see if there was a name or company he recognized from his calls from Rick and Doc. He had almost given up on finding anything when his pen light revealed a large brown envelope with Craig Benson written on it. Thirty-eight photographs later he made sure everything was in its place, he shut the door, checked to make sure it was locked and left for home. He placed the small package in the mailbox on the corner before he stopped into the diner for a meal and a beer. At least he had found something. It looked important, but the content would have to be scrutinized by Rick before Max knew if he had made a good find or not.

"Hey there sailor, what's going on with you?" Laura always made Max feel better about his job calling him a sailor. To those who didn't really know who Max was, they thought he was a veteran of the high seas, a real sailor now consigned to just moving paper around all day.

224

"Miss Laura, you look really great. I like your hair. You must have known I was comin' in tonight."

"You are the most conceited man I have ever known, but thanks for noticing. Whatcha havin'?

Mindy's cheeseburgers were more like a Texas cheeseburger and with those fries she cooked, Max ate there quite often. Put a cold beer with it, and he was in heaven. The place wasn't busy; so, Laura sat down with him and they talked while his food was being prepared. He was about to ask her about seeing a movie on Saturday when a guy walked up to the table and told Max, "You're needed at the office right now."

When Max stood up and asked who the guy was and what was this about, a small caliber gun was stuck in his side. "Buddy, I don't know why they want you and I don't care. Are you comin' or not?"

Laura looked petrified and Max was rather pale himself. He kept wondering how they knew he took photos. Guess he would know soon enough.

"Max, come in, sit down. I'm Victor Harris and this is my associate Clarence Winston. Sorry, we had to interrupt your dinner, but it has come to our attention that you had to work late tonight. I need for you to tell me why you needed to be in the office after hours, and too, how was it that you were able to work so long without any lights?"

As fast as Max could think, he began to come up with a story which hopefully would keep him from being killed on the spot. "There are some guys who think they are above the rules when it comes to changing shifts, vacation time, and frankly working at all. I was going to find out what their background was and come up with some way to help them manage their time better. I was in the personnel office for about two hours and then left. Is there a problem with that?"

"Did you write any of this information down or is it all in your head?

"I don't write things like that down because it might get into the wrong hands. I just wanted to see some names."

"Tell you what Max, let's go back to that office and you show us what it was you were looking for and what you found that's now stored in the old bean."

As he slowly unlocked the door, "I guess you think I'm a fool to arbitrarily show you files that are none of your business. Tell me who needs the information and I'll consider showing it to you."

"You sorry piece of crap, I will beat your ass into the ground and then shoot you if you don't show me what I asked for." He reached for Max's hair, pulled his head back, and yelled, "You got that sonny boy?"

Max knew the odds, but he wasn't about to leave this office without doing something. He hit Clarence with a chair first and then lunged at Victor. He knew he had to hit them hard right now or he was dead meat. He felt a sharp pain in his back and as he was falling to the floor saw two guys running away. He couldn't breathe. As best he could, he pulled the phone to the floor and dialed the operator. The ambulance arrived just in time. Another ten minutes and Max would have been dead. The police wanted to know who shot him and why. Before Max fell unconscious, he told them it was a robbery.

The surgery lasted almost six hours. The bullet had punctured his right lung and shattered his rib cage. It would be days before he would realize where he was. Laura didn't find out about Max for two days. One of the regulars was talking at breakfast about how bad Max was hurt, and when Laura heard that she dropped the order she had in her hand. She called the union office and found out which hospital and rushed to see Max. About the closest they had come to romance was holding hands on the way to his car after a movie. He was important to her, and she had to see him.

By the time they cut him open and put tubes everywhere, he looked even worse than he was. Since she wasn't a family member, about all Laura could find out was that he had been shot and was holding his own. It could take another twenty-four to forty-eight hours before they could say whether he would live or not.

While she was sitting in the waiting room, two men were asking to see the doctor about Max. They weren't the two who had taken him away from the restaurant, and she hoped they were his family or his friends.

"Gentlemen, pardon me for asking, but are you part of Max's family? I know him from where I work, my name is Laura, and if you find out anything would you tell me please?"

"Laura, we are friends of Max and do you know anything about what happened?"

She had already told the police what she remembered about them, but she told Rick and Doc what she saw and heard. Yes, one of the guys, who looked really mean put a gun in Max's side and they left. After that, I didn't know anything until late yesterday afternoon. I stayed last night just in case something happened.

"Laura, as soon as we know anything, we'll let you know. Give me a number I can call just in case you aren't here."

Two days passed, three days passed, but Max wasn't responding to anything. The doctors were concerned about pneumonia or an infection setting in while he was in this condition. After almost five days, Max began to stir. Laura had almost been living at the hospital, but they still wouldn't let her see him. When Rick found out about that, he asked the staff to allow her in to see her boyfriend. She was so happy to see him no matter how beat up he looked. She hadn't wanted to admit it before, but if she could love someone who she barely knew, it would be Max.

He still looked awful, but at least he could open his eyes. When he saw Laura, he squeezed her hand and tried to smile. Two days later they moved him to a room, and she was right there with him.

Rick told Doc to head back home and he would brief him when Max could tell him what happened. Whatever happened they were going to get him out of New Jersey before whoever did this, finished the job.

Another week passed, and Max was now walking up and down the hall. It had been an extremely close call and Rick told him that he was being moved out of New Jersey. Max didn't want to be taken away from his job, but he wasn't given a choice. When Rick left, Max left. They had what they needed, or at least most of what they needed, and Max was now a marked man. He didn't have but just a few minutes to tell Laura goodbye. When he walked out the door, she started crying and she didn't stop for hours.

Chapter 45
Putting Pieces Together

It was a really cold day in the south, the rain felt like sleet, and the Gulf was in an uproar. Doc set up this meeting with Rick, Chip, Darren, and Max to get everyone up to date and discuss some of the issues which had recently become more important.

How was the connection between Harvey and Jack Ruby arranged by Joey Dianatti, and how did Vanessa fit into all this? Why did Big Jim want to meet with Joey? Was Joey acting on his own? Did he have the backing of his father? How were the money transfers to Benson & O'Steen handled and by whom?

228

Doc was convinced that the assassination was a hit set up by the Dianatti and Vinzzetti families. Somehow, they had access to vital information about the President, and so far, the only suspect in that scenario had been murdered. Rick and Chip were convinced that Harvey had only been a disposable pawn in the game. Was that why Ruby shot him? Was Harvey that important or was it they just needed to make sure he never said anything? When asking about people being shot, who were those two guys found in the lake in Fort Worth? How did they fit?

The guys knew it was Benson and O'Steen who handled the money, but there was no solid evidence that connected them to anyone in the organization, at least not yet. Darren knew how it was done, but had not been able to come up with anything concrete to show a direct path of the money to or from the families. For the moment, Darren was stuck. There was another person involved in this, but for now, they couldn't figure out who it was.

Though Becker wasn't in attendance, his girlfriend garnered quite a bit of conversation. Chip was convinced that Nancy had killed Meriwether and Becker was going to find out if he could survive her lust long enough to verify that. Since the death of Meriwether, things had been in a very defensive mode at the agency. Some of the key analysts had left the CIA to seek employment in the private sector. The country seemed to be coming apart and it wasn't really a fun time to be on the covert operations side. Viet Nam, drugs, race, and an overall sense of doom was making it feel as though a revolution was in the works.

Meriwether's connection with the Dianatti family, and his many contacts with Johnny gave Rick a sense that Donald Meriwether was the victim of a professional hit. On the other hand, if that were true, why did it to look like the work of an amateur who just didn't like the guy? Usually, when there's a major hit, the shooter wants to leave things nice and tidy with no traces of any kind.

Every member of the group knew that this was a huge conspiracy to take the heart from the people, bring the country to its knees, and possibly cause the collapse of the economy. When they left Gulf Shores, their agendas were set to narrow in on those who had the most contact between any and all of the suspects.

* * *

In late January, Doc flew to Quebec for a meeting with a man quite close to the Kennedys. His fortune had been made in acquiring and developing real estate around the world. Charles W. Finley had been in constant contact with Bobby since the death of the President. Bobby told Charles what his family was financing, and that was a most uncomfortable surprise to Doc.

The meeting lasted almost four hours, a lot of questions were asked and answered.

"Dr. Carmichael, I thank you so much for your time and sharing the extent of what you've been doing for the country and for the family. It is my understanding that all of this started at the bequest of President Kennedy, and upon his death, your group wanted to stay together to find out what really happened. The Kennedy's have always been close friends of mine and an even closer partner in any number of endeavors. Joe and I made a lot of money over the years, and it doesn't seem right that he and his family must suffer like this. We haven't discussed what this has cost over the years, but I'm certain it's a great deal. Doctor Carmichael, do you have any figures you could share with me?"

"Mr. Finley, including the money used for the development of the false drug company, salaries, and the expenses, the amount spent to date is a few dollars over three million. Finley didn't react, but instead, took a book out of his desk and handed it to Doc.

Doctor, have you seen this notebook before?"

"No sir, I haven't. What is it?"

"Read the first page before you look at anything else."

At the top of page two was written, "There is no amount of money I won't spend to find out who murdered my brother. I will hunt them down if it takes me the rest of my life."

"You see, I want to help Bobby find an answer, if there is one, and you feel certain that there is. Is that correct?"

"Yes sir, I do."

"Bobby places a great deal of trust in you and your plans. All I want Doctor Carmichael is an estimated budget of costs for one year. God willing you will have answers within that time, but if not, we'll do the budget again this time next year. Should I die, my attorney will be instructed to carry out my wishes. I'm just like Bobby. There is no amount of money I won't spend to find out who killed the President."

When Doc got on the plane, he ordered a couple of drinks, and closed his eyes. Charles Finley had agreed to fund the group for at least another year. For the next five hours he dozed on and off, drank on and off, and was still groggy when he landed. It had been a long two days.

Chapter 46
Triple Committed

It took almost three weeks before much of anything happened. Darren was processing work as if nothing had happened, but that was mainly because of Craig and Myer. He couldn't have them thinking he wasn't taking care of the clients. He had been watching who was coming and going, and the one that surprised him the most was Francesco Dianatti himself as he arrived one afternoon around five.

About an hour after arriving, Dianatti was gone, and all Darren could do for now was to wait and see if anything had been recorded. Hudson was a real pro and had inserted a tiny bug that unless you already knew where it was you wouldn't find it. He had also devised a method to outsmart the devices being used to find listening devices. When Rick called to tell him that they had it all on tape, Darren could finally take a deep breath.

"Hey Jen, are you busy tonight?"

"Not really, what did you have in mind?"

"Would you go with me to dinner? I'm a part of an investment group which meets once a month, and I don't have a date. They do this date thing twice a year, and I forgot all about it. I could pick you up at seven if that's okay."

"What's it going to cost me?"

"Ha, aren't you cute? All you have to do is act like you know me."

"I don't know, Darren, that's a lot to ask." They laughed and then he was out the door, but not before he told her she could leave too."

"See you at seven."

Several of the major investment houses were represented, and some of the wives or dates looked as if they were trying to out dress the other women. Jennie looked very nice, but nothing too opulent or over the top. She had on a black cocktail dress, with a strand of pearls which gave her a look of simplicity, elegance, and beauty. Darren had difficulty concentrating on anything else but her. He asked himself, "Did she dress like this to drive me crazy or to attract other men?"

She had accomplished both, and Darren was realizing that there was a bit of green in his attitude. He wasn't supposed to be jealous. She had made it plain that there was to be no relationship, but there must have been eight or nine guys who were wanting to know more about her, was she married, and other assorted questions that Darren ignored. Of course, Jen was loving the attention, and thanked Darren profusely for asking her to go with him.

The next morning, she had several calls asking her if she had a moment to talk with them. At first, she was hesitant, but when Mark called, the guy who she had conversed with the night before, she did talk to him. He asked her out and she said yes.

When Darren arrived around ten, she told him about the call from Mark. "You remember the tall, good looking guy I was talking to while you were doing your back-patting?"

Trying to act like he didn't notice, he said, "I saw you talking to several guys, but not sure which one you're talking about."

The phone rang, and she didn't say any more about the call. Darren sat in his office deciding if he was mad at himself or her. At this point he didn't know anything about the date with Mark. On Thursday he would find out more after the roses arrived.

How could he have been so blind? She did want to have a relationship, but not with him.

What did Mark have that he didn't, he wondered.
For now, he would just have to live with it and go forward. He had far too much to attend to without getting bogged down in a romance. Whether he believed that or not he didn't know for sure.

* * *

Instead of the usual meeting at one of the restaurants, today Darren was having lunch at Rick's place. "Darren, I'm going to ask you to do something you may not be thrilled about, but it has to be done now. We just heard that our landlords have been told that somewhere in their offices is a bug. Fortunately, they think it's the Feds who are snooping, but we can't take a chance on them actually finding it. Paul is in Chicago, and since you are always in and around their office, it's you who has to get in, get the bug, and get out. If you need to, make it look like a burglary, because the little microphone is imbedded in the pen set on Craig's desk."

"I thought everything was clear before Dianatti came in the other day?

"It was Darren, but for some reason, someone is convinced there's a bug in there and they're going to find it. They have a guy who is with the FBI and he evidently let them know there was a microphone in Craig's office. How he knew that I don't know. What I do know is we have to get ours out of there now."

"Rick, I've never done anything like that before, and I'm not even sure I could get in there if I knew what I was doing. And what about security, for God's sake?"

"My man, we don't have a choice. It's either get that thing out of there or shut down a key part of the operation."

"Okay, but if I come up with a better way, it's okay right

"Do whatever you have to do, but do it."

Darren wasn't really the guy anyone would want for cloak and dagger thefts. He was great at numbers, loved to mingle with the rich and famous, but the idea of him breaking into a place to get something illegally, kept him from sleeping. The morning after his conversation with Rick, Darren looked like he had been on a binge for a week. Mr. Cool didn't even shave, and his clothes weren't fresh from the closet. He had thought all night about some way he could do what needed to be done without breaking and entering.

"Jen, would you do me a favor please? I need you to take this over to Craig and while you're there, make a big deal as to how much you love his pen set." That caught her off guard and of course she asked why.

"Darren, I've seen it before, and believe me it's nothing special. What would make it interesting to me today?"

"Tell him you think your dad would love something like it."

She went, she told Craig it was very business-like, and asked him where he got it. It was a gift, and he thanked her for the compliment.

That afternoon Darren asked Craig if he had a minute. Darren wasn't the most relaxed he had ever been, but he would see how his idea worked.

"Craig, I don't know if she told you, but Jen's looking for something her dad might like for his birthday. When she was over here this morning she noticed your pen set and thought her dad would really like it. Would you be willing to sell it?"

"Darren the pen set is a gift and besides, you could probably pick a new one just like it for a few dollars."

"You're right, but something about yours piqued her interest and I wanted to do something which would let her know I'm happy that she's happy."

"Bullshit Darren, you just want to do something for her to get her mind off that guy who sent the roses. How bad do you want it?"

"How much do you think a gift like that is worth?"

"It's a sentimental favorite of mine; so, I think a hundred could ease my loss."

"Are you kidding me? A hundred dollars for a pen set?"

"Darren, if you want it, that's the price. Otherwise, I've got work to do. I'm not so sure your clients have the right guy as their advisor if this is your idea of a deal."

The pen set was in Darren's file cabinet. All he said to Jen was that she needed to thank Craig for his boundless generosity. Rick had the bug in his hand and told Darren he had done a good job. If a bug were found, it wouldn't be theirs.

* * *

David Atwater had been in Chicago for a few months, and he and Vince had talked several times about various parts of the Vinzzetti operations. At first, Vince said he didn't pay too much attention to Carl's coming and goings, but he did find out that when the President was shot Carl wasn't in town.

"Vince, do you think Carl shot him?"

"Dave, Carl doesn't dirty his hands doing the deed; he has others carry out his plans. Where he gets his talent, I have no clue, but if he's a part of it, I will do what needs to be done to find out how he made it work."

David's job was in the City of Chicago's Property Tax Division. Posing as an attorney for a real estate client, he spent many an hour going over all of the tax records from early '62 through the end of '65. If there were any transactions with the names of anyone Doc had given him, it was David's job to find them and make a list. This had been going on for weeks, and so far, there was nothing to show for all the time and effort. He needed a break.

Sitting by the fire, having read the same paragraph at least three times, David was thinking about the last time he saw Vanessa. *I wonder how she's doing.* He decided to make a few calls to see if she was still in New Orleans. If not, they might know where she was. He did know she was an undercover agent for the FBI in New Orleans, but didn't know that after the President's death she was transferred to the Atlanta office. No more exotic dancing for Vanessa who was once again, Susan Arthur.

She was now a special agent, specializing in white

collar crime and its ties to the mob and money laundering. It had been a long, tedious operation, and she was looking forward to a few days off. Susan had been pulling sixty to seventy-hour weeks for the past month, and she was so tired it was difficult to concentrate. Her boss told her not to come in for a week, and she gladly accepted his directive.

In the meantime, oblivious to the intrigue of her work, in Atlanta, David asked Rick if he knew where Vanessa was. "No Dave, I don't know what happened to her. Misty told me that she left rather unexpectedly, and had not talked to her since. Let me see what I can do to help you. How are you and Vince doing in the icy cold of Chicago?"

"Vince is one cool dude and that has nothing to do with the arctic winds blowing us around up here. He's probably the only guy involved in a crime family who is in love with a first-class lady who loves him dearly. I'll be glad when he and I are both out of here. Talk to you later and let me know if you find out where Vanessa is."

Even though he was constantly tempted, ever since he and Vikki married, Rick tried to stay clear of Misty, but seeing her at the club made it impossible not to think about her. She was now general manager of the whole damn place and was pulling down a sizeable income. The club was one of the main places to be seen in the Quarter, and she was a big part of the reason why that happened.

Once she got her head around Rick's marriage, she began concentrating on her career, and making as much money as she could. What she found out about herself was how creative she was becoming by finding new ways to get people into the club. When she started having Tacky Night where the women dressed as naughty as they dared, the place was packed.

But the big money was because of the tourist business she

was pulling in with aggressive TV and billboard ads. If a person didn't make a reservation at least three weeks in advance, too bad. A concierge at the finer hotels could make a considerable amount of money in tips by coming up with reservations for their guests. The hotel would pay triple for the favor and Johnny told Misty she could name her price to stay with the club. She didn't give a damn if there was a man wanting to meet her or not, she was too busy to fool with that. Misty knew in her heart why she felt that way and wished the ache would go away.

Chapter 47
How Interesting is That?

Susan, aka Vanessa, was taking a nice warm bath, had a bottle of wine by her side, and was listening to an album of music by Nat King Cole. She had almost fallen asleep when the phone rang. She had a phone installed in her bathroom for just this situation.

"Hello . . . Who? . . . Oh yes, David, of course I remember you. How are you doing? It's so nice to hear from you. How in the world did you find me? . . . Ha, you always did seem to be very persistent . . . I do understand that . . . I'm taking off a few days myself. It's sorta like being on a mini vacation . . . That might be fun. When will you be here? . . . Why don't you do this: when you get here and get settled in, give me a call and we'll go from there. I look forward to it . . . See you then."

David Atwater felt like the third person making it a crowd. All he had done for the past year was to be available to take care of matters in Dallas and Chicago. He now spent countless hours sitting on his ass in that records room trying to find needles in haystacks. Doc had talked about adding responsibilities, but not much had come out of it. As they say, be careful what you wish for because some wishes do come true.

A lot of time had spent a lot of time working on some of the data that the guys had uncovered in New Orleans. Doing some of his own investigation, Doc had found out something that didn't make a lot of sense. When he read about Vanessa, there were a few notes indicating that on several occasions she had gone missing for two or three days at a time. When Doc had her followed, she sometimes seemed to be involved in some odd things that had no relationship to her work. How many dancers in the quarter leave packets in mailboxes at vacant homes? The guy who picked it up looked like a cop, but maybe not. Whoever he was, he tried to make sure that no one saw him.

The next time she left a packet, it was Chip who picked it up just after she left. It was a message which was in a coded format. It wasn't new recipes Vanessa thought Martha would enjoy.

Doc got back to Rick and asked him if he had seen Vanessa. He had not. She was gone. A series of calls were made and though it wasn't easy to do, Doc found out where she was. David's desire to see Vanessa again would be an ideal time for Doc to find out what her role had been in the big picture.

Vanessa looked entirely different than when they last met. Her hair was shorter, she looked as if she had been working out, but one thing hadn't changed: her style. That first date he decided she had to be the smartest exotic dancer in New Orleans. She could act the dumb blond, all she wanted or needed to be, but she was one smart lady. Her looks and her mind were a great combination. He could still remember how she moved around that stage and looked like she was really enjoying herself.

Right now, they were on their way to dinner, and Doc had told David to get to know her extremely well. She knew things and David was the one to find out what. Rick wanted to know if there were any connections she still had in New Orleans.

He thought the date went well. They weren't exactly close before, but she had gone out with him a second time before she left Big Easy. This time they talked about her move and why she was in Atlanta. She told him she was working for a security firm as a salesperson, and business was good. It wasn't her dream job, but it got the bills paid. Considering where she told him she lived, it must be more than paying the bills, she has a very wealthy friend, or maybe the FBI pays more than he thought. Susan had considered telling him the truth, but most likely he wouldn't be seeing her again. She did her best to be as interestingly boring as possible, but David liked her and was hoping she would see him again.

Both times he called her, she wasn't home or just not answering her phone. He ruled out the latter, since she told him how many projects she was pursuing.

Of course, he couldn't locate Vanessa because she didn't exist, and Susan certainly wasn't in the security business. When she got back to work, she was immediately sent to Chicago and would be there until her assignment was closed.

The FBI had been tapping phones of various members of the Vinzzetti family for the past two years, and all they had to show for it was a lot of lost time and an extreme amount of tape. The feds were trying to tie the family to corruption in local politics and sent Susan there to see if she could find a way to get on the inside.

Susan Arnold was going to be Vanessa again, but this time she was going to be a very sexy secretary for one of Chicago's city councilmen. Vanessa Tyler's objective was much what it was in New Orleans: find out who wielded the power and had the connections, then make sure she worked for that person in some capacity.

With her smarts and her looks, it didn't take much time for the new Vanessa to find a job working for Councilman Rodney

Hartford. His penchant for beautiful women was observed frequently as he attended various city functions and especially for some of Chicago's more elegant social outings.

Rodney was a graduate of Northwestern and had his law degree from Virginia. When he was a young man he found out quickly that money and power go hand in hand, and if you happen to be good looking and very charismatic, the money and power can happen a lot faster in politics.

When Vanessa walked into Rodney's office for her final interview, he made a point of assisting her with her chair and offered her some of his imported coffee. "Miss Tyler, I see on your resume that you were in the entertainment business in New Orleans. What kind of work did you do there?"

"In her best down-home impression, she explained that her work was mostly in the public relations arena and of course doing whatever she could to help the owner promote the business. It didn't really matter to Rodney because with a body like hers, he was more interested in how she might work out in his bedroom. Three days later she went to work for Rodney, but had the first week off to return to Atlanta to get her things. He would have her apartment waiting when she got back.

The new Vanessa quickly became Rodney's new best friend. He asked her to dinner, but she refused, saying that might not be conducive to their employer-employee relationship. He admired her sense of ethics, but no one really turned him down but once. He would take her to lunch where they would work on a couple of projects and get to know one another much better. She didn't choose to work on her short lunch break; consequently, she turned him down again. Rodney mused, *what's the deal here? She does know who I am, right?*

He called her in after work to discuss her attitude and found that his mention of not being a team player didn't have an effect on her one way or the other. Vanessa was sorry that he felt that way and if she needed to move on she could do that. She started to get up from her chair and say goodbye, but he asked her to stay a moment longer.

"Vanessa, you know I'm very attracted to you and I've been thinking of several ways to show you that I'm not such a bad guy. Why are you so opposed to going out with me?"

"First of all, Mr. Hartford, I thought you would be different. I'm constantly being approached, hit on, propositioned, or worse; so, I was determined that the next job I took there would be no dating the boss. I understood from the start what you wanted, and I'm flattered by your attention, but I'm not sleeping with you and that's that."

He just sat there looking at her with a rather stunned are-you-kidding-me look, but decided to accept her decision and act like he didn't care that she felt that way.

"Very well, Miss Tyler, I understand your hesitation, but I'm not in the habit of sleeping with my employees. I don't care for your attitude; nevertheless, you are very qualified to help me run this office and I appreciate your candor."

She rose from the chair, thanked him for his understanding, and walked out. He couldn't take his eyes off her cute little ass as she walked out of his office. Somehow, someway, someday he was going to spend the night with her, or at least that was what he was promising himself. As to whether it would really happen, he knew he would certainly have to try something besides the same old same old. He smiled, *baby, old Rodney boy ain't done yet.*

That afternoon, one of the calls that came in was from Carl. "Hi Carl, what can I do for you? . . . Sure, what time? . . . Do you want to meet for lunch? . . . Okay, we can do that . . . I'll have something ordered in and see you around noon tomorrow . . . You too guy."

Anytime Carl called it wasn't just to catch up. He needed to have something done or he needed information. No one in the office knew who Carl was other than that he was a local businessman who needed to see his councilman on occasions.

"Mr. Hartford, your appointment is here."

"Carl always good to see you." They shook hands, and Carl introduced Rodney to Vinnie Pertinelli.

"Mr. Pertinelli, it's my pleasure to meet you. So, Carl, what can I do for you today? Carl asked Rodney if he had noticed anything unusual with the phones.

"Like what?"

"Any clicking sounds or false rings or maybe the phones are just not working."

"The staff would know more about that. Let me ask Vanessa." He asked her to come in and when Vinnie looked at her, he knew she was Vanessa from New Orleans. He had been at the club one night visiting with Rick when he saw her with the girl Rick was dating at the time, and there were very few men who could forget seeing Vanessa. Misty had tried to get Vinnie and Vanessa together, but someone else got there first. Rick had also told Vince that Vanessa seemed to be hooked up with Johnny Faretta and that might cause a problem that would need to be worked out before asking her out.

So, here Vince was with a capo in the Vinzzetti family meeting with a city councilman and Vanessa worked for the guy. Vince knew the world isn't this small, but something or someone is making it that way.

Vince called Rick to discuss Vanessa, and that left Rick very puzzled. He was going to call David, tell him about this situation, and make sure that David's number one priority was finding out why Vanessa was now in Chicago.

Doc told Rick she was in two different places as Vanessa, and there must be far more to her than they first thought. David needed to figure out a way to meet her in the councilman's office or where she had lunch, but make contact. Rick strongly

243

emphasized: "Make damn sure you do whatever it takes for her to think you're the most incredible man in America."

When Rodney was first noticed by the powers that be in the arena of city politics, he was very self-confident, even cocky, but that only made him a better fit for the party bosses. What he didn't know at first was that a lot of his campaign funds were coming from sources which were very private. No laws appeared to be broken, but money was being distributed around town for only one purpose: getting it to Rodney's campaign. After he was elected, he was occasionally reminded from whence the money came. He had been bought and rationalized that the money was just for campaign expenses.

A month or so after he took office, he was approached by Carl Montano, who encouraged Rodney to look long and hard at the bid being offered by the Mendosa Brothers for replacement windows in the city's office buildings. Rodney's vote gave the contract to the small company in a small suburb of Chicago, and he enjoyed the case of Dom Perignon '59 which was left at the office and addressed to Gerald Johnson, an old friend of Rodney from his college days. Rodney asked Vanessa to have someone pick it up and deliver it to an address in Hinsdale. Rodney would be at his mom and dad's home later in the week to pick it up. Rodney was a quick learner and a favor next time would be worth far more than a case of expensive champagne.

Doc never said how he found out about Vanessa's real name, and her job at the FBI, but now he was determined to find out why she was in Chicago. Did the FBI know something he didn't? The same friend who gave him her name was now called on to find out what she did for the Bureau. In the late sixties, it took a lot of leg work to come up with information about someone who didn't want to be found. This was no exception, but in November of 1967 one of Doc's friends dropped him a note to say that it looked as if she was working on something involving the Vinzzetti family.

What is Susan looking for, and why is she in the same places we are? Doc needed to know more about what the woman was up to, and wanted David to know it had just become a lot more important than first thought. Now he had a real job . . . maybe even a pleasurable one.

Chapter 48
The Ties that Bind

Susan was FBI: so, was Misty in the agency too? "Rick, this is going to be somewhat uncomfortable for you, but we need to know if Misty is also an agent, and if not, did she know that her friend Vanessa was?" Doc didn't want to ask Rick to do this, but if anyone could talk to her he could. They needed to know more about what Vanessa had been up to when she was in New Orleans.

"I'll do this, but if you find out I've been shot, you'll know by whom. I've got to tell Nikki because if she ever found out that I met with Misty and didn't tell her, she might dispose of me permanently."

"That's your call, but whether she likes it or not, you have to find out what Misty knows."

It was still difficult to realize that it had been almost five years since they first met. So much had happened, so many lives had changed, and why did he feel so uncomfortable asking Misty to lunch.

Nikki had a few choice remarks about this supposed business meeting between her husband and his old friend. He saw Misty at least four times a week, so, why did he need to have lunch with her? Though Nikki could be a handful, she did trust Rick. It was Misty, she didn't trust.

"If that woman so much as reaches for your hand, I'll have yours and hers removed."

"Sweetheart, this is about Johnny Faretta's offer to sell her the club, and she wants to talk about my contract. I promise it's nothing personal."

Rick had asked Misty to meet him at a small place in Metarie. He didn't want to be interrupted while they talked. He knew she did it on purpose, but she arrived dressed in the shortest and tightest dress she could find, and how she could walk in those high heels he had no clue. There was just enough cleavage showing to remind him of what used to be one of his favorite places.

"So, what did you want to talk about, Mr. Charles?"

"Aren't we being formal today?

"You wanted to talk about something important; so, I knew it must be something other than you and me."

"I realize when I ask you this question, you're going to ask me five, but just answer this yes or no, please. Did you ever suspect that Vanessa was working undercover, and I don't mean her sex life?"

"You're right, I do want to ask some questions, but I will answer yours with yes, at times I thought she was being a little too cute and much too evasive about small things. With that said, why do you ask?"

"I'll answer that after this quick one: are you going to buy the club?"

"It's going to depend on what they're going to ask me for once they give me the money. Right now, I'll say yes, but if they try to control me because of the money, I'll turn down their offer."

"One of my good friends, Dr. Carmichael, who I think you met a few years back, called to tell me that Vanessa was really Susan Arthur and he thinks she's with the FBI."

"What? Rick, if Johnny knew that she'd be dead."

"Since she's alive and well, if he did know, there's a reason. Most likely he doesn't and can't know because he would track her down and have her killed. You promise you won't say anything about our little conversation today?"

"No, Rick, I wouldn't do that." When she put her hand on his, he immediately remembered what Nikki had said, but he'd just keep it to himself.

"Why are you so interested in Vanessa and what she did or didn't do back then?"

"My dear Misty, how did I know that would be your first question?"

"Because you are the only man who has ever known me like a book and had such a lovely way of turning my pages." It was the first time she had smiled since she arrived.

All he could think of at that moment was the countless hours they had spent loving one another. Here she was sitting next to him and though she had him remembering their time together, for now, she might as well be in some other world. He loved Nikki, but he loved Misty too. He had made his choice but had also spent countless nights thinking back to the time when he and Misty thought they would be together forever. Though she was an incredible lover, it was her heart and soul, her love for him and all his vices, that made him care for her so much. Though he could have taken her in his arms and kissed her for an hour, he didn't. He wondered if she was hoping he would.

They had lunch, indulged in some small talk, and then it was time for her to leave. She hugged him goodbye and as she started to leave, held his hand a moment and told him how wonderful it was to have some private time with him.

"Take care of yourself Rick."

He watched her walk away, but didn't see the tears.

* * *

247

Rick and Nikki had a party to attend. They couldn't just go to a party. Every one of her parties required Rick to wear a tux and a white or black tie depending on where and why there was a party. Nikki wouldn't wear just any dress; so, each event required a detailed shopping spree with exquisite dining at lunch with her friends.

Life was not easy for the daughter of John Meredith. Drowning her unhappiness in shopping, parties, and charities, not to mention the alcohol . . . plus her not working, made life at the Charles home a vacuous, emotionless cavern of despair.

They had left the party early because Nikki had a headache and wanted to leave. When they came home, she asked him if he had met with Misty. Yes, he told her, and he thanked her for her understanding. Nikki wanted to fight, and this was as good a time as any. "Did you lust after the slut?"

"Hey Nik, let's not do this. I talked to her, asked her what I needed to know, agreed on the contract, and that was it."

"It might have been that way for you, but I guarantee you, she's going to try to get you back in her bed. And, Ricky, my boy, you get in her sack, and you'll pay for the rest of your life. I hate that bitch, and I'm not sure yet, but I think I hate you too."

No one really thought it would last. A very wealthy woman with looks and talent marrying a guy who plays and sings in a small band in the quarter. He was great, but Hollywood hadn't come to town to make him a star. Combine her distrust with her angst about giving up her career, and when they did make love, it was like they were trying to punish one another and themselves at the same time. She wanted him tonight, but he was going to know just how very unhappy she was.

When they woke up the next morning, she was all loving and giving. He had begun to think that it was the amount of alcohol she was consuming that had changed her so much. She

248

had wine or a drink at lunch, in the afternoon, and at dinner. Sometimes she had a small glass of sherry at bedtime. Her drinking was getting in the way of her life. She was bored and either drank to have something to do, or to forget. Either way, it had to stop.

Rick called her old agent in New York, told him about the situation, and asked if he could get her some work. It would take her a month or two to get her voice back in shape, but she would be so much happier doing concerts or maybe an opera. Daryl Davidson, her agent, would get back to Rick to see if he could find her something of quality.

When he told her what he had done, she went off like a gun. "Damn you Rick Charles, can't I ever do anything or live my life without your help? What are you wanting me to do besides go on tour? It's that bitch Misty isn't it? You just want me out of the way, so you can have all sorts of time drilling her into the sheets. I tell you what let's do; let's just get divorced and you can have her all you want."

Nikki was out of control and something had to be done. "Hey John, you have some time to talk? Rick and John took their drinks out by the pool and since John could sense Rick's tension he got things started. "Son, what's the Princess doing now?"

"John, I'm really sorry to have to come to you with this, but I'm worried about her. She's drinking too much, sees a villain in everyone, doesn't trust me, and is now mad because I talked to Daryl about getting her some engagements. She thinks I'm trying to get her out of town, so I can be with Misty, and is even talking about divorce. Something is seriously wrong, and I can't seem to fix it."

They talked for a while, but all they could come up with was asking her to go into rehab, and they both knew how that would go over. Nikki was strong willed to start with, and whatever she was going through seemed to be really making everything worse. When Rick returned home, he found her lying on the sofa and she didn't respond when he tried to awaken her. He called for an ambulance.

An hour passed before Rick found out what the problem might be. Mrs. Charles was expecting their first child. Rick didn't know whether to start celebrating or asking himself why he never thought of the idea of her being pregnant.

When Nikki finally woke up, she had a terrible headache, and didn't understand why she was at the hospital. She wasn't fully awake, but enough to know she wasn't on her very comfy sofa. Rick was standing next to the bed when she did begin to figure things out and wanted to know why she was in a hospital. He told her that he found her asleep and she wouldn't wake up, he called an ambulance, and here she was.

"Rick am I sick?"

"No, my darling, you're not sick, but you are in a fragile condition. My love, you are blessedly pregnant."

Nikki was a beautiful woman with or without makeup, but her eyes were swollen, her lips were swollen from the oxygen mouthpiece, and she had perspired so much that her hair was matted. She smiled, "I'm going to have a baby? Rick, I love you, and she's going to love her daddy so much."

"Hey, wait a minute, you know we might have a son." She was released later that afternoon, and her gynecologist made her an appointment for the next day. Maybe now the turmoil in the Charles' house would begin to seek a lower level of intensity. John and Elizabeth Meredith were the happiest grandparents-to-be in New Orleans. This called for a party, but then again, they called for a party to celebrate the 100th anniversary of the jigsaw puzzle. Every day would be a party now.

The doctor gave Nikki instructions about exercise, a diet, a no-no as to drinking, a couple of pills to take once a day plus a bottle of vitamins. She was smiling a little more every day. The Charles family could now get some rest.

Chapter 49
Chicago, Chicago, What Wonderful Town

For whatever time was needed, David would still be David Calvin Flynn, III. Because of his various real estate interests, he would, from time to time, need to speak with the city council to discuss various issues such as zoning and permits. When David first met Rodney, it was at a meeting of the council to discuss one of David's projects. Rodney asked some good questions as he probed David for exactly what he was hoping to accomplish by building more office space.

"Mr. Flynn, I'm sure you are aware that there are thousands of square feet of unleased office space which already exists in this area?"

"Yes, I'm aware of that space, but what we are proposing is about the small business which needs an office, someone to answer the phone, access to a conference room and office equipment without having to pay for space he or she only needs on a part time basis." David went on to explain how it all worked, and the council was impressed. After the council had adjourned, Rodney invited David to join him for lunch the next day.

"David Flynn, what are you doing here?" Vanessa was quite surprised to see David, but she took him right in to see Rodney.

"Do you two know each other?" Rodney had a red light go off immediately and wondered how they could run into each other by accident in a place like Chicago.

David laughed and told Rodney he was lucky

enough to meet Vanessa at her friend's home while she was visiting in Atlanta. "We had dinner, but she was so attracted to me that she had to hurry back to Chicago to keep from falling madly in love with me." They smiled at his attempt at humor, and it seemed to make things more comfortable for Rodney. Vanessa couldn't figure out what caused David to make up a story like that. He handed her one of his business cards and wrote something on the back. If you need to talk to me or just can't keep yourself from wanting to see me, this is my direct number. Take care of yourself . . . The Dave."

When she told her boss at the FBI about the way David had created the story about how they met, it was decided she needed to find out more about David Flynn. She called to ask him out to lunch and of course he accepted. They would eat at a small restaurant near her office. Rodney was out of town so there would be no danger of him seeing her with David. He would be jealous even though they were not a couple.

She remembered that she did enjoy her last date with David, but had no idea that he was so heavily involved in the real estate development business. After their lunch date she asked him to a party on Saturday night, and once again, he was most effusive as he accepted the date.

"Vanessa, that would be a lot of fun, and if you aren't tired of me after the party, I've got tickets to see the Russian Ballet on Sunday afternoon, if you would like to go." Two dates on the weekend with them asking questions would surely give them a better idea of what the other one was doing in Chicago. Besides that, it would be fun to just get away from their day jobs. She looked smashing, and FBI or not, he wanted to get to know the real Vanessa.

The party was loads of fun and the concert was beautiful. Their Sunday dinner lasted almost three hours, but even though they arrived at her apartment at almost eleven, she asked him up for a nightcap. They both had to be at their offices by 8:30 on Monday morning, and surprisingly, they made it on time though they had talked until after two. She hadn't enjoyed a night this much in a long time, and had no idea that David had such a diversified background. This man had done a lot of things in his life, and now he was taking on Chicago.

Whether she was undercover or not, as a woman she wanted to get to know this man much better. Why he wasn't married, she couldn't figure. He was smart, wealthy, nice looking, and articulate. Maybe he is married and not letting anyone know, she thought. She decided to ask him if he was or not?

The woman had been hit on by a lot of married men, but David didn't fit that description. Damn, she thought, I'm really beginning to like this guy. He was nice on their date in Atlanta, but now he was moving up her list she reserved for being a little more special. For now, it was back to the reality of working for Rodney, and after spending time with David, Rodney was now even greasier than ever.

Chapter 50
Out West

Over the years as Lyndon rose to prominence in Texas politics and then to Washington, where he became one of the most powerful senators in the history of the U.S. Senate, Jake Winslet was always just a phone call away when Lyndon needed something done. Hell, there were times, when Lyndon didn't even know he needed something done, and then soon thereafter, he would read about some mysterious accident or an occurrence which made a difference in the outcome of certain activities.

No one who ever really gave much thought to the idea that Jake might have had anything to do with it. On the other hand, no one ever really knew where that boy was all the time either.

Lyndon used to say of his friend: "The boy could have been up to some mischief." It didn't matter where Jake might be or what he was doing, his undying loyalty to Lyndon came before God, country, or family, and that's all that mattered.

As Lyndon Baines Johnson became wealthier and more powerful, he always took care of Jake. It wasn't like giving him a crumb now and then. Lyndon set him up with a nice sized little ranch northwest of San Antonio, a herd of cattle, and a few dollars to keep the cows fed. The guy who sold Moorman's Feed to Jake was about the only one who ever saw him other than some of the people who worked where he bought his groceries. Jake just wasn't in the mood to be all that sociable.

There was a big celebration the first time LBJ was elected to Congress, but Jake stayed home and heard about it on his radio.

One day Jake was gored by a steer and damn near didn't make it back to the house to call for help. He was bleeding badly when the ambulance finally arrived, but after they got him to the emergency room, stopped the bleeding, and sewed him up, he was ready to leave. The doctor told him he had to stay a couple of days. That's when he met Ruth.

Ruth Montgomery had been working at the hospital for eleven years, first as a licensed tech assistant and then as a registered nurse. She met Jake while he was lying on his side and she was putting a needle in his butt. He said something about the pain, and she told him to kiss her ass and he said okay.

Before he left, they were pals. She wasn't much for folks and neither was Jake; so, they could talk to one another and leave everyone else to do as they wished. He told her where he lived and if she was ever out that way she could drop by to check how his scars looked.

She loved his place and she loved what that man had in his pants. Two lonely people had found a little bit of paradise. They were married four months later. Jake was damn near forty and

Ruth was thirty-four. Lyndon had just been elected to the Senate, and life was good. It wasn't like they didn't try, but for some unknown reason, there were never any children. They could have adopted, but chose not to go that route. Instead, they kept adding acres and cows to the pastureland and making more money all the time.

Four years after they married, Ruth inherited a substantial amount of money when her mom died. So, with her money, the ranch, 15,000 plus cattle, and four new producing oil wells, anywhere else but Texas, they would have been rich.

Ruth took the call, but it was for Jake. Washington was calling, and they assumed it was Lyndon. The Congressman was in a committee hearing and had told one of his aides to call Jake. Lyndon thought Jake should meet Craig Benson, who was one of his supporters from New Orleans.

"Mr. Winslet, Mr. Johnson apologizes for not being able to call himself, but wanted you to know about Mr. Craig Benson." The aide went on to tell Jake that Mr. Benson was a prominent financial advisor in New Orleans, and that Mr. Johnson wanted his friend to have Mr. Benson's phone number. "Mr. Winslet, the Congressman did say that it was up to you whether you called the gentleman in New Orleans, but from his perspective it would be a very smart thing to do." Jake thanked the young man and went to the barn to feed the horses.

Chapter 51
Come Fly with Me

Lyndon had been gathering incriminating information on everyone since he was first elected to the House. He did it for two reasons: As a weapon he could use if he needed to make sure a particular bill passed, and secondly, for nothing but pure intimidation over anyone who might get in his way.

Directly or indirectly, as the new Vice President, Lyndon Baines Johnson may have lost a chunk of his power when he left the Senate, but he was not going to go quietly into the night after becoming somewhat of second thought as second in command. Sooner or later, all of those who regarded him as finished would rue the day they even thought about that scenario.

Jake arrived at the Lakefront Airport about the time the sun was going down, took a taxi to a small apartment in the Quarter, and waited for Craig Benson. It was May 8, 1961 and they had started doing business together soon after Lyndon's office had called Jake. To be so different, there was something each one brought to the table that the other one needed. It wasn't about money, and Lord knows they had enough of that. It seemed to be more of a you do this for me, and I'll do something for you attitude.

"Craig, how difficult would it be to get me into see Francesco Dianatti?"

"Depends on why you need to see him."

"Let's say that I want to talk some business ideas with him?"

"I can certainly ask him if you wish."

"I would appreciate that very much. You can tell him it's a large undertaking, quite complicated, but there is a lot of money involved."

"Jake, it may take me a week, but I'll see what I can do."

"Thank you, my friend."

* * *

Michelle Hart was a beautiful young model living in New York and enjoyed the attention and the money of several older men. One gentleman was much richer than several of the others put together. He enjoyed her company, and though he was mostly paralyzed on one side of his body, she made him more than happy. Her Manhattan apartment, limo service, jewelry, and American Express card made her happy too. Some nights they would go out, but mostly they stayed in and enjoyed each other's stimulating conversation.

She loved his gifts, the money, the apartment, and his understanding that there were other men in her life. He particularly appreciated that she was discreet as to who was taking care of her very lavish lifestyle. Times were very good for Michelle, or at least until she got the threatening phone call suggesting she should consider finding a new sugar daddy. When she told her friend, he dismissed it as some weirdo hoping to scare her out of a few hundred dollars. "I wouldn't worry about it sweetheart, but if it happens again, I'll get the cops on it."

He was there on Thursday afternoon for an hour or so just for a visit. Later that evening he was told that she had fallen from the roof of her apartment building. He was heartbroken because he really liked Michelle and knew she didn't voluntarily jump off that building. Someone was sending a message to the old man, which he heard loud and clear. He let it be known that he wasn't going to let this pass without retaliation. After all, the man had total access to the most powerful bureaucracy in the entire world. He bought it and he was going to use it.

Carl had never liked killing a woman, but if that's what he was told to do, he did it. She was very pretty, intelligent, and as she and Carl went to the roof, she couldn't have known she was about to pay for the sins of the guy paying her bills. When you're involved with someone who has betrayed the wrong people, bad things can happen. Just to make sure the old man understood that he had fucked over the wrong friends; Carl threw Michelle off the roof to see if she could fly.

Big Jim and his friend Francesco had been approached by Michelle's friend back before Jack Kennedy was nominated. In return for Francesco's help, the friend would ask his son to ease up on the organized crime battles and concentrate more on the international affairs for a while. But Jack's brother became the Attorney General, and set out to destroy the crime families. Big Jim and Francesco had been betrayed.

Sometimes it's better to hurt someone very close to the traitor than the traitor himself. It stings so much more they say. The old man loses Michelle; he tells Bobby not to pursue his present course any further. Bobby doesn't listen, and he and his father cannot imagine the pain that's to come.

* * *

"Mr. Vice President, there's a gentleman at the gate to see you who says he needs no introduction. Should I have security take care of this?"

Lyndon laughed and told his secretary to tell the guards to let the s.o.b. come on in.

Jake, you old stud, how's it comin'."

"I suppose I'm goin' to make it if the Lord's willin' and the creeks don't rise. It ain't been rainin' much, so I guess if the Lord's okay, guess I am too."

"Mary Anne, bring me and my friend here a little somethin' to get the dust out of our mouth." She came back with a couple of cold Budweisers and they started catching up.

"How's Ruth and the ranch?"

"The woman has more energy than three of us, and she gets better lookin' every day. I'm not sure I can stay away too long. We just added a couple more wells on the far west side of the place. Sometimes I think we must be floatin' on that stuff."

"What are you doin' here? Somethin' I can help you with?"

"Lyndon, I'm fine, but do have a few quick questions which I wanted to ask you in person: How are things goin' for you in this job?

"It damn sure ain't the Senate, but at least I'm guaranteed fifty-yard line tickets at all the space launches. Seriously Jake, I'm fuckin' miserable. That bastard Bobby is driving me crazy. Just when it looks like Jack and I can have a decent conversation, Mr. Smartass comes in to tell the President he needs to talk with him. He does it just to piss me off. It's that smug little shit's way of putting me down, and he loves it."

Jake had been thinking that the President needed to head down to Texas pretty soon to get those idiots who are runnin' for office off their asses.

"Lyndon, they seem to think the President's reelection is a done deal. There's lots of infightin' which ain't helpin' much."

"You make a good point, and this about the only time I agree with Bobby. It oughta be me goin' down there. I'm the only Texan in this Camelot shit."

"Mr. Vice President, I've got a plane to catch, but one more thing: Do you still want to be President?"

"Hell yes, I want to be President, but as things are now, that ain't gonna happen. I don't think I'm even going to be on the ticket in '64. If Bobby has anything to do with it, I'll be so far away from the Whitehouse my little cabin will only be a few miles from the frozen tundra of Siberia."

They had a good laugh, shook hands, and Jake headed to the airport. Jake sat in the limo and kept hearing his friend talk about the situation. Lyndon could use some help.

Francesco Dianatti consented to meet Jake, but there would be some stipulations: Family business would not be discussed, the meeting would be in a public place in the middle of the day, and Jake would be alone. Those requirements were not a problem for

259

Jake, and the two met, along with four associates of Francesco who were sitting at various tables around the room.

"Mr. Dianatti, I am here to discuss a very intricate situation and ask your guidance as to the best way to carry out my plans. Because of the enormity of the task at hand, I am also asking for the help of some of your most trusted associates. I realize that the scope of my request requires significant funds, and for that reason, should you consent to my request, I will transfer $3 million to your personal account plus I will pay for the expenses of the operation."

"Mr. Winslet, you make a strong argument for me being of help to you, but before going any further as to whether I accept or not, I have to know exactly what it is you need my help to do."

"Sir, no disrespect intended, but at this moment, I can't give you that information. What I can tell you is that what I have in mind will change the direction of this country, remove many elements and individuals who are threatening our very freedoms, and rebuild a military structure dedicated to keeping us free from the threat of communism. Our way of life has to be preserved."

With that, Don Dianatti rose, thanked Jake for the delicious dinner, and told him quite bluntly: "Mr. Winslet, you sound to me as though you or one of your friends is running for office. I don't need another politician. If, and when, you have a viable plan in mind and are willing to discuss it in detail, I will consider meeting with you to discuss it. Until then, don't waste my time." Francesco waved to his bodyguards and the meeting was over.

Chapter 52
The Family Life

From the moment he first saw her, he was head over heels for the girl. She was the most beautiful girl he had ever seen, and not only beautiful, but loud. When Elizabeth Louise Charles was born, you could tell she was her momma's little opera star. With lungs that strong, her career was already obvious to all who came to the Charles' home to see little Miss Princess. Born October fifth at 2 am, she was 19 inches long and 7 pounds of pure energy. Rick and Nikki's lives would never be the same.

The home was full of flowers, gifts, and cards, some of which contained considerable amounts of cash. Her birth had gotten a lot of attention, but not as much as her second day at home. The doorbell was ringing at non-stop pace and Rick just wanted to find someplace in the house where he could sit back, have a sip of something soothing, close his eyes, and rest. He put two chairs together in the upstairs utility room, got himself a pillow, and did his best to be comfortable. That lasted almost ten minutes. He finished the drink and went back downstairs to the oohs and aahs. He promised himself he would be sure to sleep sometime soon.

One very distinguished gentleman who dropped by for a momentary visit was introduced to Nikki as Dr. Carmichael, a very old friend of Rick's family. As Doc left, he told Rick that the term very old wasn't necessary. Rick gave him a hug, and told him they would talk later. "Thanks for coming by Doc. I do appreciate how much you care about us all."

There was another person at the house, but she did her best not to be seen by Nikki or Rick. Misty just wanted to see the baby. Before they knew she was there, she was gone. Misty cried, but wasn't sure if it was about the joy of the birth, or the sadness that it wasn't hers. It was both.

* * *

When it came to family gatherings, the Dianattis also knew how to put on a party. When Joey turned thirty people came from everywhere to wish him a happy birthday and extend their congratulations and respect to Joey's father. It seems like they had been in New Orleans forever, but Francesco Dianatti didn't start his small antique shop until the late thirties.

Francesco feared nothing or no one. As it was in a lot of cities in those times, the weak looked to the strong to see that things in the neighborhood had some order. Francesco wasn't going to do it alone; consequently, he asked a few friends to join him and order was put in place.

There was one caveat which everyone had to understand from the beginning: In what was known as the Quarter, no one would set up an illegal activity without first running it by what was called the neighborhood management association. You could say it might have been the precursor to today's homeowner's association but with heavy backup.

In the beginning there were those who laughed at the idea, but then the derision went away. Bobby Sutherland was a small-time crook who took on the responsibility of helping certain young women obtain business. His fee was ninety percent, and he had a most unpleasant way of managing their careers. He unwisely decided that this Francesco Dianatti guy could go to hell because nobody told Bobby Sutherland how to do anything, much less take care of his girls or how he made his money. He decided that he was going to bring in a load of heroin for some of his friends, and if he had some left over, thought he'd put it on the street to make a little extra spending money.

It got around that there were some nasty problems breaking out here and there and almost always it had to do with heroin. It was making the cops antsy, and Francesco didn't like it when the police were nervous or unhappy. He called a friend who knew Bobby and asked him to arrange a meeting for Francesco and Bobby at a nice restaurant on Canal Street.

The meeting was set for 8 pm on a Wednesday night. Francesco showed up, but Bobby sent a message that he was tied up with something else and wouldn't be there. Francesco left and nothing else was said about it until about a week later when the phone rang in the Dianatti home. Joey answered and told his dad it was for him.

"Listen you piece of shit; don't you ever think you're so big that you can arrange a sit down with me. If I need to talk to you, you can drop by my place for coffee. Otherwise, keep your fuckin' hands off my business, and never tell me that you control anything. The Quarter's plenty big enough for us all. You make one more mistake and your family will wonder where you ran off to. Do you understand me?"

According to several people who were near the corner of Bourbon and St. Louis streets on the night of August 7 at about 10 pm a small truck stopped, three guys got out and took the guy right off the street. His hands had been cut off, eyes burned out of their sockets, tongue cut out, penis was missing, and then he was shot in the head sometime later. The police had never seen anything like it before. Bobby Sutherland was very dead and about all the coroner had to say was, "This guy must have begged to die, but then again he didn't have a tongue."

All the girls who had been employed by Bobby were free to do as they wish, but they immediately chose to be a part of the local management group. Order had been restored in the Vieux Carré.

Little by little, the management group gave way to how Mr. Dianatti thought things should be run, and by 1950 nothing happened in New Orleans without first consulting the Don. There was no miscellaneous crime on the streets, and several members of the police force had homes they couldn't afford on a cop's salary.

In keeping with the rules of Bourbon Street, as the Dianatti imprint on New Orleans was sometimes called, a couple of guys from New York wanted to speak to the man himself. If Francesco didn't want to see them, he would assign someone to see what it was all about and decide later whether it was worth his time or not.

Craig Benson and Myer O'Steen would be meeting with the Don at small bar a long way from downtown New Orleans. Francesco had bought a lot of property in that area and wanted to check on some construction; thus, he told the two city boys to meet him there.

"Mr. Dianatti, thank you so much for your time and for meeting with us. We are not here to ask for any special favors, but merely to let you know what we do and how we plan to grow our business. It is our hope that many of the more affluent members of your beautiful city will become our clients simply because we have some ways to help them save on taxes and if necessary, keep certain government agencies out of their business."

"Gentleman, I'm appreciative of your desire to bring me into your confidence. No one, especially those who have labored long and hard for their wealth, wishes to pay more than they have to pay to the IRS. You have my complete support and let me also suggest that at times I may have need of your services and would ask you to honor me with your financial expertise." Craig did most of the talking and was most effusive telling the Don, "Sir, you will have our undivided attention should you need us for anything. We will be honored to assist you in any way we can."

Over time the boys from New York proved to be most helpful to the Dianatti family and thus proved they could take care of the rich and infamous. The boys were rolling in the dough, and even they couldn't believe how much was in their Swiss accounts. New Orleans was their personal gold mine.

* * *

On September 14th, 1918 in a small town in southeast Louisiana, Clarisse Meredith gave birth to John Douglas Meredith.

264

The child's father, Steven Meredith was an attorney who had only been practicing for a couple of years in this small town. It was so small that there were only three lawyers and two of them had most of the business. Steven J. Meredith, Esq. had to come up with a different clientele or starve to death.

The Meredith's home was only a short distance to the Gulf and Steven loved to fish. Steven would rather spend all day somewhere in the Gulf than be cooped up in a law office. He asked himself *how he could practice law and fish too?* That's when he decided to specialize in Maritime Law. There were hundreds of ship owners who had no clue about the law of the sea, and damn sure didn't know anything about Louisiana law. Over the next few years his practice grew as did his family. When John was nine and his little sister Anne was still in diapers, they moved to New Orleans. Clarisse was raised in New Orleans and was happy to be back. To John it was the beginning of a wondrous new adventure, and would enjoy himself immensely.

And so, began the most interesting life of John D. Meredith. The girls loved him, guys wanted to be him, and he grew up with parents that let his life go where it would go. It went a lot of places and some of them he wasn't supposed to know anything about. He went to LSU for his undergraduate degree, excelled in his classes and on the basketball court. Found the love of his life one night while he was in the student center, and a year later he married Victoria Elizabeth Antoine, got his law degree from LSU, and joined his father's firm.

John's first client was a guy who stopped by the office and told Margie, John's secretary, that he needed to see a lawyer right now. Steven was in court in Baton Rouge; so, John listened to the situation and took the case.

"Mr. Broussard, do you know my father?

"Not really, son. My good friend knows your dad and told me I should meet him. You guys work together, right?"

"We'll take good care of you, Mr. Broussard. You have my word on it."

Emmit Broussard was from Alexandria, Louisiana, and was having a lot of trouble with a neighbor's cattle trespassing on his pastures. If that worrisome problem wasn't enough, Emmit feared that one of the neighbor's Hereford steers would mate with his prime Angus breed.

The firm was hired to get things straightened out, and in a matter of days, the problems were resolved. Emmit was a much happier man, and asked John if he would take care of his other business, Broussard's Import Export, Inc.

By the time John, Jr. was born, the practice was growing quite nicely. His ability, work ethic, smarts, and charm helped grow the firm to twenty attorneys by the time his daughter Elizabeth Nicole was brought into this world. Nikki would never know until she was grown that all people didn't live like the Merediths.

Chapter 53
The Journey of a Mile Begins with the First Step

A new IBM 360 computer was being installed in the office of Darren Leitner and it was going to make life a lot easier. It could store massive amounts of information, access almost instantly, and if needed could quickly print it. Jennie was happy to have the computer, but then she found out what would have to be done first.

"Are you saying you want me to type the data onto cards and then load the cards into some machine that will put that into the computer? I don't have time for all that extra work. You need to get someone to help me or you can double my salary."

* * *

Doc got a call from an old friend who once did statistics for the Agency. His friend, Cameron, had no idea what Doc was doing nowadays, but had heard that someone in the hierarchy at the Agency knew something about Donald Meriwether's murder and thought he would be interested.

"Doc, it's just a rumor, but some of the women who at one time worked for him, said it was some society dame down there who killed him. His old secretary said that she wasn't surprised considering his taste in women."

"You know Cameron, I think I may know who that woman is, and appreciate your input on this. While I have you on the phone, have you heard the name Debra Kaye Sullivan or Williams?" Doc heard that name on the tape of a phone call between Johnny and Joey. Joey had said something about her working undercover for the feds while working at itty-bitty machines. Doc understood there was an agent of the FBI or CIA now at IBM and her name was Debra Kaye Sullivan or maybe Williams.

"Doc, her code name is Stealth and be very careful with her. She has a friend high up the food chain at the Justice Department."

Rick got an early wakeup call from Doc. "There's a woman at IBM who isn't who she says she is. She's with the FBI. We need to know why she's here. Do whatever you have to do to find out but be careful."

* * *

Jennie's unhappiness could prove to be the way that Rick needed to find out more about the girl at IBM. "Darren, I want you to go to IBM, ask for an analyst by the name of Debra Kaye Sullivan, and get her to help us with the data storage problem.

Use money, your charm, or both, but make sure she starts helping us.

She was very plain, and Jennie said she must be a lonesome spinster, but who's a spinster at thirty-five?

Debra Kaye Williams aka Debra Anne Sullivan was hired by the FBI shortly after her graduation from Stanford. She had a degree in Math and Physics and finished at the top of her class in both majors. She had an incredible mind which is why the FBI recruited her. They needed her in New Orleans to keep track of those individuals who Vanessa had discovered were linked together by money, and in some respects, politics.

"Mr. Charles, you requested meeting Debra Sullivan. Debra, this is Darren Charles and he needs your help.

"Is it Miss or Mrs. Sullivan?" Rick politely inquired.

"Just call me Debra please, Mr. Charles. How may I help you today?"

"We are having a hell of a time getting data stored on the new 360 and the secretary is threatening to leave us if we don't get her some help. Your name was given to us by an associate at the Hibernia bank; so, I have come to ask you to help us with our data input. Can you help us?"

"It would have to be for a few hours on weeknights, but yes, I can help you. Any afterhours work would be at $25 per hour.

"Any chance you could start tomorrow?"

"Please give me your address and I will be there around 6:30 depending on the traffic."

"Thank you so much Debra and we'll see you tomorrow evening."

"Darren, this is Rick. Meet me at the club for lunch. It's important."

There was no need for Rick to give Darren every detail,

but he told him enough to help him understand why they were going to give her a lot of false information to store on the system. "We'll know it's false data, but she won't; so, put enough together to keep her busy for a week or two. By then we will have had time to get to know her better."

Jennie thanked Darren for getting her some help, gave him a little peck on the cheek, and went home. About an hour later Debra arrived and took a couple of hours getting things where she wanted and setting up the other equipment in the office. Darren sat in his office reading the Wall Street Journal. He didn't want to be there, but he couldn't leave her alone at that time of night. Around ten, she stuck her head in to say goodnight and that she was leaving.

He walked her to the car, thanked her and told her he would see her tomorrow night. "Be careful going home."

The following afternoon, Rick came by to relieve Darren and when Debra came in he asked her if she had eaten. He was ordering a pizza and would she like some?

"Yes, that sounds good, thank you. The only thing I can't handle is anchovies. Just too salty for my taste."

They took a break when the pizza came and that's when he decided he would use the time to see if she would talk about herself.

"Debra, the guy at IBM said you majored in math and physics at Stanford? How in the hell did you get to IBM in New Orleans?"

"I don't have any advanced degrees and I needed a job; so, when they offered me a position as a senior analyst, I jumped at it. The job could have been in Tahiti or Northern Canada for that matter. I needed to make a living, and I love New Orleans. Are you from here Mr. Charles?"

"Please Debra, call me Rick. I'm getting older, but please, help me feel younger."

"Rick, are you aware that some of your data seems to be inconsistent?"

"What do you mean by inconsistent?"

"Let me show you."

Debra went out to her desk and brought back a file marked Broussard Account. "Here on page twelve you have transactions from 1966 through 1967 and then it goes backward to 1965. That doesn't make a lot of sense to me. Also note that the amount of funds on hand in 1965 is $68,000 more than in 1967, but when you look at this accompanying transaction file it indicates you are making the client about six-point five percent a year. How can you be making six-point five percent a year and lose $68,000? You need to have your accountant go over this material before I go any further."

"Debra, I see what you mean. I will call Darren first thing in the morning. Thank you so much for letting me know. I don't know how long it will take to get things in order, but I do hope you will continue to help us."

"Certainly, I will be happy to help you. Let me know when you're ready."

"Hey Doc, you got a second? You were right on with your description of Debra's smarts. She kicked my ass last night and probably thinks we're either defrauding our clients or stupid or both. Darren doesn't know it yet, but he's about to have a meaningful relationship with Debra."

Darren took about two seconds to say, "Oh no you don't. I'm not going to get into any kind of relationship for God or country. I'm quite sure she's more than happy just like she is. I much prefer to chase Jennie knowing I can't catch her."

"Darren, we don't have a choice. I'm married, and she knows that, but you're not and she knows that as well. I have a rather tainted reputation and you don't. We've got to know why she's here. You have to find out, and you have to do whatever it

270

takes. As bad as I hate to put it like this, this is something you have to do, and you have no choice. If it means keeping her working for a few weeks, then do it, but we need some answers and soon."

All afternoon Darren sat in his office thinking about a plan of action. He didn't want to do this, but on the other hand, he understood why it had to be him. Jennie was sitting out there being beautiful and when she left he was supposed to get some washed-out looking math genius to find him irresistible. Oh well, you do what you gotta do.

Sitting on the desk, her first night back, was a dozen red roses and a card which read: Debra, thank you so much for saving us from disaster and welcome back. Darren.

"Darren, thank you so much for the flowers. The rose is my favorite flower in the world. You are too kind."

"It's the least we could do to say how much we appreciate your attention to detail. Our accountant was most embarrassed. Would you consider joining me for a late-night dinner when you're finished? If you're too tired I certainly understand."

"Let me see how I feel when I'm finished with this first section, but thank you for the invitation."

They didn't have dinner that night, but several days later she took him up on his invitation and they enjoyed the evening. Though, in Darren's mind, the girl had no clue as to how to dress, but what she did wear looked nice on her. Debra's hair was always in a bun, she looked rather ashen, but she was attractive in a simple kind of way. He couldn't help but notice that she had a great figure.

Rick decided she had seen enough data to keep her busy and by ending her time working there she would have more time for Darren. Jennie had noticed that Darren wasn't paying as much attention to her as he had been and missed his constant need to see her. She wondered, *has he met himself a new girl?*

Jennie saw Darren's American Express bill each month and couldn't believe all the restaurants and clubs where he had recently been and obviously with someone else. *I wonder who she is?*

The phone rang four times at 7:15 pm, stopped, and then rang again five minutes later. They had agreed that Debra would call a number which was a phone booth in a town south of Baltimore. "Whatcha got for me?"

She told the guy, "I've been at this for almost six weeks and all I see are client's transactions, spreadsheets, trades, and the development of twelve limited partnerships. There are no offshore accounts, Swiss connections, and damn sure nothing to link them to the guys here or Chicago. The guy who runs the place wants to get in my pants, which I may let him do. Who knows, he may be holding something back that we need to know. I'll leave you a note before our next call."

Debra was a woman of action and decided to drop the façade and lure him into her web a giant step at a time.

"Darren, have you ever been to the Sunset Club?"

"No, I don't think so, why?"

"Would you do me a favor and meet me there on Saturday night around 11 pm?"

"Sure, but why? Are you working there too?"

"We'll talk about that on Saturday. Is it a date?"

The place was packed, and a great little jazz band was playing when he walked into the place. There were two acts being featured. The under bill was Miss Double D . . . D'licious Dalilah. She had talents most women would find nearly impossible to imitate. The top of the bill was Andrea and that's all it said.

It was after ten and Darren was looking to see if Debra was anywhere around. He assumed she was working there as a waitress, but she was nowhere to be seen. As he ordered a scotch and soda, the emcee barked, "Give a rousing round of applause for the most tantalizing woman in all of New Orleans. Ladies and Gentlemen, the woman who gives you everything . . . Andrea!"

The lights went out and then a spotlight on a woman in a black dress, black gloves, and long flowing auburn hair. The music played, she moved, and moved like nothing Darren had ever seen. Twenty minutes later the crowd was in an almost mob-like mood. More, more, more they chanted, but there was no more. Her clothes were on the stage and Andrea was gone.

Darren hadn't moved since Andrea walked on stage, but now that she was gone, he assumed he had been stood up and was getting ready to leave. As he took the last sip of his drink, there was a tap on his shoulder. "Hi Darren, how are you tonight? It was Debra, but she was wearing a dress, her hair was down, and she looked great.

"I thought you stood me up."

"Darren, honey, would I do that to you? Come with me, I want to show you something."

She took his hand and led him up some stairs, then across the bar area, and down another hall. She knocked on a door, no one answered, and she took Darren's hand and went into the vacant dressing room.

"What are we doing here?"

"Just give me a minute or two and you'll find out. I hope you can keep a secret."

She gave him a drink, asked him to sit down, and went out another door. Ten minutes later she walked back in just the way she walked onto the stage an hour ago. There was no music, and she didn't waste any time taking the dress off. She crossed over to him, put her breasts in his face and told him to suck her tits. Darren figured she had given him acid, but suck he did. Debra screamed out, "Come on baby get it hard, get me wet, and let's fuck."

He didn't care if he was on acid or not, this was the most

intense sex he had ever known. *Who is this woman?*

She wouldn't allow him to stop. He came, he rested, he came again. Andrea did him on the floor, the table, the sofa, and the desk. It went on what seemed to him to be hours, and finally he told her that he just couldn't go anymore. She took him in the shower to bathe him and when he had the slightest erection, she almost ripped it off getting him into her mouth. He was lying there thinking he had never had sex that hurt so much and been so good. When he awoke on Sunday morning he was alone. He found his clothes, slowly got dressed, and started out the door. There was a note at the foot of the door.

Baby, I hope I didn't hurt you too badly. If you want more of me at any time of the day or night, here's my private number. Please call me and soon . . . Your Andrea.

For the moment, Darren just needed some time to rest and check out what may be broken, missing, or too sore to touch. Besides that, he was famished.

"Rick, we have to talk." He left the message with the answering service and laid down on his sofa. Every muscle in his body ached; some more than others and one in particular.

"Rick, this woman gives a whole new meaning to man eating tiger. I swear I can barely walk. I am still trying to figure out how and why someone would have two personas that far apart."

"Maybe she's a schizophrenic."

"Whatever she is, when I recover I will love both of them."

"That's just great Darren. So happy you had a fun-filled weekend, but we still don't know what the hell she's here for, and now she's even more confusing. Let me see: she's a math whiz, an analyst for IBM, a secret agent, and a stripper who kills her sex partners, or at least tries? Doc's not going to believe this."

Rick called Doc about Saturday night and expressed his concerns. "This woman is trouble, and if she's doing what I think she's doing, we have to know who her contact is at the Agency. I'm not one to use rough stuff, but we're going to have to find out what she knows and why she's here. She used Darren like a doormat and now we'll have to do what we need to do.

"Rick, before we consider using brute force, we're going to let Darren enjoy another night of painful ecstasy while putting her out like a light. I'm sending you a courier with a truth serum that will knock her out and hopefully get her to start talking."

Darren gave it his best Cary Grant imitation. "Baby, I haven't been able to think about anything but my night with you. You said to call soon. I need to see you."

"I was hoping you would call. When do you want me sweety? I'm ready right now if you are. Momma's waiting."

Rick emphasized, "At some point, you are going to have to get her to have a drink or a glass of wine or just water, but you have to get this into her glass. Once she drinks it, it will only be a minute or two until she's out like a light. I'll be downstairs; so, all you have to do is shut the blinds and open them to let me know you're ready."

She didn't even take the time to put on clothes. He knocked on her door, she grabbed him, started rubbing him all over, ripped his zipper open and sat on top of him all within the first five minutes. An hour later, he asked her if they could have a drink before he showed her something new he wanted to try. She finally agreed and while her head was turned he poured a small vial of liquid into her glass. She turned it up and drank it and was ready to get on with the night's playtime. Her eyes began to flutter, and a few seconds later she was out cold.

She was out about five minutes before Rick could get upstairs. He waited a couple of minutes, and asked for her name, where she lived, and other trivial questions. Darren took over. "Honey this is your Darren; do you hear me?" She smiled and muttered something which they couldn't understand. "Andrea, do you know anyone who works for the Justice Department?"

"What's that?"

"Baby, it's part of the government in Washington."

"Oh that, yeah, I know a couple of guys there, but I won't fuck 'em."

"What about someone you talk to on the phone sometime?"

A moment went by before she spoke again, but when she did, "That's my sweet Wendell?"

"Does Wendell have a last name honey?"

"He's my little Jeff baby. He loves my body."

"Did he send you to New Orleans?"

"Mmmmm, yes."

"Did he tell you why?"

"Because he loves me."

"Any other reasons?"

"Mmmmm, yes."

"Can you tell me the reasons honey?"

"Maybe, but I'm thirsty."

"I will get you a drink when you tell me the reason why you're here." Again, a minute or two passed.

"To thank Joey."

Rick backed off a second and told Darren to see if she would say why and when.

"Darling, why would you want to thank Joey?"

"Jeffrey asked me to."

She started to move around, and her eyes were twitching. Andrea seemed to be coming to, but it was too early. Darren asked if there was any more of the serum, but there wasn't. Rick decided he had better leave. Darren laid down on the bed and pulled her against him. Fifteen minutes passed before she got up to go to the bathroom. When she got back in the bed, she immediately went to sleep. Darren left her sleeping and went to his place.

He was on his way to a meeting with a client the next day and was listening to the morning drive on WNOE when the guy started the news with, "An IBM analyst was found dead in her apartment after what authorities are calling a wild night of sex. Neighbors saw two men entering and leaving her apartment at different times in the early hours of the morning. Police are searching for those two men now." Darren damn near rear ended a police car, and managed to pour coffee all over himself and the car. It must have burned like hell, but he was oblivious to the pain. "Oh my God, we killed her?"

As soon as he got to the office, he called Rick. It was all over the local TV stations and they were describing her as a highly educated senior product analyst for IBM who had been given a synthetic chemical which must have killed soon after she ingested it into her system.

"Rick, if we didn't do this, then who did, and why?"

"It's my guess that they knew someone was on to her and had her removed. They had no way of knowing that she had given us a name before they killed her. I'm sure the coroner is going to find more than one chemical in her bloodwork."

Several days later the story in the Times-Picayune said that the regional Director of Covert Operations at the CIA, Wendell Jeffreys, would be arriving for a meeting with the New Orleans office of the FBI. What the discussions were concerning, no one knew other than certain national security individuals. Doc had his answer.

* * *

Though several large corporations, NASA, government agencies, universities, and research groups were very familiar with programming, no one in Doc's group had any idea as to how to create a program. They had to have one, but it had to be based on finance rather than on putting together the pieces of a giant puzzle called conspiracy. Who could create what they needed and how could he or she be brought in without causing a problem?

When Dr. Carmichael was at Harvard one of his classmates, Lawrence Carter, was way ahead of his time with respect to the future of computers. Lawrence later became the owner of a software patent about the progression of calculations to identify various pieces of data within a selected research group. It wasn't a perfect match, but it would have to do for the moment.

"Lawrence, this is Davis Carmichael. Do you happen to remember me from our days at Harvard?"

"I do remember you Davis. Who could ever forget your treatise on the therapy of laughter? By the way, did you ever go any further with that?"

"No, my career went another direction, but thank you for remembering. Lawrence, I need to ask a huge favor, which I will be happy to pay for, but it has to be kept secret."

"Davis, I'm not much into secrecy, but what can I do for you?"

Doc went on to say, "I can't discuss it on the phone; so, would it be possible to meet at your office? Two days later they had brunch, and discussed at length what doc needed.

"Let me see if I understand this correctly Davis. You need a program, dressed in financial clothing, which will use an immense amount of data to help create a possible connection between the good guys and the bad guys in some sort of clandestine undertaking?"

"That about says it all."

"When do you need it?"

"Six months ago, if not sooner."

"Davis, something like this could take weeks, maybe months, and cost a ton of money. Are you paying for this?"

"Indirectly, but the cost isn't the issue. It's the time. If you can do this for me, I need for you to do whatever it takes to get it done as quickly as possible."

"Let me think about this for a day or two, and I will call you with my decision."

"Anything you can do will be most appreciated."

It took three days, but when Lawrence called, he said he could do this, but he would need at least a month, maybe five weeks and the cost would be $150,000. Doc agreed to that and headed to Lake Charles, Louisiana. Everyone would be at this meeting.

* * *

This was a most unusual situation, and everyone had to be together on this. Going forward was most likely going to be the most dangerous time they had known as a group. Every person in attendance would be balancing their lives on the edge of what they were calling the most vile conspiracy ever known to this country.

If they were right, it could mean disaster for a lot of lives, reputations, legacies, and the unbelievable shamelessness of those who set out to destroy this great country for money and power. The pieces had been placed on the chess board. All that remained were the moves toward checkmate.

Doc spoke first. "Gentlemen, we've been together a long time now, done some crazy things, and some of you have damn near been killed having all this fun. I thank you from the bottom my heart for your endurance, strength, and tenacity.

"Because of you, we now have dates, times, places, people, and other connecting data. What we have to do now of course is keep narrowing the players, the money, and the time sequences in

279

that order. That may require some very up close and personal work with those who may not necessarily like what we're doing.

"Because of the work you've already done, we now know that the assassination of the President began in New Orleans and Chicago. There's more to look at before we know for sure why, but we do have a good idea. I'm positive about the first two layers of the conspiracy, but without linking that to the real power, without corroborating all the pieces of evidence, we have nothing.

"Here's the last thing that we're going to talk about while we're together: What do we do with our findings, our facts once we are finished? Who can be trusted with something this large?

"How do we go about breaking it to the country? Do you give up the names of those who cannot defend themselves? Do we do anything other than write down what we have and leave it for future generations to ponder? What if we get part of it wrong? I leave you with this question: What would you do?"

The meeting went on for several more hours as they discussed the separate agenda of each man for the next few months. Sometime around ten that night they said goodbye, and though they didn't know it at the time, this would be the last time that any of them would ever see all their cohorts again.

Chapter 54
Bringin' in the Shivs

It was only forty degrees, but the wind blowing in off the lake made it feel like it must be zero. Carl called Vinnie to set up a meet at Al's on Cermak Rd. around seven the next night. Vinnie had been gone a couple of days to attend an old friend's funeral in Lake Charles; so, business was lagging a few days behind. Carl wanted to get caught up and had a new job for Vinnie.

"Hey man, sorry about your friend. Where did you know him from?"

"We went way back, but Davey boy just couldn't stay away from the broads. I told him when he married her that she could be trouble. The bitch killed him with a baseball bat when he stayed out all night with an old friend named Shirley. The Mrs. was very touchy about things like that. Whatcha got for me?"

"Vin', I'm sending you to LA for a couple of weeks. Somethin' ain't right and I want you to find out what it is and get it fixed. Here's the name of the guy you need to see, but don't let him know why you're there. I think the guy's been takin' a few dips too many in my pool and if you find out that he has, I want you to fix the problem. Got it?"

"Do I let him know who I work for?

"Let me suggest that you let him think about it for a day or two while you ask around. These are a couple of people you can trust. Joe Pistano runs a small pawn shop and will give you some contact names. Liz, and we'll leave her last name out of this, can be found working for one of those disc jockeys who do the big parties out there. She's been playin' the guy you're going to meet, and when she's not pursuin' her acting career, she works for me. Liz is a hot little broad, and always watch your back when she's around.

"I want you goin' out there like you fuckin' own the place. Scare the boy shitless and decide what we need to do with Benny boy. Do whatever you gotta do, but make sure he's the problem. If I'm right, then see to it that I don't have to worry about him anymore. Capiche?"

Vinnie was on a 10:30 flight the next morning and hoping he wouldn't be out there too long. He and Darlena were very much in love, and they both hated it when he had to leave for heaven knows where. The love of her life just got back from a funeral and now he was leaving again. Vin' told her he would be in LA and not to worry. He'd be back in two or three weeks.

They had gotten a place near her restaurant and were even talking about getting married at some point in the very near future. Her father insisted she bring Vinnie home to meet the family before going any further with all the foolishness about a marriage.

Don Cordero Velasquez had to approve of his daughter's choice, and at this point had no idea his daughter, a saint, was living out of wedlock with a man, not to mention a man who was a member of a Mafia family. Had he known about Darlena's living arrangement, she would have been forcefully removed from America, disinherited, and disgraced while Vinnie would not have seen his next birthday. It's not good to fool with old Spanish families, which have more wealth and power than most countries.

The guy's name was Benny Ludlow, and old Benny was having a little too much fun to suit the boys back in Chicago, especially Carl. Vinnie wore his best Armani suit to see Benny and was told by his secretary, Clarissa, that Benny was in meetings all day.

"Baby, I don't know who your boss is meeting with today, but give him this card and see if it frees up any of his time."

Evidently, she knew that anything about Chicago meant that she should give her boss the card. Moments later, Benny came out all smiles and apologizing for the delay. "Sometimes business takes longer than expected. How can I help you today Mr. Pertinelli?"

"Benny, I understand how things can get sort of out a control, and I'm here to maybe help you with that. Why don't we have dinner tonight and discuss my reason for being here in more detail?"

Before Benny could say anything, Vinnie suggested a place Carl had told him about, and they would meet around nine. "That okay with you Benny?"

"I'll be there."

Vinnie turned to leave and then turned back to Benny. "And one other thing, don't bring a friend. Nice to have met you Clarissa."

The rest of his day would be spent going to see the two people Carl had suggested he get to know. Joe Pistano knew Vinnie might be dropping by and had his favorite cabernet waiting for the visit. "It's always a pleasure to meet one of Carl's friends, Vin'; so, how can I help you?"

"I need to know more about Benny Ludlow."

"Oh man, you want nothin' to do with that guy. He's stupid and he's crazy. The guy thinks he's a big player out here, and some of those who disagreed may be in the tar pits. If you're trying to get yourself killed, suggest that he's a two-bit player in a C-note game. Best way to approach him is to let him think you need his expertise to get things done. Girl's say he's got a short dick and giant ego, but make sure you don't mention either one."

"One other question Joe: How can I get in touch with Liz?"

"This is her number, but don't tell her I gave it to you."

Vinnie called her. "Liz, my name is Vinnie Pertinelli, and I'm out here on some business for a friend in Chicago. Would you have some time in the next three or four hours to have a cup of coffee or a drink with me?"

"Who's your friend, Vinnie?"

"Let's just say he's a friend of the family."

"Yeah, I've got a couple of hours." She gave him her address and told him she could see him around 3:30 or thereabouts. "You might want to leave at least an hour early with all the afternoon traffic."

She opened the door, took a long look and smiled. "Well, aren't you some hot shit, Vinnie."

Liz was most proud of her looks and wanted to make sure the new stranger in town didn't forget her. She handed him a drink and showed him to the pool area.

"Well, baby, what can I do to you?"

"Tell me what you know about Benny Ludlow."

"You mean old pencil dick? Not much to say if I want to maintain my present facial structure. The boy's got a bad temper. Thinks he's hot shit, but he's scared to death of the boys where you come from. Should I be scared of you Vinnie baby? Benny can handle the wetbacks out here, but not so much you Italians back east. You got business with Benny?"

"Let's just say, I need to meet with him about some accounting questions. He ever taken you to Vegas?"

"Yeah, we've been out there a few times. He likes a beautiful woman on his arm until he starts playing craps, and then I could pretty much do whoever or whatever I wanted. Do you think I'm beautiful Vinnie?"

"Yeah babe you're a knockout. When was the last time you were there with Benny?"

"It's probably been four, maybe five months, why?"

"Liz darlin' you want to make an extra five grand?"

"What do I have to do, fuck you upside down?"

"Honey, if you're horny that's one thing, but I'm not; so, do you want the money or not?"

"You know Vin' you're not a lot of fun. Sure, I want the money, but what do I have to do to get it?"

"I want you to get Benny to take you to Vegas for the next two or three days. I need him to be gone. Can you do that for me?"

"Do I have to sleep with the bastard?"

"You can do what you damn well please, but you have to make sure he's there for at least an overnight stay. Can you do that?"

"And for that you're going to give me five big ones?"

"That's it baby."

"Honey, you can stay or go. I have bags to pack."

"Call this number when you and he arrive. If at any time he starts heading back early, call me. Here's a thou to buy something sexy you might not wear very much."

"Vin', I think I love you."

Dinner with Benny was reasonably friendly. Vin asked him a lot of questions about his business, asked about his very stunning secretary, and bluntly told him that he was out here to look at the books. Benny was incensed at that, threw down his napkin, and walked out. Vin smiled, knowing that Benny was guilty as sin.

Liz started earning her money the next day when she and Benny arrived at Caesar's Palace on a very warm Tuesday afternoon. Just like clockwork, when they arrived, he went to the bar, she went to put on something sexy, and then she joined him at the bar. He would have a couple of vodkas on ice and head to the tables. After winning or losing for an hour or so, he would give her a couple of thousand to play the slots or she could hit the roulette table when she got bored with the machines. Whichever she did, he didn't care. All Benny did was play Mr. Bigtime for as long as possible. Liz knew better than to ask, but always wondered where he got all his money. For a small-time crook, he always took a bundle to Vegas.

Vinnie watched Clarissa lock the place up and head home. He had sent her a dozen red roses to thank her for being so nice to him when he unexpectedly dropped by the office. She was carrying them to her car and was more concerned about the wind than she was about someone following her.

She didn't live far from the office, but the apartment complex was gated. There was a phone box there, but he didn't know her apartment number; thus, he had to wait a while until he could walk in behind a someone's car. Once in, he saw her car in front of number 188, he pressed the doorbell.

Clarissa stood there a second and then said, "Mr.

Pertinelli, what a nice surprise. Thank you so much for my flowers, but how did you find out where I lived?"

"I hope you don't mind, but when I'm trying to ask someone out to dinner, I'm quite tenacious."

"May I call you Vinnie?"

"Yes, by all means, please do."

"Vinnie I would love to have dinner with you, but I can't tonight. I'm sorry, but I already have a date. He's the cutest guy in LA." She stepped into the next room and came out holding Mr. Michael A. Justin's hand.

"Vinnie, meet my son Mikey. You're more than welcome to have pizza with us, but you probably don't have to eat pizza too often."

"Are you kidding? I'm from Chicago."

She fed Mikey, and let him play until eight, and then she took him to bed, read him a story, and sang him to sleep. When she came back Vinnie was looking at a magazine she had left on the sofa.

"Is this you?"

"That's me. I played a nurse one week on a soap opera, and they took a photo of one of my scenes. They were actually there to take a picture of the two main characters, and I happened to be in the scene." She smiled and told him it helped her pay another two month's rent.

"Clarissa, this is none of my business, but how did you get mixed up with Benny Ludlow?"

"He was on the set of a game show I was doing, asked me if I would like a full-time job, and offered me the job as his secretary for a lot more money than I had ever made before."

"Has he asked more of you than just being a secretary?"

"Mr. Pertinelli, I don't care for the implications you're making, and you can leave now if you are set on making me out to be a slut."

"I'm sorry; I didn't mean to do that at all. I'm just concerned about his temperament in case you turn down one of his advances. You see I know him much better than you do. My sincere apologies to you. I thank you for the pizza, the conversation, and hope we have a chance to do it again. Tell Mikey it was nice to meet him. Goodnight."

It was nine-thirty and time for Vin to head to Benny's office. Now that he knew that Clarissa was probably all tucked in next to Mikey, and Benny was chasing sevens at Caesar's Palace, he could get to work.

The security was a joke. Vinnie searched the office two or three times, and had decided Benny must keep his records somewhere else, but where? He was sitting at the desk looking the room over when he turned to look at the bookshelf to his left. His right shirt sleeve snagged on something barely sticking out from the edge of the desk. When he pushed it, a door under the middle desk drawer opened. Three hours later he had photographed every document and replaced them all very neatly. If he were in there much longer, he'd be meeting Clarissa as she came to work.

Thursday afternoon he got a call at his hotel from Liz. They were on their way back and Benny was all smiles. He had won nine thousand, but acted like it was ninety. Vinnie told her he would see her tomorrow to give her the rest of her money she so dutifully earned.

When Vinnie got to Liz's apartment she offered him a glass of wine and told him that she should have charged twenty thousand. "The guy is just greasy, and rude, and socially unacceptable. I mean it's not like I'm Miss Priss, but the guy doesn't even brush his teeth for God's sake. Yuk, and I mean yuk."

"Baby, did you have to sleep with him?"

"He was getting ready to beat the crap out of me if I

didn't, but thankfully he passed out. I left him lying in his piss. I tell you the guy's a fuckin' pig."

Vin gave her the money and stopped to call Benny's office. He told Clarissa he would be there in about thirty minutes.

When he walked in, she had on a dark red dress that fit her just right. "Clarissa, you look beautiful today. How's our favorite Hollywood child actor to be?"

"He's fine, but I always hate to have to leave him at daycare. Knock quietly, she whispered, "I think he has a hangover."

The guy looked like he hadn't slept in a week and was drinking some awful looking green goo from a fruit jar. Benny didn't get up and didn't say much.

"Benny, sorry you feel so bad, but I need for you to very carefully stand up and put your gun on the desk."

"Who do you think you are coming here telling me what to do. You can get your ass out now or I'll blow it out of here."

"Benny, Benny, Benny, settle down. You're going to have a heart attack. One more time, put the gun on the desk." Vinnie showed Benny a very large handgun he lovingly referred to as Sweety and Benny decided to place his toy on the desk.

"Now that we have that taken care of, let's move on to my next request: Benny, my boy, you've been really bad. Did you know that there is $387,658 missing from Carl's account? Where do you suppose it is?"

"Wait a minute Vinnie, there ain't none of Carl's money missing and you know it."

"The other day Carl and I were having this talk and he took time to share his concerns about money that he seemed to think was being stolen from him. As you well know, Carl has to account for everything when he meets with his boss, and you know who his boss is, don't you Benny? Carl has an excellent accounting system, and he sent me out here to, shall we say, audit the books."

When Vinnie dropped a very thick file of photos on the desk, Benny's attitude seemed to change. "Where did you get these? I've never seen these before in my life."

"There you go again, doin' that lyin' thing, and you have to know how much I hate liars. Move back and let me show you something Ben old buddy. Vinnie pressed the button and there was that secret door coming open.

"Okay, here's the deal. I want a briefcase packed with $500,000 in cash at my hotel by noon tomorrow or you and me will be going on a one-way fishing trip. Let's see that gives you twenty-five hours and eighteen minutes. See you tomorrow. Vinnie picked up Benny's gun and put it in his pocket. "Oh, and if you decide to leave, that would be a terrible mistake. The traffic in LA can get a person killed."

Vinnie had sent Rick a small package with a copy of the photographs from the desk. When he called to let him know about the parcel, he also told Rick that unless this guy came across with the goods, "I may have to kill the guy, and you know I didn't sign up for that scenario."

Rick thought about it for a minute, and told Vinnie to see what happened, let him know if Benny didn't pay, and in the meantime, Rick would call Doc. "We'll get you through this Vin. Just hang in there, and for God's sake be careful."

Vinnie had let Carl know that Benny hadn't showed up with the money. "It may take me a day or two, but I'll find him, and then I may have to tell Clarissa she's out of a job. I hate that for her."

Benny solved one of Vinnie's problems by doing a jackknife off a forty-story building. Vin still didn't know where the money was, but Carl thought Vinnie had thrown the guy off the building. "Vinnie, you're really bad. Did he splatter much?"

Carl laughed so hard he almost had tears in his eyes. "Damn boy, I would have loved to see that guy's look just as he went off the side. Good job man."

When Vinnie got back to Chicago, Carl said it had never been about the money. What he needed to know was who Benny was using to cut out part of the family's business. Benny got greedy and got caught and got dead, which meant nothing to Carl. The family now knew the names and places of those who had been getting business that didn't belong to them, and so did Doc.

Rick, Doc, and Chip had been going over every document that Vinnie had sent them from the secret file at Benny Ludlow's office. Not only was it exposing a large smuggling operation, but there had been four large payments made to one of the largest trucking companies in the Northeast. The four payments of $250,000 each came from a bank in Paris by way of Seattle. On four different pieces of paper on four different dates there was an inset of a photo of words and numbers which read: 6608-PB Party Pre-Pay. What the hell does that mean, they wondered. Attached to that information was a memorandum on CIA letterhead.

Confidential

From my perspective, it seems as if there's going to be a civilian uprising bordering on revolution. The Viet Nam war continues to escalate with more American service men and women dying for what is nothing more than a Viet Nam civil war. The military establishment used the domino effect to lobby Congress and the President to keep South Viet Nam from falling to the communists from the North. They told us all that if that happened, Southeast Asia would fall to communism. Obviously, politicians bought into it, we are still fighting, and the arms manufacturers keep raking in the billions. How many shares of their stock does Congress own?

One can't turn on the television at night without killing and mayhem overseas and in the South. Martin Luther King, Jr. got much of the civil rights legislation enacted by Johnson. President Johnson was under pressure from every front, and what he didn't need was that damned Bobby Kennedy getting in his way. He had just about enough of that arrogant little bastard, but if Bobby wants to get us out of the war, he will have to do it himself. Lyndon is done. He announced he would not be running for another term as President. Something must be done and soon.

4/1/68

Another piece of information in the copies, which didn't seem to fit, was a map of a part of Memphis. On the front was an inset of a small area of Memphis, Tennessee, and on the back were three letters: JWH. The only other item they had found which had anything to do with Memphis was a receipt for payment to a trucking company in Boston for moving office furniture to Memphis. They were mystified as to why money spent to move office furniture was in this batch of documents. After all, Benny had these in his private filing system which was primarily about various routes and financing for illegal drugs. Rick and Chip assumed that office furniture was a cover for drugs, but to Memphis?

Chapter 55
She's Back

Nancy Townsend's plane landed at LaGuardia at 9:10 am. Her meeting in downtown Manhattan was set for 10:30 with lunch at noon. From there she would have a car take her to Bristol, Connecticut, where she and her friend would have a quiet dinner and talk about the old days.

Wendell Jeffreys was as bad as they make them, and she loved him for it. The worse he was, the more it turned her on. Her favorite was the mink handcuffs he would use to completely subdue her and perform raucous and extremely provocative acts of his sexual fantasies. She loved the pain, the energy, and the feeling that she no longer had to control everything. As he slapped her ass and bit her nipples, she thought she might keep him.

There had been a lot of changes at Headquarters and after Donald Meriwether's tragic death, Wendell had been promoted to the new regional Director of Special Operations, and started cleaning house immediately upon taking over. First to go was anyone who had ever even considered that Wendell was not qualified or had discussed the possibility of someone else having the job. The second thing he did was to make a list of all the field agents who could also make extra money with a rifle.

Though he loved the title and the perks, Wendell wasn't happy about the money he was paid in such a wealth-oriented environment. A load of money had been skimmed off the top at several agencies, and he had become the master of that technique. His Swiss account had over four million dollars in it, and was available for him at any time. Myer O'Steen had set that up for him.

After Nancy and Wendell's very intense sex romp, they showered, dressed, and ordered a bottle of scotch. "Baby, you're the best, but somehow I felt you didn't have your hard in it today." To him, it appeared she was laughing at him. He didn't take disrespect well.

"Listen, bitch, I'll let you know when I need your assessment of my intensity or size. . . Do you understand?"

"Okay, oh great leader." He hated it even more when she could tell him to fuck off so casually. Wendell seemed to be under a lot stress, which made him more than dangerous.

"Sweetheart, when you get back to New Orleans, I need you to do me a big favor."

"Sweetie, I don't do favors without something in return, but you already knew that."

"There will be a special gift box waiting for you at the Roosevelt with your little happy inside. Also, inside will be the favor I'm asking you to do for me. It's not dangerous, and you might even turn it into a bit of fun time before you head home."

"You're not going to tell me now? How rude."

Wendell was dressed and, on his way out the door. "Bye babe and hope to do you again soon." She indicated he was number one.

* * *

Johnny had been a busy man lately. The organization had been growing very quickly, some of the families in the east were having a lot of problems which caused some business to literally go south.

Joey D. had narrowed in on the drugs, and was either buying, selling, smuggling, and distributing or all the above at any given time. He expected Johnny and his boys to keep things running smoothly. Almost three years ago there were several lost

293

shipments, but the losses seemed to stop around the end of '63. Though he had nothing to do with the decrease in the number of losses, Joey gave Johnny the credit and a lot more authority.
The phone rang, and someone yelled upstairs, "Hey, Johnny, some babe needs you." He yelled back, "Don't they all?"

"Yeah, this is Johnny, what can I do you for?"

"Hey love, it's your favorite ex-girlfriend."

"What's the matter baby, you get the wrong number?"

"I have something I need to give you and it looks so pretty; besides, I'm wearing something you might like to take off while I'm there. Could I come over now or are you going to make me wait?"

"Sure. Come on over."

Since Joey had decided he didn't want to put up with all her antics, maybe a little romp with her might not be too bad.

Nancy had moved a lot of money over the past three or four years and stolen even more. She was smart, devious, and if necessary, would kill in a heartbeat. She loved the spotlight, the diamonds, and men, in that order. Some had suggested that she stay out of the spotlight.

She walked up the stairs much to the delight of the men downstairs, knocked on Johnny's door, and without him saying come in, she was already inside.

The box she was carrying was wrapped in bright red paper. She tossed it on his desk, went to the bar, and Johnny barely had a moment to say hello. He didn't open it right away. Instead, he walked over to the bar, put his hands on her ass, and kissed her neck. Sure, she liked it, but what didn't she like he thought.

"Johnny, I'm staying in the city tonight. I'm at the Roosevelt, 428; so, if you have some time, let's have something to help me sleep better."

He gave her a gratuitous hug and thanked her for bringing the package over. "I'll see you later baby, and you better be there when I get there."

It was a busy day and before he could open the gift there were two more phone calls. Nothing important to concentrate on; so, while he was talking to a guy in Cleveland, Johnny picked up the box and opened it. There was a small envelope marked For Johnny Only. He continued to talk to his friend as he began to open the envelope. There was $50,000 in cash and a note which read: She's talking to the Feds. Take her for a long ride. Here's money for the gas. Johnny damned near dropped the phone. He told his friend he would call him back later.

As he looked at the blue jay on the windowsill, he was smiling; so, the bitch is trying to cover her ass and keep the money. Johnny was going to enjoy the sex, but even more was knowing he would be the last thing she would remember.

No one seemed to know where she was. Her secretary knew about the trip to New York, but Nancy was supposed to have been back three days ago. At first, her little clique of friends assumed she had met some dashing man and they had flown off to Paris or Rome. Knowing her as they did, she could be anywhere. But usually when she had one of her spur-of-the-moment trysts, she would call in laughing and say where she was. Nancy would never say how long she would be gone, but most of the time, she tired of the guy in two or three days.

"Hey Wendell, how you doin'? . . . Yeah, I got the car all cleaned up, filled up with gas, and I think I can get at least $2500 for it. Nice car, smooth ride, and you know how rough some of those roads are in South Louisiana. . . You too and talk to you later."

As far as the rest of the world ever knew, Nancy Townsend's disappearance would forever be an unsolved case.

The funeral was huge. Judges, Hollywood stars, financial magnates, the New Orleans old-money set, and everyone who was anyone were there. Had she been able to hear the accolades, she would have been so proud to find out that she wasn't really such a selfish bitch. She was more like a woman who knew what she wanted and reached out to get it. Back in a small hole deep in the ground just north of Venice, Louisiana, was a woman's body encased in a block of cement looking just as she did when Johnny had finished with her. He had merely removed the jewelry.

Chapter 56
Avast Ye Matey

On April 18, 1968, Wendell Jeffreys handed in his resignation, citing his desire to spend more time with his family and to some extent simply take some time to rest. His job at the Agency was total stress, and even more so when he chose to become involved in murder. Wendell loved to sail and just as soon as he and the family arrived in Cape Cod, he began getting his prized possession, a sleek 29 ft. Soling, ready for a run to Bermuda. He and a small crew left on April 26th, expecting to arrive on or before May 3rd. They weren't racing; just relaxing and having a great time. When they didn't arrive by May 5th, the Coast Guard began searching for the boat. It had last been seen by an oil tanker about two hundred miles NNW of Bermuda. Two more weeks went by and still no word, no sighting, no wreckage.

Somewhere in the deep abyss of the Atlantic was a small Soling sailboat. Wendell and the crew had been shot, and the small bomb in the bow had made sure the boat would sink quickly never to be seen again.

Since sailing can be dangerous at times, foul play was never considered. This must have been a tragic accident caused by a sudden storm, or a failure of the equipment. The North

Atlantic in early Spring can be deadly at times. The only problem with that type of reckoning was that they had all the latest radio and location equipment on board. What could have taken the vessel down so quickly that it didn't have time for an SOS? No one could answer that, but after four months of inquiries, it was determined that the sinking with all hands aboard was an act of God.

Carl knew why he didn't like to be on the water. On their way to meet Wendell's boat, he had thrown up numerous times, and wasn't in a good mood when he got back.

Big Jim had asked Wendell about certain documents, and determined Wendell was lying when he said he didn't have any of those documents. During that same conversation, Wendell did say that he was going to sail to Bermuda just to get away and have some time to relax.

Carl was told to do whatever was necessary to make sure not one single piece of that boat or Wendell ever arrived in Bermuda. He decided there was one way to take care of this and not worry about any signs of a hit. While Wendell's boat was in dry dock, a location device was secretly attached under one of the bunks. All the Chris Craft had to do was follow the beeping sounds until they could see the little sailboat. They caught up with it about one hundred miles from Bermuda.

Before any of the crew on the sailboat could do anything, shots were fired, and all were dead. Each body was tied to some part of the boat, the blast put a large hole in the bow and within ten minutes it had sunk, and the Chris Craft was on its way back to Bermuda. The second and only CIA link had been removed.

Vinnie had managed, at great risk of pissing Carl off, to not be available for the boat ride. He had never said no to Carl, but this was about a woman. "Listen Carl, I'm not tryin' to mess you up here, but Darlena is having two big occasions happening on the same day, and I want to be there." He lied, but it was imperative to do so. Carl as much said what he was going to do, and Vinnie wasn't about to go with him. He did call Doc, but by the time Doc got the message from the answering service, Wendell, the boat, and the crew were already gone. There was no doubt anymore as to one of the connections. David and Vince could directly link the Vinzzetti family and the money to New Orleans.

* * *

On November 17, 1963, $2.8 million was transferred from a small bank in Bermuda to a Swiss account and from there to a small bank in Seattle, Washington. The name on the account was Northeast Moving Company. That same day, another $1.1 million dollars was wired from another Swiss account to another bank in Montreal and from there to the Vieux Carré Trust in the Bahamas.

Two days later, a wire transfer in the amount of $1 million was sent from the Vieux Carré Trust to the firm of Benson and Osteen earmarked for purchase of certain financial entities, one of which was a $40,000 promissory note in the name of J. L. Rubenstein aka Jack Ruby.

No one would have ever known those facts had it not been for the information that was kept in Benny Ludlow's secret compartment. These documents should not have existed, but somewhere in the back of someone's mind was the idea that they needed to cover their ass or use it for blackmail.

In the data which Vince had photographed, was a note from Craig Benson to Joey Dianatti, which looked more like a physics problem than a letter. Darren spent almost three weeks deciphering the damn thing, but finally, something they could use.

Doc was convinced that Benson and Osteen were in the middle of the plot to kill the President. They were the money men, knew where the funds came from, and to whom and where it went. It was time to put the squeeze on the boys to see how they handled the hot seat. They knew that neither one of the partners would go down with the ship. Who would they reach out to first?

Justin Maxwell would become the perfect FBI agent, and David was going to be moved back to New Orleans for whatever time it took to make Craig and Myer uncomfortable. David had the perfect look of an SEC attorney. Doc would get whatever identification the two would use during the scam. The danger to both men was how both families reacted to the scrutiny of Benson and Osteen's financial information. The partners knew they should be constantly looking over their shoulder. It made certain people extremely nervous when suits began asking questions.

* * *

Darren and Jennie were going over some financial information when Justin stopped to ask for Craig Benson. Jennie pointed him to the other office, and Darren knew the plan was underway.

"I'm sorry Mr. Maxwell, but neither of the partners have arrived. I'm sure they will be here within the hour. Would you care to wait, or would you rather I make you an appointment?" Having seen his badge, she assumed he wouldn't take well to having an appointment; so, she wasn't surprised when he said he would wait.

Thirty minutes passed before Myer came in, telling Marjorie how much he had enjoyed getting to play eighteen holes on Sunday. "You know Marjorie, I need to take more time off and play the game more often. I might even break ninety if I had time to practice."

"Mr. Osteen, you have someone waiting to see you."

As Myer turned, Maxwell showed him his FBI badge, and suddenly the smile went away. "Mr. Osteen, I'm senior agent,

Justin Maxwell, and I need to ask you a few questions if you don't mind."

"What is this about, Mr. Maxwell."

"Just a few questions about a few of your clients."

"I'm not sure I can do that. My clients trust me not to discuss any of their business with anyone."

"Are you an attorney, Mr. Osteen?"

"No, why?"

"Then there is no attorney-client privilege, Mr. Osteen. If necessary, I can get a subpoena. Now, let's sit down in your office and visit."

"Shouldn't we wait for my partner? He's an attorney."

"Is he the firm's attorney, or your attorney?"

"No, but shouldn't he be here too?"

"Mr. Osteen, how long have you and your partner been in business?"

"Mr. Maxwell, I'm just not comfortable with this. May I call our company attorney?"

"Certainly, but be sure to tell him I'm not here to ask about anything you may or may not have done."

Craig and their attorney arrived at about the same time, and after introductions and some discussion, it was decided that they would meet tomorrow morning at ten in the attorney's office. Johnny had several calls from Craig after Justin left, and it was apparent that Craig was badly rattled.

"Hey man, settle down. You have nothing to worry about. You did destroy all those files, didn't you?"

"Sure, Johnny, but why are the Feds even here? Do you think someone has ratted on us?"

"If they had, you wouldn't be the only person they'd be talkin' to. We'd all be in the can."

In Johnny's own way, he was trying to calm Craig, but at the same time wondering how long the partners would hold up, and if they would risk bringing the whole thing down on themselves but give up the Dianatti and Vinzzetti families to save their asses.

"Craig, listen to me very carefully. If it should cross your mind to make a deal, be aware that nobody talks and lives to tell about it. You understand?"

"Yeah, sure, Johnny, I know how it works." As if Craig didn't have enough to worry about, Marjorie told him he had a long-distance call from David Flynn with the SEC.

"Yes, Mr. Flynn, what can I do for you? . . . No, I'm not sure I do, but I can check for you. . . . Certainly, I would be happy to meet with you. What day did you have in mind? . . . Tuesday will be fine. Ten o'clock okay with you? . . . I look forward to meeting you too. . . . Goodbye, Mr. Flynn." He sat there for a moment, and then went in to talk to Myer.

"What do you suppose they're looking for?"

"Hell, I don't know, and at this moment, I want to get away as far as I can. I'm not cut out for all this intrigue. We're going to have to lie a lot, and hope we don't get caught, isn't that about it?"

Craig's mind was headed in one direction: I know that they can never find the files, or we'll never see the light of day again, and I don't mean solitary confinement. Johnny will have us at the bottom of the lake and never look back. We talk, we're dead. I need to talk to Johnny about those files.

Once again, Johnny told him to calm down and quit worrying. Sources in the FBI told Joey that they didn't know anything about any investigation; so, stop worrying about it.

Tuesday morning was cold and rainy. Craig and Myer were preparing for their meeting with David Flynn at ten by going over the things which might be part of the conversation.

"Gentlemen, your appointment is here."

"Mr. Flynn, come in, and welcome to our office. Would you like some coffee?"

"No, I'm fine, thank you."

"Have you spent much time in New Orleans?"

"Yes, I'm quite familiar with your city. I love it here."

"Will you have time to have lunch with us today?"

"Let's just see how things go, and we'll talk about lunch later."

The meeting began and after a couple of hours of basic questions, they took a coffee break. It was during this time that David asked Craig a different kind of question. "Tell me, Craig, is it true that there's a lot of collusion between Dianatti family and the police here?"

"Let's just say that that they cooperate to make sure that things run smoothly and quietly. Why do you ask?"

"Personally, I think more cities should let the mob control the small-time hoods. It keeps the good guys from having to worry about the everyday problems in the neighborhood. Would you agree with that?"

"You know, I don't really think about it at all. We take care of our clients, and let everything else take care of itself."

They went back to the questions and that went on until around twelve-thirty. David was satisfied he had covered most everything, and they decided to have lunch at a small Italian café on Magazine Street.

David told them both how much he enjoyed the hospitality and thanked them for their cooperation. He hoped he would see them again the next time he was in New Orleans.

A week later, Craig received a thank you card from David saying that he appreciated the time they took to help him with his investigation.

"He's investigating something?" Myer wasn't too keen on that idea, and thought they should call him and ask him what he was looking into.

"No, Myer, let's not act like we're concerned; otherwise, he might be coming back again. We'll just leave things where they are for now."

Speaking of the devil, Marjorie let them know that Mr. Flynn was on the phone. "David, we were just talking about you. How are you this morning? . . . No, I don't think so, why? . . . Let me look at my calendar. . . . Yes, Tuesday would be fine, and may I ask the purpose of your visit? . . . I see, and what's the name of the company? . . . Yes, we'll have whatever you need. . . . You too, uh huh, see you on Tuesday at ten."

Myer wanted to know what the hell that was about. With a slight grimace, Craig answered, "He said that he had found something he needed to look into further and thought it best we meet in person. He wants to see our file on the Northeast Moving Co."

"How the fuck does he know about the Northeast Moving Co.? It's just a front for God's sake. There's a leak somewhere and we've got to tell Joey."

Craig looked deep in thought, waiting a moment to respond. "You know I'm not sure that would be a good idea. For all we know this could be a ruse to see if we've got our shit together. Let's do this: We'll meet with David, see what he knows or doesn't know and then we'll decide what our next step will be. I have an idea someone could be playing us."

* * *

Rick went to see Johnny on Monday morning to ask a question about a phone call he had received late last night. "Do you know anything about a moving company somewhere near Boston?"

"No, why?"

"Whoever the guy on the phone was, told me you and I needed to talk about the moving company, and to get our stories straight. I don't know anything about a moving company and that's why I'm here."

"Ricky boy, I have no idea what your call was about. If we move something, it damn sure isn't going to be with some moving company in Boston. I'm sorry, but I got a ton of things to do. We'll talk later, okay?"

Rick left and a minute later Joey's phone rang. "We need to talk about that new office furniture."

Fifteen minutes later at Joey's place, "Somethin's goin on here and I'm not sure I like it. My boy was just here and said he got a call about a movin' company in Boston. You and I know about that; so, who else could be makin' calls about it?"

Joey thought a minute and told Johnny to see Craig.

Johnny looked puzzled. "Does he know anything about this?"

"Find out."

Craig was extremely uptight and irritable has hell. "Johnny, I don't know what's going on here, but the guy from the SEC wants to meet tomorrow about the same damn thing. He wants to see the file about the Northeast Moving Co., and there is no file."

It was decided that Joey needed to call Big Jim and find out if anyone has been sniffing around up there asking about the moving company.

Carl got on a chartered flight and headed to New Orleans. He was to be at the meeting on Tuesday, and find out what, if anything, the SEC dude knew. Rick found out in time to have

David's secretary call to postpone the meeting. Carl was more than pissed that he had flown down for nothing.

Three days later there was another note from David to the partners apologizing for cancelling the meeting, but there was more. In the small envelope, was a set of questions typed on very elaborate stationery from the SEC office in Chicago and signed by the Director of that office.

How that was accomplished was because of Doc's old friend, Gregory Mathers, who had prosecuted one of the most successful forgers of the twentieth century. Had it not been for the testimony of some guy who sold ink, no one would have ever known about an incredible set of counterfeit twenty-dollar plates. They were damn near perfect. Because the prosecutor had worked out a lenient sentence for the guy, he could ask a favor.

"Joey, this is Craig. I'm sorry I have to bother you, but one of your bond accounts needs to be updated. Could I drop by your office, in the next day or so? . . . Great, this afternoon at two. . . . See you then."

Craig was antsy as hell. "Joey, I'm not comfortable telling them a file isn't available when it's a client's file? And if it's missing, how do you substantiate the way you have to answer subsequent questions?"

Joey sat there a minute and then smiled. "Don't say the file is missing. Answer the questions the best you can without revealing anything about the company. Make up a file and then answer the questions. Hell, they'll never know the difference. It's just a company in Boston that needs good financial advice. Get back to your office and get to work on that file." Craig had just been reprimanded like a school kid, but went back to the office to make up the file and answer the questions.

A week later a letter arrived and once again it was from the Director of the Chicago office thanking Craig and Myer for a prompt response. If any other questions arose, David would be in touch.

A sigh of relief from the two partners was evident as was the decision to have a glass of bubbly and dinner at that little Italian café. Now they could get back to work.

It was time for Justin to reenter the picture. This time he would have a senior agent with him when he met the financial gurus.

Justin and Doc unexpectedly dropped in to see Craig and Myer, but Craig was gone for the day. They knew Myer was the weaker of the two, and they would leave him with the idea there was a bigger problem. They would then follow him and also listen to any of his calls to Johnny.

Myer was a nervous wreck when he finally got Craig on the phone. "There's something going on that we don't know about, and it's making me really nervous. Are you sure we have everything covered?"

"Calm down Myer. It's okay. You know the Feds; they love to play the drama game. I have it covered so lower your shoulders and breathe. Everything will be okay. I'll see you tomorrow."

Doc enjoyed his role as senior agent and complemented Justin on his performance. "I almost believed you really did work for the Bureau." It was time to put the next part of the sting in place.

* * *

"Craig, this is David Flynn, and this is off the record. I'm in New Orleans and would like to meet with you about a personal matter. It has nothing to do with the SEC. It is important."

306

Marjorie said that was the message word for word. Craig asked her if he left a number and she said "No, but he did say he would call again around one."

Sure enough, at one o'clock on the dot, the phone rang. The conversation was short, but a meeting at the office was scheduled for seven that evening.

David was very edgy. He kept looking at his watch, then he would look toward the front door. He would stand up for a minute or two and then sit. He acted as if he was being watched.

"Are you okay David?" The constant movement was exasperating to Craig.

"Yeah, I'm fine, but I feel like I'm being followed."

"Why would anyone want to follow you?"

"It's just me, I guess. I've never done anything like this before. I'm just having a little stage fright."

"You want to tell us what this is all about?"

"Sure. Okay. But you have to swear you won't breathe a word of this to anyone."

"Okay, Dave, but for what am I swearing secrecy?"

Looking to the front door again, and sitting on the edge of his chair, he told Craig and Myer that the FBI guys weren't the FBI. It was a set up.

"And how do you know this?" Craig asked.

"Because my office set it up. My boss thinks there is something not right about your partnership and the moving company. He has strong ties to the Bureau and got their permission to put this charade in motion. I'm here to help you because I have a big favor to ask of you."

"And why should we do a favor for you, other than telling us we're being set up by the SEC?"

"Because I'm on the inside and can let you know how, where, and when things are going to proceed."

"And why do we need to know all of that?" Craig asked.

307

"Listen guys, there are several people looking at your operation here and none of them are your friends. Sooner or later they are going to find all the connections between your firm and those individuals in whom they are most interested. I'm simply offering my services, for a small fee, to help you get ahead of the situation."

"And if there was anything to this, what would that small fee be?"

"I'm certain I could keep you adequately informed for $30,000."

"Mr. Flynn, it's been most informative meeting with you, and should we find it necessary to have a mole within the SEC, we'll call you first. Now, we have actual business to attend to. Good-bye Mr. Flynn."

Immediately after leaving the meeting, David met with Doc and Rick to discuss the conversation he had with the partners.

"Doc, they didn't act like they were too concerned when I told them about their firm being of interest to the SEC. They are either cool as a cucumber under stress, they don't give a damn that they're being scrutinized, or they have nothing to hide, which we know isn't true."

"Dave, with what we know, they'll be in touch, but it may take a few days, even a week before they figure out the best way to handle you. We also need time to make sure all the safeguards are in place. I don't want you to be worrying about midnight cruises on the lake."

Rick thought it might be a good idea to send the firm another letter asking more questions. Perhaps that would give them more incentive to seek David's help. They quickly found out that a second letter wouldn't be necessary because Craig called David's office the next morning.

The message read: When you have a moment, I would like to discuss your proposal in more detail. Please call at your convenience.

"Craig, this is David Flynn, how can I be of service?" "David, could you come to our office sometime after five this afternoon?" "I will see you between five and five-thirty." The hook was set.

"Let's get right to the point David. Why does your office feel a need to delve into our firm's business dealings? All we do is manage our client's money, and each transaction has been meticulously recorded in our client's files. We are audited once each year, and there has not been one iota of variance in any of our transaction accounts."

"Yes, Mr. Benson, that's true. There is absolutely nothing but good things to say about your transactional accounts. It's more about the ones you don't have a file for, at least here in your office. For instance, there is the transfer of funds from Northeast Moving Co. to the Vieux Carré Trust, which traveled a very circuitous route from Paris to Bermuda before finally being received by your firm's account. I must admit no one would have ever known about these transactions had it not been for a discovery of several documents found in California. From those few pages, it appears your firm has been helping some of your clients hide substantial amounts of cash and other assets. That's why you are now under the microscope. Of course, you can deny it, but others may try to save their ass by putting yours under the bus. I guess it gets down to a game of chicken. Who gives up what they know first? I can help you with that, but again, it will cost $30,000. It's your choice."

"Let's assume for the moment that we agree to your terms. Exactly what do we get?"

"I can keep you informed the moment anything stirs in your file or there is any discussion of your clients and the movement of their funds. Everything goes through my office first; thus, I can let you know when and why there could be a problem. Right now, I need for you to explain why you need to route money from Paris to Bermuda to Montreal via Seattle. Secondly, to give me something for my files, what was the reasoning for a moving company in Boston sending large sums of money to the bank in Montreal? You need to think about this answer because there is no Northeast Moving Co."

"David, my clients trust me to keep my mouth shut, but in this instance, I need to confess. I was merely trying to help a friend hide a great deal of his wealth because of an impending messy divorce. The guy worked a long time to make his money, and he wasn't going to give it to a woman he had been married to for only four years. If I have to pay a penalty for helping him, then so be it."

"That's certainly a good reason to do something like this, but still highly illegal. What is your friend's name? He's not going to be happy about this, but maybe I can keep the both of you out of real trouble by acting quickly.

"Marco Vinzzetti . . . and you're right . . . he's not going to be happy."

"Are you talking about Vinzzetti as in Big Jim Vinzzetti?"

"Marco is his younger son."

"Guys, how in the hell did you get mixed up with the Vinzzetti family?"

"That's not any of your business. Marco is a good client and that's all I have to say about that."

Myer wanted to get more details about what was going on in David's office. "Are we being investigated on a criminal basis or is this about filings or lack of filings? We earned the same amount of money transferring the funds directly to Montreal. As far as I'm concerned, all this is about is getting our hand slapped. We don't need to pay you $30,000 to help us with that."

David agreed. "Mr. O'Steen, you are right. If that's all this is about, I'm not worth the money. On the other hand, there could be more to this, and only you know that. If you want my help, fine. If not, that's fine too."

Craig told David, "Let us think about this, and I will call you on Friday to give you our answer. In the meantime, should anything happen that you feel is important, call me immediately."

When David got back to his place, he took off the wire, showered, changed clothes, and called Rick. The most important thing was the doubt they had infused into Craig and Myer's thinking, and secondly, that they had it all on tape.

The tape machine adjacent to Johnny's office was also recording the calls from Craig and from Marco Vinzzetti. The pot was being stirred, and it wouldn't take too long to see what came to the top.

"Joey, call me."

Joey sounded pissed. "Johnny, what the fuck is goin' on? . . . Yeah, okay . . . I'm gonna be here another hour or so if you want to drop by." Joey tried to spend as little time in his office as possible. He was used to things being handled without getting him involved. Now that he was handling most everything for the family, there was always something getting in his way, and his social life was suffering. Johnny got there about thirty minutes later, and Joey wasn't interested in small talk. He wanted to get whatever it was finished.

"Joey, that dude in Chicago fucked up in the worst way. They gave some files for Carl to move and they wound up in California. Now the Feds know there are connections between the moving company and Craig. One small fish at the SEC is trying to get thirty thou out of Craig and says he can keep a lid on this. They are thinking about taking him up on his offer. Craig has all the codes for the money and both of them know where the bodies are buried. How do you want to handle this?"

311

"I'm tired of the whole fuckin mess and wish to hell my father and his pals had just left politics alone. Every damn thing we are doing is being watched, as if we're the only family around. You tell Craig and Myer personally that one word out of them that gives the Feds any link to us in anyway, and one or both of em are gonna be real dead."

"Joey, damn it, I already did that."

Carl was told to go to New Orleans for a sit down with the partners. They discussed all the possibilities and Carl insisted that before Craig and Myer agreed to the deal, they would have to see the papers that Flynn's boss possessed concerning the moving company. The only other matter on Carl's agenda was explaining the consequences of getting too friendly with the Feds. For the first time since Craig and Myer got in bed with the Dianatti family, they were having real doubts about their safety. In the world in which they now lived, there was no room for error. There could be no mistakes. Two crime families were watching their every move.

Chapter 57
Things Move

Craig and Myer were having a late-night chit chat and decided to shut down as many as thirty offshore accounts. They would notify clients that they were concerned about the IRS starting to investigate several of the paper trails left by other less qualified financial managers. Nothing would disturb the partner's core business in Bermuda, but certain modifications would be made. It was going to cost the firm a lot of revenue, but better to lose a few million than their lives.

Chip let Rick know that their account with Johnny was being re-directed. What that meant, he didn't know, but suggested

312

that Rick speak to Johnny about it. Chip went on to say, "We evidently stirred things up; so, let's see what and how much.

* * *

Security systems were becoming very sophisticated, but they also were experiencing glitches which an expert thief could exploit. Benson & O'Steen had installed, at great expense, the most burglarproof system ever created. It had more bells and whistles per square foot than anything designed before. The manufacturer went so far as to guarantee no one could break into electronic-eye system. They were so certain that if it did happen, they would pay the client $1 million.

It really was a dark and stormy night in New Orleans. The oppressive humidity and a cold front coming through set off heavy downpours with a lot of lightning and thunder. Rick offered Paul Hudson $100,000 to help him get into Craig's office and open the safe which Rick knew was behind Craig's desk and hidden by a large wooden panel.

There had been a recent break-in at Neilson's Electronic Surveillance Company, but it appeared that nothing was taken. It was most ironic that a company which secured many local businesses couldn't stop someone from breaking into their place. The three New Orleans detectives who had been sent to investigate the break in had a $5,000 deposit made to each of their wives' new accounts. The case never made it to the papers.

Rick had used the drawings he photographed to figure out what was being so well protected and where it was in Craig's office.

It had taken some strong pleading and money to get Paul to commit to a burglary, but if it was for the good of the country, he was okay with it. He still didn't understand what Rick had to do with the country's welfare, but he said yes.

Paul had studied as much material as he could find about the XR-750 Electronic Lockout System. His card said he was a reporter for a well-known magazine, and was meeting with an engineer who worked at the company which made the unit to do a story about this new breakthrough in security. The interview plus the photos he took gave Paul a place to start. Two weeks later he had an almost certain way to overcome the electronic eyes of light without setting off any alarms.

There was no need to cut the power because the unit went to a backup battery-powered system. Paul knew that before attempting to enter he had to disable the connection between the front door and the system. Very carefully, he removed a small hole in one of the glass panes with a diamond glass cutter. He then moved a small mirror into place and reflected the beam of light back onto itself. Rick held the mirror while Paul opened the door wide enough to place another mirror on the floor. Crawling on his stomach, he moved the mirror to the side and took another one from his pocket and set it where the mirror that Rick was holding had been. With that done, Rick moved toward the door and waited for Paul to proceed. When they were both inside, the door was shut, and no one could see that there were intruders manipulating the beams of light. They moved closer to the office by misting the air with a water bottle and refracting the light away from where they were directed. Once they moved forward a few feet, Paul would reset what was behind them so as not to cause any long delay in the pre-arranged array of lights. Each cycle was only one minute long. There were two cameras pointed toward the offices; so, when they had successfully gotten close to the office doors Paul placed a small cap on each lens. He had learned from the engineer that the company was so certain no one could break into any of their customer's locations that they didn't have to monitor with cameras. They were only there to watch during office hours, but Paul didn't want to take a chance. They were in and now it was time for the safe itself. It was behind a large wooden panel, but it wasn't hard to find out where it opened. A small button beside the panel, when pressed, caused the door to slide open. Now it was just about safe-cracking and with the equipment Paul had, opening the door took only twelve minutes.

Now the work was in the hands of Rick and his camera. It took him almost an hour and a half to finish getting the photos and putting back everything just as he found it. The journey back through the maze was supposed to take at most thirty minutes. For whatever reason, when Paul misted the way back there were at least ten more rays of light. With only the three small mirrors, they had a problem. They had to be out of there before five in the morning and Rick looked at his watch to see that it was four twenty-five. Not one to panic, Paul kept looking at the distance and each beam's direction. It finally occurred to him that he could place a mirror in the middle of three beams and deflect them while they bypassed the others with the other two mirrors. They reached the door; Rick went around to the side window and held the mirror while Paul slid out the door and closed it.

There was one last detail which had to be taken care of: There couldn't be a small hole in the windowpane. They placed a small dead bird next to the window, broke the window very carefully, and laid glass around the bird. The storm must have scared the poor bird so much that it flew into the window at full force.

No one knew there was a break-in; so, Paul and Rick got what they wanted and saved the security company a million dollars.

Rick told Paul that he hated to have to resort to breaking and entering, but it was the only way to find out if Craig and Myer were stealing money from the union pension. Paul was okay with that.

If Francesco Dianatti or Big Jim Vinzzetti had known what Craig and Myer were keeping in their safe, there would not have been a Craig, Myer, safe, or office. No one in their right mind would keep that kind of material unless they were complete idiots thinking they could blackmail the two families, or they just couldn't bear to part with old memorabilia. Either way, any knowledge that they had retained the documentation would have led to their immediate journey to hell.

The partner's incredible stupidity was all Doc and the guys needed to cement their case.

* * *

"Vince, I wanted to check on you, see how things were going."

"Doc, it's a lot more stressful around here and not sure why. Carl has had me going everywhere, taking on small jobs and big ones too. So far nothing extremely serious; just time consuming. Darlena is so busy that she barely misses me, but we do have some time together. How much longer you think I'm gonna be here?"

That's part of the reason I called, Vince. We have uncovered some material that gives us a clear picture as to how various pieces of this conspiracy fit. The one thing I need you to find out, and it could be dangerous, is when Carl met with Jake, where they met, and what Jake wanted from Carl."

"Damn, you don't want much, do you? What do you think he's gonna say? 'Hey, Vin, old buddy, I'm gonna tell everything I know about a secret meeting I had with ole Jake.' You want to hear about it?'"

"Vin, I did say it could be dangerous, but what's a little danger for a guy who has worked his way up in the Vinzzetti family? Do what you can. It's important, but not enough to get yourself killed.

Chapter 58
The Pressures of Wealth

Rick and Chip began putting things together from the photos taken in Craig's office. Since every document had dollars involved, it appeared that the partners wanted to have a safety net in case of a problem. They must have known that what they were keeping could get them killed, but who would ever know?

Withdrawals and Transfers:

October 4, 1963 . . . Carl, at the instruction of Big Jim, delivered $200,000 cash to Craig at 9:30 pm.

October 19, 1963 . . . $200,000 in cash delivered to firm from Chicago source at drop-off.

November 6, 1963 . . . Balance of $200,000 cash delivered by Carl.

November 7, 1963 . . . $550,000 deposited in the Vieux Carré Trust.

November 7, 1963 . . . $ 50,000 cash delivered to Joey

November 10, 1963 . . . $1,500,000 to NT's Swiss Account

Total: $2,700,000

Northeast Moving Co. account balance 10/04	$8,056,886
Transfer fees	1,300,000
Account balance 11/10	$4,056,886
NT Fee - 11/20	3,000,000
Balance available	$1,056,886

Two copies were made with one being sent to Joey's office and the second sent to the office of Marco Vinzzetti. Now it was time to wait and watch to see what happened next. It didn't take long.

There must have been at least five minutes of "what the fucks" and "how in the fuck did this happen" before the actual conversation began. The next bit of the tirade was getting answers and taking care of this. Marco and Joey weren't even using code words. Marco yelled, "I want the mother-fucker who did this . . . dead . . . you got that?"

Darren and Jennie were having their daily agenda meeting when there was very loud noise at the front door. When Darren looked out there were three very tough looking men banging on the door. Darren opened it, they shoved past him and headed for Craig and Myer's offices. The door slammed. A few moments later Marjorie opened the door and ran out. There were a lot of voices, but not loud enough to understand what they were saying. The three men opened the door, went to the front door, and were gone. Marjorie went back in the office and ran out again. "Jennie, call the police and get an ambulance."

Craig had a large gash on his head, which was bleeding profusely. It looked worse than it was. Myer's face looked as if it had been used to open the door. Both men were taken to the local emergency room. They would be fine, except

318

for the ongoing fear of living next to death every moment of the day and night.

Joey had changed his mind about killing them, at least for now. He told Johnny to make the boys uncomfortable, and he did. Craig met with Johnny the next day to ask him why they were being treated this way.

"Johnny, what have we done to deserve this? We've done nothing and yet you have three of your thugs treat us like we're dirt. What the hell is going on here?"

Johnny showed him the note Joey had received and asked Craig, "Look familiar?"

Hoping not to look as if he knew what it was, Craig asked, "What is it?"

"You know damned well what it is. We don't write down nothin'; so, that leaves you and your faggot partner. Blackmailin' us ain't a real good idea old pal."

"Johnny, you have to believe me, we didn't have anything to do with this."

"Then who does? No one else knows about any of this except us and you, and we didn't do this. You better make damn sure you find out and let me know or you can kiss your asses goodbye."

When Craig left, he was mostly in shock. How in the hell did that information get out of the safe? "Myer, did you give anything to anyone without telling me?'

"Craig, I would never do anything like that."

"Johnny got a note with six of the money transfers before the hit, and we've been told to find out who did this, or it will be us who pays the price."

Myer was now almost moved to tears. "Should we call the Feds?"

"Are you fuckin crazy? That's all we need."

After things settled down, Craig looked at the safe. There were no marks anywhere which might indicate there had been an attempt to break into it. At an angle he could see what look like a small circle, but didn't pay much attention to that. The pane of glass had been replaced, but that was caused by a bird. No one could get past their security system; so, how in the hell did his transaction record get out?

No one knew they had this safe, and for sure no one knew they kept records. Johnny would have already had them killed if he had found out about the safe. Craig was near panic himself. Who did this?

Then a few days later Rick had a letter ready for the Vinzzetti family, but wanted to check with Doc first.

Cover money:

> Carl . . . $50,000
> Harvey . . . $20,000
> Chicago Associates (2) $25,000 each

"Do we send this or hold it awhile?"

"You send that now, and those guys are dead. I have an idea. Let's get a note to Darren saying something to the effect that he should consider moving as soon as possible because he might not want to be in the same building with Craig and Myer. That should put them on the edge of the edge.

"You know Doc, you don't play fair. Those boys aren't sleeping too well nowadays anyway, and now you're going to make it worse? I hope you never get it in for me."

"I hope the bastards choke on all that money they have stashed away. And I'm glad things are about to get worse for the both of them. If I have to, I will be sending David back in there

320

shortly to put more heat on them. Maybe they'll start talking, thinking that David can help."

* * *

David couldn't decide whether he liked being the big-time big-deal land developer or the SEC guy on the take. Both required excellent acting skills and David's ego was happy with both scenarios. For now, he was back in Chicago, and that meant he would get to see Vanessa again soon. She had made it quite clear on their last date that she had more than a passing interest in their relationship. What she meant by that he wasn't sure, but at least she wanted to see him when he had time. David was back in town and he went to her office to ask her out to dinner. Ron wasn't all that happy to see him, but reluctantly called Vanessa to let her know David was at the front desk.

She insisted that they have dinner at her place. She wasn't promising him more than pizza, but then again, she might surprise him. She told him to come casual and be there around seven. Her jeans, Chicago Bears T-shirt, and being barefooted made her look more adorable than any cocktail dress could. She had ordered spaghetti and meatballs from the deli next door and the wine she already had. She gave him a quick kiss as he entered the door, and as they sat by the fireplace after dinner, she gave him another, more of a come-hither kiss.

After they had talked about this and that for a while, Vanessa asked him if he liked her enough to endure her true self. "I'm not sure I understand the question, but of course, I can endure anything when it comes to you."

"David, I trust you. That's not something I usually say to a man, and especially a man I have only known a short time. You haven't even tried to lure me into your web of lust yet. Now that I think about it, maybe I shouldn't trust you." She was smiling to some extent when she told him that if he had tried to use her in anyway, he would not be sitting here tonight. Not that she didn't enjoy the intimacy of sex, but it had to be about more than wham bam thank you ma'am. "If what I tell you tonight is too difficult for you to handle, it's okay. I want us to go forward and I'll know if that's possible after we talk tonight."

"Vanessa, it sounds serious, but by all means, let's get it out on the table."

"David, I'm not Vanessa. I'm Susan Arthur, and I'm not a stripper or a secretary. I'm a senior agent with the FBI. I'm here on a case of high-level fraud concerning the City of Chicago and especially in the office where I work.

He certainly couldn't act like he already knew that; so, with his best acting skills, he looked shocked and also happy that she would share that information with him. He immediately asked, "Aren't you worried that they'll find out?"

"That's the hazard of the job. I'm okay most of the time, except when I get a big surprise. I know you wondered what was going on that day in the office, but you handled it very well. I really care about you David, and with that said, I don't want to have to lie to you anymore. I am what I am, and that's all I can say."

He took her hand and pulled her to his side. "Sweetheart, that took a lot of courage and trust and you have my deepest respect. I also love your hot body and kissing you is a sexual fantasy all by itself." They kissed passionately for several minutes. She was moaning quietly, and they were pressing against one another with each breath they took. His hand cupped her breast and gently rubbed her nipples. They were hard and eager. His leg was between her thighs and she began moving her body up and down in an increasingly rhythmic pace. They were now lying on the carpet and she was kissing his face and neck and pulling him closer to her body. She wanted him now, but very gently, he pushed her back.

"Vanessa . . . Susan, there is nothing I want more than to make love to you, but we're going to make it something special when we do this. I care about you so much, and I want us to make love for hours, but not tonight. She sat there looking at him, finding it difficult to believe this man could stop in the middle of something that felt so good. "Did I do something wrong?"

"No baby, nothing wrong, but every time I've fantasized about our first time, it has always been something I wanted to be amazing for us both." He kissed her again, held her, and then told her he had to be going. As he left, she just sat there, unwilling to think he simply wanted to make a big deal out of their first time. Instead, she was confident it was because of what she had told him.

"Why did I do that?" She leaned against the sofa and tears began to trickle down her cheek.

David got back to his place and was convinced he had ruined their evening, maybe even the idea of a relationship. It just didn't seem right, he thought, and proceeded to pour himself a couple of fingers of scotch. *I could be in her bed right now, making incredibly fantastic love to a most beautiful woman, but no, I had to go and call the whole thing off. I am so stupid.*

His phone rang, and he almost hated to answer it, but it could be Susan wanting to talk. Instead, it was Doc calling to say that he wanted David in New Orleans the day after tomorrow. When he hung up, he did something completely out of character: he drove to Susan's, pounded on her door, and when she opened it up, he picked her up, kissed her, and headed toward the bedroom. As the sun rose, they were lying there both breathless, knowing they had never known such love making in their lives. She called in sick.

He didn't want to say goodbye, but she understood that when business calls you have to go. Besides, it would give her some time to rest. Their love making was non-stop for hours and hours and sleep was something they could do later. Every part of her body had been loved, kissed, and caressed. They were both very oral and both had little scratches and bite marks everywhere. Her insides ached for him, but she was so thankful she could have a little time off to recover from his insatiable need to be as deep into her as possible. It was so good that every time she moved it was about where David had been. It was so good . . . *Hurry back to me my love.*

David had a chartered flight to New Orleans and took a cab to a warehouse that Rick had rented on a month to month basis. There was a small apartment area in the building where he would stay until heading back. As he was being briefed on all that had transpired in New Orleans, he told Rick and Chip that Susan had told him she was undercover for the FBI working on a fraud case involving officials in the City of Chicago. He didn't elaborate on the relationship they had, but her job in Chicago had nothing to do with what Vince was there to do.

"David, when you get back up there, see if there's anything else Susan can tell you about Carl. Find out what you can about why she was in New Orleans." Doc reminded him to be careful, and to tell Vince that things were going to get very sticky soon, if they weren't already.

Marjorie looked up to see the gentleman from the SEC standing there, but looked more like he was on vacation than coming for an official visit. "What can I do for you, Mr. Flynn?"

"I need to see Craig and Myer right away. It's terribly important."

"I'll tell them you're here."

David wasn't greeted with much friendliness. More like, oh no what are you doing here? Feigning friendliness, "David, nice to see you again. Are you taking a camping trip?"

"No, I'm just passing through and wanted to tell you that you guys need to find a good lawyer. I've been fired, but before I left, I found out you guys will be indicted very soon. You have anything to tell me that I can use to help you, let me know. Call this number and leave a message. I've got to go, and you haven't seen me."

He was in and out of there under ten minutes, and after he left, Craig really didn't know what he had just heard except the word indict. What the fuck is going on? Someone's out to get us.

The note that Rick let Doc see, was now in the mail addressed to Craig Benson. Two days later, Craig called the number David had given him. Craig assumed that David would answer, but instead, it was a woman's voice. It was an answering service, and Craig didn't want to leave a message. He thought about it for five or ten minutes and called back. He gave the woman a number and asked that David call him back. Two hours passed before David called.

"Everything okay back there?"

"No, and I want to know what kind of game you're playing with us. Does your office have something on us or not, and if so, what is it? And this is no time to be fuckin' us around. Tell me what they've got or you're going to be history."

"Hey, wait a damn minute here. I came by to tell you to cover your ass and you're threatening me?" Forget that asshole. All I have to do is make a couple of phone calls and you and your chummy little buddy are going to go very dead very quickly. Do I make myself clear?"

"Okay, okay, let's just settle down here. Did you send this note I got today?"

"You think I'm dumb enough to send you a letter? I haven't sent you anything."

"Okay then, do you happen to know if anyone in your office has any kind of financial information which wasn't within the scope of their normal authority?"

"What kind of information?"

"Damn it David, information we might have kept secret to justify our private transactions."

"Sorry Craig, I don't know of anything like that, but then I wasn't in the unit that investigated things outside normal procedures. I gotta run, talk again soon."

Myer was now nothing more than a whining, crying bundle of nerves. He was useless to Craig, and both were on the verge of running. But to where? They knew there wasn't any place they could run to that Joey and Marco couldn't find them. The partners didn't understand that there was a lot more to all of this than just family business. David warned them not to go to the Feds because there were those somewhere in the bureaucracy who already wanted them dead.

It was too late. Myer had stopped by the local market on his way back home. As he opened the door to get into the taxi, two shots rang out. He never knew what hit him. Craig was now frozen in grief and fear. There was no way out. He had to run, and he was devastated. He wasn't going to stay long enough for Myer's funeral. Sitting at his desk trying to decide how to make his escape, he was packing as much cash as he could get into a duffle bag. Craig now knew that if he stayed they would kill him, and if he ran and they found him, they would kill him. With no choice but trying to disappear, he very calmly told Jennie and Darren that he was leaving early to take care of some things at the house.

Craig left a small envelope on Jennie's desk, and walked away. To where, no one ever knew, or if they did, never let it be known. When Craig Benson disappeared, he was 53.

Darren sat down at his desk and opened the envelope.

Darren,

Hope your business continues to grow. I have listed here a few of my clients I hope you will help. If you think you can do the job they will appreciate your input and getting them a good return.

As for me, I'm taking some time off. Maybe more than I want, but will be resting either way. It's only justice that I'm winding up like this. I really had nothing against the man. It was just about the money and power, and I only had that for a short while.

Be careful of the Dianatti and the Vinzzetti families. When they sting, it's deadly.

CB

Darren took the letter to the warehouse where Rick and Chip were still going over all the documents from the safe. It didn't say much, but that second paragraph did seem to have an underlying meaning.

The guys didn't really feel sorry for Craig. It was more about watching a pathetic human who was facing what might be the end of his life and asking, for what? A lot of money he couldn't spend, and the make-believe world of power surrounded by the suffocating blanket of the mob.

* * *

327

Monique Sanchez was a graduate of Wharton School of Finance and Commerce and had been overseeing most of the offshore transactions arriving from Switzerland. She had been hired for her excellent educational resume and her ability to speak French and Spanish fluently.

There had been a great deal of activity in three different accounts starting around the first week of January 1963. She made note of the activity and after some analysis, determined that her bank was merely a conduit for Swiss funds being routed to a large trust account in Seattle. The bank was making significant fees for handling the processing, and Miss Sanchez was driving a new Mercedes. She put the file aside and thought no more about it.

When she told her boss that she would be taking a few days off, she wasn't kidding. Her neighbors told the police they had never heard anything like it before. The beautiful Mercedes went up in a very loud explosion. There was no body to bury, but the bank expressed their condolences to her family at the memorial service.

Chapter 59
And the Heat Is On

Vince had earned his place at the table and all that was left was for him to become a made man. Carl was eager to help him with that, but had been told by Marco to wait until the perfect time. In the meantime, Vince let Carl know that he was proposing to Darlena and didn't want to have any unexpected business get in the way on the big night. He had told Carl earlier in the month that he wouldn't be around on this Wednesday. There was something he wanted to show Darlena. For all she knew, he had moved to a new apartment or maybe bought a house, but he did catch her off guard when they arrived at a small Italian restaurant which looked like it was closed.

When he opened the door for her, there was only one table and it had a candle flickering in the middle of the table. There was a bucket with champagne sitting by the table and three violinists playing O sole Mio. The owner helped her with her seat, and Vince told her how much he loved her.

Darlena was raised where things like this were common, but this night meant so much more than all the others in her life. Vince took her hand, knelt beside her and said, "My darling, I love you more than life itself, and never want to be without you for the rest of my life. Will you marry me?" Once she gathered herself together, she smiled, said yes, and they kissed. It was such a beautiful moment for them both. Now all they had to do was get daddy to accept this man into the family. They would fly to Spain within the next two weeks.

After such a wonderful night at their own little bistro, it was time for them to go home to their little apartment and savor this night forever. They talked about Paris, what she wanted, where she wanted to be, what he would do after Chicago, and that's when he decided to do what he had sworn not to do. Vince had to tell her the truth. He couldn't marry her without her knowing.

Two hours later she fell into his arms, and with tears in her eyes told him, "I knew you could never be a bad man. I love you for being who you are, and thank you so much for trusting me with your secret. I would die before telling anyone anything."

It was time for bed, but before they slept, they kissed, he held her close, and thanked God for this sweetheart of a woman. She had fallen asleep.

A couple of days later Vince was summoned to Marco's office and was told it was urgent. He had only been around Marco a couple of times, and he knew if the boss called something big was up.

"Vince, how are you? Good to see you, and I understand congratulations are in order? You know we had her checked out and Vince my man, you know how to pick 'em."

"She is a remarkable woman and I thank you for your respect and acceptance of her."

"The reason I needed to see you is twofold: First, it's time for you to move up to another level in the organization. You've earned it. Secondly, do you know a woman who goes by the name Vanessa? She used to be a stripper in New Orleans and is now working downtown."

Vince wasn't going to lie because he knew that Marco already knew the answer to that question. "Yeah, I think I ran across her once or twice down in New Orleans. Why do you ask?"

"As bad as I hate to admit it, she's damn good at her job, but she's with the FBI, and for whatever reason, she's trying to get into our business. I can't let that happen. You need to make sure she has an accident, or you can just shoot the bitch, I really don't care. Just get rid of her. Then we'll have a little party for you. Carl has a piece you can use if you decide to just plug her a few times."

Inside, he was feeling as if he could throw up, but Marco would never know it. Vince said he'd get it done, and quite reluctantly had to thank him for his trust. This was his worst nightmare. He called Rick.

"Here's the deal. I've been told to kill Vanessa or Susan or whoever she is, and it's supposed to happen in the next couple of days. Someone needs to get her out of Chicago tonight or she's dead. If I have to pick up Darlena and head for Spain I will, but you guys have to get Vanessa out of the way now. I will call back later."

330

From here he had to slow down and get in touch
with Carl. He didn't want Carl thinking he was backing away
from his job.

Rick decided to play his hand with a king-size bluff. If it
worked, there would be time to save Vanessa. If it didn't work,
she would be dead or taken to God knows where.

"Hey, Johnny, can you talk?"

"What about?"

"I have a problem and you need to tell me how to handle
it."

"Sure, come on over."

"There's a woman, who I have had working for me for a
long time and you're going to think I've lost my mind when I tell
you how I set things up. It's going to destroy my image as naïve
and nerdy, but that's okay. Do you remember Misty's roommate,
Vanessa?"

"God, I guess. That was one hot broad. And the bitch
could kill you as well, or at least I figured she could. Got my
attention right away. We had some good times together. What's
she got to do with this?"

"She's been working for me."

"Don't fuck with me Ricky boy."

"I'm serious Johnny, and she has been since she left you."

"Why the fuck do you need her working for you? She's
not your type."

"First of all, I found out she was working for the FBI
because my partner in Brazil told me. Stay with me on this
because it gets a little weird. The Bureau was trying to set a trap
for some Cubans here in New Orleans, and wanted her undercover
to find out about how the money was being handled. That's why
she was sent here. Chip told me about her a few months later, he
and I got her attention, and gave her two choices: tell you or
maybe not. At the moment she chose maybe not."

"I don't believe this Rick. Why are you telling me somethin' so absurd?"

"Do you want to know about this or not?"

"Go ahead, but you better not be fuckin' me around. If you are, you know I'll shoot your ass."

"She became my eyes and ears for our little venture, letting me know everything that was happening between Rio and the boys in New Jersey. She also let me know that one of the most dangerous members of the Vinzzetti family was copying a bunch of shit that was supposed to be destroyed. Why he was doing that, beats me.

"Now, as to why I'm here. The Vinzzetti family has put out a contract on Vanessa. I don't need for that to happen. They think she's still working for the FBI only because of something Chip said while talking to Alejandro. What I'm asking is your help in telling Chicago to cancel the contract."

Johnny sat there for what seemed like five minutes, and then picked up the phone. "Hey, Joey, you got time to see me and Ricky boy? . . . Yeah, it's real important. . . . Ten minutes. Come on kid."

On the way over to Joey's, Johnny wanted to know if she was still being paid by the FBI. Rick had already thought that one out. "No, she couldn't take the increased pressure, and besides, we paid her three times what she was getting from the government. Also, Vanessa isn't her real name."

After an hour at Joey's office, there were two choices of how to handle this: Get in the way of Chicago or do nothing and to hell with Rick's insider. Joey called Marco and told him that he needed to back off the Vanessa matter, and let New Orleans take care of the situation.

For the moment, Vanessa and Vince were spared. Rick was now wide open for a lot more scrutiny, and Johnny's trust in Rick took a big hit.

Later that evening, the Atlanta office received an anonymous call that Vanessa's cover in Chicago had been blown and that they needed to get her out of there in a hurry. A courier arrived at her home around eleven that night, she packed what she needed, and was on a chartered flight to Atlanta three hours later. When she didn't show up for work, Ron called her home, but there was no answer. When she didn't come in or contact the office for the next three days, he fired her.

In Atlanta, she was trying to find out what happened. Once the office had gotten her to a safe place they would then begin to find out who found her out and how. In the meantime, she couldn't help but wonder how David was going to find her. Was it David who did me in? She didn't want to go there right now, but then she had to assume everyone was a possible informant.

Marco told Carl that they needed to talk. When Carl arrived at their usual dinner location, Marco was going back over some notes he had on the table. "Carl, we may have a big problem. I got a call a few days ago from my friend Joey, and bottom line, asked me to back off the Vanessa problem. Something about her being valuable to them. He told me the FBI contact was a scam, but who in the fuck would run a scam as an FBI agent? Somethin' smells and I don't like it. I want you to take Vinnie for a little ride and see if he sweats. If he does, kill him."

Carl never asked why, and this time was no different. He picked Vinnie up, told him they were going to take care of some business and would then get a drink. Vinnie had no reason to be suspicious.

There were a number of turns and an hour later they were sitting on a stretch of road adjacent to an old railroad yard. "Vinnie, you and me are gonna have a little chat. You fuckin' tell me the truth or I'll blow your brains out, you understand?"

"What the fuck is this about?"

"Don't you think it's a little strange that Marco gives you the contract and just like that the bird flies?"

"Carl, I thought somethin' must have happened when she didn't answer when I called, but I didn't have anything to do with that. As far as I knew she was off. And you know what, I don't like havin' you pokin' around in my business. If I have a job to do, I'll do it. You got that asshole?"

Now it was Carl who was starting to sweat a little, but it had nothing to do with fear. He just didn't want to have to kill his partner. "Vin, I don't give a damn what you like or don't like. Tell me why that bitch is gone, and we'll just close out this conversation.

"She's dead. Check the morgue for a Jane Doe who was killed by a hit and run driver on Tuesday night."

Sure enough, a blond, 5'6" female, dressed in a pink blouse and black skirt was pronounced dead around 10:30. No purse, no ID, but they are trying to ID her by fingerprints and dental work. You remember the gold cross with the diamond she wore? With that Vince reached in his pocket, pulled out the cross and showed him the engraving on the back. There was a simple 3:16 and Happy Birthday etched into the gold.

"You wanna have a look for yourself?"

They pulled her body out, Carl took a look, and sure enough, it was her.

Three hours before, a very deceased Gina Granger was a brunette, but a makeup artist had done a masterful job of making her look just like Vanessa having been hit by a car. Darlena's good friend Martha Danziger had made herself a quick thousand and was glad to help her friend create her weird practical joke. Vince was impressed.

"Carl, I'm thirsty, let's grab a drink."

Marco took Carl's word for it, and that was that. Vinnie and Vanessa had made it another day. Rick's gigantic bluff had given Vin the extra time. It had worked for the most part, and Vinnie's status was moved up a notch. Doc was convinced that Vince had to be removed from Chicago. This couldn't go on any longer.

Chapter 60
Rocky Mountain High

David was so happy to hear from her. "Baby, where have you been? I've been worried sick about you." David had been looking for Susan for over two weeks; Ron told him she had disappeared.

Susan was happy, but she was being serious. "I'm so glad we found each other, but we can't meet anywhere around here. Can you get away for a day or two and meet me in Estes Park?"

"Colorado? Are we going skiing? Where do we meet up when I get there?"

"I have a small chalet rented near the main lodge at Estes Park. The number is sixteen and has a very green door. I'll be waiting for you. David, I love you, and be careful."

He let Rick know that he was going on a long weekend and would talk to him soon. Rick had not discussed Susan with him either. As far as David knew, she had just taken a few days off. When he did arrive at the chalet, she grabbed him as if she hadn't seen him for a year. Her life had come so close to being over that seeing him again was such a wonderful gift. She didn't want to let him go. "Darling, I've missed you so much. Let's not let time do this to us again."

They must have kissed for ten minutes before they finally sat down by the fire. "Susan, why didn't you let me know. Your office said you had just disappeared. Are you okay? Has something happened with your job?"

"Sweetheart, we'll get to all of that soon enough, but for now, let's just relax here together and never forget how it feels." She had tears in her eyes, but she laughed a little as she told him how happy she was that they were together. They had a couple of glasses of wine and that's when she began to tell him what happened.

"It all began around eleven when my doorbell rang. I first thought it might be you, but then you would have let me know you were on your way over. The guy at the door was what we call a runner, but his official title is junior agent . . . a newbie . . . who was assigned to my division. He handed me a note and said he would be waiting downstairs. The note said there was a contract out on me and that I had to leave immediately. I threw some things in a bag and the guy took me to a private plane for the trip to Atlanta. I had never written your number anywhere; so, I couldn't call you. I don't know what happened, but I assure you it was because of the Vinzzetti family. I'm sorry I had to upset you, but it couldn't be helped."

"I'm glad I didn't know, sort of, or I would have been out of my mind. What's going to happen now?"

"Babe, I don't know, but I suspect I'll be very invisible for a while. Maybe I get to see you a lot more, just as long as we're very out of sight. My bed would be an excellent hideout."

"Susan, this may be a tad too practical and unromantic, but would you marry me?" Once she got her mouth closed, she kept looking at him and asked him, "You are kidding, right?"

"No, I'm not. I want us to be together. If you don't want to get married, then will you live with me? Unfortunately, I didn't arrive with a ring, but would you say yes to one of my offers . . . ring or not?"

"Let me answer you this way: Who needs a ring and yes, I

336

will marry you, but only if you'll consent to a church wedding. Doesn't have to be a big one, but I want to make sure mom and dad and God are all there with us."

"Say Amen brother, and I'll love your cute little butt forever."

Since it was fourteen degrees outside, they decided to stay in. They were so tired. After all, it was almost three in the afternoon. Maybe a nap would help. A marriage proposal can be an exhausting experience. They had dinner at eight and David decided she had to know the truth. Just like Vinnie, David couldn't marry her without her knowing the truth.

Over the course of the next two hours she must have thought she was listening to a rerun of a Twilight Zone broadcast. The man she loved, the man she had just told yes, she would marry him, made her work seem trivial in comparison.

"David, are you really David?"

"I am, but not David Flynn." He began telling her who he really was, and no he wasn't a super-rich real estate mogul. He had a good idea he could be one with a little working capital. "I'm the son of a Colonel in the Army, a graduate of the Military Academy, and I have my MBA from Wharton. When I was in the service I was an aide to a Four-star General. I know how to fight dirty, chase bad guys, and when Doc asked me to help I said yes. Will you still marry me even though I'm not rich?"

"Only if you promise to keep me satisfied on a very constant basis."

"It's a deal. Do we need to get to work on that right now or would you rather give me another hour to recover from our nap?"

"I love you David . . . Atwater. I think I like that better than Flynn actually. Anything else you have to tell me that will blow my mind?"

"Yes, there might be one thing: My grandfather left me 10,000 shares of AT&T, which I think has split several times. I could be rich."

* * *

"I want him out of there, and I want him out now. Do we understand one another?" When the good doctor was that emphatic, things better damn well happen, or he would be all over your ass until he got his way. Doc wanted Vince out of Chicago, and he didn't give a damn if things had worked out or not. No way was he going to keep one of the most important men in the operation in harm's way.

"Rick, I can't leave now. I'm close to finding out what's been going on up here since all this started. Tell you what, give me a couple of days to think about this, and I'll call you with an exit plan."

"Okay, but you better damn well have a good one. Chip and I will come up with one just in case we think yours stinks." It wasn't much of a time for trying to be funny. "See you later guy, and be careful up there."

Sure enough, Rick didn't think too much of Vince's plan, but promised he would take both of them to Doc to see which one he wanted to go with. Another day passed by before a decision was made. Doc would go with what Vince wanted to do. It would keep Vince alive and make him invaluable to the Vinzzettis until the day arrived that there might not be a Vinzzetti family. There was risk to it, but anything was a risk at this point.

* * *

"What the fuck makes you think Big Jim would take his time to see you without you runnin' it by Marco first? And secondly, why do you think I'm dumb enough to ask Marco about this? You wanna talk to the big man, then it's your ass if it doesn't work out. I ain't got nothin' to do with it."

"Carl, I'll remember this; you can bet your ass on it."
"Marco, this is Vin and I need an hour of your time for lunch. It's more than important that you see me."

"No lunch . . . meet me at Carmelo's at eight tonight, and leave your piece in the car."

There wasn't anyone there except an older couple up near the window. Marco liked to dine in private; so, now there was a closed sign on the door.

"Vin if all the boys were as active as you we could take over Detroit. Carl told me you were going to call; so, whatcha got?"

"You know that Darlena and I are going to be married, but that first I have to go to her father, discuss it with him, and get his approval. That part doesn't seem like a problem for me, but I got to thinkin' how it might be somethin' good for you and the family. Want me to go on?"

"Yeah, sure, go ahead."

"Her old man must run at least a million tons or more of sugar and rice from Spain and Mexico into the states each year. Let's say that I can get all the loading, transportation, and delivery schedules for all that sugar and rice. How many bags of heroin do you suppose we could fit in some of those containers headed to any place we choose?" Vince went on to say, "I'm his only daughter's husband, there's not anything she can't get from him, and she'll do it for me. I thought it might be a good idea to let him know that I'm financially sound enough on my own, but together he and I can increase revenues by several percentage points. To get his attention, I need at least $5 million in a private Swiss account. This is what I want to talk to your dad about, with you there of course."

339

Marco didn't say anything. He looked at his watch, waved to one of his men in the back, and stood up. "Vince, you're too damn smart. I don't like it when someone's too damn smart. Makes me nervous. I'll be in touch."

Next morning Vinnie's phone rang while he was having breakfast. It was Marco. "Be at my place, 2 pm, and be on time." Vince didn't feel right.

When he walked into Marco's office there was no one there. Instead, some dude walked in behind him, put his fingers to his lips telling Vin to keep quiet, and then the guy opened a door in the corner of the room. They went down a long hall, the guy knocked twice, and the door opened. Sitting at a large desk was Big Jim Vinzzetti in a blue cloud of cigar smoke. There were five other very unpleasant looking men sitting in there as well as Marco, plus two huge guys standing behind him.

"Sit down Vinnie, and don't mind my friends here. We're all interested in what you have to say. First, let me congratulate you on your engagement. She is a beautiful girl, and looks like you stumbled into a gold mine too." Big Jim laughed, and they laughed too. Marco tells me you'll be heading over there to get the old man's blessing. That right?"

"Yes sir, I'll be leaving in about ten days."

"What makes you think we know anything about heroin, Vin?"

"All I know is what I've heard, and if I've heard the wrong thing, my apologies to you and your family. I meant no disrespect."

"You know Vin, I may replace my boy Rodney with you this next election. You're smooth. Ever been told you're a little too smooth?"

"Mr. Vinzzetti, let's just say I have a good line of bullshit."

Big Jim laughed, and again everyone laughed. "I like you Vin, and I think the idea you discussed with Marco may have

340

some possibilities. Just to make sure you have a successful trip. I've set up a little company for you. You and I now own Pertinelli & Associates. We're a well-connected dealer in high end antiques and art. Our account has roughly $7 million in it, and you're doing quite well. It will be up to you and your particular brand of bullshit to make this work. Here's fifty thousand as a wedding gift, but you are not to touch a dollar of our account. It's just for show. Now get your ass out of here." Big Jim didn't stand, but everyone else did. Vin thanked the Don and made his way outside where he thought he was going to throw up.

That night he and Darlena talked about everything and how it had to work. She knew her father would be most happy that his future son-in-law was well off and not marrying his daughter for the money. She didn't care one way or the other because they loved each other and that was all that mattered. Whatever Vince needed she would see to it that daddy helped.

Vince called Rick to let him know that everything was set. They probably wouldn't be talking again for at least three weeks unless there was a problem. Doc wasn't the happiest man in the world, but accepted the plan with one caveat: Don't trust anyone.

* * *

Darlena Isabella Rodriguez Velasquez was not supposed to marry just anyone. Her father had been careful to make sure only the best families and their most successful sons would be candidates to be her husband. He had been screaming at everyone since he heard the news that she was bringing the love of her life home from America. This could not be happening. Things just aren't done like this, and the patriarch of this family would have nothing to do with the situation or his daughter. How could she not know this would never work? Don Alvarez Carrillo de Velasquez didn't like it when she first called, and he was determined his only daughter would never marry an American, especially one who did not have one drop of Spanish blood in his veins. No one could trust those damn Italians.

Darlena and Vince arrived after a difficult nine-hour flight and both weren't at their best when Vince was introduced to Darlena's mother. Don Alvarez had been called away on business and could not be there. He sent his apologies to his daughter. After a quiet dinner, Vince was taken to his bedroom, which was quite lavish, without having an opportunity to tell Darlena goodnight. At this moment, Vince was thinking that this might be a lot more difficult than he expected.

He was awakened quite early the next morning and told that breakfast would be served on the patio at 7:30. When he finally found the patio, he was five minutes late, and there, sitting at the head of the table, was a most massive man that Vince thought, my God it's an old Zorro. Dark eyes, silver hair and beard, rugged skin as if he had been working in the fields his entire life, were the features Vince noticed first. And then he spoke in a rich baritone voice that was almost melodic, "Señor Pertinelli, welcome to my humble home."

"Don Velasquez, it is my honor, sir." Darlena was hesitant to embrace Vince and he could tell she was most careful not to offend the Don's concept of protocol.

"My daughter speaks highly of you young man, and says that you are an American businessman of some success."

"Yes, I have been most fortunate, sir. I could not have conceived of asking your daughter to marry me unless I knew I could give her a secure and happy life."

"Today, I want you to see a part of what we have built here over the centuries. I too have been blessed. Many bountiful harvests have been a true gift from Heaven. Are you a religious man, Mr. Pertinelli?"

"Yes, Señor Velasquez, I am."

The Don excused himself, which gave Vince and Darlena a few minutes to talk, but from across the table. Darlena's mother, Maria, did her best to limit their conversation because she too understood what her daughter could say and not say at the breakfast table. It was more about Vince answering Maria's boring questions than about idle conversation.

After four days of somewhat icy attitudes, it was announced there would be a party to celebrate Darlena's return to her home. Nothing was said about Vince, other than he was a guest of the Velasquez family. Darlena demanded that she have time with her father.

"Father, this has to stop. I love this man, and you can do all the disinheriting that you wish, but we are going to marry and that's all I have to say about it. You can either accept it or punish me as you see fit."

"My darling girl, I do not wish to punish you. It is only my wish that you marry in the style in which you were raised. Running off to America was bad enough, but falling for some common man with no family history is beyond my comprehension."

"Daddy, I love you and momma more than life, but the thought of some pre-arranged marriage is like the dark ages. This man is so good to me, cares about me, loves me, and even respects that he has to have your consent. I'm a grown woman, living in the United States, and I love Vince. You consent to our marriage, or we will be returning home as quickly as possible. I'm not a little girl anymore, and maybe it's time you started realizing that."

He smiled as she left the room, and then said to himself, "She's just like her father." Don Velasquez scheduled a meeting with Vince that evening.

It was a long hour and a half, but at the end, the two men shook hands, and when Darlena and her mother were asked to join them, there were smiles and the Don stated he approved of the

343

marriage. The party which he had scheduled as a welcome home party would become the announcement of Darlena's engagement to a fine, young American man, Vincent Pertinelli. There was only one request which had to be honored: The wedding would be in the church where she was christened. Let the church bells toll.

Vince called Big Jim to tell him about the wedding, which was scheduled for November fourteenth. He wanted to let Big Jim know that if he wished, he could remove a portion of the funds in the company account. It wouldn't be needed.

A second call was made to Rick, also letting him know that things were moving forward. Vince was going to be away for some time, but as long as Big Jim knew why, things were cool for the moment.

* * *

James Alejandro Hagen was almost three and had not seen his father in months. Camila had yet to file for divorce, but she was convinced that ending the marriage was the best thing to do for her and her little boy. If Chip was going to continue to live in New Orleans, she had no choice because Camila was not living in the United States.

Chip had flown to Brazil on several occasions and unhappily some of those visits didn't include his little boy and the woman he loved so very much. His unhappiness and his paternal instincts were beginning to effect his work. Rick, Doc, and Chip needed to have a sit down to discuss Chip's situation.

There was no doubt that Chip's mind wasn't on the tasks at hand. There was no blame going around. Just facing the reality that the man missed his family, yearned to be doing something that had a future for him, and take him out of the way of someone's well-placed bullet. Rick put in his two cents worth with one sentence: "Give Chip a good way to let all of this go."

The dreariness outside seemed to be making its way into the small hotel room where Chip and Doc were meeting. After several hours of remembering from whence they came, how things back then seemed to have more of an urgency and purpose compared to the way it was now, both men came to the same conclusion: It was time for Chip to go to home to his family and let things happen as they may. Knowing as much about Alejandro's business as he did, maybe Chip could be the wrench thrown into the machine which would bring Estoval down. If he did, it would be strictly his decision. When Doc and Chip said goodbye late that afternoon, there would be one less man to carry things to their conclusion.

Camila and James met him at the airport, and for the first time in several years, Chip was all smiles. Whatever happened now would be the direct result of Chip's decision to leave behind a synthetic, at times make-believe world, to live in the present with his wife and son.

* * *

Rick and Chip had risked their lives to get the little black box, but they had never been able to decipher the paper inside the damn thing, Doc decided to try something else. He assumed it was financial, but every possible way they could think of to find numbers in the myriads of symbols didn't come up with anything. It had to be words, but they couldn't figure that out either. Where could they get some help?

"Dr. Carmichael, it's a pleasure to meet you. My wife Claire tells me that you and she once upon a time had the same Chemistry professor."

"Yes, Dr. Reid, and that's how I found you. She tells me you can solve any puzzle ever devised. I hope she's right, and please call me Davis."

What Dr. Reid didn't know was that back in their college days, Claire Fitzsimmons Reid and Davis Carmichael were closer than her husband might want to know. Both had thought at the time that they would be married once school was done, but things happened, lives changed, and their paths went in two different directions. They stayed in touch for a long time, but once they were both married, about the only time they talked was at some medical convention. Every time they met they both could feel the physical attraction.

Doc handed the letter-size piece of paper to Dr. Reid, who at first, said nothing. He looked another minute or two then asked, "Davis, where did you get this?"

"From a boat captain. Does that make a difference?"

"It appears to be several years old by the looks of this paper."

"Dr. Reid, I have no idea how old it is."

"Are you going to be able to leave this with me?"

"I suppose I can do that," but as he smiled, he said, "If it's a map to buried treasure, I'll be watching you."

"Give me a week and I will try to have something for you. Would you care to join us for dinner tonight? We're having roast beef."

"That sounds delicious Dr., but I have to catch a plane to New Orleans. Do you want me to call you next week?"

"I've got your number Davis; let me call you."

Doc shook Dr. Reid's hand, gave Claire a prolonged hug, and was headed to the airport.

* * *

Several days later Dr. Reid called Doc to let him know he thought he had solved the code or at least had found a way to make out what the symbols meant. After breaking down the

346

symbols into what seemed to be a code for letters, Dr. Reid had given Doc the letters:

KRLNVFAM2BGD2RBLWH-PBCK-FDBJWJNMX-JRXSH
which, when deciphered, said: Carl/Big D – Two rifles below Harvey – Payback- Francesco Dianatti, Big Jim, Wendell Jeffreys in mix – Jack Ruby/X Harvey.

Had Dr. Reid seen this message years ago, and broken the code, perhaps the President could have been saved. The fact that they didn't have the message would haunt them all for a very long time. However, it now seemed this was the perfect time to let this message pop its ugly head up again and see where it went. Rick wanted revenge and he really didn't care how it played out.

Inside the package that Big Jim received earlier in the day was a copy of the decoded message. There were other copies and a couple of photographs, but the coded message along with its translation brought an ugly grimace to Big Jim's face. He had told Carl to destroy all of this, but instead, he had made copies of it. None of this would have ever been written down had it not been for Joey's stupid mistake. Big Jim flew down to meet with Francesco. The talk was long, and decisions were made.

About ten miles northeast of the small town of Cairo in southern Illinois, two cars drove into a field of corn gently waving on a cloudy, misty night. A door opened and out stepped a large man who then pulled out another man bound tightly with ropes and something stuffed in his mouth. A small lantern lit the work up ahead where three men were digging a large hole between two rows of corn which stood about five feet tall. When they were done digging, they walked over to the man bound by ropes and began hitting him in the mouth with a hammer. His screams and his blood turned the gag in his mouth into a soggy, bloody mess.

When they finished, they threw him into the grave and slowly began to cover him with dirt. Carl was buried alive.

Chapter 61
Decisions

Barbara Carmichael was a reasonable woman. She married Davis with the idea that he would build a practice in the suburbs of Baltimore, they would have a home and children, and lovingly grow old together. That's how it started, but something along the way changed things drastically, and nothing had been the same since late October of 1962. That was when Davis began flying all over the country, basically giving up his practice of Psychiatry, and leaving her alone for days at a time. At first, she did her best to roll with the punches, but after being hit so many times, she decided enough was enough. One night after he returned from one of his mysterious journeys, she told him they had to talk. Maybe closer to the truth, she had to talk.

She and Davis didn't marry until he had finished his residency at Johns Hopkins, and she had finished her Ph.D. in Chemistry. They were smart, sensible people. They even put off having children until they had time to get to know one another as a loving, giving professional couple. It was almost too scripted, and too perfect.

That all changed drastically as she considered her worst nightmare: Davis was seeing another woman. Once he put her mind at ease with that, it seemed to be somewhat better. At least there were some weeks when he was home, and things seemed normal. Then, out of nowhere, the phone would ring, he would pack, and he was gone. He only told her he couldn't talk about it as he headed for the door.

It had been like this for over eight years, and their marriage and Davis' health were on the brink of collapsing.

"Davis, I need you to sit down, be quiet, listen, and understand I'm up to here with your secrecy. This can't go on anymore. I'm very seriously considering a divorce, and you can help me with this or just let your family walk away. It's up to you."

He didn't say anything about her comments, but did ask if he could pour himself a drink and one for her if she wanted one. She had no desire for a drink, but when he sat back down, she was even more aggressive about what she wanted to say.

"If I didn't love you more than life, I wouldn't be here now. I would have long ago packed it up and told you to give 'em hell honey, whatever or whoever you were trying to do.

"Either you tell me what you've been doing, or I'm leaving. It's that simple. No wild tirades, no screaming, no crying . . . just kissin' your ass goodbye. Is that clear enough for you?"

Davis hadn't missed a word. He knew this day was coming, but hoped it could have been later. Frankly, he had figured she would have done this a long time ago, but thankfully, she had smiled and endured all his secrecy. At their age, she should know, and he should be ashamed for waiting so long to take her into his confidence. She didn't deserve what he had done to her, the marriage, and the family.

For the next several hours he did his best to cover all the facets of what he was called on to do back when his friend Jack was alive. Maybe he should have stopped right then, but he and the young men he had recruited couldn't accept that the President was murdered by a lone gunman. There was more to it, and they would find it. Doc was sorry, but he had to know who and why.

Barbara was completely mesmerized and when he was finally done, he told her to ask him anything. He had nothing to hide from her any longer. She had questions, and he answered them one by one. He had consumed three glasses of scotch during his discourse, and after the first hour she began drinking her favorite cabernet. With the air cleared, everything on the table, they had the most marvelous sex they had experienced in many years. They loved their children, but were so happy they weren't there.

The only other thing Barbara insisted upon was that Davis see his doctor. Doc had lost weight, didn't have much of an appetite, couldn't sleep at times, and a lot of the time was very lethargic. He reluctantly agreed.

* * *

Rick had thought about a lot of things over the past few weeks, and the one most on his mind was about Justin. He had damned near been killed, and other than his acting debut as an FBI agent, he had been given little to do. He was spending most of his time going back and forth to see Laura. They usually met somewhere close enough for her to drive, but far enough away that there was no danger to Justin.

Justin did confess that he told Laura some of what he was doing, but other than working under cover for a private investigation team, he had not been totally forthcoming. Rick knew it was only a matter of time until Laura would know everything; therefore, it was time to let Justin know he was going home to stay. He was free to live his life again. The same element of secrecy would be in place, but when Justin felt it was time, he would decide when to tell his loving and adoring wife the rest of his story.

Three weeks later, in a small church in Point Pleasant Beach, New Jersey, Mr. and Mrs. Justin Maxwell began their new life together. After a brief honeymoon, they found a small apartment not too far from the Naval Academy, where Justin began his new job as part of the security force. Laura found herself in a world she had never considered, but she was a quick study. Most importantly, they were together, and they were safe.

* * *

Joey wanted out of the club business and told Johnny to find a buyer. The old man had okayed the deal, but only if the new owner were someone they could trust. Johnny told Misty, and the deal was done. Her loan was at one percent and had to be repaid within three years. The seller's small import-export business was the source of Misty's funds. Everyone was happy.

Misty had now become so well known that she had a nickname. When you make it to the top without sleeping with Johnny or Joey, you are one foxy lady; thus, the club became the Foxy Lady. Rick now referred to her as boss which she secretly loved to hear, but said she hated. The club was the hottest spot in town, and as long as she could keep Rick and his band there, keep the booze flowing, and the girls the hottest in town, everything would continue to be fine. Misty was a new woman. Hell, she didn't even hate Nikki anymore.

Her latest boyfriend wannabe was a very prominent heart surgeon who she played with for almost three months. He was the number one catch, or so he thought, but she wasn't interested in anything more than attending some of his parties on those occasions when the Charles' might be in attendance. Dr. Hart did bring a lot of business to the Foxy Lady, and occasionally she would give him a reward. She once let him put his hand on her thigh under her dress. Men came and went, but there was only one man in Misty's life. She might not be able to have him for herself, but somehow, she would find a way to share in Rick's need to give back.

* * *

351

Darren had successfully moved many of the Benson & O'Steen's clients to other brokers who could give them their full-time attention. His primary responsibility now was the ongoing business which Rick and Chip had begun, and creating a financial timeline of all the activities of all the banks involved in the transfers between the suspected conspirators. They had been tracing the money for years and would soon begin tightening the noose. All Jennie knew was that her workload had become almost that of an accountant. She didn't mind making numbers her priority, but she wondered what it was all about. She knew Tony Curtis wouldn't be coming around any time soon. Since the disappearance of Craig and Myer, there were very few visitors and they were usually just needing directions to some other place.

Rick and Darren decided that it was time to bring Jennie on board. She had proven time and again that she was loyal and could keep a secret. Considering they were going to need her help, like it or not, they were going to bring her into the plans of operation.

Rick did most of the talking, explaining in an hour or so what had been going on for years. Jennie was a vital part of the operation and they wanted her to know they trusted her, needed her, and over emphasized the need for her complete silence. She was totally awed by it all, but agreed to help in any way she could, and not say a word about it. "Darren, you sure could have fooled me, and I guess you already have. I would have never taken you for a spy. Not that you aren't really smart and all that but being in the middle of something so dangerous is not how I had you pictured."

* * *

David and Susan were married in a small church in her hometown, and after two weeks in the Caribbean, she went back to work in the Atlanta office and David flew to New Orleans to meet with Rick. It would be David's job to make sure that Big Jim began having some doubts about the behavior of his son Marco. As always, the best way to arouse suspicions was to raise questions about the money. As soon as Rick was satisfied with the plan, David would be on his way to Chicago to meet with Ron.

During the course of the conversation with Ron, David let it slip that he had sent the last cash payment to Marco, but had not had a response that he received it. The normal procedure was that once the cash was delivered, Marco would send a dozen roses to Gloria Barnhardt, the President's secretary at Hibernia Bank in New Orleans, thanking her for such wonderful service. This month Mrs. Barnhardt had not received any flowers. David knew that Ron would first check with Marco, and be assured the money was received and deposited in the Canadian bank. When Ron checked the account there would be a deposit, but not the amount which he and David had discussed. Ron would then send a brief note to a friend who would see to it that Big Jim got the message. Marco assured his father that the cash had made its way to the Swiss account which in turn wired the funds to the Canadian bank. He didn't understand why there was even a question about the transaction. Ron didn't know that David had made a mistake in the amount, accidentally adding $25,000 to the cash amount he discussed with Ron.

After the second inconsistency, the old man wanted to see his son. "Marco, my son, have I not given you enough over the years to make you happy and content? Why would you want to nickel and dime me at a time when business is so good? Have you no loyalty, especially to your father?"

Marco had no idea what Big Jim was talking about, and he asked his dad if he was feeling okay. Wrong man to ask the wrong question, and Marco heard about it. Since Marco had no idea what his father was talking about, he just let the man rave and rant, and walked out.

It had to be something connected to the Dianattis, he figured, and didn't worry about it anymore. At some point, he would take care of that problem once and for all.

* * *

Chip had made the decision to leave, but only in the sense that he was no longer willing to be a part of the daily inter-workings of the group. He was still a vital piece in the on-going plan to track people, places, and the money and to eventually determine how the most horrific of conspiracies was put together. Living near and working with his father-in-law gave Chip access to almost anything he wanted to know. The one thing he couldn't find was Alejandro's private papers which he kept in a large safe somewhere close to but not in his office. Chip had to be extra careful with this aspect of his search. One mistake here could undo all the trust he had built with Alejandro since they began working together.

When Chip told Camila that Rick and Nikki were coming down for a visit, she and her mother began planning a very large party to welcome Chip's best friend and his very famous wife. Nikki had recently starred as Aida in Italy and in doing so had become something of a celebrity back home. Camila was anxious to meet the very cosmopolitan Nikki Charles. What Camila didn't know was that Nikki would not have been appearing at Teatro La Scala in Milan had it not been for the continuing emotional outbursts occurring in the Charles household. Nikki had left one rainy night screaming at the top of her operatic lungs, "You pathetic excuse of a man, you can spend all your nights with that bitch as far as I'm concerned." When her father told her, she would not be spending the night at his home, she went to the Roosevelt, had three very dry martinis and went to bed. Around noon the next day, she called to apologize, but Rick was not there.

The screaming and yelling had begun after a trip to the doctor about her back. She had evidently strained a muscle and he prescribed a mild pain killer to help her through the day and help her rest at night. As the pain increased, so did the number of pills she was taking, and now it had become a very seductive way to forget about anything she didn't want to think about. Nikki began accusing Rick of seeing Misty after the shows. When he arrived late, she would be passed out and left Elizabeth to be taken care of by the nanny. Rick told John that he was having Nikki committed to a local treatment center. Even though it saved her life, she said she would never forgive him for having her taken away in an ambulance in the middle of the night.

But after eight weeks in the clinic, she was able to face the day and face the fact that she had become addicted to pain pills. Her frame of mind was that she needed time to become better adjusted and thought the best way to do that was by working. After she married Rick, she had spent most of her time shopping, drinking, lunches with friends, parties, and doing absolutely nothing productive. Now she would find out if she still had the voice, the passion, and the stamina to become the star she had always longed to be. Even the toughest critics thought she was remarkable in the role, and Rick watched his beautiful wife once again become the elegant master of her craft. They decided to have some time for the family to go on a trip.

They had known each other forever, it seemed, and yet, without realizing it, Rick had allowed Nikki to be the last to know about his other life. She might not take it well, but with things beginning to come to a head, she needed to know the man she married. The late nights, the calls at all hours, days away from home without a word. Nikki had determined that Rick was having an affair with Misty, but what she was told the night before they left Milan left her confused, angry, and ready for war.

"Why in the hell am I just now finding out about this, and who exactly are you? You're trying to con me with this story of yours, or if it is true, you had no right to be involved in something this dangerous and not tell me about it. You are the most selfish, unfeeling bastard, I've ever met, and you don't need a wife, especially this wife. Why don't you take your spy shit, if there truly is any spy shit, and find a nice sleezy brothel to show off your trade. I'll go with you on this trip, but it's the last time you and I will ever be a couple again."

Nikki was out of control, and Rick knew how dangerous that could be. If things stayed like this, it would only be a matter of time before she began spreading the news, and that couldn't happen.

When Rick and Chip had time to get away for a few hours on Chip's boat, there was a lot to discuss. Their little marijuana business had continued to grow, but they knew it was only because Johnny and his friends needed another mode of distribution. That was okay with Rick. All he wanted out of the deal in the first place were the connections between Alejandro's and Johnny's contacts. Thousands of tons had been stolen, blown up, or gone missing over time, but large sums of money kept showing up in Rick's accounts that Darren had put in place. Somewhere in Brazil, Alejandro had facilities which took the poppy seed resin and converted it to pure heroin. It was then blended with other ingredients to create two percentages: 100% and 50%. The pure heroin was for the wholesalers like Joey and Marco, who would create their own percentages, and the rest was for retailers buying for the general population of addicts. Dock workers and those responsible for inspecting incoming cargo were paid large sums to turn the other way when the resin arrived in a Brazilian port. Now that Chip was on the inside, he had located what he told Rick was the largest of the labs. Both men knew that you could blow up one lab and another one would take its place almost overnight. There had to be some way to get Alejandro's source of the raw ingredient cut off. Joey might not be happy to find out that his Brazilian connection had begun watering down the finished product. Of course, Alejandro would never be so stupid as to do that, but all Rick wanted to do was place some doubt in Joey's mind that his partner was possibly trying to cheat him. Chip would see to it that the next two shipments would be less than pure by some small percentage. Rick would make sure that Johnny found out about the switch and see what happened.

* * *

She was a cool, tough professional woman, but Nikki Charles wasn't ready for the scholarly-looking gentleman she had met when Elizabeth first came home from the hospital. At first there was a bit of small talk, but it quickly became very direct and not so friendly.

"Mrs. Charles, I'm not happy that I have to be here today. There are any number of things I need to be doing, but since this is so important, you and I are going to have what my grandmother used to call a come to Jesus chit chat. I know your father quite well, have worked with your husband for the past nine years, and quite frankly, don't give a damn if you think you're Miss High Pissy and God's gift to mankind. As far as I'm concerned, you're a pampered prima Donna and don't deserve the man you married. Now that I have that out of the way, I have several things you need to know, and when I'm finished, and only when I'm finished, will you even consider opening your mouth. Do I make myself absolutely clear, Mrs. Charles?"

Nikki just sat there acting as if her feelings were hurt and trying to take in what she just heard from the man sitting across

357

from her. All she could do was nod in the affirmative. At the same time, she was trying to think if she had ever been talked to this way in her entire life.

Doc took the next hour or so to explain things very carefully, and described in graphic detail what would happen to her should she ever decide to speak to anyone about Rick's work or about this meeting. He was most emphatic to point out that should Rick become aware of anything which concerned this discussion that in any way had Nikki as the source, there would be no way he could guarantee her safety. "Now, Mrs. Charles you may ask questions."

Her attempt to be indignant didn't faze Doc one bit. He didn't care about her feelings at all. In her most dramatic persona pointed out that she had never been spoken to like this in her life. "My father would not be happy about this if he knew."

Doc quickly pointed out that her dad had been informed about this meeting and why it was necessary. "Now that we have that out of the way, Mrs. Charles, do you have anything else you would like to say or ask me?"

Doctor Carmichael, you have made yourself quite clear, and if I have any questions, I will ask my husband."

"Mrs. Charles, thank you for your attention, and I'll tell Rick he can come home now. I have a plane to catch. Good day and please give your daughter a hug for me."

When Rick walked back in he had no idea how direct doc had been with Nikki. She looked as if she was in some deep-reflective thought process, and waited for her to speak.

"You know, sweetheart, in some strange and eerie way, I like your friend. I have never been treated with such disrespect in my life, but considering how passionate he was about you and what you are trying to do I understand why he felt it necessary to let me know what's really important about you and me. I am sorry about the way I have treated you, and sorry I've acted like a child.

Will you forgive me, and let me have a second chance of being the wife and partner you should have had all along?" Over the next few hours, these two lovers, for the first time in such a long time, gave one another their love, their hearts, and their souls. Rick sent Doc a long thank you note, and a bottle of his favorite Brandy.

* * *

Joey arrived in Rio and checked into the President's Suite at the Copacabana Hotel. He had told Alejandro to meet him there for dinner the next evening. Johnny was in the hotel, but would not be at the meeting. He was to be close by should Joey need him for anything.

"Señor Estoval, it's always a pleasure to see you, and hope things are going well for you and your family." Joey gave no hint that there was anything bothering him or that he had any questions about the business they shared.

"Senor Joey, I thank you for the opportunity to see you again, and next time we meet, let me extend the hand of friendship at our modest home rather than a hotel."

"I hope you enjoyed the meal. I had this rather American cuisine ordered and the wine selected for this special meeting. Now tell me Alejandro, why have you treated me and my family so dishonorably?" As he asked the question, Joey picked up his steak knife as though he was examining the blade.

"Joey, I'm not sure I understand the question. What have I done to give you the idea that I have acted in a disrespectful manner?"

"We pay you a great deal of money for your supply of 100% pure product, and yet, our last two shipments were barely at 80% levels. The first shipment I thought might have been an accident, but not the second. You will ship us two more loads at once and the purity should not be an issue, or my friend, we will go elsewhere while they try to find your body . . . Ha quedado claro?"

Joey received the two shipments and they were the real thing, but the seeds of doubt had been planted. Things from this point forward might be more closely watched than before. Joey gave Johnny an extra fifty grand for letting him know about the discrepancies in the first two shipments.

Chapter 62
In the Beginning

At the 1960 Democratic Convention, Kennedy needed Texas and suckered Lyndon into the Vice Presidency letting the Texas Senator think he was going to be a powerful part of the administration. Once elected, Lyndon was treated like a country bumpkin, given the least important tasks, and told he was to be seen not heard. That much ego with all he had accomplished made for a very angry, very unhappy Vice President. Jake was determined to help his friend in any way he could.

When you have large amounts of explosives, in this case the Dianatti and Vinzzetti families, near a burning flame like Jake Winslet, the result can be a devastating explosion. Revenge, payback, and money became silent partners on a rainy afternoon in January of 1963.

Francesco had already dismissed the guy from Texas who sounded more like a guy wanting to run for Congress. He had a lot of money and wanted his friend Lyndon to have more respect and would pay a large sum to get it. The guy was back, and this time it had nothing to do with the Vice President or at least directly. Big Jim agreed to meet with Jake, and after a brief argument with his father, Joey reluctantly agreed to be there to represent the family. This was no casual dinner meeting at a local restaurant. The three men were meeting in a small A-frame cottage outside of Vail, Colorado. No one, not even their families knew where they were.

It started in Jake's court, but soon began to switch to Big Jim and his hatred of that little bastard, Bobby. He wanted to put a contract on the kid, and that would take care of the problem. Joey made good sense saying that once Bobby was killed, Jack would bring down the entire Justice Department on their heads and they would be relentless. Killing Bobby wasn't the answer. Jake sat there listening to these two guys, and then quietly said, "Why don't we kill Jack?" Joey and Big Jim had a rare moment when they couldn't think of anything to say.

Jake went on to say, "Think of it like this: We kill the President, Bobby is no longer the Attorney General, Lyndon is President and runs old Bobby boy right out of town, and I can suggest to the new President that there are bigger things to take care of than reaming the mob's ass. It will take the country and the government years to get over this." There was a lot of discussion about how to do it, but nothing was said about not doing it. As they shook hands the next afternoon at the airport, Jake would put a plan together and get back to the other two as soon as he was ready.

"Joey, are you fuckin' nuts? I send you to a meeting, and you come back with this idea that we're all gonna join in this plan to kill the President? You've lost your fuckin' mind." Francesco hated the President and all the President's men, but killing him, wasn't a good move at all. "The minute that gun is fired, they'll be all over us." Joey spent the next hour trying to calm the old man down, and explaining why the Feds wouldn't be bothering them. "Sure, we'll be a suspect, but think of it as a typical hit, and so what if we are a suspect. They won't be able to prove shit, and there won't be any more of little Bobby meddling in our business. Do me a favor and let's wait until we see what Jake comes up with. If you still don't like it, we'll withdraw our support. Old

Jake may have more money than all of us; so, if he wants to go it alone, let him. Right? Now relax, pops."

* * *

The summer of '63 was nearly over, and things had to get settled into place. Jake worked alone and wanted no one telling him what to do or when to do it. It was his idea for the hit on the President, and he would make certain that it worked. He wasn't going to leave something so important to a bunch of thugs with an IQ of ninety.

Who would know more about undercover agents than the CIA? That's how Jake figured he could find the perfect candidate for the hit. Being used to covert operations, the individual would understand the necessity for complete secrecy, deadlines, obeying orders, and not asking questions. Now Jake had to come up with a way to find that person. Although Big Jim and Joey thought that one of their own would be the best choice, Jake knew that whoever did this had to be someone no one had ever heard about. Lyndon wondered why Jake needed to speak with Wendell Jeffreys, but he arranged it. As far as the Vice President knew, it was about the immigration problem in south Texas. A lot of Mexicans were setting up shelters on Jake's land, and he needed an agent who could find out who was bringing them into the state. That was good enough for Lyndon.

Wendell was born suspicious; so, he was made for his job at the Agency. Some would say ultra-paranoid would be the best description of the clandestine bureaucrat. Jake couldn't have asked for a better contact.

"Wendell, I do appreciate your time to let me tell you what we're facing down home. It's becoming a real pain in the ass to keep running these people off the property, but then another bunch takes their place. Lyndon and I talked this over, and he thought

362

maybe you could help me with an idea I had about taking care of the problem once and for all. I need a man who is a great shot, a marksman would be best. He would have to camp out for a week or so before making his move. The reason he needs to be an excellent shot is that I want him to fire into the crowd, but not hit anyone. Just scare the shit out of them. They'll know that my property is protected, and I can have him back to his regular job in three weeks. Can you help me with this?"

"Jake, we're not set up here to arrange sharpshooters for ranchers. If I tried something like this, I'd be out of here so fast I wouldn't hear the door slam. I'm sorry, but I just can't help you."

"I thought maybe my idea would pose a problem for you; so, I put together a little somethin' that could help you in case your job here was put in danger. It's about the only way I could think of to offset any problems you might have." Wendell opened the case to see a that it was full. "Damn, how much you have in here Jake?"

"I believe I counted out $500,000."
Wendell took a very deep breath. Almost stuttering, he looked at Jake and told him, "Sure, Jake, I'll find someone for you, but it may take me some time. When do you need the guy?"

"Thank you for reconsidering. How about in two weeks? I'd like to meet with him, tell him what I want to do, and then have him ready when it's time for his services. I would need him for a couple of weeks or so during the summer if that's okay with you?"

"I'm sure I can meet your deadline. Obviously, this is a very secret operation; so, I need a cover for it. Any suggestions?"

Jake thought for a moment. "Yeah, let's call it Payback."

* * *

Harvey was a Marine at seventeen, and it didn't take Captain Mallory long to notice the kid could hit a half dollar at fifty yards. He was good enough that they gave him a promotion and moved him into a different group which allowed him to be on the range as often as possible. Though he loved being able to have target practice most anytime, Harvey grew tired of shooting and the military. Too much bullshit for him. The boy wasn't necessarily the sharpest knife in the drawer, and for some odd reason thought he would be better off in Russia. It took him a while, but he finally got there, but it didn't take long to find out it wasn't what he thought it would be. Except for marrying a beautiful Russian girl, he was very unhappy and wanted to go home. He was there a little over two years, and sometimes the KGB would have him followed, but to them, this American, was just a fool.

A couple of weeks after he got back, Harvey met some dude who said he was from the CIA. The elderly looking guy told Harvey he was in charge of covert operations and that he wanted to hire Harvey. Two weeks later, Harvey was given an official looking document welcoming him to the CIA.

His cover would be that of a communist sympathizer. Being the excellent marksman that he was, his contact told him there would be a high-risk operation which would require his services and that he would be paid $20,000 for that job. Besides, when this job was pulled off successfully, there would be other groups needing his skills and willing to pay what he charged plus a bonus. In the world of covert operations, his name would soon become a legend. Now that Jake had the decoy in place, he still had much to do to see that the real shooter was given all he needed for the hit.

Jake had to meet with Big Jim Vinzzetti to hire the use of two of his men as backups for the job, and make sure there were no cracks in the security. Marco could not know about this until it was over.

Johnny would be the go-to man for the Dianatti family, but would not be told the details until Joey gave the word. All Johnny knew now was that it was big, very secret, and there were only six men who knew about it. That made Johnny feel important.

Jake wanted Johnny to be his money man for part of the plan. Johnny was chosen to handle the physical movement of cash. He would meet with Harvey to tell him how and when his money would be delivered. Harvey was to be the single sniper, but at this point, there was no location, no time, and no victim. As Jake saw it, the last piece was the most important part of the entire operation: What to do with Harvey once he understood that he had been had. Joey had an idea, but it could be a risk that Jake might not like. *Who cares what Jake likes or doesn't like, I can handle this.*

Johnny took $50,000 in cash to Dallas, knowing that if the guy didn't go for this, he would have to kill him.

No matter how you described Jack Ruby, he was still a fuckin' sleaze bag to Johnny. Why they chose him, he didn't get, but it wasn't his job to think about it one way or the other. He would do what he was told or die. It wasn't much of a choice. In Johnny's mind, if you're going to do a guy in, you don't send an amateur. Johnny Faretta was thinking too much, and that can get you killed.

They met in Jack's office, if you want to call it an office. Stripper's photos, in various poses, were all over the walls. Tacked to the wall with no apparent order were women who had either worked there, been laid by Jack, or covered up the cracks in the plaster. It smelled like mold and marijuana and Johnny quickly told Jack they were going someplace that didn't smell like an outhouse.

"Jack, I'm here on behalf of the entire Dianatti family. I am honored they chose me to meet with you about this most important request. I hope you understand that our time here is extremely confidential, and no one must know of our discussion. Do you swear your silence?" Jack was overwhelmed, but managed to eke out a quiet "yes, yes, of course I do."

"Sometime later in the year, there is going to be a hit on an extremely important man. At this moment I don't know where or when, but I do know how and who's gonna do it. I am here to offer you the job of making sure the shooter never makes it to trial."

"Johnny, I've never killed anybody. I wouldn't know the first thing about where to start and not sure I could pull the trigger. I appreciate the confidence in me, but I have to pass. Please explain to Joey that I just can't do this . . . I just can't."

"You know Jack, I don't blame you for backing off, but let me put things in a different way: You don't have a choice. You'll be paid a lot of money, given all the instructions about how to do it, and won't ever tell a soul the truth. Does that make it easier for you my friend?"

"What do you mean I have no choice. You said that they were making me an offer."

"And the offer is this, Jack: You agree to take care of the shooter or I'll blow your brains out while I'm in town. Now, it's up to you."

Jack didn't move, almost couldn't breathe, but nodded his head yes when Johnny asked him again. He would do whatever he was told to do. Johnny laid three hundred-dollar bills on the table and they walked out. Johnny would catch a cab and head back to New Orleans. Jack drove back to the club and puked.

The one thing that still had to be decided was where and when. It had to be crowded and noisy, which ideally would be during a motorcade, but when would the President have a reason to be in a motorcade? Lyndon would know, but wouldn't even be able to tell Jake because it was highly secret. Harvey would have to know at least a week or two before the hit because he would have to pick out where to fire and how to escape. Time was quickly passing by, but for now, Jake could only wait and see how things worked out.

* * *

Rick wasn't exactly sure how to handle this, but it's not every day you tell the boss you're retiring. That's how he was going to approach the meeting with Johnny and que sera, sera.

"Ricky, my boy, this is no time to leave the boat. This is the easiest money you'll ever make, and it just keeps growing. I can't let you leave now; we've got too much in this."

"Johnny, believe me, this isn't easy, but I never intended to be in the marijuana business to start with, much less, shipping tons of it all over the place. You guys are much better suited for this than I am. Chip and I talked on our last visit, and both of us have families to take care of and need time to enjoy the kid's lives. And on my end, you know that Nikki is a load most of the time. We'll sign over the stock, no money required, and we'll go about our business doing what we do best."

"I don't want to do this, but I'll run it by Joey. We like you kid, and maybe we can change your mind. I mean you're a celebrity around here and I only know one person who isn't a big fan. Just kiddin' you, my man. She's probably waiting for you to have the seven-year itch right now." Johnny told Rick he'd take care of things.

Rick failed to see anything funny about Misty's attitude about him or his music. She was his boss and never let him forget it. He was thinking on his way back to the club, she may still think about me, but I'm sure it's not good.

After a couple of run-throughs of some new arrangements for the band, Rick was headed to his car when he heard his name called out. It was Misty, telling him, "Johnny needs to see you as soon as possible." *Maybe I'm clear to get out of this business,* he thought.

"Rick, I need for you to sit down and take a deep breath. What I have to tell you isn't good, and it's going to hurt like hell. I'm sorry I have to be the guy with the bad news. Last night Alejandro was giving a party for a few of his friends and family on his yacht. Around one this morning, there was a tremendous blast, and everyone on board was killed. It's not for sure that your friend Chip and his family were on board, but if they were . . . I'm sorry man."   For a minute or two, Rick just sat there in a stunned silence, not believing what he had just heard. Chip couldn't be gone. The guy was invincible. Finally, he looked at Johnny, and asked if it was on purpose or not.

"There's been some talk about skimming, but I can't tell you any more than that. Marco told Joey a couple of weeks back that about fifty g's was missing, but Alejandro denied any part of it. If you hear anything about your friend, let me know." Rick wouldn't allow himself to accept that Chip was dead. At the same time, if there was a party, Camila would be there, and Chip was always by her side. First, he would let Doc know and then hope he could find his friend.

Word got back to Marco that everything had been taken care of, and to let him know if there was anything else he might need. Jimenez Diego was more than happy to take out the Estoval family. They had been a thorn in the side of the Diego family for a long time. Marco didn't know it, but Jimenez would have done it for free. Maybe not free, but for much less than $75,000. He hated Alejandro that much.

Many of the bodies couldn't be identified. There were five or six children on board that night; so, if one was Chip's son, almost certainly one of the bodies would be his father. The police investigating said it looked like a bomb blast, but didn't yet know for sure. Rick was sure that it was. All Chip had wanted to do was be with his family more. All the narrow escapes he and Rick had made gave them both a feeling of immortality. Rick prayed for a miracle, and at this point that's all that would save his friend. Rick never thought much about tears, but now they possessed him.

Marco had a beautiful wife and three children, a beautiful home in a very upscale part of Chicago, and a luxury apartment downtown where his mistress Tina stayed. Marco told his wife that he worked so hard that sometimes would need to stay in town to be able to get some sleep. His wife Anna was no fool, but she wasn't about to give up the life she and the kids had because he was seeing another woman. Sometimes when the kids were with their grandparents, Anna's tennis lessons went on much longer than originally scheduled.

On this Thursday morning, the doorbell rang while she was watching out the kitchen window as the kids got on the bus. "Mrs. Vinzzetti, may we come in?" The Chicago police department was calling on her at this hour to let her know that her husband had been murdered. They were sorry to have to be the ones to tell her, but they needed her to come downtown to identify the body. She fainted.

They lifted her to the sofa, and as she came to, began crying. "Are you sure it's Marco," she asked. Yes ma'am, we are, but we still have to make it official. When you're ready we'll take you with us.

They had warned her ahead of time that it wasn't going to be easy. Marco and his girlfriend had each taken three shots to the head. It wasn't a hit, but more like a jealous husband. They took her back home, she went to get the kids out of school, and called Big Jim. The man had issues with his son, and didn't trust him, but he was still his son. Someone was going to pay for this . . . bigtime.

Nikki couldn't sleep; so, she was up looking at books about remodeling and having a scoop of ice cream. The phone rang and when Rick didn't answer, she did.

"Hey, Nikki, this is Chip." She almost dropped the phone. "Chip, where are you? Are you okay? Is Camila with you?"

"Nik' is Rick around?"

"Let me get him."

He was in the shower and when she told him who was on the phone, he almost fell out of the shower trying to get to the bedroom phone.

"Chip, where are you?"

"That's not important right now, but I need you to do something for me in a hurry."

"Sure, Chip, whatcha need?"

"I need a place to stay for a few days. Think you could find me somethin' where no one would be pokin' around?"

"Something hell, you will stay with us."

"Rick, I appreciate that, but that wouldn't be a good idea right now. Your place is probably being watched right now. Just find me something, pay for the place, and I'll call you back to find out where you're leaving the key. Gotta run."

"Thank you God." *He's alive, but he must be in some kind of deep trouble.* He told Nikki that he was going to find Chip a place to stay, and flew out the door. He went straight to Misty's place. When she first saw him through the peephole, she told him to go away, but he was almost yelling to let him in. It wasn't about him; it was about Chip.

It took him a couple of minutes, but when he explained the situation, she told him no one would look for him at her place.

She had a spare bedroom with a bath, and he was welcome to stay as long as he needed. She wasn't there that much anyway.

When Rick got home it was almost three in the morning. Nikki was asleep on the sofa. He waited for the phone to ring. He took the call in the bedroom so as not to wake Nikki and Elizabeth. "Okay, Misty is letting you stay at her place for as long as you need. Tell me where you are, and I will take you there." Chip had been hiding at the bus station and would be outside waiting.

"Chip, God, it's so good to see you. I have been so upset, but I know it had to be horrible for you. Tell me did Camila . . .?

"She and my son are dead. The bastards slaughtered almost sixty people to punish Alejandro. I would have been dead, but he sent me to the lab to get things shut down and moved. I didn't know anything until I got back to the house. I was going to call you then, but a couple of guys came to the door, and pointed a gun at me. One of them was straight out of the movies with the wise guy talk and waving his gun. He told me to tell everyone that Alejandro got what he deserved and now no one would try to fuck over Marco or else. I thought he was going to shoot me, but they just walked away. They didn't know who I was, or they probably would have killed me right there."

"So, when did you get here, and why do you have to hide? Johnny was really upset when he thought you had been killed."
"Rick, it's not Johnny I'm concerned about. I just killed Marco Vinzzetti, and there was probably some kind of cameras in that apartment. If they've seen my face, I'm dead unless I stay out of sight."

"You killed Marco? My God, Chip, if they don't kill you, the Chicago police will nail you to the wall. Does Doc know about any of this?"

"Just you, and I'm sorry to do this to you, but I need time to think, to figure out a way to disappear. I haven't slept in days, and not sure how much longer I can keep going."

Misty had all the lights off, and when Rick knocked, he was very quiet. There was brief hello and Rick took Chip to the bedroom. Before he could get him on the bed, the guy was asleep. She put a small blanket over him, turned off the lights, and closed the door.

"Misty, I can't tell you how much I appreciate this, but I have to get him out of here as quickly as I can. He killed Marco Vinzzetti."

"What? Rick are you crazy? He can't stay here. Does Big Jim know Chip did it? If they do, they'll kill me too. Baby, I love you and will do anything for you, but I'm not stupid."

"Sweetheart, I will have him out of here just as soon as he wakes up. Let him sleep for now, and just go about your business like nothing happened. You'll be okay. I will take care of you, I promise."

Chip didn't wake up until the next night, but Rick was there waiting for him to clean up and get ready to move. While Chip slept, Rick rented a room in a house owned by the Dianatti family in the ninth ward. Rick had to lie to Johnny, which he didn't want to do, but he needed something close by that was safe for Chip. Once he was settled in, Chip began to talk about what he had done.

"The son of a bitch killed my wife and child, and he had to pay for that. I hid for a few days near the old lab, and that's when I decided what I had to do. I got a job on a steamer headed to Miami, and took a bus from there to Chicago. It only took a few hours until I knew where his apartment was and then I waited. He had a couple of heavies with him, but they weren't at his door for some reason. The lock was easy, and thinking that he might be there when I opened the door, I had my gun ready. I could hear her moaning, and she never saw me when I opened the door. Marco turned, I fired three into his skull and shot her too. I am sorry about her.

"I ran out, and was ready to shoot his men if it was necessary. I'm sorry Rick, but it's done. If you need to turn me in, let's get it over with, okay?"

"You stay here for now, and give me time to think. No one is going to know you're here, and Johnny thinks you're one of our guys from the rig. Whatever you do, don't leave here, for any reason. There's plenty of food and drinks so rest and stay out of sight."

Rick knew what Doc would say, but he couldn't turn in his friend. There might be a better way. There was a woman on Carondolet Street who made a nice little pile of money giving people new identities. He told her what he needed, and handed over the money. She said it would take her a week, and the deal was done. Before Dr. Arnold Fitzsimmons boarded flight 726 to Berne, he shook his friend's hand, gave him a hug, and said goodbye. It would be the last time Chip and Rick would ever see or speak to one another again.

* * *

Jennie started crying around ten in the morning and hadn't stopped since. Her dream job was over, and the man she had come to care for a great deal was leaving her too. Darren had accepted a job with Merrill Lynch in Tampa and would be closing the office at the end of the month. He and Doc had talked and they both thought it was the right time for Darren to move on with his life. He had no trouble finding something he wanted to do for the moment, but knew at some point that he would open his own investment house. He didn't know where, but someplace warm. He told Jennie right after she got to work, and she was crushed.

They had become quite close, and they had started dating for real. She asked him if she could go with him to Tampa. "Jennie, are you sure you want to move? Besides moving, you would have to stay with me until you found something of your own. I don't mind, but I'm not the most organized guy in town."

"Darren Leitner, you're either acting or you are the most naïve man I have ever met. I just asked if I could go to Tampa to be with you . . . as in live with you . . . as in I think I love your dumb ass, and that we need one another. Do you now understand the question?"

"Jennie, I really don't know what to say. I have dreamed about this moment from the first time I ever saw you, but couldn't imagine a woman as beautiful as you wanting to be with Mr. Klutzdrawers. Of course, you can come with me, and we can start all over again. We'll be a family. I love you so much.

All of Darren's work was now in three safe deposit boxes at Hibernia. He had mapped the last eleven years of all the transactions he had been given, and they all led back to the same place. Doc had more than enough data, and he and Rick would take it from here.

* * *

Two days after Lyndon made the announcement on national news, he told Jake that he should have never given up the nomination for a second term. One of the Presidents plants in the Kennedy family indicated that he was certain that Bobby was going to run now that Lyndon was out of the way. "That pompous little son of a bitch makes me so mad I could spit. Hell, the only thing he knows about politics is what his daddy told him. I hate this damn war, but Bobby will just bring the boys home and give the reds everything they want. We're gonna look like a bunch of cowards because of that boy. Far as I'm concerned, Oswald shot the wrong guy. The other thing that he's gonna do is give the credit to Jack for all the legislation I got passed. And I'll tell you somethin' else: Martin is becoming a thorn in my side. He's losing his followers and wants me to take care of the situations he has stirred up and can't control." Johnson laughed out loud and said, "I think old Edgar is about to let the cat out of the bag about Martin. When he does, everybody better batten down the hatches because all hell is gonna break loose." Jake just sat there and listened to his friend rave and rant while they drank Lyndon's favorite bourbon.

*　*　*

Jake no longer required the services of the Dianattis or the Vinzzettis. He would handle this himself. Regardless of what everyone else thought about Martin Luther King, Jr., Jake was not a fan. If the head of the FBI were going to spill the beans on the guy, what difference would it make if he had an accident. Jake was convinced that the whole civil rights movement was just one big grab for control of the country. Some members of the House and Senate would sell their grandmother for a few more votes. Between Martin and Bobby, the country was headed toward a revolution, and by God, Jake wasn't going to let that happen. He didn't have to explain to a committee, ask for money, or rationalize what he thought needed to occur. All he had to do was do it.

On April 1, 1968 Ray was introduced to a guy who looked something like a cowboy, and sort of talked like one too. "Jimmy Ray, I've been told you're an excellent shot, and know how to keep your mouth shut, is that right?"

In his rather southern drawl he said, "Yes sir, I can hit just about anything from a good distance, and sure, I can keep quiet. Why you askin'?"

"Would you like to make a bunch of money, Jimmy Ray?"

"Depends on what a bunch of money is."

"Would $100,000 help make the decision?"

Ray laughed and asked, "Who we shootin'?"

"Martin Luther King. He's going to be in Memphis, and that's where I want it done. Can you do it?"

"Hell yes, and it will be my pleasure to get rid of that black son of a bitch. I've had just about all I can take of his peace shit while his cohorts tear the country apart. They get any more power, and white boys like me will be choppin' their cotton. I'll need a couple of days before the hit to decide when and where to do it. When do I get my money?"

"Here's $25,000 and once you've decided when and where, there'll be $25,000 more. When you're safely out of the state, you'll get the rest."

"You gonna help me get the fuck out of here?"

"All you have to do is call this number, tell me when and exactly where you'll be when you take the shot, and I'll handle the rest. I can only help you if you give me the exact site of the shot."

What Jake didn't explain to Jimmy Ray was that it didn't make any difference if he could hit a guy at one hundred yards or a mile, he wasn't going to be making the hit. Freddie Jones was a stone-cold killer. Jake paid him three million to kill the President and was now offering him the same to blow King away. Freddie would do it the same way they did it in Dallas.

Lee Harvey was set up for the shot when Freddie came running into the room where Harvey was set up for the shot. He told the kid to get the hell out because the cops had been tipped off. Freddie told him he would get rid of the gun while Harvey got out of the building. Freddie took care of the rest.

Just like before, Jimmy Ray would be all set to take the shot, Freddie would rush in to tell JR to run like hell to the van. Freddie would take care of the gun, and see to it that it was destroyed. When Freddie made the hit, Jimmy Ray was already in the van and leaving the chaos. He had been told the van would take him to a deserted airfield in north Mississippi. Jake knew Ray would start running when he thought there was a problem, which would make him the suspect. From Mississippi, he would be flown to another small airstrip in southern Georgia, and then head to Jamaica. He stayed in a small hut for a couple of days, and then a larger business jet took him to Barcelona.

While America burned, Jimmy Ray, as Jake called him, was taken to a small village near the border of Portugal. There he received a Canadian passport, driver's license, and the rest of his money. He was told to stay put for at least four months, but he didn't listen.

Freddie Jones was back in Duluth enjoying his two million dollars, and Jake was most pleased with himself. In less than a week, he had managed to unleash the rage of millions of black and white Americans.

Jake's next target wouldn't be so easy. Bobby Kennedy was loved by millions and there was always an incredible amount of security around him. To make it happen, he would have to pick a site before or after an event where Kennedy would be speaking. Once he decided to run for the Presidency, things got a little easier.

Whether he won or lost California, he would have to celebrate or concede afterwards. He knew the Kennedy camp would have to book rooms ahead, and once they did, that's where things would go down. Jake met Freddie in St. Louis the first of May to discuss the details. Since this was going to be a lot more dangerous for Freddie, he wanted an extra million for the job, take it or leave it. Jake never blinked an eye, but had one provision: He wouldn't give Freddie the cash for at least three weeks after the hit. Freddie said no to that; so, Jake gave him a million dollars up front, and the balance would be paid three weeks afterwards.

Freddie put an ad in the paper for someone to help him with a catering job. There were several applicants, but he picked a young Arab guy by the name of Sirhan. All the kid had to do was be in the area of the kitchen and to let Freddie know when Bobby was on his way. Sirhan thought it was going to be a surprise ending for winning the primary. Freddie also hired another person to be in the same area, but he was there to hand Sirhan a gun in a towel just as the candidate was coming into view. Sirhan was so stunned by having a gun in his hand that he didn't even hear the shots. Next thing he knew he was being thrown to the floor, and Freddie quietly took off his waiter's jacket and went out the back of the kitchen to throw away some garbage. When the other young man was leaving the hotel, Freddie put a bullet in his brain, and put the body in his trunk. He threw the guy into a drainage ditch and headed to the airport. Two weeks later, while watching a baseball game at one of the local bars, Freddie felt a sting, like a bee, on his neck. Forty-five seconds later, he was dead. Jake saved three million dollars.

The old cowboy friend of Lyndon's had three of America's greatest men assassinated: Jack, because daddy double crossed two mob families, Martin Luther King, Jr. probably because he was black, and Bobby because Lyndon hated the little s.o.b. There was no CIA, no FBI, no crime families involved in the last two. It was just Jake, who had learned how to get away with murdering Jack, and did nothing more than copy what he did before. Jake had even had the balls to call Martin to tell them he had less than a day to live.

Rick was aware there was one last thing that had to be done, but it might take him another year or two before it happened.

Doc was really having a hard time, and looked awful. He had lost a lot of weight, was having difficulty breathing, and was so lethargic he could barely respond to regular conversation. He and Rick spent a lot of time together, but they both knew it wouldn't be much longer until Doc would take his last breath. He died on May 19, 1978 with his wife and family and Rick by his side.

Rick was the only one of the men who knew where everything was. The safe-deposit boxes would be emptied a little at a time so as not to draw attention. He now had only three things to think about: first was his family, which was about to grow by one; his job at the club; and one other thing that he didn't want to discuss.

There had been an attempt at a hit on Joey, but it failed. The two guys who were found to be responsible were sent to Big Jim's home in an airtight container. They had been rearranged to make sure they fit.

Johnny and Joey reached a business decision and Johnny took his earnings and his part of the business to Florida where he lived like a king until he died in his sleep in August of 1997. Joey was killed in a boat accident on, of all places, Lake Pontchartrain. He was drinking and driving and didn't see the pier.

Darren and Jennie were married less than a year after they arrived in Tampa. He had a great business and she helped in the office whenever she could. It wasn't long before they just drifted into the background of day to day living.

Max died of colon cancer in December of 1986. David and Rick were at his funeral, gave Laura a small envelope, and went their separate ways. David and Susan moved to Italy and never came back to the States.

Vince and Darlena had four children, and lived the life of luxury in a home bigger than some hotels. At first, Vince helped Big Jim, but when he and his father-in-law visited the Vinzzetti home, it was made quite clear that Vince would no longer be in the shipping business. Big Jim agreed and put the $5,000,000 in his safe. He didn't have long to enjoy his new-found wealth.

Eight months later he had a heart attack and died while talking to his wife.

Becker stayed at the University for two more years before moving to Atlanta. He met a Delta stewardess, Harriet, on a flight to New York, they began dating, and two years later were married in a small church in her hometown of Columbia, South Carolina. They had three children, Susan, Gabe, and Josh. Becker Caldwell was the coolest and most respected school administrator in Atlanta until his death in 2011.

Misty had made the Foxy Lady the place in town to be seen. She had worked her way up from waiting on tables to owning the damn place. It had been eating at her for a long time, but she had finally had enough. Rick and Nikki now had two children, and they seemed to be at peace. Misty had made him an offer, the deal was done, and now Rick owned the Foxy Lady. Misty took her three point eight million and went to Honolulu. She bought a club, some investment property, and Rick wasn't sure the guy who told him was right, but he said Misty married an Episcopal priest. Rick smiled, thinking how many times the guy had thanked God for that woman.

One afternoon, Rick sat down with Nikki and they talked about the kids, some of the places she wanted to go, and maybe even having another child. When they finished their drinks, he told her that he had to make a quick trip to California in a few days. He was going to meet with a producer in L.A. and who knows he might be able to get a record deal out of it. She wanted to go, but she was the new President of her women's club and had to stay behind for a meeting.

Rick had bought himself a very expensive Mercedes SL and decided he would drive it to California. Nikki thought he was crazy, but if that's what he wanted to do, have at it. He wasn't going to California. His trip was going to take him up the road a piece to see a cowboy in Texas. Rick had a huge decision to make because the team had pieced it all together, figured how Jake had been the key player in the killing of Jack Kennedy, Martin, and Bobby. It was all written down, and all that was to be decided was Jake's fate.

The old man who came to the door, was frail and looked like he was wearing an old beat up robe. "I saw you drive up. We don't get a lot of fancy cars out here. How can I help you?"

"Mr. Wenslit, my name is Rick Charles and I just need to spend a few minutes with you. I've driven here from New Orleans to meet with you; so, I would be most appreciative if you could give me some of your valuable time."

"Sure son, come on in. Can I get you anything to drink?" "No, I'm fine, but thank you. I'm here to tell you that I know who killed President Kennedy and how it was done. I also know that you're a quick learner, and that you had Martin Luther King and Bobby Kennedy killed the same way. I have transactions, all sorts of connections, deposits, and other assorted papers which explain everything. With that said, you have two choices: You can confess to what you did, or live a most uncomfortable life. It's your decision."

The old man just sat there. It took him at least five minutes before he spoke. "How much would it take for you to forget all of this and just go home?" I can give you whatever you want. I'm richer than all get out."

"Jake, I don't want or need money. I just want you to tell this country what you did."

"I'm afraid I can't do that son. Too comfortable here on the ranch to risk being put in a cell. Besides, no one is going to believe you when I take this to my grave. If you shoot me, I win; if I tell you to go to hell, I win. So now what?"

"I thought maybe you might respond like this: so, I came prepared." Ruth had died a couple of years back; so, there was no one else around.

"You came prepared for what?"

Rick got up from his chair and began to walk around the room admiring all the beautiful antiques, the pottery, and the man owned two Van Gogh paintings which were breathtakingly beautiful. "Where did you buy the art?"

"That was a gift from a friend. Why don't you come back over here and sit down? You can tell me how you came prepared."

"You know what Jake, I had rather show you." At that moment he plunged a small syringe into Jake's neck.

"What the hell have you done, you little asshole."

"Jake, it's a little something I made up just for you. Do your fingers feel funny yet? Do you hear a ringing in your ears?

"Am I dying?"

"Good heavens no, Jake. Do you think you deserve to die? I'm not sure I could ever kill a bug much less a human. I guess I could have it done, but I'd still feel guilty. God would still blame me. Do you believe in God, Jake?"

The rather thick chemical was now coursing through Jake's veins, and his face was beginning to look twisted in a way. When he tried to talk, Rick couldn't understand him. A few minutes passed, and Rick rose to say goodbye.

"Jake, death is just too good for you, and I'm hoping you have a wonderfully long life. Of course, your skin will always feel like it's crawling, you won't be able to talk much, and besides not being able walk, that damn ringing in your ears will be there for the rest of your life. You take care of yourself, and Doc wanted me to be sure and tell you to have a good day."

Chapter 63
Not Much Left to Say

Rick's life was filled with hope and love for Nikki and the kids. His music became even more popular, and he did get that record deal. What he loved most was his back porch. He and Nikki would sit out there in the afternoon having their afternoon toddy and telling each other what happened that day. Their first child, Elizabeth, followed in her mother's footsteps majoring in music at Julliard's, David, the second child, was the lawyer in the family, and Sherry, the baby, was the apple of the old man's eye. She was one spoiled little girl, and she loved it. Sherry married one of the wealthiest men in New Orleans.

Rick would spend a few hours each day going through some of his old papers and writing down something in a leather journal. He kept it in the safe. Before he died, he wrote a note to his son, and when his will was read, David was given the note and the journal.

The funeral was in the fall of 2015. There were hundreds of people at the service, and though her heart was broken, Nikki knew that the man being remembered today had lived an incredible life. He met challenges with his heart and soul, and gave back the only way he knew how. Doc had trusted Rick to lead the group, and the young man never wavered from doing the best he could do. He did violate Doc's most important rule: He kept notes on everything and later wrote more extensive details in his journal.

He wrote what he saw and heard and left his words to validate the lives of Doc, the lives of his closest friends, and all those who loved these men.

SO, NOW YOU KNOW?

Made in the USA
Columbia, SC
03 December 2020